The Nominal Theory of Good Art

This is a work of fiction. The names, characters, places, and incidents described herein are products of the author's imagination, or are used in a fictitious context. Any resemblance to actual persons living or dead, actual incidents, or real locations, is coincidental.

Copyright © 2010 by William McCauley

All rights are reserved. No part of this book may be used or reproduced in any manner without written permission, except in the case of brief quotations embodied in critical or review articles.

Scriptoria Publications
Auburn, WA 98001

ISBN 978-0-578-05465-0

For information, contact 253 804-2631
or
billmccauley@comcast.net.

Cover art by Roger Lake, Virginia Street Studio, 1976

To Cam and Jake

Other Books by William McCauley

The Turning Over (1998)

Need (2004)

Adulteries, Hot Tubs, & Such Like Matters (2007)

Texas Hold'em: A Starting Hand Strategy for Internet and Live Play, with Robert McCauley (2008)

One

Elevated triglicerides, LDL at one-ninety, and drinking too much coffee. Pete had been nagging Wally for years about the coffee, reminding him very time he went in for his EKG or a blood profile or to fine-tune his warfarin dose, that coffee was irritating his kidneys, exacerbating his bladder, unsettling his bowels, swelling his prostate, getting his electrolytes all out of whack, stimulating his edema to pump his legs full of water, and setting off those ventral fibrillations, which set off the implanted defibrillator, which always knocked him flat on his ass. Stop drinking coffee, Pete said, drink water. But coffee is water, which is a little bit colored. So how come water doesn't do to him what coffee did to him? He used to drink coffee all day long. Fifteen, twenty cups. Now if he has a measly six or seven cups his heart is flipping and skipping until he's light headed and he's in the john so much he might as well have a desk in one of the stalls.

Wally dragged his attention back to the meeting. He raised his cup and sipped, wondering if they were gonna talk all day.

"It'll take two days," Kimberly said. "She's got a cancellation and can give us Wednesday and Thursday next week. After that she's booked for months. We need to get her in here now."

Browning scrutinized the paper on the table in front of him. His muscular, athletic neck pushed out against his tie, and his bunched shoulders stretched the fabric of his jacket. "Okay, okay. I see the problem. What I don't see is the solution. How does your proposal solve the problem? It looks like another time-and-money gamble that you can find a solution's in there somewhere if I just give you a bunch money. The GUI team's a month behind now—*that's* the goddamned problem. And if we take them off line to do this they'll slip another two days."

"Summarized in table one," Kimberly said crisply, reaching across the table and stabbing her finger down on the paper. "Column three of the table shows we make up the two days within two weeks, and you'll note that in another two months they'll recover all of the lost time, *and* be on the original schedule."

Browning studied the paper. He looked up at Kimberly. "This is pie in the sky. Your conclusion rests on assumptions that you don't identify, *or* evaluate."

"Every number in that table is validated by this team's past performance under the very conditions I want to implement. I discuss that in paragraph eight-dot-four. You missed it. They're behind on this project because management pushed them into the design phase without proper usability studies, and experience should make it clear that the schedule's gonna keep slipping until we solve the fundamental design problems that come out of that situation. The way to solve the problem is not more overtime; that'll simply add to their frustration. The only way to fix the problem is to stop doing the stuff that makes it worse. We have to stop, back up, and do the usability evaluation. The cost is trivial. It's two days, not two weeks."

Wally wasn't listening to Kimberly. He was observing Browning, to ascertain how he was leaning. With so much crap on his desk Wally hadn't had time to read the proposal, so he took it home. But with the new TV season and all those new shows he had to watch, he hadn't had time to even glance at it. Besides, the proposal title suggested the project required an outside consultant, which would mean out-of-budget expense, and he didn't have to guess what Browning will say about a pro-posal that requires out-of-budget money for out-of-house talent.

All that coffee: Wally's bladder had been crowding him for a half hour, and now his bowel was beginning to rumble. He needed for the meeting to be over. Believing he'd figured Browning out, he spoke: "It's an interesting proposal—if we had money to spend on science projects and if we weren't so far behind. But I don't think this is a time for experimenting."

Browning raised his eyes from the paper and looked at Kimberly. "All right, we'll do it." He slapped his daybook closed, a sign he was ready to move on to his next meeting. "Kimberly, it's your proposal, you lead the project. If it works, good for you; if it fails, it's your ass. Between you and me, I don't believe your usability expert will do anything but suck money out of our depleted treasury. But it's the best proposal I've seen, so get your expert in here next Wednesday. I'll fund two days. And one more thing. I like this kind of work, because it's imaginative, and you presented it aggressively and thoroughly. Even though I think it's bullshit, it's an excellent example of the thinking we need around here. Now: is that it?"

Wally reddened and looked for the agenda that he'd asked Kimberly to prepare, and which he couldn't find in the stack of paper she gave him just before the meeting. "I don't think there's anything else," he muttered.

"The Gearheart contract," Kimberly said. "We need to deal with it today."

Wally shuffled papers. "Right, yes, we, uh—we need—um—" he stammered, hoping Kimberly would jump in again (like she usually did) and reiterate whatever the hell she'd said about the contract an hour before, as he was leaving his office to get another cup of coffee on his way to the crapper. Something about looking at something or other.

"It's up for renewal," Kimberly said.

"Exactly," Wally agreed. "And I think—" He shuffled papers some more. "That is—Gearheart's done a great job—"

It's out of control," Kimberly said. She pulled a sheet of paper out of a file folder and pushed it across the table to Browning.

Out of control? Was that what she'd said?

"The bottom line is we should not renew the contract," Kimberly said. "They've overcharged on every billing for the last six months. Could be sloppy bookkeeping, of course, but that is not a good argument for renewing. I've prepared an RFP that I'd like to send out to a list of vendors I've identified as candidates."

Browning's brow wrinkled into a scowl. "I want background!"

"I asked Accounts Payable to summarize the last four years of Gearhart invoices, showing unit costs of manuals as a function of order size and page count." She passed another sheet of paper to Browning. "The important numbers are these—the last six months."

By now Wally did not know and did not care where she was going with this. Nor did he understand that she had set a trap for him, and that he had stepped right in it. His attention was focused now on the ominous rumbling in his gut and the increasing pressure on his bladder.

Browning turned to Wally. "*You're* the Tech Pubs Manager. Why is the fuck is Kimberly doing this and not you?" His face was red from his crew-cut scalp down to his bulging neck.

Kimberly looked on angelically. "I'm really sorry if I've stepped out of line, I was just—"

A stab of pain deep in Wally's gut. An infallible signal.

"Why are we not reviewing Gearheart's billings?"

"Um—can you excuse me for a uh—for just a minute?"

With his chubby thighs pressed tightly together and his oversized ass pulled in, Wally pushed himself up out of his chair and minced out the door. Behind him Browning rolled his eyes over at Kimberly, who shrugged innocently.

—

Wally smirked. "Fifteen-two, fifteen-four, fifteen-six, three for a dozen, his nibs for thirteen—and out."

Roy's jowels quivered. He slapped his cards down on the table.

Wally scooped the cards up and began shuffling. "That's nine in a row."

"My ass," Roy muttered.

"Here's the score sheet. Count 'em. Three games this afternoon. Six on Saturday. That's nine. You ain't won a game since last week. Want me to play with one hand behind me? That's what I used to tell George, when he was little. Sometimes he'd win when I did that."

"Deal."

"Winners tell jokes, losers say deal. Ethel! Roy's bitchin' 'cause you haven't brought the dessert out yet. Says if he has to sit here all day and get his ass kicked, he ought to at least get some cheesecake out of it."

"I didn't say a word," Roy shouted.

"It's in the ice box," Ethel called from the living room. "You'll have to get it yourself, I'm busy watching Jennifer. She's got these newlyweds on—they're really cute—with the girl's new boyfriend. They're trying to figure out which one gets her, 'cause she loves both of them. Now be quiet, I want to see what the audience decides."

Wally offered the deck for a cut. Roy waved it off and Wally began dealing. "Looks like we got time for one more game, if you got the balls for it. Then there's a *Maverick* rerun I want to watch. It's on at five. Maybe we can get Ethel to cut that cheesecake while we watch it. If we can get her away from her programs. You'd think these women have something better to do than watch that crap. And there's a *Matlock* rerun after that. You might as well stay for supper and we can watch that while we eat."

"Sure." Roy sorted his cards and played an Ace. "One."

Wally tossed a queen. "Eleven. You're probably tired of gettin' your ass kicked, so my guess is you'd love to watch some TV."

Roy played a four. "Fifteen two." He moved his peg.

"*Matlock's* okay, but it's not as good as the old Andy Griffith stuff," Wally said. "These days Andy just stands there, like he's propped up so he doesn't keel over, while all these youngsters do the acting around him. Presence. That's all they got him on there for, to get us old farts to watch the show, and to prove that sometimes youngsters actually do listen to what some old fogie's got to say. Which is bullshit, they don't. Sometimes I get the *Mayberry RFD* tapes out and I'm always shocked at how much difference there is."

"What d'you expect? He's an old man. Play."

—

Wally picked up the phone.

"Wally, do you have plans for lunch?"

Wally recognized Browning's voice. "No, I don't—"

"We need to talk, Wally."

Wally's face reddened pleasurably: Browning didn't say things like that to him very often. "Sure Jim. What time?"

"I'll come by for you in seven minutes," Browning said. "We'll go down to the Crab Pot."

Wally leaned back in his chair, bridging his fingers over his belly. Well—this was interesting. He'd begun thinking maybe they weren't even considering him. He rose and went down the hall and into the men's room. As he stood before the urinal he reviewed his thoughts about the promotion Browning was finally going to offer. He'd considered every argument for and against, and had begin to think seriously that it might be better to decline the offer. In his heart he really wanted nothing more than to coast along as Tech Pubs Manager until they turned him out to pasture. He was an old man in a company from which the other old men had long departed. Now the place was crawling with kids vibrating with energy and new ideas and exuding such a cloud of arrogance they couldn't even see him and they moved so fast they didn't even notice he was in the way. There wasn't a director or a VP over forty, and no one in the company was older than Wally Walder.

On the other hand, that could be the reason they wanted him: for his experience and his wisdom. After all, he was the senior Allied employee. Those in front of him gone now—each into a nursing home or a hole in the ground. Wally had experience, all right, lots of it, and it was good to know that Browning valued it. He was like one of those Japanese living national treasures, or whatever they called them. A repository of priceless experience.

He glanced down to see if his bladder was doing its job, saw that it wasn't, and looked back up at the gray and ivory tiles. Yes, experience is what they want. They have too little of that around here, particularly in the senior positions. Too much testosterone, too little wisdom. The youngsters rule, because they have more energy. But they spew it out like sunlight, spilling most of it wastefully into the void. Wally knew how to operate on low output, how to focus a tiny laser beam of energy precisely on the task at hand.

He thought about the lunch meeting. Browning would make small talk about one of his mountain climbing trips to Switzerland or Katman-something-or-other, or his recent sailboat race around Antarctica, and then, after they'd finished their crab cakes and were sipping coffee he'd tell Wally that the selection committee has decided they need the experience of someone who has matured with the company, someone from the inside. And then he would offer the ritual questions: "Are you up to the challenge? Are you big enough for the job?" And Wally would raise an eyebrow and say: "Can I run IS?" Wally smiled at the gray and ivory tiles. "Can *I* run IS?"

"What?"

Wally tensed, glanced sidewise, and went red in the face. "I was asking what time is it."

Gary stood at the next urinal. "Thought you said something about IS." He looked at his watch. "It's nearly noon."

Wally decided that he should not make Browing wait for him while he waited on his bladder to act. He'd take a leak at the restaurant. He zipped and turned to the sink. He heard Gary flush and then the young man was at the second sink and turning on the water. Wally thought about the empty offices on twenty-five, wondering which one they'd offer him. Probably the corner office down at the end, by the IS staff cubicles and the server room. That'd make sense. He'd have to be close to his staff (*if* he accepted the offer). He didn't know all that much about network technology, and he knew almost nothing about UNIX. Only enough to get into trouble—like last month, when he inadvertently erased the entire documentation directory tree. But what the hell, directors didn't actually *do* anything. Directors were decision makers, not doers. You don't have to know all that much to be a damned good director. Besides, it was his wisdom they were after, not his expertise.

—

"Then he told me."

Ethel rose and came around the table. She drew his head into the soft pillow of her bosom. She held him for a time, then drew back and looked down into his tired eyes and smiled.

"It's okay, I'm glad."

"I didn't really want it—not in my heart, but—I don't know, I felt like it was important to be offered to me, even if I didn't want it. Hell, I might have accepted right there if he'd offered it, but I've known all along that it's a job for someone with a future, not a worn-out old man who only has a past."

"You're not a worn-out old man. You're still young and springy, and I'm glad they're too stupid to see it, because I don't want you taking on something as hard that. Not at your age."

"Rumor is they've made an offer to Kimberly. Can you believe that? A little girl."

She drew him to her breast again.

"Ethel—"

She looked tenderly at his upturned face.

"I pissed my pants again."

She sucked her breath.

"I couldn't help it. He was telling me about the reorganization, how I wouldn't be reporting to him any more, but to the new Director of IS. He kept saying it wasn't a demotion, that it was just a horizontal move, a way of bringing functional groups together and—oh hell, I don't even remember what he said after that, I was so shocked, so humiliated. He didn't even wait 'til they brought the menus. Just started right in, like I wasn't worth a few minutes of small talk. I felt so insignificant. Goddamn it, I was wearing my twenty-year pin when he started training his hair. Saying those things to *me*. And then I had to pee. One minute I didn't and the next minute I had to go so bad I could feel my bladder giving up. I got up and rushed into the bathroom—" He sighed. "It just let loose on its own—before I could get it out it was all over the place, all over my hands, on my pants. The guy next to me moved away and gave me such a look—like I was some kind of freak or something. I took off my coat and carried it over my arm so it covered the front of my pants. My god, Ethel—how can I make it for five more years? They're gonna have me working for a little girl I hired two years ago as an assistant to an administrative assistant."

Two

Charles got off the bus and entered the café. He slid into a window booth and ordered a cup of coffee. The natural high, which had been absent from his life for a long time, was back, and so was his confidence. He felt good; the cold sky looked good; the rain seemed abrim with promise; the morning commute, hissing excitedly by the window, seemed exuberant and optimistic; his cold hands, which would soon surround a hot cup, tingled in anticipation of the palette and the brush; the stickiness of stockingless feet inside broken shoes—Christ, even that felt good. The world was a good place on this good-feeling portentous morning. *Change* was in the air! The word itself had the suddenness and the movement of action. Change was newness, and newness was discovery. Change got your blood surging, made you rosy and cheerful and venturesome; made you smile. Change was excitement. Change energized curiosity, spawned ideas, and the excitement of those ideas got your work moving into discovery mode.

For the first time in months he couldn't wait to get to work. But first he had to complete the change of old self into new self, and he'd start by making the long-planned change of his address. This was a must, a thing he had to do before he could even think of lifting himself out of the psychological rut that was so deep he'd begun to believe its muddy walls marked the limit of his world.

He smiled at nothing, sipped his coffee, moved his ass on the plastic seat of the booth to confirm the presence of his fattened billfold, and felt the power and the energy that comes with nascent revival of hope, and nascent vitality of pocketbook.

He rehearsed, mentally, the next part of this momentous morning. The old man would raise his cold eyes from his account book, look out from under snowy eyebrows and over that ridiculous pince-nez, run his contemptuous gaze over the white-haired fellow with round bifocals and battered jeans, paint-splashed parka, and a flannel shirt redolent with turpentine and body odor. Wordlessly he, Charles, would haul his now prosperous billfold out and start counting the fifties onto the desk in front of the old man and say, "Here's the first two months." Old Nussbaum would raise his head in new respect, and Charles, showing nothing in *his* face, would add, "And here's another hundred—for my part of the dumpster and the utilities. I'll need two keys." And old Nussbaum would push himself to his feet and shuffle back through those junky islands of dingy glasses and dust-dimmed flatware displays and light-faded linen samples and pans and pots and skillets and cooking utensils—to the back wall and get the key ring from its nail.

Charles waited through two refills, content to laze like a fat cat in the steamy warmth and clatter of the café and think about the morning just past. Janice had surprised him—he'd counted on getting *some* money, maybe a couple hundred. But all of it? A grand? What had tipped her over? His appeal to the old days? No—she was used to that. Complaining about her cruelty—was it that? No, it wasn't that, either, though he had certainly embarrassed her by calling her on it. No, it was his reminder that he was still going after what she'd long ago given up on—but still wanted. He'd made her remember when he was still, after the decades of struggle, exactly what she always wanted to be, and had quit trying to be.

—

Fifty years of junk filled the huge space. Broken parts of display islands, boxes of shopworn linen and faded promotional displays, broken-handled pans, dented pots. Stuff stuffed into boxes and stuffed up here to be sorted later, and then forgotten. All to go out the back window into a dumpster. Decades of letters and ledger sheets that detailed the history of a business and a family. Charles climbed through the dark mounds of trash toward the gray cone of light spilling dimly down into the center of the long room. He put himself in the center of that cone of light and picked up a box and heaved it off to the side, raising a cloud of dust. He lifted the broken side of a display gondola and pitched it aside, raising more dust. When he finished clearing the area under the skylight the air was murky with dust. He looked twenty feet up at the big wire-reinforced glass, which a half-century of accumulated grime had rendered almost as opaque as the tar roof. The first thing he would do is climb up on the roof with a scraper and a brush and a bucket of soapy water and clean it. And then he would construct his studio right here; he would position his easel right in the center of the cone of light. He turned and looked toward the door, which was hidden behind dark mounds of trash.

"Boyce!"

A voice came from the darkness. "Whut."

"You ready, man?"

"I guess."

"You feelin' okay?"

"I guess."

"See if you can get that window open."

"Which one?"

"The one over there by the office wall—I mean my bedroom wall. The dumpster's below it."

A tall shadow moved out of the darkness and into the edges of the cone of light, the light just sufficient to reveal the elaborate blue paisley tatoos that covered his face.

"Man, you didn't tell me there was *this* much shit up here."

"What difference does it make? You want to live here, you contribute. That's what a co-op is. Open the window and let's get busy."

"You been sayin' that for months," Wilma Hatchet said, trying to see past Charles into the apartment. She'd heard the stairs creak and had lumbered down into the basement hoping to trap Charles.

Charles spoke through a narrow opening between the door and door jamb. "It's just taking more time than I thought, but I'm delivering the paintings today. I'll bring you the money in the morning."

Mrs. Hatchet narrowed her eyes. "What're you hiding in there?"

"Nothing."

Mrs. Hatchet tried to look into the tiny hutch of an apartment, where she would have seen garbage sacks filled with his belongings and the open window, had she been able to see past Charles.

"My girlfriend—she's not dressed, or I'd invite you in. Listen, I have to go now, got to deliver the commission. I'll come to your apartment in the morning and pay you."

"You better not be fucking with me again. I'll lock your fucking stuff up if you're fucking with me again."

"You'll get your money, Mrs. Hatchet."

"You'll be sleeping in the freeway hotel with nothing but the clothes on your back."

"I have to go now."

"Because I'll lock this place up."

"You'll get your money, Mrs. Hatchet."

"Tomorrow morning."

"Right."

"What time?"

"Whatever you say."

"You can't believe a word artists say," Mrs. Hatchet informed him. She crossed her arms over her breasts. "They say whatever they think you want to hear."

"Whatever you say, Mrs. Hatchet. How about nine?"

"I'll believe it when I see it. And if I don't see it, I'll be puttin' a padlock on this door."

"You'll get your money tomorrow."

"At nine."

"Nine sharp."

"Better be there, by God, or I'll padlock this fuckin' door."

"You won't have to do that."

"I will if I don't get my money."

"I have to go now. Got to deliver the painting."

She didn't move.

"So. I'll see you at nine?"

"You better not be messin' with me."

He closed the door.

Boyce started to say something but Charles held his hand up. They stood still, listening. Finally, they heard the heavy creak of Mrs. Hatchet dragging her three hundred pounds up the stairs.

"It'll take her a couple of minutes to get situated with her food in front of the TV," Charles said. "She won't move after that."

They took the important stuff first: the big, sturdy easel, the boxes of paints and brushes and spatulas, the tens of canvases, many of which he'd painted over two or three times, and which he would paint over again. They passed all of it out the basement window into the alley, temporarily converted the easel to a litter and carried the boxes and the canvases on the improvised litter down the hill past other decaying brick apartment buildings and over the freeway, carried it a mile through gray rain to the Co-op. They trudged back up the hill, entered the alley, and slipped into the apartment through the basement window. They filled plastic garbage bags with Charles's clothes, boxes with books, letters, and odds and ends of dishes and pots and pans. After more trips down and back all that remained was a broken-backed old sofa and a chair with exploding cotton arms and the mattress and a few canvases he had over-painted so many times they were cracked and stiff as plywood. They rolled and tied the mattress, covered it with plastic, and managed to shove it through the window.

Charles went through the remaining canvases, pulled two of the worst out of the stack and left them on the sofa with a note: "Mrs. Hatchet, the guy didn't have the money for the paintings so I'm giving them to you for the rent."

Three

Wally beheld shoes moving in a confused and hesitant shuffle, and gray and ivory tiles. The shoes moved hazily in and out of view, and he heard frightened murmurs: *"Wally? Wally? Can you hear me?"* A thick warmth tickled his face as gleaming red spread over the squares of gray and ivory. It was a startling, astonishing red, the like of which he had never seen. How could he have lived so long and never seen so brilliant a red? And then he discovered that he was no longer leaning on his arms. His arms had disappeared like his legs and he was floating down into that astonishing red.

Why this *pain*? And why this horrendous roaring, this shuddering sky-filling roar—thunderous, huge—rushing down on him like a roller coaster. He struggled for the strength to look around, to discover what was making the racket, but the pain immobilized him. He couldn't raise his hand, turn his head, couldn't even open his eyes. He kept trying, each attempt ending in failure and each failure exhausting him more deeply; bringing him closer to what he began to think was his death.

The pain surged! Oh, God, the pain! Pushing him right up to the edge, tilting him over into that infinite emptiness. Was this ignominious wallow of pain his dying? He felt the slipping again, and decided he wasn't going anywhere. No way was he going, not like this.

He surfaced, gasping. The pain still thundered, the roller coaster roared, the world heaved and shivered; but not so intolerably now, not so overwhelmingly. He worked at opening his eyes. Failing, he called for help and found that his words were soundless against the roar. He gave up and let himself lay in the hot blast of his pain, stoically awaiting deliverance or death.

From behind the roaring came Ethel's voice, faintly: "Sweetheart, it's me, can you hear me?"

More voices. A distant clatter. Shuffling and grunts, hands on him, hands under him. Ethel again, dis-tantly: "It's okay, it's all right, sweetheart. I'm here."

Summoning himself to one grand effort, he managed to crank an eyelid open—open, it turned out, to a shocking flare of color: electric yellows, drenching blues, mouth-puckering oranges, sour greens, screaming reds, rumbling tumbling purples. And behind the convulsion of color, a papery rustle of voices. Ethel's, George's, even Pete's. The reckless flamboyance of all that color got his heart pounding hard, pumping up the pain to unbearable levels. He closed his eye against the terrible colors and felt himself subsiding.

Worn down, exhausted, he wished for an end of pain and noise, even if it meant end of self.

—

Kimberly and Gary brought flowers and chocolates and a card covered with scrawled signatures. Gary sat in a chair at the end of the bed and ate the candy while Kimberly sat on the deep window sill swinging her sandaled feet and telling him not to worry: even with her new responsibilities as Director of IS she was managing to do his job in addition to her own. Gary mentioned that Browning was telling everyone what a brilliant job she was doing. She interjected that she was really surprised how easy it was to manage Tech Pubs. Piece of cake. As a matter of fact she'd turned some of Wally's responsibilities over to her new administrative assistant, who was also being brilliantly successful at it, even though she was just out of high school and had never had a job before. Now Kimberly was thinking of giving the youngster even more of Wally's responsibilities.

Gary said that Professor Rader's usability evaluation was a brilliant success and the Senior Management Team asked Kimberly to present a talk on the results. The talk was also a brilliant success. As a matter of fact, the SMT asked Kimberly to bring Professor Rader back in, when she has time, to evaluate the GUIs of all thirteen of Atlas' software products, and then make follow-up evaluations a routine part of every release cycle. It was turning out to be a brilliantly successful strategy. Wally closed his eyes; he'd heard all he needed to hear about Kimberly's brilliant successes. To cheer Wally up Gary repeated the jokes circulating on the thirtieth floor. By the time he got to the one about the vigilante groups that had been deputized in every department to subdue killer bathroom doors, tears were streaming down his face and he could hardly speak through his awful, snorting, hacking laugh. Wally gazed at them through a morphine haze and wondered why they were tormenting him. Even when he felt good Gary's laugh irritated him; now it came at him like an electric cattle prod. And the relentless brilliance of Kimberly's dress! How could she wear that disrespectably tiny, unbearably gaudy rag into the room of a very sick, and possibly moribund, man? Where was her sense of decency? The whole thing wan't bigger than a hanky. Hardly covered her lap. And the way she sat—she was as careless as a little girl about keeping her legs together—you could look right up that shadowy valley between her athletic thighs and see the international orange and neon yellow of her floral panties. She might as well just throw her legs wide open and *show* you her panties, they are that close to being out in the open. Barely concealed behind a dress so flimsy you could wad it up and stick it in your pocket and it wouldn't show a bulge as big as a handkerchief.

They left after Gary finished the chocolates. Wally fumbled with the call button. When the nurse came he whispered that his head is exploding. She said she'd bring his medication. He raised a hand to stop her, gathered his strength, and murmured, "The flowers—"

"Yes—aren't they're beautiful?"

"Please—get rid of them. So bright! So much—like Kimberly's panties."

—

George came in. "Good news, Dad."

Wally hoisted an eyelid at his son, noted the salt and pepper of his hair, which he wore pulled down against his scalp by a pony-tail, and his habitual jeans jacket, buttoned rather high over a pot belly, and the dingy gray of his once-white shirt topped by the shining black of his plastic bow tie. Familiar—and yet there is an element of newness in the picture. He opened the other eye. Was it the shirt lapels? He considered the way the lapels nested the shiny bow tie. Before this moment he never noticed those triangularities in that congruence of lines. Most interesting.

"I just saw Pete in the elevator. He said he's happy at how good yer scan come out. He's gonna be in in a few minutes."

"Strange, I didn't notice it before," Wally murmured.

"Whut."

The familiar scent that Wally associated with his son, that fecund aroma of nutrients just one or two steps of decomposition removed from the rawness of human waste, was spreading ever so faintly in the room. And, remarkably, it seemed to color the air—with a tinge of tan, he thought, or perhaps light brown.

"Whut're you talkin' about, Dad?"

"The color of the air."

George looked around.

"Very nice," Wally said dreamily, his attention wandering back to the place at George's throat where those triangularities co-existed so interestingly. "The blue of your jacket—what an attractive dusty, powdery blue. It's like a soft pillow for the black—but I don't know, maybe it's too—maybe—oh, I don't know. Why aren't you working? No jobs today? Where's your mother? I never noticed how hefty you're getting. You're getting fat, George, and you're starting to look old. I never noticed that before."

George grinned. "Man, they're givin' you some good shit."

—

Ethel and George drove Wally home. As they levered him out of the passenger side and stood him quivering beside the car, they heard a door slam. A moment later Roy came striding around the corner of his house.

"Hey Wally, how you doin', boy? Jesus, look at your head. You look like a sheik or something. When Ethel told me what happened I like to 've died—went right in and took out every one of my bathroom doors." He grinned and punched Wally playfully on the arm. "Seriously, though, let me give you a hand here. You okay, ol' buddy? You look bushed."

Roy's meaty face reminded Wally of his favorite sweater, an old maroon V-neck he liked to wear on cold evenings. Wally's stomach quivered unpleasantly. He turned away from Roy's varicose nose and reeled up the driveway.

George and Roy jumped to Wally's side and each took an arm. Wally managed a dozen steps before his legs went rubbery. He paled, put his head out past his gut, and puked, splattering hospital oatmeal in glistening beige gobs over the gray concrete. He pulled himself up and looked around for Ethel; and saw, through his own wet eyes, her wet eyes brimming with pity and love, a double chin and fat pendulous cheeks, and a pert little nose all pinked with cold. She was so beautiful with all her love and pinkness. She touched his face and whispered that everything was going to be okay.

They got him into bed and he swallowed some more of the pills and slept.

—

"Just eat your breakfast and stop worryin' about it," Ethel said. "If you knew how close you come to dying you'd be thankful you're even alive. You looked so awful with those tubes stickin' in you and those machines blinkin' and flashin' I couldn't hardly make myself go in the room. On the night Pete come out of that ICU and told me to prepare myself for the worst—well, I just about come apart. It's a miracle you're even here. And a bigger miracle you're not a vegetable or something. I just thank God we even have you."

"But a *month*?" Wally had just found out, once again, how long he'd been in the hospital.

"I told you, they wouldn't let you go home as long as you were having those seizures."

"I don't remember any seizures. I don't remember anything but headaches."

"You had 'em every day, but now you don't. You don't see the progress, but I do."

"But every morning—"

"You *are* getting better," she insisted. "Pete said it would be like this. He said it would be slow."

"Getting better?" he murmured at his orange juice. "I get up every morning thinking it's three months ago and time to go to work and you tell me about the accident all over again because I don't remember anything about it—and that's better?" Ethel has just told him that they've had this conversation many times. It frustrated him greatly to find out they'd talked about these things so many times, but not know that until Ethel told him. He wondered if time had slipped a cog, wondered if he'd continue looping back on himself like this forever. It was so discouraging. He felt tired.

"Your eggs are getting cold."

"I'm not hungry."

"Sweetheart, you've got to eat—you're skinny as a rail."

"I'll eat something later. Right now I'm too tired."

"You want to rest for a while?"

He gathered himself and pushed the chair back. Ethel came around the table and took his arm and helped him up. He caught his pajama bottoms before they slipped off his bony hips. Holding them up, he let Ethel lead him shuffling into the living room, where he fell into his Lazy Boy. She stepped back and looked down at his face. Eyes closed, mouth hanging open, breathing shallowly, stubbled cheeks hanging in loose folds of white skin, he looked a hundred years old.

She went to the kitchen and was at the sink rinsing the breakfast dishes when she remembered she was going to call Pete. He'd told her to call if there was any change, particularly concerning the headaches. She went to the phone and called his office. The nurse told her he'd call back. She hung up and looked at the phone, and recalled that she was going to call George. She dialed his number.

"Septic Concepts, Wanda speaking."

"Hello Wanda, this is Mom, I just called to tell you that Wally woke up this morning without a headache. *And* he knew where he was."

"Thank the Lord! Oh, I knew it, I knew God would be merciful if we prayed long enough and hard enough."

"Well, he's better, that's true, but he woke up thinkin' he had to get ready for work, as usual. And he didn't know nothing about the accident or the hospital, but he did remember some things that happened just before the accident that I don't remember him remembering."

"Well—long as he don't have them headaches."

"That's the main thing. Is George there?"

"He's out on a job."

"Will you tell him to call me?"

"He'll be so thrilled. I'm gonna call Reverend Stammer and tell him."

—

Wally started having the dream soon after the headaches stopped. He woke feeling worried, but with no notion of what was worrying him. Then he worried the rest of the day because he couldn't quite remember what he was worrying about. And then one morning he woke with "*a piece of cake*" echoing in his head. The phrase lingered as he began dressing for work, and was still there as Ethel served him eggs and bacon and explained to him, as usual, why he wasn't going to work.

"But I have to go to work. They think it's so easy and I have to show them it's not."

"What's not easy, sweetheart?"

He didn't know, exactly. All he knew for sure was that threatening phrase, "a piece of cake."

"It's not a piece of cake, damn it."

Ethel waited for him to finish. When he didn't, she murmured, "I'm sure it's not, honey."

He thought irritably that she couldn't possible know what he was talking about. Hell, he didn't know what he was talking about.

The phrase—"*a piece of cake*"—ricocheted through his thoughts for the rest of the day, conjuring concepts like *insignificant* and *trivial* and *inconsequential*. It wasn't until the next morning, as Ethel finished telling him, as usual, about why he wasn't going to work, that his brain connected Kimberly to the phrase.

"It's her, by God! She's the one who thinks it's a piece of cake. But she's wrong, it's not."

"Who thinks it? What isn't a piece of cake?"

"Kimberly thinks it. But it's not."

"What isn't, sweetheart?"

"Hell, I don't know! I just know it isn't."

That morning was the last morning he woke thinking he had to get dressed and eat his breakfast before driving down to the Park-and-Ride to catch the 250. Thereafter he woke remembering just enough about the accident and its aftermath to know he wasn't going anywhere. On that day he started calling Kimberly to see how things were going in Tech Pubs, hoping thereby to assert his relevance. He also offered advice she was not interested in receiving. Within a week he was calling her so often that one morning when she heard his voice for the fourth time that day, she didn't even give him a chance to make his suggestion.

"Wally, stop bothering me with these annoying and stupid suggestions."

The rebuke shocked him, but not for long; he reminded himself that she was a director, so she was supposed to talk like that. All those responsibilities, making all those decisions that directors have to make every day, and managing his Tech Pubs group in addition. And being so brilliantly successful at it that a brand new admin who's never had a job before can handle most of the details. Apparently no one in Tech Pubs even missed him, for they were putting out the whole suite of manuals that accompany two major software releases, all at one time. And on schedule! His peace of mind did not need her to be so brilliantly successful at things he had never been able to do. His peace of mind needed for her to need him back at his desk, managing Tech Pubs.

He drank his seizure medicine and slept. And worried, even when he was so drugged that he couldn't keep two eyes open at the same time. Ethel noticed his worrying and worried about how much he worried. She stopped encouraging him to remember and began encouraging him to forget. And to rest. That was what he needed; to rest and let himself heal. Rest and watch the TVs and forget every-thing else. That was her prescription.

To please her he tried to do as she wished. He watched the TVs, but the TVs didn't make him forget his worry about his job. All the TVs did was get the headaches going again. He found the morning shows particularly painful. *The Jennifer Show* hurt his head so much he had to turn the sound completely off. Even his favorite evening shows got his head throbbing with pain. Eventually Ethel just turned the TVs off and kept them off. Even her kitchen TV. But the mere presence of their blind and muted faces was enough to drive him from a room. He complained so often about the damned things staring at him that Ethel got to worrying more about his TV aversion than about his headaches. She was convinced it was temporary, like his memory loss, but she gave in and hauled the portables out to the garage and covered the 54-incher in the living room and the 39-incher in the bedroom with table cloths and doilies and potted plants. Amazingly, within days of de-TVing the house, Ethel saw the changes she wanted to see in Wally. He began relaxing, and was soon eating with a healthy appetite. His color returned, his eyes brightened, he seemed to worry less. It wasn't perfect—there was still a strange absentmindedness, but Ethel wasn't looking this gift horse in the mouth. She was thankful she even had him.

Roy saw the strangeness that Ethel saw, but he was not alarmed by it. He saw improvement beneath the strangeness. He came over every afternoon, ready to encourage further improvement in any way he could; which was usually by offering to resume their cribbage battles and by inviting himself to stay for supper. At first Wally was reluctant to accept Roy. Ethel attributed this behavior to Wally's uncertain memory. And she was right: as Wally remembered more of his past he began to look forward to the cribbage.

One afternoon they were playing cribbage at the kitchen table while Ethel peeled potatoes at the sink. Wally, who was looking up at the ceiling, said reflectively, "It's amazing all the stuff that goes on in your head when there's no noise from the TVs."

Roy sorted his cards, studied his hand, selected and played a jack, saw that Wally was still staring at the ceiling. He glanced up and saw nothing but off-white flatness. "Your play," he said.

"Look at the way the light makes the ceiling seem different from the wall."

Roy glanced from one side of the ceiling to the other.

"I figured out why," Wally said. "I noticed it yesterday afternoon when I woke up from a nap in my Lazy Boy and saw that the living room ceiling seemed like it was a different color from the walls. At first I thought it was just shadow, but then I realized there was no shadow, the light was the same all over the room. It came to me that it was the same reason the night seems darker when you're driving on wet pavement compared to driving on dry pavement."

Ethel had gotten quiet. She turned from the sink and faced them, holding a half-peeled potato and a paring knife. She stared fixedly at Wally, as if dreading what was coming next.

"You want to know why a dry street is brighter at night than a wet street?" Wally asked.

"Play," Roy said.

"It's because the street's got all these tiny little voids and bumps in it and when it's dry your headlights hit the sides of the little irregularities and some of it reflects back at you. The key to the problem is the angle of incidence equals the angle of reflection."

"Play," Roy said again.

"See, when rain water fills in the voids and smoothes over the little irregularities, the light from your headlights, which hits at a low angle, reflects off the water at that same angle, but away from you. Almost none of the light is reflected back at you, so it seems darker when it's wet than when it's dry."

"Okay," Roy said. "So play."

Wally picked up his cards, fanned them, and played a five. "Fifteen-two," he said, moving his peg.

Roy played a five. "Twenty for two," he said, moving his peg.

"See, it's the same idea with the ceiling. The light from the window hits the ceiling at a low angle, and it reflects away from you so your eyes don't see much of it, whereas you do see a lot of the light reflected from the walls because the angle of incidence is greater and the reflected light comes to your eyes. Makes the ceiling seem darker than the walls. At first I thought it was just shadow, but then I realized it couldn't be shadow, 'cause the light was the same all over the room. So—"

"I said, twenty for two," Roy said. "It's your play."

Wally dropped another five on the table. "Twenty-five for six," he said, moving his peg six pieces. "So, anyway—"

"Christ, where does this man get his luck," Roy muttered, playing an ace. "Jesus. Twenty-six."

Wally played the fourth five and moved his peg. "Thirty-one for two."

"I'll bet the lucky bastard's got a ten, too," Roy muttered, playing a ten.

Wally played his last card, a ten. "Twenty for two and one is three." Wally moved his peg again, then reached across the table to the TV shelf, which now bore a stack of books and a pencil jar. He grabbed a pencil and began drawing on the table cloth. "I'll show you what I mean."

Roy watched Wally draw lines and angles and Greek characters. He looked back at Ethel with a raised eyebrow. She stood as before, the potato in one hand, the knife in the other, her face pale.

—

"George, it's not just some quirky little thing he does once in a while," Ethel said. "It goes on all the time now. First it was these headaches and he couldn't remember anything, then he comes out of his headaches and starts rememberin'. Then he starts worryin' about gettin' back to work. That goes on for a while, and then he forgets he ever had a job and starts this discovering business. It's like—it just seems like he's going backwards, that he's behaving just like a little boy, and it scares me to death. He'll discover— that's what he's always talking about now—he'll discover something or other and it's all he can talk about until he discovers some other thing. Then that's all he can talk about."

George listened patiently enough, but his body language (glancing at Wanda knowingly, looking down at his coffee with a frown, tapping on the table with the fingers of one hand) communicated very clearly what he was thinking. He was thinking that his mother just isn't up to handling this situation; he was thinking maybe *he* ought to step in and show her how to handle it.

Ethel read her son like a book. She knew exactly what he was thinking, all right, and his thoughts weren't helping the situation one bit. It was hard enough having to watch Wally all the time without George acting like she's as inept as Wally, who'd gotten so absentminded now that you had to watch him all the time or he just wandered off God knows where.

"I don't care what you think, I'm gonna ask Pete to bring in a brain doctor."

"Mom, Pete's looked at Dad hundred a times in the last few months. What Dad needs to do is to get back to work and—"

"Oh, sure, Pete sees him all right. Says 'Hi, Wally, how you doing?' Listens to his chest, thumps him on the back, looks in his eyes, says 'You're looking good, Wally.' And if he asks me what I think, it's while he's looking at his watch like he's run out of time, or scribbling on a piece of paper. No one sees it but me, because I'm with him all the time. Roy comes over every day and even he doesn't see it."

"You got to be firm with him," George began irrelevantly. "You got to make him—"

Wanda interrupted. "What *does* Roy think?"

Ethel sighed. "Wally's got him buffaloed; even got him interested in those discoveries. Sometimes they're both like little boys."

Silence for several seconds, then Wanda spoke again. "Mom, it's not that we think you're wrong. We're seeing the same things you see. We just— sometimes we just see it differently. Maybe we should ask Reverend Stammer to help us pray on it."

"You ask me, all he needs is to get back to work," George blurted, unable to contain himself in the face of all this female foolishness. "If all I did was lay around the house all day long I bet I'd be mak-ing discoveries, too."

The discoveries came fast and furious. Discoveries about light, mostly, because the more Wally discovered about light the more time he spent thinking about it. The thing about light was you can literally *see* the evidence of it everywhere. Without light you can't see evidence of anything. With light, every parameter of measurement became evident: dimension, mass, proximity, velocity, acceleration, color. But there was a problem with light: you don't really see it. Looking at light is like looking at a sheet of the purest glass: the only evidence your eye can give you of its existence is your own reflection in it.

For all of the wealth of data his eyes collected about light he could not attain an understanding of it, could not come up with a reasonable hypothesis that explained it. It was just too abstract, too defiant of intuition's guidance to make sense to him. So he kept going to his physics book for help. Wave *and* particle? He tried to visualize a wave, saw in his mind a sinusoidal shape of water surface moving out in a circle from a point, then tried to see that phenomenon as particles moving sinusoidally. He saw it, but just could not make sense of it.

His inability to solve the mystery of light did not dampen his enthusiasm. Far from it. His lack of understanding incited his eagerness, which led to the discovery of other marvels. Not big discoveries, not like his discovery that the angle of the incidence of light equals the angle of reflection, which led to all kinds of other discoveries. Most of his discoveries were simple hypotheses that explained one observation or another. Like the way a dark background gave a scene an apparent depth of field even when you close one eye and see the scene two-dimensionally—for example, the fruit trees in the back yard against the darkness of the woods across the creek.

Insignificant phenomena that he'd lived with all of his life and never thought about became subjects of intense scrutiny. He discovered, for instance, that a grouping of shapes and textures and colors in a certain arrangement can seize his attention and so please him that he thinks of the grouping as a thing in itself—not as an assortment of things. He looked for but did not find a description of that phenomenon in his physics book. Surprisingly, he found it in an article about composition in an architecture magazine at Pete's office.

This led him to the discovery of the principles of composition. Something about that topic captured him, mesmerized him. He became quiet and, for a couple of weeks, introspective. Ethel often found him staring into space for minutes at a time, with such concentration that he looked like he'd gone into a kind of suspended animation. Or she'd find him looking at some grouping of shape and color and texture—an insect in a spider's web, or the sienna in the murky shadows in the cheap print hanging in the entry hall, or the glisten of morning frost on drooping rhododendron leaves, or a cottony lens of fog hanging in the quiet air over the creek beyond the fruit trees. In those moments she had a dreadful feeling that irretrievable loss was close upon her, and she remembered what she felt like when her mother fell over dead one morning, and when she found her own dear first-born, a daughter, dead in her cradle.

—

Pete turned off the light. "Your eyes look better, Wally. How's your sleep?"

"Okay," Wally said.

"Any double vision?"

Wally shook his head.

"Dizziness? Faintness?"

"Nope."

Pete opened up the file folder and scribbled something. "Ethel tells me you've been making discoveries."

Wally nodded.

"I'd like to hear about them."

"Okay—what do you want to know?"

"Tell me about something you've discovered."

"Well—strictly speaking they're in the physics books already. And in the drawing books. What I'm doing is discovering them for myself."

"Tell me about one of them."

Wally thought for a moment. He decided on the angle-of-incidence discovery. That was a good one because there was nothing subjective or abstract about it. It was pure physics, and being physics, was easier to talk about than color and texture, because discoveries relating to those attributes tended to be abstract. He couldn't find the words to articulate intensity of color, for instance; and it was impossible to convey how the beauty in that intensity moved him, how the arrangement of color in shapes and textures mesmerized him. And disturbed him—that above all else: how the shapes and textures and colors seemed to grab his soul and drag it right out of his body. He had tried many times to explain it to Ethel as a discovery, so that she could share the emotional lift, but she always turned the richness of his discoveries into a frailty by insisting that she could help him overcome his problem. Of course he didn't think of any of his discoveries as a frailty or a problem. Now he tried to make Pete understand that very point as he told him about how he had thought through the principle that the angle of incidence of light equals the angle of reflection, and how he had proven it with mirrors and flashlight and tape measure.

"Wally, when did you develop this interest in physics?"

I never thought about it until the last few months."

Ethel did not like the way the conversation is going. Wally was making it sound like it was *normal* to think about stuff like physics and art, and Pete was just going along with him.

"Wally, tell him how you don't think about work anymore," Ethel suggested.

Wally obliged. "That's right, I don't."

"Why not, Wally?" Pete asked.

"Because it's not as interesting as physics?" Wally said it more like a question, as if he wasn't sure it was an acceptable answer.

Ethel frowned.

"Let's talk some more about going back to work," Pete said.

"You mean I'm ready?" There was no enthusiasm in Wally's voice.

"No, not yet, I just want to know what you think about it."

"Well, a man's gotta work. That's the way life is. When I'm ready I guess I'll just go."

Little blotches of red showed on Ethel's cheeks. All this talk sounded like Pete was trying to make her concerns seem—well, stupid. But she wasn't going to take it lying down.

"Wally. I want you to tell him about how when you're making a discovery you just forget everything and wander off, and how we have to go find you."

Wally nodded. "That's right, sometimes I get so wrapped up in a discovery that I just forget everything else—where I am, what time it is."

Pete smiled. "Reminds me of a book I read about Einstein, how he'd get so wrapped up in one of his thought experiments that he'd forget where he was."

Ethel's lips tightened. "Wally's not Einstein. He needs to know where he is."

"Are you taking your medication, Wally?"

"I guess so."

"Ethel gives you the pills?"

"Yes."

"I give him his medicine exactly like the bottle says," Ethel said.

"Put your shirt on, Wally," Pete said. He watched Wally button his shirt and tuck it into his pants. "You look fit, Wally. I think you're ready for more exercise. I want you to walk. Start with a half mile every day, and very week increase the distance a half mile until you're walking three miles. As for work—I think you need to be stronger before we can release you to go back to work." He talked as he scribbled in the file folder. "Ethel—about the discoveries. I understand your concern, but I wouldn't worry too much about behavior changes like these. Head injuries have a variety of transitory effects. And so do the drugs. We'll reduce the medication, see if that helps." He tore a prescription off the pad and gave it to Ethel.

"I don't think it's the medicine," Ethel said. "I think it's the injury. I think he hurt his brain."

Pete nodded. "Indeed he did. He's lucky to be alive. But he's made a remarkable recovery, and there's no reason to think he won't continue recovering. Changing the medication might deal with your concerns."

"Well, I think he's in no shape to be doing all that thinking. I think it's dangerous for a person with a brain injury to be thinkin' as much has he does. Stands to reason it's hard on your brain. *I* think you ought to caution him about all that thinking. Maybe talk to him about watching more TV. That's bound to make him stop thinking."

Pete closed the folder. "What d'you think, Wally? Do you think you're thinking too much?"

Wally thought about it for a second, then shook his head. "I don't think so."

—

Ethel hoped the new medication would waken the old Wally, but it didn't. The new medication incited even greater curiosity in Wally, and got him making even more discoveries. His mind hummed as he darted about looking for something to discover.

One drizzly morning he entered the kitchen to get his coat before going for his walk. He looked out the window. There, just beyond the crease of land in which the creek flowed, in the shadows of that alder thicket where the neighborhood kids made their fort and fought their summer battles, he saw the black center of a lovely composition. Over the years he had seen the thicket in every season, in every con-ceivable light, always as a tangle of saplings and underbrush, never as the central element of a composition. He studied the scene for a while, then went out the back door and stood on the steps looking out past the line of ancient fruit trees and the overgrown lau-rels and the patchy lawn.

Still thinking about the thicket, he walked out to the creek, crossed the foot bridge, and followed a path through knee-high yellow grass. He came back along the path an hour later, sweating under his jacket, his shoes soaked, his pant legs wet to the knees, tired but exhilarated. He saw Ethel move into the frame of the big kitchen window, then out of it, then back in. He continued along the path to the foot bridge, crossed, and came up the sloping back yard and paused at the line of ancient apple trees—survivors of an orchard that had produced fruit before he was born—and remembered that he was going to prune the trees. He looked up into a tree, thinking maybe he'd do it today.

As he gazed up into the tree he was struck by the graceful, straight-up reach of last year's growth: young runners rising up out of knotty arthritic limbs, growing strong and straight, while the parent limbs—well, the combination of age and insects and disease and weather and their own weight had done to them what the same effects did to all things. He swept his gaze over the landscape: the grandfatherly cedar rising out of the alder wood, the lone survivor of an ancient cedar forest, towering over alder youngsters; the back yard sloping down to the creek; the gnarled plum and apple trees; the arbor of grapes; the creek, now running full enough for a spawning steelhead; and that lovely dark thicket of alder. It hit him then—a realization as real as God. No, *more* real than God. He ran inside, practically pushed poor startled Ethel out of the way in his rush to his desk. He shoved a piece of paper into the old typewriter and started pounding away.

Ethel stood in the kitchen and listened to the clacking, which went on for one minute, two minutes, five minutes. When it stopped she went trembling into the hall and peered around the doorway into the room he had always called his study, but which, like every other room in the house, had for decades been just another TV room (the TV now resided on a shelf in the garage with the others). Wally sat at the desk beneath shelves and shelves of video tapes of TV programs going back to the seventies, leaning over a sheet of paper. He had a blue pencil in his hand.

"Wally?"

He looked up. "Ethel, you have to read this."

"Don't you want take off your hat and coat? And change your clothes? You're all wet."

"Oh, sure," he said, but made no move. "It's the most incredible thing. I was in the back yard looking up at one of the apple trees and I thought of something amazing—" he held up a sheet of paper "—I had to write it down before I lost it. No question about it, it's my most important discovery. I'm not the first one to discover it, of course. Because Newton and Einstein and, well, you know what I mean, those physicists back then discovered it too, but—" He paused. "You following me?"

—

Pete wrinkled his face. "Gravity? I don't understand."

George cleared his throat. "Well—it's kind of hard to explain, but Dad has this idea that he's discovered the—what'd he call it? Oh yeah, the *mechanism* of life. He says it's gravity, an' that it's the closest thing to God." He paused, squinting in concentration. "He said maybe gravity is God. I guess. Even told Reverend Stammer that the proper study of God was not the scriptures, but Newton and some other names—I don't remember who all else he said."

"It was awful," Ethel murmured at her purse. "Reverend Stammer even agreed with him. Which I'm sure he didn't really, he was only being nice."

"Dad's saying some strange things," George added.

"I been telling everyone that very thing for months and no one believed me," Ethel said tiredly.

"He don't even think about work no more," George added.

"Tell me how he's behaving," Pete said.

"I been telling you," Ethel said. "For months."

"He walks a lot. And reads—I guess." George looked at Ethel, who nodded sadly.

"What's he reading?"

"Strange stuff," George said. "Physics an' art an' stuff like that."

"He goes to that used book store down by the Safeway and finds these books on drawing and painting. Says it's all physics."

"I think you better bring him in."

—

Wally had gotten dressed for his morning walk and had gone to the back door and looked out the window to check the weather. His eye caught the glint of a star in the southern sky, and below it a thin, delicate scimitar of silver. A new moon. How lovely, he thought. He went outside, to see it better.

Although shadows of night still lingered between the house and the rhododendrons the sky glowed with daylight. And in that bowl of spreading brilliance that single star still shown—alone of all its billions of companions, refusing oblivion. He admired it greatly, was deeply moved by its audacity. He moved out from under the apple tree and around the house into the openness of the front yard, the better to observe it. He continued walking down the long driveway and across the street, to improve his view of it. He walked south on Juanita Drive, his eyes on the delicate silver scimitar and the gleaming hot dot of the morning star.

Two hours later he crested the hill on Market Street and looked down at Kirkland and the lake. The sun was bright and the wind had swung around and now came strong out of the southwest. With its ten-mile fetch the wind had raised whitecaps on the lake, and breakers at the boat ramp. A sailboat heeled over far down the lake, along the southwestern horizon where the Seattle skyline stood out against a clotted purple sky. The weather was turning, there would be rain. He continued down the hill to Lake Street, passing upscale boutiques and real estate offices and restaurants and art galleries. Cars coasted lazily along the street and pedestrians walked more hurriedly than normal, to get out of the sharp-edged wind that whipped at trouser cuffs and skirt hems. His eye caught a flash of color in a window across the street. He saw that the color came from a painting behind a big window. He went across the street to the window, on which gold leaf lettering stood out in a simple arch: *Janice Cushion Gallery*.

Four

Wally had never experienced anything like this. Mere words could not describe the extremity of the pleasure he felt as he viewed the painting. This spendid discovery was an event of total pleasure, of pleasure exploding inside him with the velocity of the big bang. He was having his own private big bang; a new universe coming into being in him; an exquisitely rich hunger that, in being satisfied, is marvelously never-satisfied. He stared at the painting until his eyes hurt. Wanting to penetrate it, to get inside it, to be in it.

He was discovering. Big time. Discovering ways of looking at it: as a unit, as a collection of objects embedded in planes, as shadows and curves and lines, as brush strokes, as daubs and streaks and splashes, as discordances of color; discovering finally that he was not capable of seeing all of it at once. He concentrated on its parts: a polygon of yellow here, a block of red and orange and green there, a series of lines spiraling down to a point, colors showing through colors. And all of it against an intricate pattern—like objects strewn over a coarsely woven cloth. After a while he expanded his gaze to encompass the whole of it and tried once again to penetrate the bigness of it, which he began to see was the barrier to his understanding. His head swam.

"What d'you think of it?"

The voice came from far away.

"You been here a half hour—you must think something about it."

Wally realized the voice was aiming words at him and he felt himself drawn back to awareness of the street, the cold gray sky, the concrete sidewalk, the window on which rain beaded up, the wet wind that gusted between the buildings, the coldness of his hands and feet and nose, and a lanky white-haired fellow whose jeans and coat looked like the floor of a paint store and who studied him through small round bifocals.

"Pardon?"

"I asked you what you thought of it."

"The painting?"

The white head nodded.

"Well—that it's beautiful. I guess."

"Beautiful! A strong statement. But what does that mean?"

A tallish, slender woman was holding the door. "Charles, are you coming in?" There was more command than question in her voice.

"In a minute. I'm talking to my friend here about this—painting, I think is what he calls it." Charles turned back to Wally. "Beautiful is a meaningless word in the world of art. To say a thing is beautiful is to say it is attractive—which in no way implies that it is art. In the interest of precision, let us look at what you mean when you say this—painting I think you called it, which, by the way, is a good example of how imprecision in language can lead one astray—you have called that object a painting and you have said it is beautiful and yet a reasonably discriminating eye might judge it otherwise on both counts. Let me tell you why."

The woman let the door close and came to the white-haired man's side. "Charles," she said, "if you start one of your little episodes anywhere near my gallery, I will eighty-six you forever, and then no one in the whole world will show your work."

The lightness of her voice suggested she was making a joke, but Charles' response suggested she was not. He followed her inside.

Wally looked back at the painting, then let his eyes wander beyond the painting through the rest of the gallery behind it, which was now brightly lit. The white-headed man and the tall woman had walked to the back and were talking beside a desk. Wally looked at the wall between them and the door, recognized imme-diately that the person who had painted the canvas on the easel had also painted the canvases on the wall. He opened the door and entered. The man and the woman stopped talking and looked at him, but Wally didn't even see them. He went right to the paintings on the long wall. The man and the woman continued talking.

"Just a few weeks ago I gave you five hundred. Do you have any idea how much you're into me for? I'll bet you can't guess within a thousand."

"Well, I don't have my accounts with me right—"

"Your accounts!"—but I'd guess—two thousand? Maybe a little less? But one show—"

"Sixteen-thousand five-hundred."

"You sure of that? Okay, okay, sixteen it is. I guess I lost track."

"You lost track. Of sixteen-thousand five-hundred."

"I'm sure you're right. But that's not even one show. One show is all I need and you'll get your money back. One show."

"You have never done a six-grand show, Charles."

"I have, too. That show for Whipple, on Occidental Park. You ought to remember that, the summer you moved in with me. That was an *eight*-grand show. I had six red dots on opening night. You were there. My new stuff—"

"Charles, this is Janice you're talking to, not some twenty-two-year-old groupie."

Charles's face collapsed. "Christ—don't you understand what—" He brought his hands up in front of him, dropped them. "You're an artist. Or you were, 'til you sold out—"

"You're holding your hand out to this sellout."

"You were an artist, you were there. With me. Why do you *do* this? Why do you put me through these hoops? Just say no. Say, I don't have it. Say, I'm not giving you any of my fucking pile of money. Say, I'd rather burn it first. But you shouldn't do what you're doing. Making me beg."

Five

"I saw him! There, in the park!"

George wheeled the Ford into the empty parking lot, drove to the end, and stopped. The wipers thudded back and forth. "Where?" he said sullenly. "I don't see nobody."

Ethel was already opening her door. "Down by the boardwalk. I know it was him." She stepped into the rain.

George watched his mother pull her coat close and move off down the path. He sighed long sufferingly, turned the engine off, got out, and pulled his jacket up around his throat. Ahead of him the grassy hillside tapered down to a soggy flat that ended in the cattails of the lakeshore. Farther out the gray surface of the lake merged with the lighter gray of rain and fog. A quarter mile across the bay the south flank of Finn Hill rose out of the mist, showing haloed splashes of yellow light. They followed the cinder path around the knoll and saw him standing behind an easel, ankle-deep in water, down where the grass disappeared into cattails.

George called.

Wally glanced over his shoulder, waved, and turned back to the canvas.

George splashed up to the easel. "What in hell are you doing out here? We been looking all over the damned countryside for you."

"Trying to get the fog. But I'm making a mess of it."

"Get the fog? Dad, you're standing in the goddamned *lake*, and it's raining."

"It's all right, this is just a practice canvas."

Ethel came up behind George, one hand at her mouth. "Oh, Wally—"

"Ethel, you're crying again. You've been crying a lot lately—you used to do that before your period, but you haven't had one in years."

"C'mon, Dad. Let's pack this crap up and get the hell outa here." George leaned over and picked up a plastic sack that was half submerged in the ankle-deep water.

"Look how the fog comes off the water." Wally pointed with his brush. "Like gray fingers coming up out of gray water. Isn't it magnificent?" He lowered the brush, looked at the square of canvas. "It's such a simple scene— just a couple of colors, but I can't get it. I've painted it and scraped it off four times. I was telling Janice how hard it is to paint the evening light, because it changes so fast, and when it gets dark the colors just go together. Reds turn black, yellows turn gray. Janice was telling me that we see colors differently at night, mainly we see grays, and of course it's true, it's just one of those things you don't notice for some reason. She was explaining some things about an abstract painting of a waterfall she has in her storeroom. No matter how much I looked I couldn't see how the artist abstracted what he did from that water fall. But she said I shouldn't worry about it, it will come naturally, as long as I keep myself open. But I don't think I'm the type to paint abstract stuff. And she says it doesn't matter one way or the other, because whatever way you paint you have to master your tools. Take drawing, for instance. Janice was firm about that. She shows a lot of abstract stuff in her gallery—Patternism, Extractionism, Distractionism—of course most of her own work was in the Distract School of Extractionism, but she insists it doesn't matter how unrepresentational your work is, you have to learn to draw. To paint it the way you see it, you have to know how to use your tools, and use them fast, otherwise you get cramped and cautious and you can't paint truly if you paint cautiously, because you have to take chances to paint truly. Don't you love that? 'Course that's the reason why drawing's absolutely fundamental—like tonight, if I'd been able to work faster I might've been able to get the fog—"

George was pawing about in the plastic bag. "This stuff looks new. Dad, you're buying this crap again, aren't you. You promised."

"I needed a little paint, and a couple of brushes."

"Mom, look at this."

"There's a couple of colors I still need, but it's okay, I think I got enough for tonight. Maybe you'd like to come with me tomorrow, George. Why don't you take the morning off. I'll show you Janice's gallery. And I want to—"

"There must be twenty brushes in here. Jesus Christ, this one cost twenty-five bucks!"

"—show you what I saw at Whipple's Gallery—Janice took me over there and Mister Whipple let me see some of his private collection this morning. I'll ask him to show you, too. He's got a Jack Peacock. Can you imagine that? Now there's an abstract painting you don't have to understand. It's just plain beautiful. I'm sure Mr. Whipple will show us. He traded for that Peacock in the sixties, when he was a youngster living in Long Island and trying to be a painter. And of course there's Janice's gallery. You still haven't seen it. It's not as big as Whipple's and she doesn't have many well-established artists, but Whipple says she has some up-and-comers. When I'm in there and I look at that art all around me I can't understand how it's possible for a man to get through a lifetime and not see any of that stuff. Can you imagine, not seeing it when it's all around you? But I think I know why—because it's hidden by all the crap. Our eyes take it in, but we're not trained to filter out of the crap. Sensory overload, we just shut down, we stop seeing. Sweetheart, I wish you'd stop crying. Come here, let me hold you. My God, you're shaking. George, why'd you bring your mother out here when she's sick like this?"

"Dad, can't you just shut up? For five minutes?"

"Well, I guess so. Here, I'll carry the easel."

He folded the easel, slung it over his shoulder, then turned and faced the hill across the bay, now a dark hump behind the translucent gray of straight-down, pounding rain. Yellow lights glimmered weakly through the rain and the filaments of fog hanging above the water.

"Maybe I should just try to get it in my head and paint it from memory," Wally said. Then he leaned over and picked up a canvas floating at his feet. He studied it.

"Dad, come on."

"Look at this, George, look how the gray—"

—

Pete fell silent and watched Wally.

"Dad, pay attention," George said irritably.

Wally was working on the shading. This was his sixth try and he still hadn't gotten it right. He flipped the page of his sketchbook and began another drawing. "I am paying attention, son. I heard what Pete said. He said Doctor Ramsay thinks I've got some pieces of skull in my brain."

Pete raised himself and leaned over his desk to see the drawing; he held himself thus for several seconds and watched Wally move the charcoal swiftly over the pad. He wrinkled his face thoughtfully. "Wally, you're a wonder."

"It's not very good. These shadows—I don't like the way they make your nose so big." Wally held the pad up so Pete could see.

"It looks just like me," Pete said.

Wally scrutinized the drawing. "It isn't right," he said and went back to work on it.

Pete observed the charcoal, which seemed to scratch the features of his face right out of the paper: the eyes coming alive; the mouth becoming the mouth he saw in the mirror every morning as he shaved; shadows modeling the forehead and nose into a three-dimensionality that seems to lift it off the page. He settled back in his chair.

"As I was saying, the scan and the EEG came out normal. The fracture's healed very nicely and the subdural hematoma is completely resorbed. And as for the bone fragments that Doctor Ramsay is talking about—physiologically they're probably harmless enough; you have no symptoms that suggest there's a serious risk. People have lived for decades with bullets in their brains, so there's little likelihood a couple of pieces of your own bone will be life threatening."

Wally moved the charcoal over the paper, looked up at Pete, studied his face for a couple of seconds, looked down, and continued working.

"Did you hear what I said, Wally?" Pete asked.

Wally nodded slowly as he stroked the charcoal over the page. "Yes. You said that my scan came out fine; that my brain seems normal; that I don't have to worry; that people—"

"There's another part we need to talk about," Pete said. "Doctor Ramsay believes there is a behavioral consequence to your injury—he believes there's a connection between your recent behavior and the presence of the bone fragments in the frontal lobes of your brain. He's thinking Pablo Piccolo Syndrome. He wants to do some more testing."

Wally looked up. "Pete—would you mind moving that lamp just a little. The other way. This problem with the shadowing—I need stronger side light. I'm just not good enough to get the subtleties of—"

"For Christ's sake, Dad! Will you please pay attention? This is important stuff. We need to make an important decision here."

"I'm listening, George. As a matter of fact what Pete's saying about Piccolo is very interesting, though I'm not so sure that Piccolo—"

Pete interrupted gently. "Wally, this Pablo Piccolo Syndrome isn't about Piccolo himself—"

Wally continued shading the side of Pete's face.

"—it's about a behavior problem some researchers think he had. It seems he carried creativity to obsessive extremes, and that this problem had organic roots—probably a serious injury to the left side of his brain—just as your injury was. Doctor Ramsay thinks your injury resembles Piccolo's, and that your behavior is similar to his."

The charcoal scratched busily over the rough-textured drawing paper.

"What do you think, Wally?" Pete finally asked.

"I bought this book of Pablo Piccolo's paintings—"

George interjected: "For one-oh-nine-fifty! Can you believe that? For a goddamned *book*. One-oh-nine-fifty for *one book*. I could've bought twenty-five Louis L'Amours for that."

"George, this isn't about books," Ethel said.

"—and his letters," Wally went on. "If you read the letters he wrote to his brother Pako Piccolo you'll see he didn't get his talent from some injury. People thought he was crazy, but I don't think so. Crazy people don't write like Pablo Piccolo wrote or make art like Pablo Piccolo's art. I think he was so full of talent and love for people and art and nature, that everyone thought he was crazy." Wally looked up at Pete, then down at his pad, then back up at Pete again. "It helped. Moving the light helped."

Pete's face wrinkled up again. He didn't like this territory. He liked Wally's incontinence and edema and heart palpitations and shortness of breath and obesity and that occasional numbness in his hands and the skull fracture and that subdural hematoma and the seizures. This syndrome business—or whatever the hell it was—he had a feeling there was precious little medical science behind it. Physiological medicine—that was real, its reality validated by the way symptoms respond to artful hands and knowledge and the logic of science. Physics and skillful hands and detective work, guided by the rules of science: the tracing of effect to cause. Not a collection of disconnected behaviors as rootless as voodoo, which is what he half believed young Ramsay had got him dabbling in. Still—how do you explain symptoms like Wally's aberrant behavior? The connection of his present behavior with his injury is inescapable. Before the accident Wally was that, now he's this; and the this is as fundamentally different from the that as black is from white. And yet—even if you could say with certainty that the injury explained Wally's behavior—can you also say that the new behavior is bad, that it's a problem? A problem that requires life-threatening intervention? Brain surgery, for God's sake? When is a man sick? When he says he's sick? Or when a doctor or a wife says he's sick? When a man has a cancer there's no doubt about the sickness or the prognosis, and it is because of those certainties that you feel right about slicing him open and whacking the bad meat out of him. You know you are doing the right thing, even when you fail. You almost-kill him in order to kill the bad meat. Because the bad meat is worse than the trauma inflicted by cutting the bad meat away. But this situation: he wonders: where the hell is the bad meat?

"Did you know that Gorganzola wouldn't paint Piccolo until he knew him well enough to paint him from memory?" Wally asked. He looked up at Pete's face, which was still wrinkled in perplexity. "I didn't understand why until one day when I was trying to draw a banana. I couldn't get it right. I finally gave up and ate the banana. Then I tried one more time—from memory—and it was the best banana I ever drew. Wasn't it, Ethel."

Ethel nodded sadly.

"I don't believe I'm hearing this," George said to the ceiling.

"See—when I drew the banana after I ate it I was creating it; when I drew it before I ate it I was only copying it. That was a powerful demonstration of how important it is to develop technique, so that when you free your imagination, your hands just take over the job and do it all by themselves."

"Wally, I wish you wouldn't talk like that," Ethel murmured. "When you say things like that I get scared and all cold inside."

Wally stopped drawing, and looked sidelong at Ethel, sitting beside him on the leather sofa. He dropped the charcoal in his lap and took her hand in his own charcoal-blackened hand. "Sweetheart—"

"You've changed so much I hardly know you," she said plaintively.

"Sweetheart—"

"I want you back, Wally."

"Sweetheart, you've got this idea in your head that I've changed, but I haven't changed. It's true that I'm painting and I'm drawing, which I didn't used to do. And I'm reading more than I used to, about things I didn't even know existed a few months ago. And I never watch TV anymore—which I admit I used to live for. And I walk more in a week now than I did in any year of my life before this happened. And I've lost a good deal of weight. And I guess I think about different kinds of things than I used to think about. But all the rest is the same. I'm just the same as I always was. Oh yes, and I don't piss my pants any more. That's a big change, all right. But otherwise I'm just the same as—"

"Jesus Christ, Dad—"

"Wally, you're *not* the same," Ethel said. "All you do is draw and paint and read, and when you're doing that you're as alone as if you were on a mountain top, and when you're not doing that you wander out of the house, without telling a soul, walking God knows where. And when we talk it's never about the things we used to talk about—like what's on the TV and who we're going to invite for Thanksgiving and if we're going to plant a garden next year, and—oh, Wally, most of the time you're as remote as the moon and you don't even know it."

Wally reddened. "Of course I know it. I'm not crazy, you know." He looked down at the drawing, frowning, flipped the page, and began another drawing of Pete's face. "It's these ideas I get—when they come to me I just have to shut other things out for a while. But it's only for a while. It's not like you said, like I go off without knowing what I'm doing, because I do know, I know exactly where I'm going."

"It's dangerous, Wally. I want you well, so you don't get hurt."

"I am well. I never felt better in my life and I'm not letting Doctor Ramsay do a bunch of tests on me to prove he needs to cut my head open and poke around in my brain—if that's what this is about. All I need is to get back to work. Get a little discipline in my life. That's the best thing for me. I need to get back to work—"

"Get back to work? Get back to work? Get real, Dad. How the hell are you gonna supervise the work of five technical writers? You can't even supervise yourself."

Six

As the winter days lengthened, so did his workdays lengthen beneath the big skylight. He had never had such wonderful light in which to work, and he wasted not a photon of it. Nor had he ever possessed such an abundance of space. Now he could view his paintings from any distance—ten, twenty, forty, even sixty feet. For decades he had worked and lived in cramped little warrens of misery, like that cell in Mrs. Hatchet's basement, with its peeling wallpaper and piss-yellow light and pissy, cabbagey stench, with walls so close he couldn't get five feet from his easel without standing on his bed. But not any more. *This* is his life now. Painting under one-hundred and forty-four square feet of blue sky in the middle of half a football field of solid plank floor. So huge was his studio that the light from the big windows along the exterior walls was not sufficient to illuminate the long windowless wall of brick opposite. It was a studio for big canvases.

Like the painting on the easel under the skylight. A six-foot square of canvas, its surface an ornate pattern of tiny polygons combining to form larger polygons of swaying alloys of black, gray, blue, and purple. Tiny patterns merging to create a field of larger patterns, the field surrounding a white island of raw canvas on which the penciled form of a woman waited patiently for his attention; waited more patiently than he, the creator of this series of paintings, who in this eighth of the series was bored to death by the background pattern they all shared. That was the problem with Patternism. It was so repetitive, and as demandingly detailed as an acre of Maori body tattoo.

While he labored on toward his appointment with the canvas lady, he created her mentally. He had her in his head (an idealized Janice), could visualize her now in great detail. He had the challenging set of her hands upon her hips, the wide plant of her slender legs, and he knew exactly how the texture of her skin would brighten in curve and sink in shadow, knew how he would bloom that gleaming coppery pubic overgrowth right off the canvas.

It was when he got around to painting the subject that his stylistic variation of Patternism got interesting. When he did it right his Patternistic work had greater dimensionality than even a Neo-Renaissance Perspectivist painting. But when done poorly it was as confused as the flat intersecting planes of Abstract Distractionism, a movement in which he (with Janice) wasted precious years.

He placed his coffee, which he had been cupping in his hands to absorb its heat, on the paint table and picked another brush out of the tens of brushes poking up out of the coffee can in the middle of the table; flexed the bristles as he had flexed his own fingers to loosen them; took up a tube of white and squeezed some into the bottom of a cut-off beer can gobbed an inch thick with hardened shades of blue. He searched through the crushed pigment tubes strewn among cut-off beer cans and pieces of paint-daubed cardboard, found a cadmium orange, squeezed a dot into the coil of white, worked it in with his brush, thinned it, brushed a little on the corner of a small discarded canvas that he used for testing color. He faced the big canvas and stroked paint lightly over the bottom half of a small black and blue square. It went on too thickly. He cleaned it off with a rag and thinned the paint, took up his brush again and stroked paint over the bottom half of another of the dark shapes, letting the dark show through by painting light and high on the canvas texture. He painted a dozen of the tiny shapes and stepped back and studied the effect of his changes.

He painted until his arms felt heavy and his hands had stiffened before putting the brush and the can on the table and moving back to study the painting. As usual he could not tell if it was working or not, whether he had a good painting going or a bad one. In that respect this painting was like every one of his paintings: as he got deeper and deeper into it he lost critical objectivity. He wouldn't know how good it was until he put it aside and out of his mind for several weeks and then looked at it afresh. And of course he never did that until the painting was finished. Once he started a painting it was in his mind all the time. Until he finished it or discarded it, he couldn't not work on it.

He and Boyce argued about that. Boyce liked to work on four or five pieces at one time. Charles told Boyce that's why Boyce's work was so indecisive, so disjoint, so confused—which always pissed Boyce off. He hated Charles' paternalistic commentary about his work, particularly on this point, because he regarded Charles' work as indecisive, disjoint, and confused, because he could focus on only one piece at a time.

But what could you expect from Boyce, who's been doing art for maybe five years, and, moreover, doesn't possess even the hope of talent. Who should have kept his day job as a bus boy, a career to which he was perfectly suited—or he was until he got those tattoos.

Charles became aware that Boyce was making cooking sounds in the walled-off space in the corner. The space had once been the office of the factory that, decades before, had occupied the entire floor. Because it was confined, it captured at least some of the warmth put out by the portable heater; therefore it was where they slept and cooked the food they managed to shoplift or fish out of the Albertson's dumpster. Charles saw Boyce's tattooed head in the windowed wall of the office, moving about like a twenty-first-century Queequeg. It looked like he was stirring something. Had to be rice or pasta—that's all they had. That and a little coffee.

"Boyce!" he yelled.

Boyce looked up.

"Make some for me!"

Boyce nodded.

Charles turned his attention to the canvas. On the technical level it was good. On that score he has always supremely confident. Even artists who hated him admired the technique they saw in his work. It was usually the content of his work that drew criticism. And no one criticized more devastatingly than Philip Dillip, in his dismissive eleven-word review of Charles' last show some thirty months before: "A Charles Gas painting is a well-written poem of banalities." That was it. Eleven words under a five-word lead: "Go to a Movie Instead."

Charles tried to ignore what Philip Dillip wrote, like he'd tried to ignore the opinions of critics before Dillip. The problem was, the critics were the priests, the gatekeepers; they were unignorable. For decades he had longed for just one single critic to come forward, even a stupid one like Dillip, and discover enough Art in his art to permit the public to buy it.

This series would change all of that. His new interpretation of Patternism—which he is thinking of renaming Traditionalistic Patternism, because he was developing it out of the roots of Patternism and his own love of Post-Neo-Realism, with a strong element of technical control—will be his rocket to the top. Only a master of technique could invent *this* school of art. If he had been painting this stuff twenty years before, he'd be rich now, and art students would be stretching his canvases and doing the repetitious work of painting background designs, and poster companies would be clamoring for his work, and assholes like Dillip would be begging for an interview. When he thought of all those years he wasted mucking around in fads like Relativistic Polyhedralism and Abstract Distractionism—

But he allowed himself no regrets, allowed nothing to dampen his enthusiasm, not even Boyce's sneers about painting-by-the-numbers. Charles went into the office and warmed his hands over the red coils of the hot plate. Beside the hot plate was a bowl of steaming rice and a cup of coffee. Boyce sat cross-legged on his mattress, spooning rice into his mouth, rolling it around, swallowing it carefully. From time to time his watery eyes blinked and a tear spilled down over his tattooed cheeks.

Charles found a spoon and picked up his bowl. "Still hurt?"

Boyce nodded and spooned more rice into his mouth.

"Tim Leuter'll fix you up. He did me."

—

A pretty woman in baggy slacks with a frizzy angora sweater and frizzy black hair opened the door.

"Hi, Shelley," Charles said breezily. "This is Boyce LaFree, the guy I told you about."

Charles stepped past her into the big octagonal entry hall, leaving her to face face-tattooed Boyce all alone. She stared up at the blue visage that Boyce himself had confronted with a similar shock one morning five years before, when he woke from the coma that ended his worst and longest binge of drugs and booze—which turned out to be his last binge—and found to his horror that the intricate Patternistic decorations on his face would not wash off. Boyce watched Shelley Leuter back away, making croaking sounds and a little gesture, which Boyce thought might be an invitation to enter.

"Look, Boyce," Charles said, gazing up at the walls. "What'd I tell you?"

Boyce looked down and wondered how he was gonna get across the Persian rug without treading on it with his sodden Converses. Glancing up, he saw that Shelley waited nervously, so he took a deep breath and stepped on the rug—but lightly, very lightly—and moved to the side so she could edge past him and close the door before hurrying across the hall and out of his reach. Charles followed.

Only then did Boyce notice the walls. Clutching his newspaper-wrapped package against his side, he gazed open-mouthed at the foyer's high walls. Paintings hung everywhere, covering every square inch of wall space all the way up the staircase. Boyce spotted pieces painted by young artists he knew, and he also recognized paintings by artists whose work had taken on importance because they were dead: an anguished piece of Papist Suppressionism (probably executed during the Irish Artistic Renaissance of June and July of 1963); a work of 1960s Tubism; an early work of Jacque Mattress; even a painting by one of those grim, nihilistic Post-Modern Neo-Repressionist Aushaus Grupe youngsters.

Boyce was impressed. Though not particularly well informed about schools and movements in art, he sensed that this display, while limited by the absence of the work of such giants as Piccolo and Brick, amounted to an epitome of Twentieth Century art. Fifty bitchy, bickering, bellicose schools of art warred fratricidally right there in front of him. The violence of the battle left him breathless. He heard a door close and looked up the stairs. A delicate, elfin man started down. Boyce felt himself eerily transported out of reality: freckle-faced Howdy-Doody himself was surrealistically descending the stairs, without strings. And then the creature's big blue eyes discovered Boyce's tattooed face and registered the usual shock and fear—the fear endowing the big blue Howdy-Doody eyes with a humanity that they otherwise lacked. The creature stopped.

"I'm with Charles," Boyce murmured, in case the little man was about to panic.

"Oh. Yes. Shelley told me Charles was bringing someone." Fear still showed in his eyes, which were fixed on Boyce's blue tattoos. He did not continue down the stairs. "I'm Tim Leuter," he said finally, because it seemed necessary to say something, if only to keep this face-tattooed menace at bay.

"Boyce, we're in here," Charles called.

Boyce raised a hand, as if to gesture a goodbye at the Howdy-Doody creature, and sidled toward the door through which Charles and Shelley had disappeared. The tiny Howdy-Doody creature watched.

"And that's the Bill Basturd I told you about," Shelley was saying. She stood beside a rosewood pedestal that was like a miniature stage illuminated by miniature, ceiling-mounted stage lights. On the pedestal a miniature bronze horse was bucking a miniature bronze cowboy into space. "We were in Jackson Hole a few weeks ago and walked into this gallery, just to browse, and there it was. Well! You can imagine how excited I was. Naturally I bought it on the spot. Mind you, I am not fond of Wyomingism—too unsophisticated for the west coast, though I'm sure the critics in New York have not caught on yet, so even though Basturd's prices seem a bit high, they'll definitely go higher, particularly since he's dead now. I do think this piece is exceptional because it so clearly shows Basturd's influence on the cosmopolitanism of the Western Montana and Spokane School, and though Basturd doesn't belong precisely in those schools, his influence on them is seminal. Don't you agree?"

Charles nodded thoughtfully and thought, *what a piece of shit*. He hoped she paid way too much for it.

As Shelley spoke she darted nervous glances at Boyce. She moved to the fireplace and put her hand on the mantle beside another bronze, positioning herself to keep an eye on Boyce, who stood in the middle of the room, unmindful that he still clutched his newspaper-wrapped bundle, unmindful of Shelley's nervous chatter, unmindful that his sodden tennis shoes were despoiling an eleven-thousand-dollar rug, that his coat hung coldly and wetly and heavily, that tiny Tim Leuter hovered Howdy-Doody-like nearby, watching him like a bank guard might watch a thuggish customer with a violin case. Boyce was mindful only of this cornucopia of art, this warehouse of art, this incubator for the ripening of green art into good art, and, over time, into succulently expensive art. There was no scheme or theme to the display, it was just there, in bewildering fecundity, so densely jammed in that it diminished the enormous room. Of course the room was only relatively small; in absolute terms it was huge—at least thirty by fifty feet—and it had no window, no bookshelf, no interruption to one hundred and sixty running feet of wall except a fireplace and a door. One hundred and sixty feet of wall as densely populated by paintings as the walls of the entry hall. Boyce's head spun, and he wondered what the rest of the house looked like.

"I could use a drink," Charles said.

"Of course," said Howdy-Doody, not taking his eyes off Boyce. "What do you want?"

"Some of that Livid Glen? Or Lidit. Or whatever it was I had that time. A double. No, a triple."

"What would you like—um—"

"His name is Boyce," Charles said.

"Right. What would you like, Bryce?"

"Uh. Warm beer. I guess."

"Warm?" Tim Leuter said.

Boyce nodded. Leuter left the room and Boyce drifted to one of the walls. Shelley eyed him as she told Charles about how much certain pieces in the Leuter collection had increased in value, particularly the ones by dead artists. They had just gotten the good news that one of their most promising young artists had died of a drug overdose. It is always a windfall for the collector, she observed, when you own the work of a dead promising-young-artist. Boyce recognized Charles' immaculate technique in one of the paintings. Its presence here confirmed what Charles had told him, and what he had already noted, that the Leuter collection also contained some garbage. Maybe there was hope. Tim Leuter reappeared with a glass of scotch and a bottle of warm beer. Boyce took the beer and as his lips parted to sip, Tim Leuter's eyes locked on Boyce's disintegrating mouth. His professional interest immediately supplanted his nervous apprehension.

"Charles has told us some good things about your work, Bryce," Leuter said, staring at Boyce's mouth.

"He said you could be the next Pablo Piccolo," Shelley added in a voice that sounded like she was trying to placate him. She stood in front of the fireplace, in which gas flames danced along the upper surfaces of perfectly shaped concrete logs.

"He's gonna be big," Charles said. "I been telling him he needs to show in a gallery, to build his following. Takes time to build a following, as I know all too well. But Boyce just won't put anything out there before its time. You have to respect him for that. He thinks it's about time now. So does Dillip, by the way."

"Dillip? I thought you said Bryce hasn't shown."

"I tipped Dillip. Called him and told him he had a Pablo Piccolo working right under his nose. He came up to the studio and looked at Boyce's work. Blew him away. When you have a guy like Dillip—a sharp cookie who knows a lot about art—when you have a guy like that saying things like he said about Boyce¾well, I think you get the picture."

Shelley forgot her fear. Against a topic as intellectually stimulating as capital gains, fear was nothing. "What did he say?" she asked, eyes aglitter.

"Like I said, Boyce has been pretty cagey about showing his stuff—but he let Dillip come up and see a couple of pieces—I think the ones Boyce brought tonight. That right, Boyce?"

Boyce blinked. What the fuck was Charles talking about? Dillip? In the Co-op?

"What did he say?" Shelley asked again.

"He said Boyce was gonna put the Pill Hill School on the map. Matter of fact, Boyce was gonna invent it. But I think the work should speak for itself. Show 'em, Boyce."

"First things first," Tim Leuter said busily. While Charles talked he had moved the pedestal and bronze out from under its cone of display lighting and put a chair in its place. Now he motioned to Boyce: "Sit right here, Bryce, we'll get right to it."

"*Now?*" Boyce said incredulously. "You gonna do it now?"

"Of course. Sit down."

Boyce looked at Charles. Charles nodded reassuringly. Boyce sat, reluctantly, still clutching his newspaper-wrapped bundle. He squinted up into the lights. "What about your—you know, your stuff?"

"Stuff?"

"You know—drills and things."

"Don't need it for this," Tim Leuter said busily, leaning over, bringing his face close to Boyce's. Boyce drew back. Leuter grabbed Boyce's upper lip with the fingers of his left hand and Boyce's lower lip with the fingers of his right hand and pulled them apart. "Open wide, Bryce," he commanded, in charge now.

Boyce closed his eyes and surrendered to the wiggly penetration of Leuter's fingers. For one minute, two minutes, three minutes, Shelley and Charles watched. The only sound was the flutter of burning gas logs and Boyce's grunts of pain as Tim Leuter's fingers probed the ruin of Boyce's mouth.

Tim Leuter straightened. "I never saw such a mess. Nothing but mossy stumps. There's stuff growing in there I've never seen before. My guess is nobody's brushed these teeth in the last ten years."

"Hurts too much, man," Boyce muttered.

"This could be a hundred-grand mouth," Leuter said. "It's a dental retirement dream—gold, silver, platinum—bridges, crowns, implants—the whole works—this fellow needs a bionic mouth." He stepped back. "Yep, it's a dentist's dream—if the owner's rich. No way it can be under a hundred."

The room was silent for several seconds.

"A *hundred*! For an unknown artist—" Shelley murmured.

"But not for long," Charles enthused. "Wait'll you see his work."

Shaking her head: "A hundred thousand. I got the *Basturd* for fifty grand. And he's dead. Bryce isn't even dead yet."

Charles persisted. "Well, okay, Boyce is young, no doubt about that—but you can see how unhealthy he is. He's got rotten teeth—good odds for heart disease, right?—and he's malnourished; and his eyes are so yellow it's obvious he's got jaundice, and I can vouch for his chronic cough—all winter long—undoubtedly consumption—not to mention what he looks like with those idiotic tattoos all over his face. The man's out of his element in this world. He hasn't got a chance. I'm betting he doesn't live five more years."

"Even then, I still don't think—"

Charles wasn't giving up. He went to Boyce and jerked the newspaper-wrapped bundle out from under his arm, ripped the paper away, went to the nearest wall and found a pair of paintings of similar size, removed them, and hung Boyce's.

"Let's just take this one step at a time," he said, turning back to them. "Forget about the money. Look at the art. I'm telling you, this guy is another Piccolo. I grant you that he ain't dead yet, but you gotta give it time. Art's an investment, and it takes time for investments to pay off. When he gets dead he's gonna be great and you're gonna wish you had a wall of this guy."

Shelley looked doubtfully at Tim Leuter, who stood, arms crossed over his chest, studying the two paintings. He didn't have a favorable expression on his Howdy-Doody face. It was clear he was thinking that even death would not improve *those* paintings. Even if Dillip did like them.

———

"Man, I told not to say anything negative," Charles said. "Why the fuck didn't you just let me do the talking, like I told you. I had 'em."

Boyce looked straight ahead, saying nothing, his tattooed face dripping icy rain that was turning to be snow. The light changed and Boyce stepped into the street.

"I had 'em, goddamn it," Charles said again.

"You didn't have nobody."

A spasm of shivering rattled Boyce's bones. He controlled it, and pulled the sopping wet collar of his coat up under his chin. He was so cold he had no feeling in his legs, and his head felt like someone was shoving ice picks up his nose. The paintings slipped out from under his arm and he caught them before they fell to the pavement. And then he stopped, suddenly furious at the absurdity of these fucking things demanding any more from him. He raised the paintings to pitch them into the gutter, but hesitated, then held one over his head and offered the other to Charles, who took it and raised it over his head.

"You had to start arguing—"

"Motherfucker wanted to pull my motherfuckin' teeth out, man."

"That was just their starting position."

Rain drummed on the two canvases and cars hissed by in front of them, throwing spray against their legs. But it was hardly noticeable: their clothes were already soaked with icy water. Lights gleamed everywhere, the crystalline light of car head lamps and storefronts enlivened by the gaudy excess of a mile of multicolored neon and the red and green of traffic signals.

"I don't know nothin' about no starting position, man. The motherfucker said he was gonna pull my teeth, man."

"I could've got him down to a dozen of the worst, but no more than that, with caps and bridges for the rest."

Boyce did not respond. He walked, head down, holding the painting over his head. Rain drummed against the canvas and spilled off the front.

"You're right, man," Boyce said after a while.

"You should've listened to me and kept your mouth shut like I told you."

They walked in silence all the way through the offensively cheerful Broadway district with its youth-focused, glitzy shops attended by successful resourceful young men and women ardently selling useless objects of bad taste to other successful resourceful young men and women of bad taste. The street's crowded restaurants were bright with laughter and shouted conversations. Beyond the brightly lit business district were the darkened brick structures of the community college and beyond that, Pike Street, which they would follow down the hill to Virginia Street and the Co-op.

"You think it's too late?" Boyce asked.

"I don't know."

Silence for a while. Then Boyce spoke again: "They didn't like 'em anyway, man."

"You still ain't hoisted it in, have you. *Liking* art has nothing to do with whether they buy it. This is about collecting art, investing in art. It's about selling art to people who don't give a fuck about art. That was a warehouse of art and you were looking at inventory. I already told you, those people are *investors*. You'll never be an artist until you understand the difference between people who like art and people who invest in art."

Defensively: "I know the difference, man."

Silence for several minutes as they trudged through the rain, their impromptu umbrellas spilling water.

"You see that Aushaus piece?" Boyce asked.

"Yeah, sure, the VW. Piece of shit."

"Naw, it's not shit, man. It's a piece of art, man."

"It's shit. The only reason they own it is the artist is dead. Probably AIDS. Most of those Aushausers get AIDS. They like AIDS."

Boyce wished he'd let Charles do all the talking like they had planned, because Charles was good at talking. He wished Leuter had just gone ahead and pulled his fuckin' teeth. Wished every motherfuckin' one was out of his head, right now, taking the pain with 'em. He could not remember *not* living with pain. What was he to do now? Continue to live with pain, that was what. Charles was right. He should've kept his mouth shut and let Howdy-Doody come at him with his pliers or whatever the fuck fancy name they got for pliers and do whatever the motherfucker wanted—long as he yanked the pain out with the rotten teeth. What good is a mouth full of teeth you can't use? He thought about that Aushaus piece. The vee-dub. A little yellow vee-dub so perfectly rendered it was photographic. Boyce revered the determined isolation of those Aushaus artists, admired their philosophy of single-minded dedication to death as the high point in life, and who developed their work toward achieving that moment. Das Aushaus Grupe was the only one of all the hundreds of childish quarreling bickering battling schools of twentieth century art that made any sense at all.

Seven

"Wally, we need to talk about money," Ethel said, wiping her hands on her apron.

Wally had put his jacket on and was heading for the back door. He stopped. He'd been expecting this talk-about-money meeting since the visit with Pete, when she'd become very upset at his refusal to submit to Ramsay's examination. But right now he didn't care about how upset Ethel was, or what Ramsay wanted to do: all he cared about was getting another tube of white. He was always underestimating how much white he needed.

"When I get back we'll sit down and—"

"We need to talk about money, Wally. Right now."

They'd had some money talks already. Unpleasant talks, confrontational talks, like some of the talks Kimberly had trapped him into. He had never been good at confrontation, like Kimberly. Confrontation energized her. To forestall the unpleasantness of this particular confrontation, which he knew was coming, he had devised a new promise, this one even more binding than the other promises he'd made. He would absolutely stop spending money. No more new books. When he needed a book he'd buy it only if the library didn't have it. And no more stretched canvases. He'd buy a roll of canvas and some framing material and when he needed a new canvas he'd stretch one. And he would also stop buying paints and sketchbooks and pencils and brushes, except of course for the most essential re-supply. Like today. Today he needed some white, and he needed to get that canvas stretcher and the roll of canvas and the framing wood, and since the library did not have that book of Piccolo's drawings that he needed, he guessed he'd go ahead and order it.

"I was just going out for some white, but after that I won't need—"

"Let's sit down and talk, Wally."

Standing there blocking the door, with tight lips, arms folded aggressively over ample breasts, hard unblinking gaze, she reminded him of Kimberly. This was going to be unpleasant. In recent weeks she had been doing that more and more often—reminding him of Kimberly. She had been like that since the visit to Pete's office when he'd refused to let Doctor Ramsay do any more tests on him. She pointed to a kitchen chair and he sat and looked down at his hands. She pulled a chair out and sat across the table from him.

"Wally, our savings are disappearing."

"I've been giving that a lot of thought."

"We're spending more than we bring in. We've never done that before."

He nodded agreeably. "I see what you mean. And as soon as I get a little white and the canvas and—"

"We have to cut back, even on your paints and books."

He nodded again. "Right, I was thinking the same thing. And as soon as I get a tube of white and the canvas—"

"We're going to do things differently, Wally. I've canceled our Visa and Mastercard and I've closed our checking account." She observed his reaction, and seeing that he was meekly acquiescing, added with greater firmness: "And I opened another checking account. In my name. To pay bills."

She waited for him to protest this act of emasculation, but he didn't care what she did about credit cards or checking accounts, the important thing was getting a tube of white paint. "Okay. So—I guess we're through—? Can I have ten dollars? To buy some white? I really do need it. I'm always underestimating how much white I need."

The rich dark stink of human humus, which always followed George around, filled the kitchen. On this day it was strong enough to overpower even the ripe pungency of Ethel's baking bread. Every day was a shitty day for George, but this one had been particularly shitty. A customer had asked him, after he'd finished pumping, if he'd mind lowering himself into the septic tank to inspect the walls. It was a very old tank and she feared its walls were crumbling. George declined. Methane gas. Dangerous stuff. But George needed the money, so when the lady said she would pay him extra to do it, he told her a hundred and fifty bucks. That seemed like a lot, she murmured, but wrote the check, he'd climbed down into the shit.

"You can't just *make* him do anything," Ethel continued. "He tries, but he forgets what he's supposed to be doing. Yesterday I asked him to get the gardening tools and the lawn mower out of the storage shed. When he didn't come back I went and found him sitting in the shed drawing a picture of a shovel on the side of a cardboard box with a ballpoint pen. When I tell him he has to do this, or he can't go out of the yard, or he has to be home by such and such a time, he never argues, he just agrees. He always agrees to anything I say, and then he just does what he wants. And you can't just take him up and bust his bottom. He isn't a child, he's a grown man."

"Well, you have to make him," George said dismissively, in exactly the tone of voice that most irritated his mother. George knew that, of course. He said it not to inform her of how he thought she ought to be directing the recovery (and retraining) of his father, as much as to inform her how pissed *he* was at having this problem in his face all of the time. As a matter of fact, he'd had a goddamned belly-full of this problem. Yes, his father's injury had been serious, but he'd recovered, and it was high time he stopped this artsy-fartsy bullshit and started putting his life back together. But he wasn't even trying. Well, he, George, had had it. He had real problems to deal with. Like how was he going to pay a five-hundred-and-twenty-three dollar truck payment from a bank account that contained maybe a hundred dollars. Not to mention how he was going to pay for a new six-hundred-and-fifty-nine-dollar pump. Of course he seldom mentioned these problems to his mother, because when he talked about them, it never came out right. She always looked at him like he was whining.

"Well, I'm here to tell you, you can't make him go where he's not pointed."

"He's forgot how to work, Mom. He's just got to learn again. Thing to do is start him on something easy, like you would a kid, and then—"

"Getting the garden tools out of the shed isn't easy?"

"What I'm trying to say is—" "I know what you're trying to say, George, you say it all the time. But it isn't some easy thing like you seem to think. What he needs is a simple, uncomplicated job to get him used to bein' busy doing things someone wants him to do."

George snorted. "He's already busy. Jesus, if it wasn't for that fuckin' art."

"Will you please not talk like that to me? You know I mean busy with something that's not fun, something that he doesn't like, that he has to go and do every day, like everybody else. If he has something like that—well, maybe he can relearn how to work. A little at a time."

George rolled his eyes. "He can't think about anything for two fuckin' minutes before he's drawin' it."

"George!"

"Well, it's the goddamn truth."

"I been thinking about this a lot. I have this idea that maybe we can lick this thing little by little by getting him going to work on a real simple job. Something that pays him a little money."

"Well, why the hell else would you go to work?"

"We can even let him buy some paint with the money. A sort of reward for working. We might be able to get him weaned from this art business by getting him back to something productive, like earning money like he used to. I was thinking you might take him with you on the pump truck, say for a couple days a week—now don't you look at me like that—and put him to work handling the hose, or maybe digging for the tank lid. There must be lots of ways he—"

"Mom, you don't listen to a thing I say. Haven't I been telling you for months how bad business is? I am behind on every bill I got. I ain't took a paycheck in two months. If Wanda wasn't working down at the Safeway we'd be fucked."

"George!"

"Well, goddamnit, it's the goddamned fuckin' truth. That's exactly what we'd be."

A long, tight-lipped silence. Then a sigh and a murmur: "Well. It was just an idea."

George gave the ceiling one of his long-suffering looks. "Okay, okay, okay. See he's ready at seven in the morning. I gotta pump a tank at a farm house up on the plateau. I'll take him along. But I can't pay him, 'cause there just ain't no money to pay."

When George left, Ethel got the bread out of the oven and dropped the loaves out of the pans onto the cooling rack, then resumed her seat at the table to wait for Wally. When she wasn't preparing a meal or baking bread or dusting or pushing the vacuum cleaner or washing and ironing clothes or digging in the garden, she was in this chair. Except in the evening when their programs came on; then she used to sit in the living room in a Lazy Boy on the other side of the lamp table from Wally's Lazy Boy; the both of them across the room from the 54-inch TV, which they used to have on a low platform right in front of the fireplace so they could see it better. But not any more. The TVs were covered or gone to storage in the garage. Only the little kitchen set was still there on the shelf that Wally had built many years before so he could watch TV while he ate his breakfast and his supper.

Now she watched it only when he was gone from the house. She always took it down and put it in a cabinet when he came in, because Wally said that even when it was off it made him feel like someone was yelling at him. She had a hard time getting used to the silence, which went on until she began to feel like something bad was building up to happen. Even in her own house, which she knew like she knew her own body. Sometimes the silence made her look deep inside herself.

That was the real problem with the silence: she got too much inside herself. Like now. Right now, inside was an awful place to be. Problems twisted and turned in there like a pile of worms on a hot sidewalk. Family problems and health problems and money problems. She rose and went to the TV and turned it on. All the networks were showing the evening news, more things to make you fear something, so she kept turning the channel selector until she found an old movie. She turned the sound up louder than she would normally have it, then went back to the chair and sat and looked up at the flickering screen. She didn't care about the movie, but she forced herself to continue watching it until she felt her self-consciousness fading and the problems drifting out of focus. But the problems were too monstrous to stay in the background for long. Soon the most serious of them muscled its way in front of the blaring TV: what was she to do about Wally going off to those art galleries on Lake Street? Particularly that Janice Cushion Gallery. Those gallery people were the real danger. Showing him all that stuff and talking all the time about painting pictures—deliberately encouraging the behavior that she was fighting so hard to suppress.

She thought, in her most depressing moments, that she was in a struggle against evil. Was it evil? She had her Christian faith, but the spiritual aspect of life had never been very compelling to her. When everything seemed okay she never gave much though to spirituality. Concepts like evil and good had a cartoonish quality when she thought about them, and she had no idea whether Satan was a fictive idea or a reality, whether angels were just the descendants of minor animistic gods or were, in fact, God's little helpers, like Santa Claus' helpers.

Who, or what, was doing this to her and to her Wally? Was it Satan acting through evil people? When she made herself sit there and look at what had happened, and the problems that had come out of that single unbelievable moment in the men's room when Wally had bent over to see if he had dribbled on his pants again—when she thought about such enormous consequences from such an inconsequential act—well, that was when she thought yes, Satan was abroad in the land. Either that or she was insane.

As if Wally's injury and all its complications was not problem enough, now George was becoming a bigger problem than he'd always been. Plodding, less than bright, but a good-hearted and dutiful son as long as his father was there to keep the world safe. Now he'd grown fearful and angry, defeated and despairing. A weak child needing his father's solidity. Always too weak to succeed on his own. Those were very serious problems—but there were more! The money! All those problems at her feet, grabbing at her hems. All of those problems needing her solutions. And she had no solutions. But she had never had the solutions; she needed her Wally for that, her Wally who, for all his inadequacies, had been the keystone of their family. The rock. Always showing up. Always going to work. Always coming home. Bringing money. Mowing the lawn. Pruning the fruit trees. Being there. Answering the easy questions and guessing at the hard ones, but in the end keeping things together. A mediocre man in all ways save one, the most important of all qualities: he always knew his duty and always did his duty. He had no passions, no hungers for what he didn't have, no drives to great stature or important achievement. But he knew his duty.

How had such a man fathered a son like George? For the first time in his life the forty-year-old son was without his father's support and the son was falling apart. Not noticeably, not in sudden collapse; just pieces of him falling away and him not even noticing. Petulantly falling apart, like a man whose thumb falls off, then his toes, then his fingers and his hands, then his feet and his legs, and while this disintegration proceeds he observes only that the car is getting harder to drive. How had a man like Wally sired a son of such inconsequcnce? An able-bodied man of forty who still got money from his parents, a monthly allowance fictionalized as loan. Wally had made payments for George all his life, without complaint; but now he was no longer able to do it, and the son, in consequence, was falling apart.

She got up, went to the window, and looked for Wally, but he wasn't there. She knew he wouldn't walk up the driveway until late. He was in Kirkland, at that gallery. God, what was she to do about that gallery?

—

The truck careened down the road off the plateau and down toward the junction on the eastern shore of Lake Sammamish, George gripping the wheel with whitened fists, leaning forward with whitened face, with whitened lips taut across clenched teeth. Smelling like human shit, the worst kind of shit to smell like. His khakis sopping wet and speckled brown with flecks of shit and bits of toilet paper, his hair still sticky with little gobs of shit, even after he'd hosed himself off in the front yard of the farmhouse. And beside him his father—engrossed in his sketch pad—creating a credible drawing of his son in spite of the lurches of the careening truck.

The cop pulled them over when George ran the light at the bottom of the hill; got off his motorcycle and walked up to the window on the driver's side, opening his ticket book as he came.

"In a big hurry, are we?" the cop asked as he came up to the window. The sun glinted on the big bug eyes of his aviator sun glasses. And then the cop recoiled, catching himself just before he stumbled back into the traffic that whizzed behind him.

"What—what—"

"Had a accident," George said tiredly. "Tryin' to get home, to get this shit off me."

"Accident?" the cop called. He moved upwind, which was just off the left front fender. "Where? What kinda accident? Traffic?"

"No," George said to the floorboards: he had lowered his head to the steering wheel.

"You all right in there?" The cop kept a wary, respectful distance.

George raised his head. "Hose come loose in the yard. The shit was everwhere. Had to cap it."

Wally was looking at the cop, intensely, as if memorizing him. He flipped a page in this sketch pad and began scratching the charcoal over the coarse paper.

"Say, what's that old guy doin'?" the cop asked suspiciously. He brought his hand to his pistol.

"He's drawin' a picher. He's always drawin' pichers."

The cop closed his book. "Get on outa here. And watch those red lights." He moved across the front of the truck to the shoulder and motioned for George to continue on.

George didn't go in when he stopped to let Wally off at home. When Ethel smelled Wally she made him go to the back yard and take his clothes off and then go right in and take a shower. After she put the clothes in the washer she got on the telephone and asked George what happened.

"Just what I told you would happen," George said. "He fucked it up."

"George! Don't you talk to me like that! Now you get a civil tongue in your mouth and tell me what happened today."

"I should've known. I put him on the pump while I was handlin' the hose at the septic tank. When the tank was empty I signaled for him to turn it off." A sigh. "By then he had his pad out and was drawing somethin' or other and didn't have a notion of where he was or what he was supposed to be doin'. When he saw me wavin' he turned around and started uncouplin' the hose. He got it off just about the time I got there. Shit went everwhere."

Eight

Charles and Boyce were standing before the flood-lit easel under the dark skylight, looking at the painting, Charles sucking on a roach. Absently, he offered it to Boyce.

"You know I don't do that shit."

Charles expelled a cloud of smoke into the twin cones of light. "I know, and you should."

"It's bad shit, man."

"No, it's good shit. You just think it's bad shit because you're always in a bad space."

"Bad space's got nothin' to do with it, man. Pot's a drug and I don't do drugs."

"All pot does is exaggerate the stuff that's already there inside you. If you're feeling good, pot makes you feel better. If you feel bad, pot makes you feel worse. So what you need to do is train yourself to feel good, then you can smoke pot all you want, which will make you feel even better."

"You are so full of shit, man. You ought to listen to yourself."

"You got to train yourself to feel good *inside* yourself, *about* yourself. I'm talking spiritual here, not physical. Pot is spiritual, man."

"Spiritual, my ass. It's a drug, and I don't do drugs. 'Cept pain killers. You get some pain killers, we can do some business."

Their quarrel had started when Boyce once again brought up the allocation of space in the Co-op. While Charles was trying to persuade old Nussbaum to rent them the second floor, the Co-op was all Charles could talk about, to every artist in sight. Boyce had been the only one so desperate to find a place to live that he would go in with Charles. They'd agreed to share the rent and the space, fifty-fifty all the way. Now every time Boyce mentioned the subject Charles started talking about something else. Charles didn't want to talk about the Co-op because he didn't want to give up any of his precious fuckin' space under the skylight, which Boyce figured he had as much right to as Charles, and which was what Boyce wanted a piece of right now.

To deflect Boyce, Charles had brought up the visit to the Leuters, accusing Boyce once again of fucking up his, Charles', opportunity to trade for more dental work. By then Charles had rolled another joint and left the tiny living-eating-sleeping space that they shared and gone out into the cold vastness of the studio and turned on the two floods he had set up to illuminate the painting on the easel. Boyce had followed him out.

"Pot is not a drug," Charles said, to keep the quarrel going. "It is a quasi-religious ritual."

"You're changin' the subject again, man. We were talking about the Co-op, about dividin' it up."

Charles moved off into the deep shadow cast by the easel upon the long windowless brick wall, the wall on which he and Boyce hung their finished work. Boyce heard Charles pissing in the toilet bowl that sat incongruously along the wall beneath some of the paintings.

"I said, we were talking about dividin' up the space, man," Boyce said loudly.

He heard the toilet flush, and then Charles reappeared, carrying a six-foot by six-foot painting: his last completed work. He went to the easel.

"Drag that table over here," he said. "I was thinking maybe I should have the unfinished one up on the easel and a finished one leaning against the table. What d'you think?"

Boyce dragged the rickety table closer to the easel. Charles leaned the painting against it, then stepped back and observed the effect.

"I like that," Charles said. "Seeing a finished piece against a work in progress—it grabs you." Charles moved up to the easel and studied the unfinished painting.

"She's late," Boyce said.

"She said after eight," Charles said absently. He stood with his hands on his hips, staring at one painting, then the other.

"It's nine."

"Boyce, I got a hell of an idea. It just came to me. For the show."

"Whut."

Charles patted his pockets, found matches, and relit the roach. He drew deeply, held it for several seconds as he gazed at the painting, then expelled a blue cloud.

"Whut about the show?"

Charles adjusted one of the light stands. He studied the paintings as he spoke, as if he talked to them and not to Boyce. "I got eight good paintings now. That'll be one part of the show—a time series of paintings showing Janice from age nineteen to now, like I planned. The other part, the part I'm gonna paint next, is a series of progressively finished pictures—of her at a single age—I'm thinking maybe nineteen."

"*Whut?*"

"I'm talking about Neo-Realistic Patternistic Progressivism, that's what. Never heard of it? Well, that's because nobody's done it. Not yet."

"You're talking about showin' a bunch of unfinished shit?"

"No. Not unfinished shit. Neo-Realistic Patternistic Progressivism pieces. It's gonna be as big as Relativistic Polyhedralism—no, bigger, 'cause no one really understood the physics behind Relativistic Polyhedralism, and this is way easier to understand."

"I can always tell when you're smokin' that shit, man. An' we never finished talkin' about the Co-op."

"Should I do her at nineteen? Or now? I think nineteen, because I can make her sexier. And sex sells, particularly young sex. And my, oh my, was she sexy! Fucked my brains out. Fucking and painting, that was all she cared about. Of course that was all I cared about, too, so that's mostly what we did. But how many should I do? A dozen, I think. There's a nice balance in twelve—maybe I'll group them in four threes. They'll all be exactly the same size, same pose, same color. They'll be like the one on the easel. The first one will be a pencil layout on canvas, with one brush stroke of paint, and each one after that will be a little more finished than the last. Isn't that far out? No one's ever done that, man. Shown a piece of art progressively. It's like the Italian Instantaneity Movement, only this will be progressive." He faced Boyce, who now regarded him with contempt. "And you know what?" he added.

Boyce knew he was supposed to say, "Whut?" but he refused to be a straight man to this shit.

"And you know what? I'm the only artist I know of who can pull it off."

"You're nuts."

"I don't know of anybody who can control paint and composition well enough to pull it off. Except me."

"You're nuts," Boyce said.

—

"You're nuts," Janice said, "but I'm not. No way I'm gonna show a dozen unfinished pornographic paintings— *Penthouse* nudes, for God's sake—of me. Did you actually think you could talk me into a public showing of pornographic pictures of me?"

"This isn't you, it's art. Your body is simply the inspiration—and it isn't *Penthouse* shit. Pictures of pussies are just pictures of pussies when there's no underlying esthetic. Pornography is meant to incite appetite. This is art, because it's meant to lift the viewer spiritually, not incite appetite." He paused, to let her absorb his words, then continued sarcastically. "You do see why this is art, don't you? You should. Because art is your fucking business. But you can't see the difference, can you—between art and pornography. You never could see the work mentally, in an intellectual and aesthetic frame of reference. That was always your problem, you can't see the future."

"You're stoned."

He had moved the two light stands closer to the display wall and they were looking at the eight unfinished paintings and the single finished work hanging side-by-side. He pointed at the unfinished works. "There it is. The future. Neo-Realistic Patternistic Progressivism. It's coming. And you're gonna be famous, 'cause they'll say you showed it first. And there's irony, too, in that the subject is you."

"Why does it have to be so perfect, so realistic about my face? Can't you change the face? Anybody who's met me once will know it's me."

"It's not you, goddamn it, it's art. What's wrong with you, anyway? Where did all this modesty—which seems pretty fake to me—come from. You used to prance around me—or anybody that came by the studio, if I remember correctly—as naked as when your mother squatted and dropped you in that cotton field, or wherever it was. You didn't care who saw your goddamned pussy. Hell, I've spent more time with you when you're naked than dressed."

"Charles, you're asking me to pander a pornographic portrayal of me to people I know." A long pause. "And besides, I'm not twenty years old now, my body's not—"

"It's not your body, it's art. Now here's what I want to do."

Nine

"If it's that big a deal, maybe I'm with the wrong gallery," said Carnita Vovo.

"It's not a big deal," Janice told her, but of course it was. It was going to be very, very difficult. She moved the telephone handset to her left hand so she could pick up a pencil.

"Yeah—maybe I *am* with the wrong gallery." Carnita repeated her words, making sure Janice got the point.

Janice heard the door open, glanced up, saw that it was only Wally. His hand came up in greeting but she had already turned her attention back to the call. "I'll get the money."

"When?" Carnita demanded.

"When do you need it?"

"Now."

"I'll have it for you in the morning." Another silence, then: "Against the June show, right?"

"No, not June."

Janice tensed.

"I can't be ready by June. Maybe in September."

Janice drew a circle around the five digits, thinking about the words, then tried to think past the words to what Carnita was leading up to. "I don't understand. Is there—"

"It should be obvious. If you cared about me as much as you care about the money I make for you. I can't *work*, for God's sake! You've *seen* the stuff I'm doing now. I'm burned out, everything I *do* I've already done, and I'm bored to *death* with it. What I need is to regenerate my creative juices."

"Carnita, your work is rich with originality—"

"Rich? Yeah, for you it is. At forty percent you get rich while I wreck my reputation showing the same stuff show after show. Wikka says I shouldn't be putting out so much stuff. She says I should put out less and get more for it. It cheapens my work to produce so much."

Janice proceeded patiently. "Carnita, every artist goes through periods when it's hard to work, and you just have to push through it. That's how the ideas come, by working with your brushes, by painting, and—"

"As if you'd know where artistic inspiration come from," Carnita said petulantly. "And I'm not a child. I hate it when people think that just because I'm only twenty they can tell me what to do, like I'm not even an adult or anything."

"I only meant—"

"And I'm not every other artist."

"I only meant—"

"I don't wanna talk about it. I already made up my mind. Wikka says she sees this huge yellow aura around me all the time, and it's a sure sign I'm about to run out of creative juices. She said if I don't take the time now to regenerate my creative juices I'm gonna drain it all out and I'm gonna be empty and in danger of having a creative implosion. She's surprised I haven't already had one, what with that yellow aura and all that. So that's what I'm gonna do, I'm gonna take some time off and regenerate my creative juices in Greece, with Wikka, and while that's happening I'm gonna think about where to take my work."

—*think about where to take my work*—the words rattled through Janice's brain. Was Carnita toying with her? Having a little fun with a double ententre? No—the concept of the double entendre was way beyond Carnita.

"How many pieces do you have now?" Janice asked.

"Not enough for a show," Carnita said irritably.

"But how many?"

"Seven."

Janice saw that Wally had browsed his way along the big wall and had stopped once again before the pair of gaudy Vovos. He had come to her with questions about the two paintings a few days before. Her answers had generated more questions—about Patternism and its place in Twentieth-Century art—and a discussion of surprising complexity had followed. Since then he had come in every day to study paintings, and to talk about art, and he surprised her by how well he understood the art he thought he knew so little about, and how quickly he grasped the most arcane distinctions.

"We have two here," Janice reminded Carnita.

"I'm counting those. Look, there's no use talking about it, there's no way I'm gonna take a chance on having a creative implosion just to give you another show. The signs are terrible. I'm not gonna pick up another paint brush until I get my aura under control. I was about to have a creative implosion, and if it hadn't been for Wikka noticing and suggesting we need peace and quiet, like in Greece—"

As Carnita babbled on Janice saw Wally come to the end of the wall and turn into the second room. She saw him stiffen in surprise.

"What time can I get the money?"

The dollar sign and the five digits glared up at Janice from the notepad on the desk. "Call me tomorrow at eleven. I'll try to have it."

Muffled sentences came from another voice, the words distant and unintelligible. Then Carnita again: "I'll be there."

"Okay."

"Wikka says we're depending on it."

"Okay," Janice said, but the line was already dead.

She lowered the handset to its cradle, wondering how she was going to get the money. Load up her Visa, clean out her checking account, refinance the car? Yes—and borrow from Whipple. Again. That was the part she hated.

The dreadful, insistent question came back: what *would* she do if Carnita took her work elsewhere? How long could she limp along without at least one bankable artist before she had an artistic implosion? And what then? Work for Whipple. Again. Maybe she and Carnita would both end up there. Carnita's talk—in which Janice heard the influence of her mother, Wikka—about better galleries bringing more money for art, the talk about how important it was for an emerging artist to associate herself with the best gallery she could get herself into—Janice knew where it was leading. But what the hell, maybe they'd both be better off at Whipple's. She got up and came around the desk.

"Hi, Wally," she said.

Wally didn't hear. The twin nudes had pinned him to the carpet like a bug on a board. Twin nudes, in brazen self-display, with a three-dimensional fidelity that floated them right off their complex purple-black backgrounds; their upright marbly breasts looking wall-eyed into space; the glowing creaminess of slender thighs and flat bellies evoking the short-lived but influential Tijuana Velvetist Movement. Wally's eyes were big and his face was red. Janice smiled. He was such an odd-ball blend of liberality and conservatism: at one moment capable of embarrassment by the subject of a painting—so embarrassed, as now, that he squirmed in its presence—and in the next moment forgetting embarrassment as admiration of the art took over.

"I said, hello, Wally."

He stood there, gaping at one of the twins.

She leaned playfully close and spoke loudly: "Anybody home?"

He looked at her.

"What d'you think?" she asked.

"They're you," he blurted.

"Yes. But what d'you think?"

He stared at the paintings.

She prompted him: "Remember our talk about Patternism? Where do these fit in?"

He didn't say anything.

Raising her voice: "I said, these are Patternistic, like Vovo's."

"Yes, yes, I see that."

"What do you think?"

"I don't know."

"You had lots to say about the Vovos."

He did not respond.

"Wally, it's okay to be critical."

"But I don't know what to say."

"Do you like them?"

"Yes. The technique, the brushwork, it's wonderful. So controlled."
"What else?"
He stared at the paintings.
"You're supposed to say what you think. That's what we agreed."
"I know. It's just that—they're not like the Patternism I've seen. Not like Vovo's, for instance—" His voice trailed off.
"Yes?"
"Hers are very crude compared to these."
"What else?"
"Well—"
"You mentioned Vovo's work," she prompted. "How is this different?"
Hesitantly: "You can see they come at the work differently. She paints fast, and her palette is so outlandish, like she just reaches for a tube of whatever paint's handy and lays it on with big brushes. But this work—it's meticulous." Wally's eyes fell from the nude twins to the title cards: *Old Friend 3, Charles Gas* and *Old Friend 4, Charles Gas*.
"He wants me to give him a show. What d'you think?"
"I don't know anything about that."
"What's to know? Is it good art?"
"You know what sells, I don't."
"You can't approach the question about whether it's good art by talking about money. Is it good art? That's what we've been trying to get at when we talk about paintings—how you can tell good art. Or can you tell good art? Some people say art is a meaningless term, because it is entirely subjective."
"Well—you can't help but admire the technique. The paintings grab you. But maybe for the wrong reasons." He blushed, adding: "The poses kind of get in the way. It's like the artist wants to shock, wants to generate something inside the viewer that doesn't have anything to do with art."
"That sounds like something Charles might do."
Silence.
"What does that make the painting, Wally?"
"What d'you mean?"
"Is it pornographic?"
"Oh, no, not pornographic—"
"But doesn't it generate desire?"
"I think so."
"Isn't that what pornography does? Generate appetite? And can that be art?"
He looked at Janice, his face crimson.
"I didn't mean—"
"It's okay, Wally. I'm just trying to get you to see that art works or doesn't work for lots of reasons."
Wally turned back to the paintings.

"I'm sure I'm wrong," he said finally, "—but—they seem more like illustration than art. I've been trying to find—that thing that we talked about before, the quality that stops you and gives you that aesthetic thrill that you get when you see good art. There's something in Vovo's paintings that do that, that make you feel that way. But I don't feel it here. I get the feeling that maybe the artist is trying to shock the viewer, because he can't do the other thing—but it's probably just me, I'm probably wrong."

"You're not wrong."

"I don't mean these are bad paintings," Wally added hastily. "But we're supposed to look for the thing that makes them good art. Or bad art. That's what we said."

"Stop apologizing, Wally, you're going in the right direction."

"Are you going to give him a show?"

"I don't know. I've known him for a long time. It'll be very difficult not to."

"Oh."

"You met him."

"I did?"

"He was here the first time you came in."

"The white-haired fellow with the bifocals who didn't like the Vovos?"

"Yes."

"You've known him a long time?"

"A long time. He did these from memory." This time she blushed, which surprised her as much as the necessity she felt to lamely explain that the lewdness of the poses came from the artist's memory of distant events. "I had no idea he was doing them until he was finished."

"Oh."

"The paintings are embarrassing. But I don't want that to be a factor in whether I give him a show. I'm trying to base the decision on the merit of the work."

"Yes, of course."

They looked silently at the two paintings.

"You're not going to give him a show?"

"Probably not."

"Because of—what you said?"

"Because it's not good art."

"But it is good painting—"

"Oh, yes, it's fine painting. Charles is a fine painter. From time to time he comes close. He's always on the edge of making some very good art, but he always misses, or simply manages to destroy the chances he's given."

"Don't you think his work would be more interesting, maybe look better, if you showed it with other work? Maybe with other Patternists? Like Vovo."

Janice looked at Wally and smiled, as if enjoying his joke, but her smile faded immediately, and her eyes took on a distant look. Wally, oblivious of her gaze, brought his face close to one of the paintings, studied the minute complexity of the creamy tone-on-tone pattern that made a leg, followed it up to that startling pubic bush. He put his finger lightly on the coppery bush, as if to confirm that it was paint and not a blooming mound of curly hair.

"Look at how perfectly he's got this."

But Janice had disappeared and was returning with one of the Vovo paintings from the main room. She rearranged Charles's paintings so that the Vovo hung between them.

Ten

"Why'd you bring him here, anyway? Who the hell is he to critique my paintings?" Charles glared over Janice's shoulder at Wally, who stood before the long wall, staring at Charles's most recent painting, a finished half-finished canvas he insisted was not in the least bit unfinished, that was in fact exactly, precisely, and perfectly finished. He and Janice had been arguing about how you could tell that a Neo-Realistic Patternistic Progressivist painting, like that very portrait of twenty-year-old Janice—painted as he liked to remember her, standing in defiant spread-legged nudity—was finished. Three other finished paintings hung to the left of it, each progressively less finished than the one to it's right. "Who the fuck is he to talk like that? What does he know?" Charles spoke belligerently, and so loudly that the words echoed back from the other end of the long room.

"It was a compliment, Charles."

"It was stupid."

"He's right, Charles—they look unfinished."

"They are perfectly finished."

"They are not going to sell."

"They won't sell if you've made up your mind not to sell them."

"Boyce doesn't like them either."

"What does he know about art?"

Boyce was behind them, at his easel by one the windows, painting. "He knows enough to finish painting his painting," he said to his painting.

"Even if the idea itself was any good, each painting depends for its value on the context of the whole series," Janice said. "When you take them out of that context they're just unfinished paintings. Don't you see that?"

"This is what I see: art is what *I* do, selling is what *you* do. Get it? I paint, you sell. You get your forty percent for *selling*, not *telling*."

"Forty percent of zero is zero."

"He wants you to show 'em as triptyches," Boyce said to his painting.

"Who asked you," Charles snarled over his shoulder.

"See what happens to a man when he smokes that shit for forty years?" Boyce said. "He starts thinkin' shit like that. Triptyches, my tattooed ass!"

"Triptychs?" Janice said.

"Triptychs," Charles said firmly. He pointed at the wall of paintings where Wally stood, adding condescendingly: "Let me explain what a triptych is, first. Maybe that'll help."

"I know what a triptych is. The thing I need a little help with is how to sell twenty running feet of paintings to a customer with a house that doesn't have twenty running feet of open wall."

"What you see there, where your idiot friend is standing, is one triptych. To his right is the start of another. The first triptych is called *Triptych Number One*. There'll be a *Triptych Number Two* and a *Triptych Number Three*. A triptych of triptychs. You got that? Okay, then that grand triptych of triptychs is gonna be called—yeah, you guessed it—*The Grand Triptych*. Nine pieces of Neo-Realistic Patternistic Progressivism in three groups of three. It's perfect numerology."

"Did you guess yet that he was stoned when he come up with that?" Boyce said to his painting.

"Can't you see the impact?" Charles said. "C'mon: stretch yourself just a little bit. And try to be optimistic. For a change."

"He wants you to find a corporate buyer to take 'em all," Boyce said, as he stepped back from his easel and looked critically at his own painting.

"Why didn't I think of that," Janice said. "Nine giant pussies lined up along sixty feet of wall in the main lobby of the Washington State Bank Building. That should be an easy sell."

"They're not giant pussies, they're only life-sized."

"Are you stoned now?"

"No, I'm not stoned, but this conversation makes me want to be stoned. How did you get so uptight, so narrow-minded?"

"When I started writing so many checks. To my landlord, the grocery store, the insurance man, the gas company, the electric company. And to my insane artists."

"C'mere, I got it all worked out."

He dragged her across the coarse planks of the floor to the corner office with its cots and table and boxes of odds and ends. Grabbing a bucket, he held it next to the table and raked dirty dishes and pans and forks and spoons off the table into it with a clatter. He brushed bread crumbs off the table with his hands, motioned for her to sit in one of the two chairs. She sat and watched him paw through a box of books and papers. He found a notebook and came to the table and flipped through several pages of sketches that she recognized as interiors of her gallery.

"Here's the way we'll show them."

She saw that he planned to show one of the triptychs on the big wall, a second on the opposite wall, and the third triptych on the back wall.

"There's one problem," she said.

"What?"

"There's not enough wall for all these paintings."

"Sure there is—I measured the walls."

"You're gonna have to share the walls with Vovo."

"Vovo? What d'you mean?"

"I'm showing your work with Vovo's work."

"You're gonna show my work with that teenager's graffiti?"

"Charles, she's—"

"Me? Appear in the same show with that brainless twit? No fucking way. She's not even pubescent. She's not an artist, she's a *joke* about artists."

"She didn't like the idea either."

"Two out of three of us agree."

"But after I explained my idea—actually it wasn't my idea, it was Wally's—"

"Wally's? Who the fuck is Wally?"

"Wally. The guy over there."

"That figures. Well fuck Wally, there's no way—"

"She didn't like it either until I told her how I wanted to promote it. I'm gonna call it *Directions in Patternism: Two Artists, Two Generations, Two Worlds*."

"No fucking way. No—"

She reached out and put her hand on his arm. "Charles. Listen to me: it is the only way I'm gonna give you a show."

Silence.

When he spoke the bluster was gone. "I don't get it. Why would you even think about showing my work with hers?"

"I will say it as plain as I can. I will give you a show, but only if it's a two-artist show with Vovo."

Charles got up, went to the open doorway, looked up the length of the long room at his easel and the shaft of yellow light angling down from the skylight toward the long wall where Wally stood gazing at one of the paintings. The bright patch of light on the floor indirectly illuminated Wally and the paintings, from low, like the footlights of a stage.

"Why?"

"Context. There's no way I can sell your work unless there's a context for it."

"Context, my ass. My work doesn't need a fucking context. My work is art! Art does not need a context."

She sighed.

"Vovo's work needs a context," he yelled. "I will even tell you the context. A toilet bowl."

"Charles, this—"

"Why would that cunt even think about showing with me?" he asked, still standing in the doorway, looking across the studio at Wally and the wall of paintings.

"Because she realizes it's a good idea. Patternism's the unifying theme. You're both doing good work, but you are isolated at the two ends of the spectrum of Patternism and—"

"Where are you getting this bullshit? From Wally?" "—and Patternism is hot."

"That's not the reason Vovo's going for this." He came back into the room and stood over her. "She wants my scalp."

"Charles—"

"She hates my guts and she wants to humiliate me."

Janice waited for him to get it all said.

"That stuff out there is the best work I've done in years. As a matter of fact it is better than anything I have ever done. I didn't think I'd be able to pull it off—didn't think I'd be able to drag you out of thirty years ago. But I did, goddamn it. That is you out there, that is the *essence* of you, the *soul* of you—now and then. That is exactly the you I wanted."

She waited for him to get it all said.

"You do see that's you out there, don't you?"

"What difference does it make?"

"Well it is you, and when I look at those paintings, and know that it's from memory, and that I got it right—don't you know what a big deal that is? That I conceived this terribly hard, impossible thing, and then did it? Working entirely from memory. Filtering you through me, through all those years between us then and us now. When I started on the first one I had no idea how I was gonna dredge you up from way back there"—he slapped the back of his head— "but it came out of my hands onto the canvas, just like it's supposed to. My head wasn't even involved. And it's good art. Now you want to demean it by making it a contest between my shit and her kindergarten finger painting."

"You're wrong, Charles."

"Okay. I know when I'm beat." He turned away and sagged into the other chair.

"It's not a matter of your work being against her work."

"Of course it is. That's the only reason the cunt would agree."

"About those unfinished paintings—"

"They're not unfinished."

"I'll go this far with you: give me ten finished pieces to show with Vovo's seven in the main room and I'll give them half—"

"They're all finished."

"—of the best wall and you can have the back room to show your triptychs."

"The back room? My triptychs in the back room?"

—

They were driving north on I-5, approaching the exit ramp to I-520. Janice looked over at Wally. "What are you drawing?"

"You."

"Hold it up."

Wally raised the tablet and turned it toward Janice.

She glanced at it, smiled, and turned her eyes back to the traffic. "You amaze me, Wally. I can't keep up with you."

"I've got too many lines in it. I never know when to stop. I wish I could draw like Charles. Did you see those sketches on those unfinished canvases?"

"He's been doing it a long time," she said.

"I couldn't find one line that wasn't important."

"Like I said, he's been doing it a long time."

She turned the car into the I-520 ramp and merged with the traffic of the evening commute. She looked at Wally, saw the charcoal pencil dancing over the page, saw it stop for a moment as he raised his eyes to study her face. She felt his gaze, but knew it wasn't Wally looking at Janice, that it wasn't the eye-touching-eye soul contact that friends make; his gaze was distant and unselfconsciously searching—like a doctor's gaze, only he wasn't searching for affliction, he was searching for what she was, searching for the *her* that was there in the shape of her. She felt a twinge of resentment. He was already better with pencil and charcoal than she had ever been, even at her best, when she was living with Charles and drawing and painting all of the time she wasn't loving him or battling him—and in her youthful conceit believing that she was being an artist, not knowing that she was no artist, not knowing that all-important fact for years thereafter, not knowing it even after she had put the brushes aside and picked up the sales pad.

For a moment she resented Wally, because he was becoming the artist she had determined to be and could never be. Yes, he was becoming an artist—at a speed that took her breath away. And ironically enough would never be known for it, because his Ethel wouldn't allow it and because he himself did not have the conceit to make it happen. She thought about the juxtapositions of their experience and their talents. He with his nascent talent and need for experience, she with her lack of talent and her vast experience. But experience could come to him and talent could not come to her. She pushed the resentment out and leaned toward Wally so she could see the drawing better.

"You could be ready for a show in a few months, Wally," she teased.

Wally looked at her again, studied her face for a few seconds, looked down at the pad and continued drawing.

"Wally!"

He looked up.

"I said you could be ready for a show within a year."

"Me?" he said incredulously.

She laughed.

He gazed at her, his look now open and full of intimacy. "I'm not an artist, I write technical manuals. And I can't even do that anymore."

"You are an artist," Janice said, not joking now. "I wish I had your talent. Christ, I wish Charles had your talent."

Eleven

The gold embedded in Carnita Vovo's face gleamed yellow in the candle light. She listened without a word until Janice finished. "I don't get it. Why would he want to do that?"

"It wasn't his idea, it was mine," Janice said. "But as soon as he heard it he knew it was perfect."

"*I* don't think it's perfect. He hates my guts. He wants my scalp, that's the only reason he'd do it."

"He doesn't hate you. I suppose he resents your success. And your talent. And why wouldn't he resent you? Anyone would like to have your talent. But he doesn't hate you. Actually, he spoke very respectfully about your work."

"He did?"

Janice nodded. "Look. Just put yourself in his place for a minute. He's sixty years old, he's worked like a dog all his life, and he hasn't had a fraction of the success you've had in just two years. You exploded on the Seattle art scene—which he's been trying to crack all his life."

Carnita glanced at the mountainous, shadowy Wikka, who leaned back against the plastic upholstery in the corner of the booth, out of the shaded light, staring inscrutably at Janice. Carnita looked back at Janice. "Yeah, I guess I did. I see what you mean. I'm successful and he's a failure."

Janice hesitated. "Well, he's not really a failure. I wouldn't be asking you to show with a failure. What I was trying to say was he hasn't had the commercial success you've had. He's kind of an artist's artist. Every artist I know thinks he's a great technician. But this whole thing isn't about him anyway, it's about you."

Wikka spoke for the first time since they'd come into the restaurant. "This is a setup."

Janice raised her glass of wine, sipped, and observed Carnita's reaction.

"What d'you mean?" Carnita said, looking at Wikka.

"She's setting you up," Wikka said. Her eyebrow rings and nose rings and ear rings, which were almost as big as bangles, glistened and tinkled, and her shoulder tattoos rolled and jiggled as she leaned forward, into the light, resting her elbows and her breasts on the table. Beads of sweat gleamed on her forehead. She stared expressionlessly at Janice.

"They're gonna make a sandwich out of you."

Janice lowered her glass. "We are?"

"You are."

"How?"

"I haven't figured that out yet."

Janice addressed Carnita. "I can't defend myself against such a—nebulous attack. All I can say is look at the record. Look at our relationship. I've never done anything that has cost you money or reputation. I've given you money when you wanted it—the last time, a week ago. And in the two years you've been showing in my gallery you've come from obscurity into a reputation as an important young artist with a great future. In all modesty, I did have a hand in that success, I did provide guidance and opportunity and support. Don't forget it was me that got Dillip there to review your first show. I have always been reasonable with you and loyal to your interests. Like agreeing to represent you for thirty percent instead of forty. No gallery does that, not even Whipple with George Gorgeous." She shrugged. "So naturally when I am accused of fucking you I ask: how am I fucking you? And Wikka says, 'I haven't figured it out yet.' That's just plain not fair."

Carnita looked uncertainly at Wikka, who glared at Janice.

"Wikka, she's right," Carnita said.

"This is a setup," Wikka said. "I can see it in her aura. It's money green."

Carnita looked at Janice. "I can't see her aura."

"Of course you can't. You're not gifted."

"But she's right, she did all those things, and she did give us the money. I don't see what can happen. And we'll get more money out of it." She looked back at Janice "Do I have to, you know, *be* with him?"

"You need to be present at the opening, because Dillip is sure to be there. He likes your work, and if you spend a little time with him he'll let people continue buying your work. But you don't have to talk to Charles, or even stand with him. You can even leave early if you want."

"But what about the prices? My work is selling for a lot more than his. Don't I lose something by showing with someone whose work is so much cheaper?"

"If that's a problem, it's a good one to have: your work sells, even at three times the price of his work."

Carnita looked down at her glass of wine. Around them the level of noise had picked up as the tables filled with early diners.

"Well. Okay. I guess."

"We'll regret this," Wikka said.

Twelve

"For cryin' out loud, Mom, didn't you even talk to her?" George let his hands drop helplessly.

Ethel bristled. "How could I? She wasn't even there."

"Where was Dad?"

"Off somewhere, drawing something or other."

"Off with her, likely as not," George said. "You want *me* to talk to her? Maybe I better handle this."

"No, I don't want you to talk to her, and don't you speak to me in that tone of voice, neither. I'm not your father."

George frowned.

"It's hard enough carrying this load without you adding your little bit to the burden."

"Addin' to the burden? I give him a job, didn't I? It's not my fault he couldn't hack it."

"Doesn't give you the right to come in here and talk like that."

"I think them two got something going on between 'em—that's what I think."

"They certainly have not," Ethel said indignantly.

"I don't know how you can be so sure, he's over there ever day."

"Well, I am sure."

"I don't see how you can be."

"Your father has not bothered me for fourteen years. Because he can't. That's how I'm so certain. Does that satisfy you, mister nosy?"

George's cheeks flamed and he frowned at his hands, then dug into his pocket for his knife, unfolded the blade, and began scraping at his blackened fingernails. There was a knock on the back door. George got up and opened it. Ethel heard Roy's voice.

"Come in, Roy. You want some coffee and pie?"

"No thanks. Still on my diet."

"You can eat a small piece."

"No, I can't, really—but, well—maybe a small piece. But no coffee. Gotta watch the caffeine."

Ethel rose and went to the refrigerator. "Glass of milk?"

"You got skim? Gotta watch the cholesterol."

"No, all we got is two percent."

"Two percent ain't much. I'll have a glass." Roy pulled a chair out and sat at the table. "What're you up to these days, George? How's business?"

"Ever thing'd be fine if it wasn't for them goddamned environmentalists. They're at it again, tryin' to outlaw new tanks."

"Um."

"Getting' so pumpin' old tanks is all the business I got now. And them that's got 'em think they ought to just last forever, trouble-free."

"Um."

"Think all you got to do is pump it to fix it, but half the time they don't need pumpin', they got lateral problems, 'cause o' roots or they drove a truck over the drain fields."

"Big or little?" Ether said.

"What kind is it?"

"Banana cream."

"My favorite. Maybe just a little bit big."

She brought a quarter of a pie and put it on the table in front of Roy, who had drawn his chair close to the table.

"Um-um! Will you look at that! High as it is wide. That's the way to make a cream pie."

He cut a corner off with his fork and lifted it to his mouth.

"Your pie crust is heaven, Ethel," he mumbled.

He loaded and unloaded his fork several times before he paused and drank some milk.

"Maybe you ought to think about gettin' into the repair part of the business," he said to George. "Sounds like some opportunity there."

"There's opportunity, all right, but it takes big money. Back hoe ain't enough. You got to have a truck and a trailer to haul it on, an' tools to keep it running. An' you got to have a root-rooter. That's not cheap neither. And like I said, when they call you all they want is for you to pump the tank, they're not interested in no thousand-dollar repair job."

"Finish what you got, there's more," Ethel said.

"I couldn't manage another."

"Don't know why I bother makin' pies anymore, nobody around here'll eat 'em."

"I ain't had my supper yet," George said defensively. "I'll take a piece with me."

"Wally hardly touches sweets anymore."

"Where is Wally?"

"In his studio."

"Paintin'?"

"Drawin'," George said. "Mom won't let him paint at home no more. He does that down to that gallery. I been tellin' her if she'd let him paint here, maybe he'd stay home."

"Smells like paint," Roy said. He pushed the plate away.

"We already been over that," Ethel said to George. "I'm not about to let him turn this house into no studio, it'd be a complete surrender. We'd never get him back then." She picked up Roy's plate. "Here, I'll get you another piece."

"Just a small one," Roy said, belching. He wrinkled his purple nose: "I do smell somethin'."

"That's George you smell," Ethel said over her shoulder. "He came directly from his last job of the day."

"It's not me," George said irritably. "I wash up when I get through. You always say that, but it ain't me you smell, it's the paint."

"That's not a paint smell," Ethel said, as she cut the pie. "I know the smell of those paints, because he comes home with paint all over his pants and shirt, even has it in his hair. And his good shoes are just speckled with it."

"For the life of me I just can't understand it," Roy said.

"Gets worse and worse," George added. "For a while there I thought the medicine that Pete give him was gonna help, but Dad won't take it no more. Claims it makes him sleepy."

"It did make him sleepy," Ethel said as she put the plate in front of Roy. "Making him sleep his life away is not curing him."

"My God, Ethel, that's bigger'n the first one."

"Well, someone's got to eat it."

"I don't mind tellin' you it's been hard on me, too. It's like losing your best friend," Roy mumbled through a mouthful of pie. "Only it's never over with, like it was when Grace died. I thought I'd never get over that, but I did. But the thing about Wally is he's not gone. He's kind of gone, but some part of him's still here—or someone is. It's like someone took over his soul, just moved into his body and—"

"For goodness' sake!" Ethel snapped. "I have never heard such talk! Wally is not dead and no one's got his soul. He's the same Wally that he always was—except he's sick."

"I only meant—" Roy started, but fell silent. He looked embarrassedly at his piece of pie, belched again, picked up his fork.

"And this kind a talk doesn't help none," Ethel added tartly.

"We was just talking about what to do next," George said, to relieve the tension.

"Um."

"I'm thinkin' surgery," George went on. "That's what that Doctor Ramsay wants to do. He's the young one."

"Um." Roy kept his mouth full of pie and milk—he wasn't saying anything more until he saw where Ethel stood.

"It's Wally's decision," Ethel said, in a voice still a little sharp edged. "It's his brain they want to cut on."

"That sounds wise to me," Roy mumbled cautiously.

"Well, this situation can't go on forever," George said. "Where you gonna get the money to pay bills? Sell this house and live in a tent? And how you gonna pay some fancy brain surgeon two years from now, when they cancel the insurance and you're broke and you finally decide there's no other way?"

Ethel had gotten up to prepare a cup of tea. She brought it to the table and resumed her seat.

"I never said we wouldn't do it," she said. "Maybe it is the only chance he's got of being normal. All I'm saying is, I'm gonna have to believe it is the only thing that will save his life before I make him do it."

"And all I'm sayin' is you need to get things prepared—just in case you need to make some decision or other. Don't do no harm to get the legal part set up. Just in case."

"Being his guardian—it just don't seem right to be able to make him do things. Like he's a child."

"You been his guardian for months. All I'm sayin' is you ought to make it legal, just in case you got to make some decision or other. I don't know what difference it'll make."

"It'll put too much power in my hands, that's what difference it makes. I don't want that kind a power."

Wally appeared in the hall doorway with a two-foot by three-foot drawing tablet. He held it up. "I did it, Ethel. You remember when I was telling you about what Piccolo and Brick did with Intractable Perspectivism. Of course, nowadays it's easy to see that would have to evolve into Relativistic Polyhedralism, then Tubism, because that's the way art is—going along with history, sometimes even leading history when you got a guy like Piccolo out there doing the leading, like I was saying about how some critics think Patternism is forecasting the collapse of society, and all that's needed is for some Patternistic Piccolo to come along and maybe we'll see they're right also, just like the prophets were thousands of years ago—some people argue they were artists, too, you know, and I think it's not that farfetched—and like the artists of Rome were, when Rome was decaying and falling apart and classical sculpture was evolving into primitivism—that was when the Dark Ages really began, when the artists saw it, which was before anybody else and even they didn't know it was happening, though their art knew it; it was their art that was prophetic. So the concept is really not new, it's just hard to understand—so anyway, now it seems logical that Piccolo and Brick were starting all that at the same time Einstein was writing his Special Theory of Relativity. Isn't it marvelous how it all ties together? Art and mathematics and biology and physics and religion—everything changing all the time, with art right out in front showing the way. When I look at Piccolo's first pieces of Relativistic Polyhedralism and think that just a few hundred miles away Einstein was writing his Special Theory—well, it just gives you goose bumps, doesn't it? Particularly since I've been working for days on a simple Polyhedralistic still life. And by golly I finally got it. What d'you think?"

He'd been holding the pad up in front of him like a little boy showing off for his parents; now he turned it around and held it at arm's length and admired the drawing. He raised his eyes a little and noticed Roy exchanging a look with Ethel.

"Roy! Don't move, stay exactly like that. Let me get my pencils."

"I rest my case," George said.

"It's very pretty, Wally," Ethel said loyally. "Wouldn't you like to sit down with us and have a piece of pie?"

Thirteen

"It's nearly ten, Wally. I've got to open up." Janice closed the book and put it on the side table.

"Just a couple of minutes more," Wally said from behind the easel.

"I've got to open up." She rose from the chair and stretched her arms above her head.

"I don't like it," Wally said.

She came around the easel and looked at the canvas.

"It's like the last one," he said. "I get it sort of finished, almost finished, and then everything I do to it is wrong. Whatever I do makes it worse. I wish you'd let me do something else—maybe if I did something Polyhedralistic—" His words trailed off hopefully.

She studied the painting. He had fixed the light on her hair and forehead exactly as she'd suggested, and he'd pushed the background farther back by darkening the wall and window detail. The woman was now unmistakably Janice. He had her. And yet this portrait went beyond the narrow didactic of portraiture: Wally had managed to portray her in the universal language of art—of good art. She felt a minute ripple of goose-bumpy emotion, a feeling akin to awe. It was a simple work. Head bent a little, eyes downcast toward the book: the pose as traditional as she had insisted, his composition as direct and simple as she had required, rendered from the basic palette she had chosen: constraints she had imposed weeks before to keep his attention focused on fundamentals, to force him to control his enthusiasm, which ran away with him every time he let it loose. He had bridled at the closeness of her supervision, had even argued with her about it; but as he ruined one canvas after another he'd gradually surrendered to her guidance.

"You're too critical of your work, Wally. This painting is very good."

"I can't finish it. I don't know where to take it from here."

"It's finished, Wally."

"But I can't tell when to stop. The more I look at this canvas, the more unfinished it seems. It looks as unfinished as those paintings Charles Gas was doing."

"You need to do a little more copying."

"I do?" Wally said incredulously. "I don't see how that'll help. I thought we were through copying."

"It will help you see when to stop."

"But I don't like copying, I want to do some Polyhedralistic work, or something in Patternism. I think I'm ready for that. Maybe that's what I need."

"Copying is what you need. For a while longer."

A defeated sigh. "Who."

"I don't know yet. Let me take a look."

"How about a Piccolo?" Wally said hopefully "Can you find a Piccolo? Let me do an early Piccolo."

She went to the bookshelf in the living room and removed a book and returned to the dining room where Wally had set up his easel, and from where they had removed her dining room table and chairs to give Wally space for the easel and a small work table. She leafed through the pages, then stopped and looked up. "Oh, of course," she murmured. She closed the book and went into her bedroom and returned with a painting of a young woman in a robe that had slipped off one shoulder, exposing one breast. The woman's face was in shadow.

"I want you to study this one. And then I want you to copy it. It's a Charles Gas. It's not very successful as a painting—much too academic—but the technique is excellent. I want you to look closely at how little paint he's spreading. And look at what he does with very few hues, how much he gets out of shadow and saturation."

Wally already had his face close to the canvas.

—

"Stop that," Janice said. "Keep your hands to yourself."

Charles grinned. "Let's go upstairs. We got all evening to hang the show."

"We're not going upstairs and I want you to keep your hands off me. We have work to do."

"Screwing'll be more fun."

"I don't screw people I'm doing business with." "When did you start that policy?"

"Very funny."

"Well, who are you fucking, then?"

"No one—not that it's any of your business. And I don't want to talk about it. We have a lot work to do."

"No one, my ass. The only time in your life you weren't fucking someone was before you started fucking. And that must have been a few years before puberty."

Janice put her hands on her hips and looked around the room. The boxes were empty now and the paintings leaned in two stacks against the wall. "The first thing we got to do is break the boxes down and put them on the upper shelves. We'll need this space."

"Can't be Whipple again. He had that prostate operation and the word is he can't get it up anymore. Is that true, by the way?"

"I wouldn't know."

"C'mon, who is it? Do I know him?"

She brushed hair out of her eyes. "I'm going to lock up in a few minutes. When I do we'll move your paintings out to the second room, then take down the stuff in the main room and bring it in here. I want to paint the main wall before we hang it. While the paint's drying we'll hang the second room. We'll do Carnita's at the same time we're doing yours."

"Fuck Carnita. I'm not her garbage man."

"Or we could get her down here and we'd have a fun evening with her and Wikka discussing who gets what place on the best wall."

"We'll hang her show."

Charles cut the tape on an empty box and collapsed it on the floor, then did the same thing to a second box. He paused.

"It's Wally, isn't it? He's always around here. That's why you won't tell me, because you're ashamed to tell me it's him." When she ignored him he grinned. "I thought so. Well, if I was you I'd be ashamed, too."

His laughter followed her out of the back room into the gallery. She went to her desk, picked up the telephone and punched Carnita's number. Only then did she notice the short, plump woman standing before the two Gas paintings still hanging in the second room. Carnita's answering machine told her to leave a message.

She hung up and approached the lady.

"Can I help you?" Janice asked.

An expression of surprise came over the woman's face. She looked back at the painting, then at Janice again. Then her lips tightened and one eyebrow arched up and her head went back.

"I am Ethel Walder," she said coldly.

Janice waited.

"Missus *Walter* Walder?"

"Oh-h-h—of course. I'm sorry—I've only heard Wally's last name once or twice and it didn't register. I'm so glad to meet you, Mrs. Walder. I've really enjoyed knowing Wally. He's a remarkably talented man."

"He is a sick man." Ethel said grimly.

Silence for several seconds.

"You may know he was injured several months ago," Ethel said. "It was a brain injury. We've been trying to get him well ever since."

"He told me about the accident."

"Then you must know that he can't work any more, because he has this brain sickness they call Pablo Piccolo Syndrome. It's a sickness where all you can think about is art."

Ethel spoke the words with cold restraint, but Janice felt the anger beneath the words. She chose her own words cautiously. "Wally told me what the doctor said."

"Did he also tell you how much it's costing our family?"

Janice studied the stiff-backed, round-faced woman, trying to figure out where she was taking this. When Janice said nothing, Ethel continued.

"I'm telling you this because I want you to know what this—what this art adventure of Wally's is costing us, so you can understand why you have to tell Wally to stop coming in here. And why I want you to stop telling him he's got talent." She spat the last word like it was hateful thing. "You need to know you are encouraging a sick man toward self destruction."

Janice's face suddenly felt hot. Momentarily disoriented, she looked down at her hands. Embarrassment flooded through her, as well as anger, because she had done nothing to be embarrassed about. She had offered kindness to a harmless old eccentric with a naïve passion for art—and, it turned out, an unbelievable talent.

"There's no way I can get him back to normal unless people like you stop leading him on with all that talk about talent. We were making progress before he started coming to this gallery. You probably think you're doing something nice, giving him paint and canvases and all, but you're not. All your encouraging talk has undid all the progress we made. He's not an artist, he's just a simple old man who works hard and comes home tired and watches TV until he can go to bed and sleep. At least that's what he used to be—'til all this art stuff come along. Now I don't know how he's gonna end up. Maybe it'll kill him."

Janice's face was hot and tight. "Being around art is not going to kill Wally. And I am offended that you would suggest that my attention to his talent is destructive."

Ethel sniffed. "You? Offended?" She looked meaningfully over her shoulder at the two Charles Gas nudes hanging in the other room. "This would be a evil place for a man to come to even if he was well."

Janice stiffened. "Who do you think—" she began, and then a heavy clump-clump-clump sounded on the stairs and the stairwell burst open and Wally lunged into the room, a brush in one hand and a canvas in the other. He held the canvas up.

"Janice, I want you to look—why, Ethel, it's you! Janice, look. I got your face and breast. Maybe not perfectly, but it's good. And I can tell it's finished! You were right, I was putting too much paint on the canvas. What d'you think? Look, Ethel."

"Well I'm a sonofabitch—"

Ethel and Wally and Janice turned toward the door to the back room, where Charles stood, holding one of his nudes of Janice.

"That was *Wally* comin' down the stairs, wasn't it? No wonder you wouldn't take me upstairs. So it is Wally. I'm a sonofabitch!"

"Hello Charles," Wally said. "I was just looking at one of your old paintings and—"

"Wally, you sly dog! Who'd a thought it'd be you that kicks old Charles Gas out of Janice Cushion's bed."

Wally looked quizzically at Charles. "Pardon?"

Charles's laughter caromed round the gallery walls.

Fourteen

"When she missed the driveway and knocked them mailboxes down and run across the lawn and ever one of my rose bushes I suspected there was trouble," Roy offered. He stood off by himself, as befitted a non-family person in the present circumstance. On the other hand, he was a close-enough friend to speak about it, and to remain in the kitchen during the crisis.

Ethel sobbed and hiccoughed. "—ur—right—that—ohmygod—wo—man—Wal—ohgod—oh-h-h—t'gether—both—oh-h-h—t'die—just want—know—just—can't—"

Wanda stood beside Ethel's chair, unconsciously twisting her face and her handkerchief in sympathy. As fat and round-faced and pink-cheeked as Ethel, Wanda was often taken by others to be Ethel's young sister. The anguish in her face now made her look like Ethel's twin.

"Mom, you need to calm down," George said.

"Leave her alone," Wanda said. "Let her finish."

"But, what the hell's she sayin'?"

"She's sayin' that your Dad and that—" Wanda bit her lip. She just couldn't say the words. Couldn't hardly even think the words. Her pink cheeks flooded with red.

George looked blankly at his wife. "Whut?"

Wanda touched Ethel's shoulder. "Is Dad over there now?" she asked gently.

Ethel sobbed and hiccoughed and nodded.

"Where?" George interjected. "Where's Dad?"

"Over to that gallery," Wanda said.

"He is?" George looked expectantly at his wife.

Wanda leaned down and put her arm round Ethel's shoulders. "Mom, you want us bring him home?"

Ethel sobbed and hiccoughed and nodded.

"You want to pray about it first?"

Ethel sobbed and hiccoughed and shook her head. "—n't help—"

"It might. God'll hear. He always hears."

George looked heavenward. "I wish to hell someone would just tell me what the goddamned hell is goin' on here."

Wanda looked coldly at her husband, who sat in the kitchen chair he always sat in at the place at the table he always sat at when he visited his mom and dad; which was the place he'd always sat at when he ate his meals for the first twenty-five years of his life. The fingers of his right hand drummed impatiently on the table. His baseball cap was pushed back, his jeans jacket half-opened over a gray shirt that had once been white. He had loosed his plastic bow tie.

"George, sometimes I just wonder—don't you understand that your dad and that gallery woman—" But she couldn't finish. She put her face near Ethel's and hugged her. "It's okay, we'll do the prayin' for you. And God'll hear, you'll see. He always does."

"—ll Reilly—going on—going—on—papers—"

"I think it'd be better if we call him tomorrow morning, Mom," Wanda said gently. "You need to be able to talk a little better. And besides, they're closed now. Tomorrow morning's soon enough, don't you think?"

"Soon enough fer whut?" George said.

Ethel sobbed and hiccoughed and nodded. "No—oh-h-h-h—guess—right—"

"We'll go and get Dad," Wanda said. "You gonna be all right?"

Ethel sobbed and nodded.

"Soon enough fer whut?"

"C'mon, George, let's go get your Dad."

"Soon enough fer *whut*, goddamnit?"

"Soon enough to see Reilly. Now get up, and let's go get your dad."

George rose and led the way to the back door. He opened it and stood aside as Wanda walked through.

"What's she want to see Reilly about?"

"About the papers."

"Jesus H. Kee-rist! Can't you women say a whole sentence? *Whut* are you talkin' about?"

George slammed the door behind him and followed Wanda around the house, leaving Roy standing beside the sink, wondering how to console poor Ethel.

Fifteen

Charles and Boyce got off the bus quarreling about Neo-Repressionist Aushaus Grupism. Charles held that it was a philosophy for morons and photographers and New-Neo-Modernists, whereas Boyce claimed that Charles was "so full o' shit, man, it's what's movin' Post-Neo-Modernism, it's the heart of Post-Neo-Modernism, man," and that Charles should read the fuckin' aesthetic theories of the early Neo-Repressionist Aushaus Grupists before "running off at the mouth like that, man, because you're just showin' off your ignorance, man. It is existentially inevitable, man. Shit, man, it's ever-where, it's inner-national, man, it's on ever continent."

Charles observed that popularity wasn't an indicator of anything except mediocrity. As a matter of fact, popularity defined mediocrity, didn't it? This really got Boyce going, as Charles knew it would, Boyce being essentially brainless. Boyce responded excitedly that lots of things were popular and that didn't mean they were mediocre. What about the Bulls? And Christianity? And what about—

My point exactly, interrupted Charles: that an idea is popular is proof that the idea is spent.

So it went, as they went down the street flailing at one another with arguments no more substantial than the breeze generated by their flapping lips, loving the meaninglessness of these word-games that artists play with such deadly intensity about the only thing they give a fuck about: playing with ideas about art, tasting art, smelling art, talking art, living art.

They went into a drug store on Lake Street, both talking at once, and while Charles looked out for clerks, Boyce shoplifted several bottles of aspirin and a handful of Aspergum packages. Back on the street they continued walking toward Janice's gallery. Boyce opened a bottle of aspirin and popped several into his mouth. He swished the tart spittle over rotting stumps of teeth as he unwrapped Aspergum. He stuck several pieces into his mouth and let them soften, then started chewing gingerly.

"They might come tonight," Charles observed as they waited for the light to change.

"Don't matter," Boyce mumbled through his Aspergum. "The man don't like my shit."

"Shelley's the one that counts. If she shows up I'll work on her."

The light changed. They went across the street and down the block toward the dock below Lake Street. At the corner, a block from the pier, they stopped and waited for a traffic light to change. Across the street was the gallery. Its interior, seen through floor-to-ceiling plate-glass windows, against the gray evening, was a stage setting. Janice was visible in the main room talking to

Carnita, who as usual wore black blouse, black pants, black lipstick, and black hat, to compliment her many gold earrings, her half-dozen lip rings and nose-rings, her exposed belly-button rings and her eyebrow-rings. Beside her was an enormously fat woman with gold rings as big as bangles drooping from nose, eyebrows, ears, lower lip; whose floral-patterned tent of a dress gave her the look of a flower-covered hillside. Nearby, an elderly couple admired one of Carnita's paintings. The completeness of the scene—paintings spewing color, cars hissing on the damp street, gray scudding clouds, the long pier, the dark wind-roughened water, the light-spangled city across the lake—provoked a rare surge of appreciation, even gratitude—in Charles. Goddamn it, she is something, isn't she? What she does with other people's art is—well, it is art: bringing art together into new art; combining art to make art. That's her art. The effect of all that exuberant color framed by cold shades of evening gray was of a single piece of living, many-dimensional art. He thought about the previous evening, when he and Janice had battled, again, over the placement of every painting in the main room. He realized now that Janice had been right—except for the fucking Vovos. He was right about that shit. The Vovos belonged in boxes in the back room. Or, better yet, on the walls of small-town cafes with signs like *Autumn Light, $30* or *Crying Clowns, $25*.

"Fabulous," Charles said.

"Wish she'd show my shit," Boyce mumbled through a mouth full of Aspergum.

"It's a performance piece," Charles said, his voice wavering with reverence at seeing his work so profoundly displayed. "She's creating her own performance art out of art. My art. God, it's so fucking good. You can see it happening, you can feel her grabbing you and dragging you into the art, making you part of it."

Boyce popped a couple more aspirin. "I can always tell when you're smokin' that shit."

"It's perfect. Except for those fucking Vovos."

"The Vovo's look good, man. They even help your shit."

"My shit doesn't need any help. But I do. I need a joint. So I can be nice to all those people."

"Whut people?"

"The people who're gonna crowd into that piece of performance art and pay me a lot of money for my art. Let's go down to the pier and smoke a jay, then go dispense some culture to the masses."

—

Women and men are antipodal creatures. Women are inward, men are outward. As much as women are acceptingly positive and loving and empathetic, that much are men thrustingly negative and vengeful and violent. Honesty, nobility, integrity, beauty, pacificity: these are the attributes of women. Corruption, pettiness, hypocrisy, ugliness, violence are the terms one associates with men. Even men know this to be true. Men know how ugly and violent and spiritually corrupt they are, and with a perfect consistency of character deny it, even as they exult in it. Not one of 'em would change it if he could. All men know they are either rapists or potential rapists, batterers or potential batterers, murderers or potential murderers. Every man of them knows it and celebrates it triumphantly, even as he shows a fake solicitude and a phony good will to the poor foolish bitch who never stops hoping that *her* man will break the mold and be different, will change and stop using her for a punching bag.

Some women manage to see through the fakery of men. Wikka Vovo was one of those women. Men's auras unerringly told Wikka what was inside them, just like stink told you what was inside an outhouse. Wikka could read a man's aura in practically any circumstance, even in the rainbow of auras that you find hovering over a crowd. Men's blood-red auras flamed above them like Satan's battle flag, advertising to all and sundry that it was fucking they wanted; first and foremost fucking, and after that the other brutalities. No act was too hurtful or disgusting or demeaning for a man to perform, particularly if could he use his penis somewhere in the process.

That women are not given to violence is a well-known fact. Less well-known is the reason. Wikka had it figured out. It was because women are penisless. The absence of penises from women's bodies make them much more pacific than men, not to mention more complex and humane, which makes them a lot less dangerous. Women display a cheerful rainbow of aural hues, an indicator of the range and delicacy of their emotions. Men's auras, on the other hand, throbbed redly with anger and sexual aggressiveness more or less all the time. Even when they slept.

Wikka had studied Janice for months. Janice had an amazingly stable aura, considering the fact that she dealt routinely with predators like Charles Gas and Whipple and Philip Dillip. When Charles arrived at the show with his disgusting purple-red aura pulsing like a jellyfish round his snowy head, Janice's delicate blue aura barely flickered. She calmly grasped the hand he flung possessively around her waist to draw her near and kiss her, and handed it back to him, then sent him off to the table in the back for a glass of wine—while her aura glowed its cool blue and she continued her conversation with Whipple and Carnita.

Wikka observed all of this and more. Observing Janice and Whipple was Wikka's goal for this evening, because she had to make a decision. For some time she'd been thinking about transferring Carnita's loyalty from Janice to Whipple. Whipple's galleries were the most successful in the Northwest, and he got top dollar for the work of his artists. This was important, for it proved to his customers that the art they paid so much for was good art. And of course selling art for a lot of money encouraged his stable of artists because it proved to them that they were creating good art. It was one of those deals where everyone profits. Especially Whipple, for his were the only galleries west of New York that took a sixty-seven percent commission from most of his stable of artists. The artists bitched about that, saying they did all the work and got a only third of the take, but that kind of talk only demonstrated the obtuseness and the ingratitude of artists. When push comes to shove, however, even artists are smart enough to understand that thirty-three percent of a lot of money is better than one-hundred percent of no money.

As Carnita's business manager and mother, it was Wikka's responsibility to understand these arcane matters of business so she could guide her daughter. And she did: she had a calculator and she knew how to use it. Indeed, she had worn the keys down to numberless blocks of ersatz ivory. And, regrettably, the calculations were pointing the way to Whipple's. Regrettably, because Whipple was a man and Janice a woman. But you can't argue with numbers. Numbers couldn't care less about loyalty. The numbers dispassionately said, *Go With Whipple.* And so she was leaning that way, despite the undeniable fact of Whipple's penis. That he had a penis bothered her greatly; though by no means did it intimidate her: she was a woman (by nature penisless, and therefore more intelligent and clever), so she could manage him. No, her reluctance had more to do with fundamental values. It was against her fundamental values to do business with people who have penises. She didn't even like to shake hands with people with penises. The very thought that she was touching a hand that only moments before could have been handling a penis made her stomach churn.

She was proud of the fact that her authority on the topic of penile encounter was theoretical, not actual. Of course she readily admitted that her one pregnancy was the result of penile encounter, but she insisted that because the encounter was indirect, it did not count as a real encounter. Indeed, Wikka made sure that the world knew that she did not violate her fundamental principles to get pregnant. She still boasted that her one pregnancy resulted from artificial insemination. (What Wikka did not admit was that the impregnating semen was not inserted by a doctor. She'd tried to find a doctor to artificially inseminate her, but could find no one who'd do it for five dollars. They all wanted five-thousand dollars. She solved the problem at the Blue Moon Tavern one evening by inducing a drunken artist who needed money for beer to go with her to her nearby rented room and masturbate into a shot glass for five dollars. She then kicked the fellow out and inseminated herself with a turkey baster.)

By such cleverness she held to her fundamental values. But in the matter of those fundamental values—as in matters of philosophy, ethics, morality, and religion—it all came down to money. Money balances things. In fact, money weighs so heavily in the balance that it always tips the scales; in this case, in favor of doing business with whoever has the money, even if that person also has a penis. Besides, Wikka had heard rumors that Whipple's prostate surgery had retired his penis from active service. That improvement made him at least a little like a woman.

This question of whom to do business with was an urgent problem. Wikka had only a few more years to milk Carnita's talent. Her influence over Carnita would inevitably wane as Carnita experienced greater success, not to mention carnal experience with men, which had already begun. Carnita would become increasingly confident in her work and as her confidence grew she would become increasingly difficult to control—particularly when she figured out how to use a calculator and saw how much of what she earned went to Wikka. The dependency of daughter on mother was eroding.

———

Dillip was nervous about the face-tattooed creature lurking by the wine table. Looming among the potted plants like Death, he seemed to loom most in Dillip's direction. The fellow's face was coarse and balefully multicolored; a face that expressed cruelty and seethed with hatred. Another vengeful artist, in all probability. Or maybe a hit man hired by an artist. No—artists can't afford hit men, even cheap ones; the only thing artists can afford are drugs. He had to be an artist—or maybe a derelict, in from the street to freeload a glass of wine. Sometimes it's hard to tell the difference. Look at his rags. And that expression of anger, the brutal mouth, the blue and red tattoos, those vicious eyes expecting rejection. The image of an artist, with rage simmering beneath his Patternistically pictoglyphic skin like Mount St. Helens the day before the big one. Dillip had seen the fellow conspiring with Gas a couple of times. Was he Gas's man, here to help Gas get his revenge? Dillip had dissed Gas's work at every opportunity for years, and Gas, like the other artists whom Dillip destroyed, had often threatened to return the favor by dismantling Dillip. But Dillip was no fool. Gas had never managed to get close to him when he was crazy enough to do what he told Dillip he was going to do to him. Except a couple of times, when Dillip had first started his art-critic business, and he'd been careless enough to respond to his own doorbell, unarmed.

Notwithstanding his precautions, Dillip was nervous. Why did these artists have to take it personally? He wasn't singling anyone out. Writing bad reviews was his job, for God's sake. It was what the paper paid him to write. Why would anyone want to read something good about art? Except, of course, for expensive art, because the people who paid him to write about art owned expensive art. So of course he wrote good things about expensive art. What was he going to do, write bad things about the expensive art his bosses owned? People who'd paid a lot of money for art had every right to expect that you'd write good things about it, because the very fact that you pay a lot of money for art makes it, *ipso facto*, good art.

That, of course, was the intellectual center of art criticism: how much the art cost. The more the art cost the better the art. And it was the critic's responsibility to enforce the aesthetics of art by protecting the value of art, which of course means making sure the market (the true arbiter of artistic merit) weeded out bad (cheap) art. Thus his mission, Dillip reminded himself often: to cultivate the garden of good art by weeding out the bad, which you accomplish by telling people what art is good and what art is bad. It was all there in the Philip Dillip Aesthetic Theory of Good Art, which had a profound effect on art critics everywhere (for one thing it made their jobs a lot easier: all they had to do was look at the price tag to determine if a piece art was good art or bad art).

Of course this made the makers of bad (cheap) art angry, which highlights the problem with artists: they just don't understand aesthetics. When Dillip first got into the art-criticism business he disdained such stupidity. No skin off his nose if you resented the fact that he dissed your cheap art. But it turned out that from time to time there was a little skin off his nose. The more dissin' he did the more threatening calls he got, and while most threatening callers were drunk or stoned on glue or pot or PCBs or PBCs or CBPs or meth or coke or crack or horse or ecstasy or LSD or God-knows-what and called from noisy places like the Blue Moon or the Central or the Continental, a few spoke with a blood-chilling sobriety, in terrifyingly soft voices, about breaking legs and arms and gouging out eyes and cutting off ears and noses and penises. After such a call—for a few quivery sweaty minutes—he swore that that was it, he was through, he was quitting. It was after *those* kinds of calls that he had gotten his broken noses and every one of his concussions and four of his broken arms. The drunks and pot-heads and snowballs made him nervous, all right, but it was the quiet ones who scared the hell out of him. Like that weirdly tattooed Queequeg creature looming like Death in the back by the wine table.

Dillip stood in a circle of sycophantic art collectors who were trying to flatter him into saying who among the current crop of cheap artists he was going to elevate to expensive. And though he was not about to divulge that information to any of these philistines, he kept his place in their circle, for in their numbers he felt at least a little protected. And the fact was, he didn't feel like looking at art. Coming into the danger of an art show always got him out of the mood to look at art. And this was only a Charles Gas show anyway—in part, at least—so he didn't have to see the paintings to write his review. As a matter of fact, he had written his review of Gas's part of the show that afternoon, at his office.

No, it wasn't Gas's work that brought him out, and it wasn't Carnita Vovo's work either. It was Carnita Vovo herself. He'd wanted her from the first moment he saw her, at her first show two years before. He'd written a rave review, called her the next great Seattle artist, but the ingrate had spurned him. She had actually turned Philip Dillip down. Well, okay, her price was apparently higher than he thought. He raved about her work in another article, and then another. And then people started buying her stuff and her price went up—not sky high, but high enough for you to begin calling her stuff good art.

"—in your Brick book, where you discussed his influence on Piccolo, it was brilliant how you introduced the idea that jealousies between Brick and Piccolo over women were in fact an integral part of Tubist theory of aesthetics—that without eroticism Tubism is just exercise with a paint brush."

All the heads in the circle turned toward Dillip. The dentist's wife had been talking to him, but his mind had been on Carnita.

"What?" he said shortly, irritated at the distraction.

She deferentially repeated her words while he frowned.

"I laid it out perfectly clearly in the book," he snapped. "We all know what moves artists."

Silence for a moment, then the dentist's wife's head bobbed contritely, signifying that she understood. The heads of the others bobbed also, as understanding came to them as well.

"And anyway, that's the way artists are," Dillip said, to nail the argument.

"Oh, yes, don't we know," the dentist's wife murmured with a wry smile and a glance at the others, who also murmured and nodded. "Tim and I have been investing in art since he got out of dental school and that's the thing we say most often about artists. That that's just the way artists are."

The other collectors nodded to one another and murmured.

Philistines, thought Dillip. At least artists managed to be amusing once in a while—because of their ingenuous deviousness usually, or their corruption. Unlike these nincompoops, who were simply boring.

"My husband and I were wondering if you thought Boyce LaFree's work was investment grade."

The dentist's wife again.

"What?"

"Boyce LaFree," she said. "The tattooed artist, whose work I believe you looked at a few weeks ago? We were wondering if it was worth invest—?"

"A tattooed artist? That fellow over there in the bushes?"

The dentist's wife looked where Dillip pointed. "Yes, that's him."

"I don't like the looks of that fellow."

"I thought you'd looked at his work and—"

"I never saw him before tonight. He looks dangerous to me."

———

Ten o'clock. Two hours and twelve minutes have passed since Charles entered the gallery, two hours and twelve minutes since he sauntered in, high on pot, drunk on confidence, glowing with expectation. He had smoked a jay on the pier and felt the high radiate euphorically into gut and groin and arms and legs. He'd stood with Boyce and looked out across the black water at the sparkle of city lights, toked on the jay, and had contrite thoughts about Janice.

There he had admitted to himself that his behavior with her in recent months had been something less than that of a gentleman. How long had it been since they'd been together and simply enjoyed one another without art intruding? He didn't know—which was probably why she was screwing that creep Wally. Well, tonight he'd make it up to her. He was going to sell out, and she would get her money back, which would ratify her trust in him. And then he'd take care of her. She would be as ready as he. She always was, after a show.

He felt confident for the first time in a long time—but he also wondered ruefully when it was that he started needing encouragement to get it up. He used to get a hardon as soon as he became aware that he didn't have one. Now he had to have confidence to get it up. But tonight would be different, tonight he had the power in his belly, the stirring of pent-up energy that would stiffen his tired old warrior, on command, for yet another battle. The power was back. Standing on the dock he'd felt the stirring. So the answer was no, he wasn't done yet. And the proof of it was right there in Janice's gallery. Seeing his paintings in the window like that—God! So fucking beautiful, so fucking majestically sensuously wondrously gorgeously beautiful—had actually stimulated a hardon. The paintings were his best work, and this night would be his best night. This was the night toward which he had labored for all of the forty terrible years he had been fighting his war with art.

And now it is ten o'clock. Two hours and twelve minutes later. He is no longer high; he is no longer confident; he no longer returns the greetings of the artists who drop in to see his show and to wish him well—that singularly humane thing that artists do, even the ones who hate one another. He no longer even knows Boyce, who as usual feels completely out of place and has retreated from the crowd to lurk resentfully in the back by the wine table.

For Charles it's *deja vu* all over again: it is a Charles Gas show and not one Charles Gas has sold. Anticipation has withered to humiliation, joy congealed to rage. And those fucking jeering red dots make him want to tear the place apart. The swarming jeering red dots, the walls pimpled with taunting red dots: where a Carnita Vovo hangs, there is a title card with a red dot, while every one of *his* title cards remains virginally white. The contrast of his title cards with her title cards is an outrageous joke. In fact, he is the joke. He knows it, too—knows the joke is doubly amusing because he is the last to get it. His art is a joke and he is a joke. The whole fucking room—no, all of the Kirkland art community—no, all of Kirkland, even the housewives and the software-engineer husbands planted in their Lazy Boys in front of the TV who browse their art in *Penthouse* during commercials—no, the whole motherfucking Northwestern United States smirks and elbows one another over this delicious joke. They are sniggering about it on the ten o'clock news, and he is certain that in an hour it's going to be Letterman's standup topic. This old fool, this never-has-been-and-never-will-be actually believed that his work was there for someone to buy! Can you fucking believe it? He actually believed that someone might give money for his shit. Well, he doesn't believe it any more. Now he understands. He finally gets it. He is here to decorate Carnita Vovo. Orange petals strewn before Carnita Vovo's jack-booted foot. His work was brought here for viewers to nibble on to clear their palates between the more substantial courses of the evening: the robust repast of her work. His pieces are condiments on the banquet table of Carnita Vovo's art. He is a frame for Carnita Vovo, his work a frame for her work. Such a delicious joke: the frame thinking it's the art, the framer thinking he's the artist. Everyone's laughing at it too, everyone is enjoying the joke. Look at them! The fucking gallery is crammed with people smirking at one another.

For this entire evening he has scarcely talked to the cunt who set him up for this humiliation. But he knows exactly what Janice is thinking and he knows she knows he knows what she's thinking, and he's loving the thought, loving it with an exhilarating murderous recklessness. No, no, no, not loves. He doesn't love anything, he hates everymotherfuckingthing. Knowing that she knows he knows she knows exactly what he is thinking is a high, a murderous antipodal-to-pot-high, a hateful, non-loving high. This is a non-hardon-high (at this juncture he could no more experience a hardon than Carnita Vovo could experience a hardon). He watches Janice, knows precisely how worried she is, though she smiles and laughs, touches an arm, leans closer to a graying head and says something, touches the arm again, then glides away to talk to a youngish couple whom she has observed looking at the one fucking Vovo that remains unsold, and as he watches her sell the piece of shit to the dumb shits, scribbles a receipt, deposits another fucking red dot (the last red dot of the night, he guesses, since it is the last unreddotted Vovo), ushers the lucky shits (who have just spent several thousands of their six-year-old son's college fund dollars) into their paid-for audience with the Princess of Art and her flower-spangled, gold-dangled, expressionless, mountainous factotum, that insufferable inseparable pair around whom Dillip has hovered and fluttered like a needing-to-mate mayfly for the last half hour. Fuck, he thinks, there they are, all my enemies, all of them in one place. And me without a hand grenade. Janice is worried all right, and if he was her he would be too.

Sixteen

Wally stopped when he turned the corner from Market to Lake Street and saw the gallery window. A young couple walking behind him toward the entrance to a restaurant stumbled into him, but Wally didn't even notice, so captivated was he by the brilliance of the big window, behind which a rainbow of fifteen paintings hung above the heads of people who drifted about or stood in admiring groups.

He was struck by the perfection of the composition and immediately felt a need to draw it or paint it. But he had no paints, no brushes, no canvas, not even the sketch book he usually carried. He'd been in such a hurry to escape the house before Ethel caught him that he'd climbed out his studio window with nothing but his clothes. But wait—the apartment! He had some in Janice's apartment, above the gallery.

He hurried across the street, entered the crowded gallery, and edged through a crease in the crowd behind an elderly couple who were looking bewilderedly up at one of Charles' nude portraits of Janice. The painting stopped Wally. He paused beside the couple and looked intently at it, drawn, in spite of the urgency of his errand, to studying it. He had seen it in Charles' studio, but it looked so much richer hanging in the gallery. He moved on to the next painting, a Carnita Vovo. A big canvas—five feet square—it was dominated by the undisciplined cacophony of color that typified Vovo's work. Remembering his mission, he turned away from the paintings and threaded his way through the crowd toward the back of the gallery, toward the desk and the wine table and the wide archway that led to the second room, and just inside the archway, the door to the staircase that led to Janice's apartment. He passed behind Janice, who was speaking to a frizzy-haired woman and a tiny big-eyed fellow. Janice was too intent on the little man's words to notice Wally working his way through the crowd. And Wally was too intent on his mission to notice Whipple, nearby, who nodded a greeting. When Wally got through the last cluster of people near the wine table he heard his name. He looked around.

"Boyce," Wally exclaimed. "Good to see you. It's wonderful, isn't it! Where's Charles?"

Boyce shrugged. "Disappeared."

"I'm gonna paint it."

"Don't bother goin' in there, man," Boyce said, nodding toward the archway to the second room. "He's got his progressive shit in there."

"I got the idea when I saw the window from across the street ¾"

"Hanging that shit's a waste of wall space."

"—because of the composition. It's perfect."

"He ain't sold a single piece. Which I coulda told him. Which I did tell him."

Wally had turned and was looking at the crowd.

"But Vovo sold out," Boyce continued glumly. "Wish I could paint like her."

Boyce's words weren't registering now. Wally's mind was shifting into discovery mode, in which all extraneous input was rejected and his consciousness was cleared for action. There was only his mission now, and nothing else. Any action that didn't contribute directly to painting this scene—all these lines and colors; these juxtapositions and groupings and associations that composed this perfection of dynamic form, in lighting that was all angles and brilliance and hard shadow—in a word, anything that didn't contribute to his mission of rendering *this* on canvas, he simply tuned out. He was painting the scene in his head, the composition emerging like photographic paper in developer; parts were materializing in shape and line and color: that mountain of a woman in the flowery dress with metal hanging off her face like woody plants growing in the face on a cliff¾she would be at the center of the composition, against that shaft of stage lighting that flooded one of the Vovo paintings; and Janice, standing there talking down to that tiny man—they would be off to the side, along the window edge; and that old couple still gazing in bewilderment at the life-sized nude—they were exactly where they should be. With the composition now in his head, he turned and headed for the archway. He had to get those paints.

Boyce watched him open the door and head up the stairs.

—

Charles listened to the clumping on the stairs. Couldn't be Janice, he decided—the tread was too heavy. And it wouldn't be her, anyway—the murmur coming up through the floor told him the gallery was still full of people. And if it wasn't Janice and it wasn't Charles (he was still straight enough to realize it couldn't be Charles because he, Charles, was already here, smoking this joint in Janice's big overstuffed reading chair) then it had to be Wally. Because only Charles and Wally had the run of the place. Then again, maybe it was Whipple, climbing the stairs to wait for Janice to follow him up for a quickie. Yeah, Whipple. So she was fucking Whipple again, like he'd suspected. If Whipple could still fuck. He released a billow of smoke and watched a human form emerge behind it and move like a ghost into the darkness of the dining room. The light came on, silhouetting Wally's slope-shouldered gauntness.

So it was Wally! The fool who'd fooled Charles Gas. But fooling Charles Gas was no big deal. Any fool could fool Charles Gas. Apparently there was no end of ways. One of his enemies used brushes and paints, another had done him in with dollars, still another had humiliated him with words. This enemy had stuck it to him with a stiff dick. Was that the worst of the many betrayals he had suffered? On another night the answer might be no, but on this night the answer was yes. For on this night he had strutted cock-of-the-walk sure of himself into the gallery, his red aura glowing as brightly as his revived libido, expecting to top off a night of artistic redemption with another kind of redemption in Janice's bed, the redemption of getting it up, all by himself, with no help at all—and found instead that a world of brand-new hurt waited for his discovery.

Over the years his enemies had contrived many clever ways to humiliate him, but in the humiliation of this evening they had reached epic destructiveness. This one was positively diabolical. The devil himself should be taking notes on this one. They had somehow sucked him into exhibiting his best-ever work in a show that was designed to make that work look idiotically unhip, unwithit, uncool; in which regard it succeeded, as it succeeded in portraying him not as an artist, but as an impotent joke-of-an-artist. And, as a perverse fillip, they'd thrown Wally into the brew—to cuckold him.

Well okay, maybe that was stretching it a bit. They hadn't cuckolded him. Wally had. Wally and Janice. But wait a minute—what claim did he have on Janice's loyalty? Okay, so he didn't have a claim on Janice, or her loyalty. Still. What about loyalty? Did all those years mean nothing? All those years of living together, of sharing? Well okay, they'd actually lived together for maybe eighteen months. If that. But what about the sharing? Well okay, about all they had really shared in those months were orgasms and battles. No, that wasn't true. He remembered loving her, though most of all he remembered loving fucking her. He smiled wanly, thinking of days when he was so sore he couldn't wear jeans and she was so sore she couldn't sit down. Loving her? Oh yes, he'd loved her—and still did, apparently.

Those months had been stormy. Storms of fucking, storms of fighting, storms of painting. The painting: oh, the painting! The center of life. The brawling a mere background to the painting; the fucking a contrapuntal to the brawling, the scratching of a persistent itch, brief, ecstatically intense. And then, when she'd gotten enough of him, she'd moved out. Out of his life and into Whipple's, when Whipple promised her a show. Which of course he didn't deliver. Had no more intention of showing her work than he had of showing the work of any of those young feminist dabblers of the eighties who thought having artistic sensibilities was the same as having talent—of whom there had been many, and many of whom Whipple also promised a show in order to get into their skivvies. Charles had never held it against her. An artist does what she's gotta do. Or Whipple, because a stiff dick has no conscience. Still, after all those years you'd think the cunt would possess at least a primitive concept of loyalty. He wondered how many men like Wally she'd invited between her legs while he'd blithely assumed her loyalty. What did all those years mean, anyway? Did all those shared battles mean nothing?

Apparently. So yes, this betrayal does hurt more than all the others: for here Charles is, waiting for his woman, in her living room, with his battered and bowed libido and who comes in? Not Janice. No—in comes the fellow who's displaced his dick with his dick. This is too much! This is intolerable!

While Charles sucked on a jay and inventoried his storehouse of grievances, Wally stood in the dining room before the old easel—the big, sturdy, studio easel Janice's father had given her when she began her studies at the University of Washington—staring at the painting resting thereon. Beside the easel was a work table on which were arranged Janice's box of paints and her paint-encrusted palette and a jar full of brushes. The easel, the table, the palette, the paint box, the brushes, even the old Mason jar¾all were artifacts of the life she had shared with Charles, who had bought the paint box for her in those first months, in one of the few periods when he'd had enough money to buy something besides drugs, food, and paints. And he'd bought the palette, too, as well as most of the brushes. And now she's dragged them out of the closet and converted her apartment into a studio, so Charles' cuckolder can use them, as the cuckolder uses her. This is more than a man can bear! This is intolerable!

The odor of marijuana smoke was heavy, but Wally noticed neither the smoke nor the smoker, who slouched in the big overstuffed chair in the darkened, far corner of the living room. Wally was busy studying the painting on the easel. He had picked it up to move it and had paused to look at it. He liked parts of it, thought he'd done a creditable job. Janice had insisted that it was finished, and he'd thought so, too. But now he saw many places where the rawness was obvious, where just a little more work—

He put the painting back on the easel and stepped to the wall and removed Charles' original. He held it at arms length and studied it, looked back at his copy, then looked at the original again. Then he placed the original beside his copy on the easel and stepped back and looked at both paintings. To an untutored eye the two paintings appeared to be identical. But he could tell the difference. Charles' was finished, his wasn't. That was the difference. He moved closer to the easel, studied a place on his painting that looked like it needed more work, and then looked at the same relative location on Charles' painting. Perhaps he'd take a few minutes and fix—

"Plagiarism," a voice accused.

Wally turned and saw a movement in the shadows of the living room. He recognized the voice, noticed then the odor of marijuana.

"Hi, Charles."

"It's plagiarism."

Wally didn't respond; he had turned back to studying the two canvases.

"Plagiarism is stealing."

Absently: "What?"

"Showing me you can steal my woman *and* paint her better—that's the deal, isn't it?"

Wally's attention was zeroed in on the two paintings. "Janice says it's finished but I don't think so."

"What does she know? She's no artist. Never was. She *sells* art."

Wally looked over his shoulder at the vaguely human shape draped over the chair in the darkened living room. A spot of pink moved in an arc upward, then it stopped and glowed brightly for a couple of seconds.

"Yours looks so perfectly finished compared to mine," Wally said. "Will you look at mine and tell me what's wrong with it? Please?"

"The man steals my woman, steals my work, then asks my advice on how to do it better." A laugh, ending in a hacking cough, then a wheezy: "But give him credit for balls."

Wally had turned back to the paintings.

Charles rose and came into the light of the dining room and stopped before the easel. He looked at his own painting and felt a warmth flood through him and momentarily gentle him; felt his anger soften to poignancy, to a yearning for the richness of the life he lived at the time of the painting. But that short-lived life was forever gone—the richness of great potential on the edge of realization, which had given that life its electric vibrancy, now a bitter dust that so coated every part of his present life that he tasted it every time he drew a breath. He thought about the moment and the event he had captured on this canvas—of lithe young Janice, naked except for that drape of cloth across her shoulder and one breast—and grieved for his loss: *then* he was entering his forties, potent, brash, full of the present, eager to battle the future. He sighed and sternly pushed memory aside, brought himself back to the present. He studied his own painting for a moment longer, looking for aspects that would justify what he was going to do next, which was disembowel his enemy with ridicule so sharp that he would expire in the same bog of humiliation that *he* had long occupied. He turned his attention to the plagiarism, ready to begin its destruction.

He shouldn't have. He should have averted his eyes and fled. With the devil in charge of this evening's festivities he should've known some new horror waited for him. It was that and more. It was a punch in the solar plexus. A karate chop to the back of the neck. It was yet another proof of the meaninglessness of life—as if he needed yet another proof.

Or was he so completely fucked up that he no longer possessed the ability to ascertain good art? Had all the overdoses of pot, wine, anger, disappointment, and betrayal so mushed his brain that he could no longer separate good art from shit? Had they destroyed him all the way down to that inviolable core of himself, to the only thing he trusted, to his sensibility of what was good art and what was bad art? Without that sensibility, how could an artist be an artist? Was this Kafkaesque hallucination that he called his life really just some echo of a life abominably lived and miserably terminated? Was he a ghost inhabiting someone's neurotic dream? He stared at the two paintings, holding desperately to his preconception of the superiority of his and the inferiority of Wally's. But his artist's sensibility, battered and bloodied though it was, was too honest to let him get away with it; his traitorous artist's heart told him that his enemy's painting was best. In fact, it told him that Wally's painting was achingly, sublimely good. Just looking at it generated a flood of pleasure in that private core of himself, and this core of him, this soul of him, this part of him that he loved best of all, this part now turned on him like all the rest of the world had turned on him. So this was the end, the devil was in charge. He closed his eyes, groaned at the pain of a knife thrusting up toward his heart, hoping *this* attack would terminate him, like this night of humiliation was terminating his ill-starred career. This humiliation the coup de grâce, the worst and thankfully the final of the many horrors he had suffered in this infinitely horrible evening. Why, he wondered, did God hate him so much?

"Am I imagining it?" Wally asked.

Charles felt a cloud of tranquillity settle gently around him. God must have heard his question and felt bad about all the afflictions He had inflicted. Charles looked around: nice—a peaceful space to die in. He was grateful.

"They look alike—mind you I'm no artist, I'm just an amateur, and not a very good one at that, but¾but don't they look kind of—kind of alike? Don't get me wrong, I'm not comparing yours to mine, because mine is so amateurish. And that's what I don't understand, how can they look so much alike and yet yours looks so perfectly finished—not one brush stroke too many—and mine looks like I just stopped painting it."

Charles felt life peacefully arranging to depart his body and he welcomed the event, welcomed the mental health that death promised. And yet something about this situation—oddly enough, something hopeful—interrupted his dying. What was it? And then he knew: Wally's self-doubt was reaching out to rescue him; and the self-doubt that Charles had learned through all the years of humiliations now caused Charles to doubt even his own self-doubt. Of course! That was the key to understanding: if Wally's self-doubt was right, then his self-doubt had to be wrong: he was wrong and Wally was right. He shivered convulsively, relief flooding as madly through him as the electric ripple of an orgasm. His own self-doubt, fed by the manifold humiliations of this night, had tricked him into believing the worst about himself and his work. He grinned lopsidedly and gratefully clapped Wally on the back. Wally had saved his life! A moment before he was dead; now he jubilantly celebrated his rebirth. He could beat these motherfuckers!

"You're right, Wally. This painting needs more work, needs more paint, lots more paint."

Wally leaned over the canvas. "Lots more?"

"All over. It needs a lot of paint, all over it. No doubt about it."

Silence for several seconds. Then, hesitantly: "Well—okay—if you say so."

"I was you I'd go over the whole fucking thing, top to bottom. Needs work everywhere, lot more paint, lot more work. You need more paint on there."

"Maybe I should just paint over it. Use it again."

"You're right," Charles said agreeably. He was terribly excited and cheerful. Feverishly excited. Feverishly cheerful. Maybe the pot. Or the wine. Maybe both. Whatever it was, he was feeling very positive. Even about Wally. He was feeling more like Wally's mentor now, more like Wally's friend than his enemy. Maybe he'd misjudged Wally. Even if he was fucking Janice he seemed like an okay dude. Besides, you couldn't blame him: a stiff dick does what it's supposed to do, and in doing it, simply drags its possessor along for the ride.

"It's just a practice canvas, anyway. I'll use it to paint the exhibition."

Charles blinked. Paint the exhibition? Paint the exhibition? The phrase seemed like an echo. Where had it come from?

Wally began collapsing the easel.

Then Charles remembered looking at the gallery window from across the street, remembered telling Boyce that exhibiting other people's art was Janice's art; that her art was making art out of art. Well okay! Now he was about to make art out of Janice making art out of art. And in the bargain, he would be making art out of his own artistic destruction! Oh, the symmetry of it! And out of that would come rebirth. This evening wasn't the devil's work; not at all; it was God's holy work, God's way of leading him out of the wilderness to witness the destruction of his enemies. Charles felt a wave of manic confidence lift him, and while he could tell that he was crazy, he didn't care. He was used to manic craziness: he'd been doing art for forty-some years, so he knew manic, and he'd been a pot-smoking artist all his life, so he knew crazy. The thing that counted was this: that it was so right, this manic confidence. And it felt so fucking good to be so manically confident. He stepped to the table and swept the box of paints and the jar of brushes and the palette up under one arm and grabbed Wally's painting with his free hand.

"Wally, you take the easel, I'll get the rest. Hurry up."

"Jeez, thanks, Charles. That's really nice of you. I wonder, would you mind telling me how you'd—"

Charles, holding the canvas and the paints and brushes, paused impatiently. "What? What is it?"

"Well, if you could just take a minute or two and tell me how you'd compose it? I have an idea, but I'd sure like to hear how you¾"

"Fuck yes, I got it right up here." Charles tapped his forehead with the painting. "I know exactly how to do it."

Charles turned and thumped down the stairs, kicked the door open and rushed into the back room of the gallery, in which he and Janice had hung the nine pieces of his Neo-Realistic Patternistically Progressive triptych of triptychs. The room was empty. There were no people and no red dots in this room. All the people and all the red dots were in the other room. There, through the archway, clusters of people lingered admiringly before each of Vovo's red-dotted paintings, wishing there were more of them, and thirty or forty other people, in groups of two, three, four, stood in the center of the room or at the wine table along the back wall, talking about Vovo's genius. A grand total of two admirers stood before one of Charles' un-red-dotted paintings: two teen-aged boys, checking out Janice's pussy. Charles hesitated in the archway leading into the big room, saw Boyce standing in the greenery beside the wine table, saw Carnita Vovo and her mountainous dyke factotum-mom standing in the middle of a worshipful circle that included Janice, Shelley and Tim Leuter, Whipple, and even that asshole Dillip.

Charles studied the room, looking for a way out. But there was no help for it; if he was going to paint this scene from across the street he had to get out of the building, and to get out of the building it had to be through the front door, and to get to the front door he had to traverse the main room of the gallery. Had to pass through the gauntlet of these enemies' contempt. But what the fuck, the contempt of philistines was no better and no worse than their approbation. He charged into the room, head down, toward the front door. And ran smack into a little old lady who screamed, tossed her wine stem and her purse and bounced back against one of Charles' paintings. Charles grabbed reflexively at her, catching her by the arms before she collapsed. The brush jar fell and shattered, sending shards of glass and brushes skittering across the floor. The paint box opened as it hit the floor, sending tubes of paint bouncing across hardwood, and the canvas went skidding right at Dillip, who ducked and yelped in panic at the sudden crash and scream behind him, convinced he was under a Gas attack. The painting slid to a stop against his left shoe.

Dillip wheeled to face his attacker, cringing, his hands uplifted in supplication. He saw Charles, not looming over him with uplifted club as he expected, but halfway across the room, holding the little old lady; saw the broken glass and the brushes, the box and the tubes of paint. And the canvas. The fear drained out of him, leaving him limp with relief. He glanced down at the painting. Immediately his attention focused on it. Something about it. He leaned over the canvas for several seconds then picked it up and held it at arms' length. The room, which had been startled to silence by the racket that accompanied Charles' collision with the old lady, buzzed for a moment or two, but fell silent again as Dillip studied the painting.

When Dillip raised his head his eyes shone and his face was red with excitement.

"This is a Gas," he murmured, in a voice filled with awe. "It *is* a Gas, isn't it? It *has* to be, it's got Gas all over it. And yet—it is—it's the most remarkable piece of work I have ever seen. How can it be so wonderful and also be a Gas?"

Tim Leuter had edged over to Dillip's side and was on his toes, looking over Dillip's left arm at the painting, then up into Dillip's face. "Does this mean it's good, that it's good art?" he asked hopefully. "We've had some Gases for years, hoping they'd would get good. Does this mean those are good art, too?"

Dillip nodded dazedly. "I think you can bank on it."

Bank on it! A murmur went round the room: Dillip had shocked everyone; had pulled another one of those surprises that marks a good critic. Just when no one was expecting it he had apparently anointed the next great artist in the Seattle art scene. For those on intimate terms with the world of Seattle art, it was an incredible turnabout. Incredible because Philip Dillip had anointed an ancient enemy. Incredible because Philip Dillip had apparently not even considered what he could get out of it. He had confounded everyone once again. But what everyone didn't know was that he couldn't help himself.

Wikka was shocked at this unexpected turn of events. How would this influence Carnita's rising-star status? And would this latest great-artist discovery catapult the Janice Cushion Gallery into the forefront of Kirkland galleries (after all, Janice Cushion had discovered Carnita Vovo as well)? Maybe jumping ship and signing with Whipple was a mistake. She looked at Whipple. He had gone white in the face. It was clear that he understood the implications of Dillip's pronouncement. This was not going to be good for his business. He might be renegotiating some sixty-seven-percent commissions.

Shelly and Tim Leuter looked sharply at one another, then turned and went to the closest Charles Gas painting and looked up at nude Janice and began conferring. Others followed suit, going to other Charles Gas paintings, even into the back room, to the Neo-Realistic Patternistically Progressive triptych of triptychs. The bargain hunters were moving in, staking territory, readying themselves to defend that territory until Janice could get there with her red dots and her sales pad. And as for Janice—well, it appeared she was more shocked than anyone. Or was that horror written across her face? Her eyes big, her face white, her hands covering her mouth.

Other than the obvious fact that Dillip had just anointed Charles, Carnita hadn't hoisted any of this in. She looked at Charles, then at Dillip, then at Wikka, then at Janice, dimly aware that something momentous was happening. Carnita opened her mouth to ask Wikka "Whut," but Wikka's expression was so full of alarm that Carnita became alarmed and forgot what she wanted to ask.

Charles had gone glassy-eyed, his mouth had slackened and dried up, his face was as white as his disheveled mane of hair. Even his flaming aura had dimmed to dusty beige. He aged fifteen years as he watched Dillip move dreamily across the room toward him, as if advancing through a haze-filled tunnel, still holding the canvas. He saw fat pink lips bouncing enthusiastically between fat pink jowls, heard a sound that seemed to be associated with the movement of the lips. But Charles' brain had short-circuited, so he did not receive the message contained in the noise.

Seventeen

Janice looked from Whipple to the waitress, who had approached with the bill.

"I'm really sorry to hear what happened," the young woman said. "I watched you and Mister Gas hanging the show. I stopped at the window and watched and I thought it was so brave of you. Hanging all those pictures of yourself." The young woman fell silent, but she didn't move away from the table.

Janice didn't think of herself as brave and had never thought of the paintings as beautiful. But how could she disagree? The young woman was offering kindness, but also a question: why? Like the police, the reporters, neighboring gallery owners, and of course the artists—she'd had so many calls from artists in the last two days that she'd quit answering the telephone.

"He was nice," the young woman went on. "At least I thought he was. When he came in here he was always nice to me. I read the story in the *Times* and it just seems so—ironic or something. I mean like how he worked all his life to get his work accepted and then he just—well, you know."

Whipple smiled. "We have some business to conclude, so if you'll excuse us."

"Oh, sure. I didn't mean to intrude. I just wanted to—you know, say how sorry I was." She put the bill on the table, gave Janice a sympathetic look, and turned away.

"So what's your plan?" Whipple asked.

Janice shrugged. Plan? Planning is what you do when you have a future. All she had was a past. And a barely-breathing present.

"I've always said you have a job at Whipple's any time you want it."

"Yes, you have."

"I meant it. I want you back."

"Thanks."

"Why *did* he clobber Dillip?"

"I already told you I don't know."

"Did he hate Dillip that much?"

"Of course. Dillip's a critic."

"But that really doesn't explain it, does it? If he'd ambushed Dillip in an alley and cracked his skull¾well, that's a sensible action, and 'Dillip's a critic' explains the action. But how does one rationalize such a rampage of self destruction?" More silence. "I think you understand, but I can't because I'm missing something. What am I missing?"

She didn't say anything.

"There is something grand about it, of course—even if it's inexplicable. Something arresting, mysterious¾even ironic, as the young lady suggested. A third-rate artist makes an apparent breakthrough with one piece of work and rather than accept success, throws it all away in one grand gesture of self destruction. Is it irony? Or is it karma? Perhaps he's just following his karma, and we are fascinated because it has that tragic inevitability. It that it? Is this the stuff of tragedy? Or is it merely farce?"

She shook her head slowly. "I have no idea."

"Of course you do. You and that lout have been pals since he robbed your cradle. You know more about him than his mother."

"Whatever."

"It's not surprising the newspapers ran with the story. Human interest, irony, mystery. Fascinating stuff." Silence for several seconds, then: "So what about my offer?"

"It feels good to know you offered it."

"What does that mean?"

"It means I don't know. It means I suppose so. It means I'm broke and I had an art gallery a couple of days ago and now I have a room full of trash and a Visa and two Mastercards at the limit and a beat-up Toyota that needs work and I can't pay my rent—and it means that there's nothing good going on in my life right now and I don't have the energy to do anything about it. It means I need to veg out more than I need a job but I have to have a job."

He leaned back in the booth and crossed his arms and studied her. "You do need to veg out, don't you. Okay. Come stay with Karen and me for a few weeks. Read books, eat food, sleep, think of nothing, get well. We have so much room you could hang around for weeks and we wouldn't even notice you."

"I was not under the impression that Karen encourages you to bring female friends home as house guests."

He grinned. "You're right. She'd come unglued."

"But it was decent of you to offer."

"I'm not giving up, you know. I always wanted you back working for me. Now's my opportunity and I'm determined to get you back. Did I tell you I'm planning on re-opening on Occidental Square? In October. I'll move it forward if you'll take it."

"Whipple, I'm worn out. I can't build another gallery."

"I'm not talking about building anything. I want you to run the gallery, not build it. I'll take care of getting it together."

She drew breath to speak, but he interrupted.

"Look, I won't accept 'no.' You're too irrational right now to make decisions. We'll just leave it this way: you're on the payroll."

She looked down at the plate, on which untouched eggs and bacon and hash browns had congealed in grease.

"The first thing I want you to do is take some time off. You're dangerously worn out."

"Whipple, I can't take your money."

Whipple was already sliding out of the booth. He dropped a twenty-dollar bill on the table. "C'mon, I got work to do."

She followed him out the door, moved up beside him as he strode off down the street.

"Whipple, we need to talk about this. I'm just not ready for the pressure¾"

"What pressure? You just started and you're already on vacation."

"I don't—"

"One of these days you're gonna tell me."

"What?" she asked.

"Why Charles clobbered Dillip."

They walked down the street of unopened shops and restaurants. The trees and the narrowness of the street and the color of the gallery fronts made it seem cozy and friendly. When they got to Lake Street they stopped at the big glass door, which was painted opaque now. She unlocked it. They stepped in and the door closed behind them, bringing darkness. Broken shards of glass had been removed from the big window and the opening was covered by sheets of plywood. She turned on the light. The broken-legged desk sat crookedly in the back; the walls were pocked with ragged, fist-sized holes; and the once-lush greenery of the plotted plants along the back wall had become a pile of wilted yard waste. Tatters of painted canvas and pieces of framing wood and shattered window glass and wine bottles littered the floor. The telephone was ringing.

"Looks like he missed the telephone," Whipple said, grinning.

She shrugged.

"What's next?" he asked.

"Haven't a clue."

"Just gonna sit here and listen to the telephone?"

"No, I'm gonna go upstairs and take a nice long hot bath and then I'm gonna take a walk along the lake, then I'm gonna visit Charles."

"He didn't hurt you enough yet?"

She didn't respond. In silence they listened to the ringing of the telephone.

"What about after that?"

"Told you. I haven't a clue."

The telephone stopped ringing. The silence lengthened.

"Call me," he said at last. "I'm worried about you."

"I'm all right."

He turned and opened the door and bright daylight streamed in. He paused. "Wikka called me. You knew that?"

Janice smiled. "I assumed it."

"No hard feelings?"

"No hard feelings."

Eighteen

While he was incarcerated, Boyce asked about Charles but none of the jail guards knew anything about him. Boyce was glad that his friend had apparently eluded the police, though he had to admit that it pissed him off that he, Boyce, was apparently the only dude they'd busted. Shit, man, it wasn't even his fuckin' show. Still, you could understand the underlying logic of the cops busting him, he being the weirdest dude there.

The cops had grilled him for two days, mostly about various open cases of burglary, rape, and assault, trying to get him to confess to something. But Boyce knew how to deal with this shit. Just keep your head down and your mouth shut. Don't say nuthin'. Don't even say you're hungry, no matter how fuckin' hungry you are. As he expected, the cops got pissed, then they got bored, then they kicked him out. When he got back to the studio he found it empty.

That was when he started worrying about what happened to Charles. He called Janice's gallery and got no answer, so he panhandled a couple of bucks from a startled tourist down on Pike at the Market and took the bus to Kirkland where he found the gallery boarded up, the door locked. He went down to the park on the lakeshore to think about what to do next and found an unoccupied park bench and sat in the sun. By then all he could think about was the pain of his mouth, which had been getting worse all day. After a while he got up and walked to the drug store and shoplifted some aspirin and went outside and opened the bottle and popped a half-dozen into his mouth and swished them around until they dissolved. He went back to the bench and sat in the sun and watched the ducks and the Canadian geese shit on the grass and looked out over the lake, squinting into the brilliant glitter of reflected sunlight. A couple of sailboats were heeled over on a starboard tack a mile of so offshore.

Five years of this shit, Boyce thought morosely. Doin' art for five years and what've I got to show for it? A paisley face and a mouth full of rotten teeth and empty pockets to go with an empty belly. His poor dead mom was right: art is a dangerous activity.

His inactivity and the aspirin and the heat of the sun on his face quieted the pain enough for him to become sleepy. He closed his eyes against the brightness.

"I saw you at the show."

Boyce jerked his head up and squinted at the silhouette. The sun, hanging in the sky above a right shoulder, blinded him. But when she spoke he knew the voice.

"I saw you talking to Charles Gas. You a friend of his?"

Still squinting, he nodded, wondering why she would bother talking to him.

"I'm Carnita Vovo."

"I know. What happened to Charles?"

"You were there."

"Yeah, but all I saw was Charles wreckin' the place, then the cops busted me."

"Yeah, I saw that. Why'd they bust you?"

He shrugged. "Always happens to me. What'd they do to Charles?"

"They took him away in chains. I heard he's in the loony bin at Bayview. Or something."

Boyce looked back out over the lake.

"You an artist?" Carnita asked.

Boyce shrugged. "Yeah. I guess."

"What's your name."

"Boyce LaFree."

"You with Janice?"

Boyce shook his head. "Ain't got no gallery."

She sat on the bench beside him and squinted into the sunlight coming off the lake.

"Bummer about Janice. I feel really bad about leaving her, when she's down like this, 'cause she's the one who discovered me. I went by her place to tell her why, but she wasn't there. It was Wikka's idea, changing to Whipple. I didn't want to, 'cause I like Janice, but Wikka says we got no choice. She did her numbers and showed me we had to get some money. That was why we got in the show with Charles in the first place, and now that all the paintings are ruined the only way we can get any money is to get an advance from Whipple. She told him we want an advance, so we can go to Greece, and he agreed. Wikka says the light's really good there."

Boyce rose, and a wave of pain engulfed his head. He groaned and sat back down.

Carnita looked at him through her sunglasses. "You okay?"

"I gotta find out what they're doin' to Charles." He rose again, steadied himself against the pain. Then he realized he had no money. He looked at Carnita. "Spare a couple bucks? For a bus?"

"Oh, sure." She stuck her hand in her jeans, pulled out a handful of bills, handed him a ten. "Here, take this."

"Thanks."

"You gonna go to Bayview?"

"Yeah."

She rose. "I'll take you."

—

"I like your shit a lot more'n Charles' shit," Boyce said, returning to the topic that had occupied them during the drive from Kirkland. "Your shit's got energy."

"Thanks."

"Reminds me of Aushaus Grupism."

"It does?"

"Sorta, I mean."

"Well—"

"A little. Not much, maybe, but a little."

"I never thought of my work as Neo-Repressionist. I kind of think of myself as a Distracted Patternist, mainly. You know?"

"Oh, I can tell you're a Distracted artist, but your shit does kinda remind me of the way them Aushaus Grupists do their shit. You know?"

They were quiet for a while, then Carnita spoke again. "I really like your tattoos. I never met anyone with tattoos like that. All over their face, I mean."

Boyce looked surprised. No one had ever spoken to him about liking anything about him.

"It's cool. I never knew anyone who had the balls to do face tattoos like those. They're awesome."

He sighed. "Didn't do it on purpose."

"You didn't?"

"Got drunk at the Blue Moon one time and met this dude who said he was a tattoo artist. I told him I didn't think tattoos was art and we had this big argument about it. Next thing I knew I woke up with this shit all over my face. When I tried to wash it off and found out I couldn't, I flipped out." He glanced at her. "It's how I got into art. Couldn't do anything else with this shit all over my face. Couldn't even be a busboy any more. Which is what I was before I was a artist."

"Wow."

"Ain't no fun havin' this shit on your face. Got me into a lot of fights at the Moon and I ended up getting eight-sixed for wrecking the place. Got busted so many times the cops kind of got me in their sights. You know? I mean, they see me and they know I must've did something. It's a drag."

"Yeah, I'll bet."

"Yeah, an' people are always lookin' strange at me, like they're worried I'm gonna mug 'em or somethin.' Pretty soon you get to thinkin' that's what you're supposed to do."

"Yeah, that's a drag, too."

"Yeah. I never mugged no one. Broke some heads, but never once mugged anyone. Busted for shopliftin' aspirin, but that's all."

She turned the car to the right and up a long drive into the hospital parking lot.

"Aspirin?"

"For my mouth."

"What's the matter with your mouth?"

"Rotten teeth."

"Oh. Bummer."

The information lady saw a tall young man with a tattooed face and a pallid girl with a metal-studded face coming toward her across the lobby. She glanced over her shoulder to make sure the doorway was open behind her.

"We're here to see Charles Gas. You got him in—" Boyce paused, looked at Carnita. "What d'you call it?"

"The nut ward. Or something like that."

The information lady backed out of the information booth and a minute later a burly young man in a white suit entered the booth. He frowned. "We have Charles Gas, but you can't see him."

"But doesn't it get cold up here?"

"Yeah. In the winter I didn't even get outa my sleepin' bag some days."

"How do you paint without light?"

"Well, me and Charles argue about that. He's got the area under the skylight and he don't think he needs to share it." He shrugged. "But we usually got power so we got lights. Old man Nussbaum turned it off couple of days ago 'cause we're behind on the rent."

Carnita was walking slowly along the brick wall, Boyce beside her, pausing before each painting to study it in the fading light.

"Wish I could see 'em better."

Boyce shrugged. "They ain't very good."

"Oh, I can see good enough to tell I really like 'em," she said.

This embarrassed Boyce. He was not used to people saying they liked anything about him. He thought she probably didn't mean it. "They ain't very good. Not like your shit. Or even Charles'."

"Oh, you're wrong, these're much better than Charles'. I think they're even as good as mine. Maybe even better."

"Nah."

"Oh yes. I'm sure of it."

"No shit?"

"All you need is a break and you're on your way."

They came to the end of the wall, where Boyce had opened the window to let in a balmy breeze. The window faced north. Boyce's easel stood near it. On the easel was a half-finished painting, illuminated by the northwestern sky, which was still a bright blue, the blue separated from the horizon by bands of red and yellow. A half-dozen dark skyscrapers with glowing squares of window obscured the boundary of horizon and sky.

"You got good light."

"Charles's got the best light." He nodded toward the easel in the center of the big room, under the skylight.

"I got some dope," she said.

"I don't do drugs."

"No shit? That's amazing. You're the first person I ever met who doesn't do drugs."

"Quit after what happened with the tattoo artist. So all I do now is booze and pain killers, when I can get some. But you can toke if you want. Don't bother me none. Charles's always toking."

She opened a small leather bag that she'd carried slung over her shoulder, removed a delicate little wood box, opened it, and extracted a tiny pipe. She removed a vial from inside the box and shook a bud of marijuana into her hand, scooped it into the bowl, and flashed a lighter over it. She sucked the flame down into the bowl and the smoke down into her chest, and held it there while she looked out over the city.

"I don't like Charles," she murmured through a stream of white smoke.

"Most people don't."

"What he did to my shit at the gallery cost me a lot of money."

"Yeah."

"But I feel kind of sorry for him, too. Like, he's such a loser, you know? Why'd he do it?"

"Just went crazy, I guess."

"You hungry?"

"A little."

She looked at him with dope-lazy eyes. "But I can't be pissed at anyone, now. You know?"

He stood with his hands in his pockets, looking out at the darkening sky.

"Am I bugging you? Do you want me to go?"

"No, man, it's nice you bein' here." And it was nice. It felt good when she told him she liked his shit. He was sure she didn't, but that made it even better, somehow—saying it so insistently and so sincerely when she didn't even mean it. Like it mattered to her that what she said mattered to him. It felt good to think that, particularly when it came from a woman. Boyce had always been fearful of women. So fearful that he was still a virgin when he'd had that fateful run-in with the tattoo artist. And of course with a face tattoo that made him look as fearsome as a man-eating Maori, he remained a virgin. So the feeling he got from her attention was a new and pleasant experience for Boyce, even if it did make him nervous. No woman had ever said anything nice to him. Except his mom, and she was crazy.

"I could order a pizza."

"Well, see, my mouth—"

"Oh! Man, I'm really sorry, I keep forgetting. How about Chinese? Can you do Chinese?"

"Noodles are okay. If they're soft. An' rice is fine. But nuthin' sweet or sour. Yeah, Chinese is fine. I ain't ate since yesterday, so I'm pretty hungry."

—

"I paint and Wikka takes care of business. It's a good arrangement, 'cause I don't like to worry about money. You know? Worrying about money is such a drag."

Boyce had scrapped the last of the egg foo yung sauce out of one container into the remainder of a carton of rice and was scooping the gooey mess into his mouth. He liked this shit particularly, because he could swallow tons of it without ever touching it with teeth. A half-dozen empty paper containers lay on the table around a single candle. Boyce had eaten all of it after Carnita said she wasn't very hungry after all, that she'd just toke on a joint, maybe eat one of the fortune cookies. Which she did while she talked and watched Boyce shovel the food down.

She spoke again, lazily: "Money makes some people feel good. But it makes me feel bad, 'cause it's just another thing people want from me. You know? All I want is for money to be there when I want to buy something. You know?"

Boyce nodded. Another thing they had in common: that was exactly what he wanted. And he also thought it was a drag worrying about money. Still another thing they had in common. He nodded as he scooped food into his mouth—this young lady and he had a lot in common. It was almost like they were friends.

"The thing is, I'm kind of easy to influence? That's what Wikka says. That people talk me into things. Like, because I like them. I like them, so I want to believe it when they say that something is good for me. You know?"

Boyce didn't know, because people never wanted anything from him, except maybe for him to be farther away from them. But he nodded anyway. He liked this young woman, so he thought what she was saying probably made a lot of sense. He covered his mouth daintily and ripped off a huge belch. He dropped the paper container on the table, leaned over and looked into the other half-dozen paper cartons, just to make sure he hadn't left anything. Seeing he hadn't, he leaned back and sighed contentedly, ready to listen to Carnita talk some more.

"Like Wikka, for instance. When I was a little girl she told me that people with penises are evil. I didn't even know what a penis was, but she's my mom, so when she said it I believed it. Though it seemed odd when she told me that the only people who have penises are men, and like all men have penises. I was really surprised at that. Like what a strange coincidence? It meant that all men were evil. And as I grew up it seemed like she was right—

people with penises were always doing bad things to me. Or trying to. Wikka says they can't help it. Like it's their karma? You know? They're evil, and maybe the people they put their penises into can become evil from it. Like the evil is catching? Like AIDS. You know?"

Boyce stirred self-consciously. *He* had a penis—another thing getting in the way of friendship, like his personality, and his tattoos.

Apparently Carnita was thinking the same thing, for she smiled and said: "I'm not saying you're evil, even though—well, you know—like you got a penis. Because you don't want anything from me, do you."

Boyce shook his head.

"When Wikka showed my stuff to people like Dillip they always said what a genius I was and then they'd tell me that if I'd fuck them they'd make me successful. I did a couple of times, but found out they were lying. After that I never did. And then I got successful. Because of Janice and Wikka, not because of people with penises." She studied him for a few seconds, then added: "Wikka told me I didn't have to fuck people to be worthwhile. She tried to convince me to avoid penises so I wouldn't become part of the evil. You know?"

Carnita permitted a silence to settle. A white silence, like noise-canceling snow. As if she wanted to give Boyce time to consider what she had said. The silence got longer and longer. She was leaning back in the chair, all in black, hands in jeans pockets, the gold in her face gleaming in yellow candlelight, the blood-red of her mouth gone almost black in the dusk, looking at him lazy-eyed. Waiting for him to say something. And Boyce sat there, wishing he had more rice and egg fu yung and wondering if he was supposed say, or do, something. Two sensibilities existed in him at that moment: hunger and something vaguely emotional. The hunger was the most noticeable sensation, because he had a lot of experience with that feeling. The emotional one he didn't know much about. The silence lengthened and he began thinking uneasily that maybe she did expect him to do something, maybe that was the reason she was silent. But she wasn't letting on what she wanted him to do. Maybe nothing. Maybe she was just resting. Still, he couldn't help wondering. So he just sat there looking at her, thinking about egg fu yung and waiting for whatever was going to happen to happen.

"I don't think that anymore," Carnita said.

He had lost track of what she'd been talking about. "Whut?"

"You know—that people with penises are evil. A lot of them are, but you aren't. I can tell you have a penis and you're not evil. You're nice, because you don't want anything from me."

He blushed, and let the silence lay there undisturbed while she stared at his face and his tattoos—a friendly stare with no hint of the fear he was used to seeing in people's faces. He seldom saw friendliness, and the strangeness of the experience made him uncomfortable. He looked away, first at the scatter of empty paper containers, then at the darkness above her head, then down at his hands.

Something new came into her voice, a huskiness: "I can tell you don't want anything from me—and that's really a turn-on. You know?"

He didn't know.

She smiled again, the pallor gone from her metal-studded cheeks, which now glowed pink enough to almost see in the growing darkness. "I can tell you don't want anything from me."

He stirred. Something made him want to move, made him need to move. But he couldn't move a muscle. He was stuck to the chair, as if his pants were glued down.

"Do you want me?"

"Hunh?"

"Do you want me?" Coyly: "I can tell you don't. It's plain as day."

He stared at her, puzzled and alarmed. No woman had never talked to him like she talked to him—the only way women reacted to him was to show fear, and of course disgust.

"You don't want anything from me. Do you."

He shook his head.

"That's such a turn-on. Are you sure? You don't want anything from me? Nothing?"

Silence again, but there was no peace in this silence. This silence was as fiercely threatening as a long-held breath, more aggressive than any police interrogation he had ever experienced.

She was leaning forward now, hands on her knees: "Are you sure?"

He sensed that this was a decisive moment, that what he said in the next instant would decide something important. "Yes," he croaked, wanting to please her.

As quick as a cat she was on her feet and wiggling out of her black jeans and black panties and whipping her black blouse up over her head, unfastening her black bra, which slipped off her torso to expose tight little cones of white, dark-tipped tit. And he noted, with surprise, how animal-like the female body seemed when you see it real and moving and close with nothing on it that doesn't grow there—except, in her case, the gold in her face and belly button. He looked modestly away while she patiently and gently cajoled him into uncrossing his legs. Several minutes later she got him to unclasp his hands and drop them to his side, then after another five minutes or so got him to let her unfasten his belt. Thus, bit by bit, she wore him down, until she had his pants clear of his hips and down to his ankles.

He began to perceive—unbelievably—that she actually liked him. Liked him just like she—unbelievably—liked his art. And he felt a heady rush of gratitude, a rush of warmth in his chest, in his face, down his arms and his legs, which was all mixed with that rush of pleasure that you feel when someone regards you with pleasure. Such a strangely powerful feeling; a fearful, fierce new feeling. And as much as he feared it, he loved it.

"Oh," she breathed, "it's so beautiful."

Before he was even aware she had it in her hand, she had it in her hand; and he went light-headed, thinking, just before he fainted and fell off the chair, that this must be what love was like, and he wondered, as the darkness closed the world down, if he could take it.

Nineteen

"It was the most awful thing I ever saw. People were rushing out of there like a maniac was loose inside. Even through the window, which by then was broke out. There was this crash and a chair come bouncing into the street and there was glass all over the place." Ethel reached into the cabinet and got a package of chocolate chips. She looked back at the table where young Reverend Stammer sat fooling with his unlit pipe and watching her mix the cookie dough. "Where's Wally?" she asked. "He was here a minute ago."

"He went out the back door," Reverend Stammer said. He rose and went to the window. "He's in the back yard, on his knees in that sandy place between the trees. Looks like he's digging in the dirt with a stick."

"He's drawing. Doctor Ramsay said to take away his paints and drawing stuff, see if that helps; but it hasn't, he just finds some other way. Or he gets restless and wanders off. He's always wandering off. We have to watch him like a hawk."

Reverend Stammer resumed his seat at the table.

"Thank God that Cushion Gallery's closed. That devil's den was a magnet. So anyway, there we was in the middle of all this screaming and yelling, and cars was lined up honking their horns, and then this man with blood all over his face and the front of his suit come running out. Of course I was crazy with worry, not knowing where Wally was. By the time the police came, there were hundreds of people watching from across the street as that crazy man tore that gallery apart. He was a wrecking machine. Turned out Wally was inside with him, and while he was tearing the place apart Wally was gathering tubes of paint and brushes so he could come outside and paint the gallery. That's exactly what he told me when the police brought him out, that he wanted to paint the gallery. Can you image?"

Reverend Stammer stirred uneasily. He already knew the story—he'd read it in the Times—now he was waiting for her to get to the point: what did she want from him?

By now she had turned to face him, mixing spoon in hand. "Anyway, the police brought that wild man out in a straight-jacket and then they brought Wally out, carrying them tubes of paint and the brushes. Soon as I saw them I went up and took charge of him, him saying all the time that he had to go back in there and get his canvas, because he had to paint the exhibition."

But Reverend Stammer wasn't listening; he was thinking once again about how much he disliked this part of his job—this tending of the flock. As a matter of fact, his job would be perfect if it wasn't for his flock. He'd much rather be back at his desk smoking his pipe in peaceful solitude, while he listened to Rachmaninoff and sipped green tea and finish editing the sermon that *Sermons for Today* had accepted for their June number. His flock got in the way of his creative moments. At its best, the flock was a pain in the ass. At its worst, it was a mine field of very real dangers. He'd entered the Walder house wondering nervously what kind of explosion he'd face this time. Fortunately, it had turned out that the dangerous elements of familial dysfunction were not present in this situation. There was no sullen-faced, metal-studded teenager toying with knives or drug paraphernalia in the living room. And there was no drunken husband to stumble in and demand belligerently what the fuck he was doing there all alone with his woman. Nor was this woman likely to come pawing at the front of his pants like Margaret Horney had.

While Ethel talked she populated a cookie tray with little blobs of dough and put the tray in the oven. Wiping her hands on her apron, she faced Reverend Stammer. "I just wish Wally'd cooperate. That's what makes it so hard. He won't listen. Not to me, or George, or Pete, or even Doctor Ramsay. I was hoping you could convince him that he's sick and he needs this surgery to be well."

Reverend Stammer cleared his throat. "It uh—sounds like—that you've thought this out carefully," he said carefully, to gain time to think this thing out. He was looking for the complications he knew were there, waiting to ambush him.

She nodded.

"And now you want me to—ah—and you're confident that—that this surgery is the only solution?"

"Everbody's been telling me we've got to do it, but I've been saying we got to wait for him to get better. But he's getting worse. And that makes me worry that waiting is wrong. Maybe waiting is going to make him so bad he'll never be better. We tried everything we could think of to help, even took away his art supplies, but that hasn't done a bit of good. Only makes him miserable."

Reverend Stammer began to see messy complication. He retreated farther into the noncommittal. "Well, sometimes prayer helps us discover the answers to problems."

"I was hoping for something more concrete, something a little more direct."

He fooled with his pipe. So—she wanted more than prayer. The potential for complication was definitely increasing.

"I was hoping maybe he'd listen to you. Maybe you could tell him¾you know, what we said."

"That he needs brain surgery."

She nodded.

"That's all?"

She nodded.

Reverend Stammer thought about this. Sounded simple enough. No real involvement. Very small potential for complication. Just tell Wally he needs brain surgery, then leave. "Okay," he said. "I'll do it."

"I'm glad you agree. It's a load off my mind."

Reverend Stammer rose and moved toward the door before Ethel could think of something to complicate the situation. "I'll talk to him right now, on my way out," he said over his shoulder.

"You don't want to stay for some cookies and milk? The cookies'll be out in a minute."

Reverend Stammer opened the back door: "Love to, but mustn't. So much to do. Another time."

He walked down the steps and out across the yard to where Wally crouched on his knees, stick in hand, making a pattern in the dirt. He looked up as Reverend Stammer approached.

"Hello, Jerry. Do you have any pencils?"

Reverend Stammer, whose first name was James, touched his breast pocket. "No, all I have is a ballpoint pen."

"Paper?"

"Beg pardon?"

"Do you have any paper?"

Reverend Stammer sensed complication. He glanced over his shoulder, saw Ethel's face in the kitchen window. "Ah. Well, no, actually, I don't. I—"

"In your car?" Wally asked hopefully. He pushed himself to his feet. "Let's look in your car."

Car. That was where Reverend Stammer wanted to go. "Okay," he murmured, and turned and hurried across the yard toward the walk that led around the house, Wally close on his heels.

"Is it drawing paper?"

"Ah—no, just a spiral notebook."

"Lined?"

"Ah—I never noticed."

"I always buy plain. Plain is a lot better for drawing. Maybe you've got some pencils in there, too. Sometimes people have pencils in their glove box. We could look there."

"Ah—yes, I suppose."

They were at the driveway. As Reverend Stammer opened the passenger door he looked past Wally and saw Ethel's frowning face in the front window. Complication was closing in.

"I'm afraid I need the notebook," he said to Wally, to head off the complication. "And besides, I've already written on a lot of the pages. And I'm sure I don't have any pencils in the glove box."

"Okay, I'll just take a few pages. And we might as well look in the glove box, now that we're here. Just to make sure."

Reverend Stammer realized that avoidance of complication was complicating things. The thing to do was get out of here quickly. He reached into the car, withdrew the notebook, and handed it to Wally, then leaned back into the car and opened the glove box and slid his hand under the pile of papers therein and withdrew a handful of ballpoint pens and pencil stubs. He thrust them at Wally.

"Wally, Ethel says you need brain surgery."

Wally had opened the notebook and was riffling through the pages, grinning. He looked up. "There's no writing on these pages."

"About the brain surgery, Wally—"

Wally was looking at the pencils. "Oh, this is a good one. A number four."

"About the brain surgery, Wally—"

Wally glanced over his shoulder at the house, saw Ethel's angry face in the window, then turned back to Reverend Stammer. "I gotta go." He started walking toward the street, clutching his pencils and pens in his left hand, holding the notebook firmly under his left arm.

Reverend Stammer slammed the passenger door, hurried around to the driver's side, got in, started the car, and got the hell out of there.

Twenty

Charles dropped his arms to the table with a clunk and looked around the room, which at the moment was being converted from project room to cafeteria. White-smocked aids and servers were wheeling steam tables, condiments, trays and plates and silverware, through the double doors from the hall. At a nearby table a purple-haired boy of perhaps fourteen sat gazing slack-jawed and wet-mouthed at some distant vision that only he could see while his companion, an orange-haired girl of about the same age, leaned across the table and talked in his face. Both wore blue, pajama-like overalls, the same sort of clothing that Charles wore. Brother and sister, Charles had guessed when he saw them in crafts that morning.

Charles looked across the table at Janice. "I need it, and it won't hurt you a bit."

"I'm not doing it," Janice said again.

"It's not even out of your way. All you gotta do is go by Harold's and tell him I'll bring him a new painting when I get out. He'll give you some duff. He always saves it for me."

"I'm not bringing you any dope."

"You don't know what it's like, being here with all these nuts and weirdos."

She smiled.

"What's so funny?"

"You. Talking about nuts and weirdos."

He sighed. "Of course you're right. This is where I belong. I am crazy. I'm poison. I destroy." He held his hands up, as evidence. Both were encased in casts from elbow to finger-tip.

She didn't say anything. Just sat there across the table looking at him.

"Just a couple of jays. Or a brownie. Hey, that's it, bake me some brownies."

"I'm not bringing you any pot. What are they doing to you?"

He shrugged. "Nothing. I go to crafts at ten. Lunch at twelve. Nap at one. Group at three. Snacks and crafts at four. And pills. Lots of pills. I tried one, but it was a downer, so I don't take 'em any more." He paused, then grinned. "So how's Dillip? Does he have any nose left?"

"Ask him yourself. He's here."

Incredulously: "He's here? In this ward?"

She shook her head. "Second floor. Reconstructive Surgery."

"Well I'm a sonofabitch. That's made to order. I'll just pop down and finish the job between group and crafts."

"Keep talking like that. They might think you need to be in jail instead of here. That could be even more fun."

"What *are* they gonna do to me?"

"My guess is you'll end up in jail if they remember you rearranged Dillip once already."

"Twice—we go back a long way. But they won't jail me. I'm crazy."

"I wouldn't depend on it."

"I'm sorry about the gallery. I was crazy then. For real. That was the worst thing I ever did to you. And I've done some bad shit." Pause.

"Yes, you have."

"I freaked. It wasn't the pot, either. It was seeing—" He looked down at his two immobilized hands. "It was seeing how good he was, how much better—and then Dillip—"

Janice watched him, her hands clasped together on the table beside her purse. "I know," she said softly. "I know that feeling."

"Where'd he come from, anyway?"

"You were there. He came in from the street one morning."

"Yeah, but where did he come from? He can't be human. His painting is uncanny. It's impossible. That copy of your portrait? When he showed it to us the day we were hanging the show, when he came downstairs with it and his old lady was there, I didn't even look at it. It was only later, up in your apartment, that I really saw it. It destroyed me. Right there, in one instant, seeing that painting destroyed me."

She smiled wanly.

"I'll never paint again. Never."

"Yes, you will. You're not fit for anything else."

He studied the casts encasing his hands. "I don't know—I been thinkin' about doing something else."

"What can you do besides paint? That's all you've ever done."

"Maybe I'll open a gallery."

—

"You know why you're here, don't you Charles," Doctor James said.

Charles nodded.

"Can you tell me?" Doctor James said.

"Sure. Because I kicked Dillip's ass and wrecked Janice's gallery."

Doctor James leaned back in his swivel chair, bridged his fingers together over his vested paunch. "That's right. You're here because you had a psychotic episode, in which you went berserk and destroyed an art gallery with your bare hands and inflicted serious bodily injury on an important art critic. Not to mention yourself."

Charles nodded. "That's what I said. A psychotic episode. I particularly like the word episode. Episode implies episodic, as in temporary. Like temporary insanity. I think I can agree that you accurately characterize my behavior as temporary insanity. On the evaluation you're gonna write."

"Giving you an escape hatch is not my purpose. However, if it satisfies you to hear my professional confirmation, you are insane. You possess so many symptoms of social dysfunction and such a distorted sense of reality that even a casual reader of *Popular Psychiatry* could pin a half-dozen serious psychoses on you. Any one of which could put you in the loony bin for decades. But I'm not thinking temporary. No, I'm thinking permanent. Because you will do it again when you get the chance. That makes your insanity permanent. Your record shows a pattern of problem resolution through violence."

"Not really."

"I'm the psychiatrist, you're the patient. When I tell you you're crazy, you can bank on it."

"You're wrong about the record. The record shows that the only people I hurt are art critics. And beating up on art critics is perfectly reasonable artistic behavior. It is simple self-defense."

Doctor James blinked. He used to hearing gibberish from his patients. He pursed his lips thoughtfully. "Well—okay, I take your point, up to a point—"

"Artists and art critics are like dogs and fleas. You don't classify a dog as insane for biting at his fleas. It's natural for an artist to feel like the critic is eating his flesh, one tiny bite at a time. It feels like that. And so it's also natural for the critic to feel threatened, because he is threatened. When artists and critics come together in a gallery, violence is always a very real possibility."

"But we can't just succumb to the urge to violence, even when the circumstance seems to justify it. What kind of world would we have if we all did that?"

"Surely you agree that self defense is justified. And maybe the world would be better off with fewer critics and more artists."

Doctor James stroked his goatee.

—

"I didn't know what to say," Charles said.

"I don't get it," Janice said.

"I don't either. But it's working out okay. Yesterday I'm a nut in a nut house. Today I'm a guest in a hotel. With room service. You want anything? A beer? A sandwich? Coffee? All I gotta do is call and the nurse will bring it."

Janice shook her head.

Charles rose from the leather chair and went to the bed and looked down at the jeans she'd brought. He had to use the fingertips of both of his immobilized hands to unbutton his blue overalls. He shrugged it off his shoulders and let the garment fall to his feet. He stepped out of it and looked down at his nakedness, then looked at her with a coy smile.

"Don't get any ideas," she said.

"They won't come in unless I push the call button."

"I'm not in the mood."

"They always knock."

She shook her head.

"I never saw you not in the mood."

"Yes you have."

He looked down at himself. "It's been like that two or three times today. Maybe it's something they're giving me."

"I don't get it," she said.

"I don't either. Maybe you're right about the pot. Sometimes I think pot isn't the best thing for your libido."

"I mean I don't understand why they're doing this."

"Doctor James is as crazy I am, that's why."

She didn't say anything.

"Look at it," he said, looking down at himself. "You sure you don't want this guy to come calling?"

"I'm sure."

"You're missing an opportunity here."

"I'll take a rain check."

"Hate to waste it. Maybe I'll just give it to one of the nurses. Couple of 'em act real interested."

"Let me know which is the lucky one and I'll send her some flowers."

He waved at the jeans laying on the bed. "Help me put 'em on, will you?"

She got up and came to the bed and picked up the jeans. "Where's your underwear?"

"Don't want any. Too hard to pee if I have to get through two layers."

He sat on the edge of the bed. She pulled the jeans up on his legs, told him to stand, then pulled them up over his hips.

"Now tuck it in," he said.

"You tuck it in."

"With these?" He held his plaster-encased hands up.

She tucked him in.

"Strange thing was, he came in as soon as they got my room set up yesterday afternoon and spent two hours talking about critics and artists. Even had a tape recorder. T-shirt now."

She helped him get into one of the T-shirts she had brought. He dropped back in his chair, which faced hers. The window was on his right, and her left, and a small table was between them. On the table was a lamp and magazines and books and a tray containing a bowl of peanuts and a bowl of candy.

"What about you? You gonna move in with Boyce and me?"

"Whipple's offered me a job."

"Fuck Whipple. What's he offering you?"

"A lot more than I ever made running my own gallery."

"He wants to fuck you. Again."

"So do you."

"That's different. I love you and he doesn't. Besides, you got to start painting again. Move in with Boyce and me."

"Right. Then there'd be three artists starving in that chicken coop, none of whom can sell anything."

"Don't you understand? It's not about money."

She laughed. "Three days ago you gave up painting."

"I changed my mind."

"I thought you would."

"It's not because I want to paint. I have to paint. You do too, you just don't know it. You need to paint. You need the drug, the lift, like every other artist. You've been on your downer for so long you don't even know you're down. All this bad shit that's happened to you? It's because you defy your karma."

She allowed a smile.

"Think about it. Do you ever experience the lift you used to get all the time out of painting?"

Silence.

"I asked you a question."

"No, I don't. Nor do I experience the poverty."

"Really? I had the impression that's what you're experiencing right now."

"There's poverty, and there's poverty."

"You've surrendered completely, haven't you."

Silence.

"I'll be your teacher."

Her smile broadened lazily. "Like before, when I was a child?"

"You weren't a child. You were a woman. In a child's body."

Still smiling: "You loved that hard skinny body, didn't you."

"Sure. Who wouldn't. And I never stopped loving the woman inside it."

"Is that what it we had? Love?"

"I did you a big favor, you know," he said.

"You've done me a lot of big favors. Which one are you talking about now?"

"Wrecking your gallery."

"I never thanked you for that one, did I."

He grinned. "No."

"Do you still love me, Charles?"

"Shit yes, I love you." And he did—at that moment he loved her very much. "Every painting in the show showed it."

"Even when you don't have a hardon?"

"Well. Kinda."

"Love, even without a hardon. The truest kind."

"But can there *be* love without a hardon? That's a hard question."

She laughed.

"Sure I can't induce you to seduce me?" he asked.

"Thinking about it."

Silence.

"Besides, it would never work out," she said.

"Sure it would. Plenty of room."

"Not for the two females who'd have to share it."

"What are you talking about?"

"When I went by the studio to pick up your clothes Carnita was there."

"Vovo? In my studio? What the fuck is she doing in my studio?"

"She's fucking Boyce's brains out. She told me she can't stand being away from him, so she's moved in and set up her studio. Boyce is so exhausted he can't work."

"Boyce? He's the only virgin I ever met."

"Really? Well, that condition is history now."

"The cunt! Taking over Boyce *and* my studio."

"She paid your back rent."

Silence. Then, "All of it?"

"And she brought in a lot of paint—boxes full—and couple of rolls of canvas. And some lights for working at night. For the Co-op, she said. She made a big point of that, saying it was for the Co-op. Sounds to me like a gesture of peace."

"No shit?"

"And a refrigerator. With food. Also for the Co-op."

"Fuck."

"Life gets simple, no matter how hard we work at keeping it complicated."

"How can I kick someone out who's paying the rent and buying the paints and canvas and food?"

"I know. It's a problem."

"So when I get out of here I'm gonna have to listen to Carnita fucking Boyce's brains out all night long."

"From what Carnita told me, and from the look of Boyce, it'll be all day too. Until Boyce dies."

"I hope for Boyce's sake that she fucks better than she paints."

She began unbuttoning her blouse. "You sure they always knock?"

He smiled. "You're such a pushover. Dirty talk's all it takes. I figured that out two hours into our first date, as we were fucking. Or you were giving me a blow job. I can't remember which."

"It wasn't on our first date."

"Strictly speaking, you're right—I fucked you before our first date. Picked you up at my show, as I remember, at Whipple's old gallery on Occidental. He was hot for you, too, but you wisely chose me. Did you make me fuck you in the back room or did I persuade you to wait until we got in the cab? I can't remember."

She laughed and he watched her remove her blouse and bra, push her skirt and panties down; then she helped him push his jeans down.

"I believe your libido is better. Apparently crazy is good for it."

"This is what's good for it," he said, putting his hands on her head and trying to draw her to him.

She pulled away. "It doesn't want to be a lollipop."

"It does too want to be a lollipop."

"Nope, it wants to be a hotdog bun in a bun." She climbed up on the bed. He followed her, pulled her legs apart, and with no more preliminaries than that, lowered himself into her.

"O-o-o," he whispered. "Goodness gracious, you were ready, weren't you? Maybe they should write some stuff in those women's magazines about the lubricating effect of dirty talk."

"They do, all the time, which is why women read 'em."

He was moving, and, he was thinking, moving pretty effectively, when the door opened. She heard it and tried to buck him off.

"No," he whispered. He turned his head toward the door. "What d'you want?" he said hoarsely.

"Whoops," Doctor James said. "Didn't know you had a guest."

"Get off me," Janice hissed.

"It's all right, I'm his doctor."

"Get off!"

"Shall I come back in a half-hour? Or do you need a little more time?"

"Yes," Charles croaked. "Half-hour. No, an hour."

"Okay, see you in an hour."

The door closed.

"You sonofabitch."

"They're supposed to knock."

Twenty-one

"We have to let him have a lawyer, unless you can convince him not to contest it," Reilley said. He leaned back in his swivel chair and waited for Ethel to make up her mind.

"We been trying to convince him for months," Ethel said. "He won't do it."

"Then he's contesting, so he's got to have a lawyer."

"But you been his lawyer for twenty-five years," Ethel insisted.

"I can't be the lawyer for both sides. The judge won't let me."

"It's not fair, making us hire someone else who's just gonna make it more expensive for us to do what we're gonna do anyway."

"All the law requires is that we make it *look* fair—so we can save some money by using Bobby Reilley. Bobby's rate is only a hundred bucks an hour, 'cause he's just out of law school. Didn't finish very high, but then we don't need talent here, all we want him to do is represent Wally."

"I still don't see why we even got to have a hearing. He's my husband. I ought to be able to just tell the judge and he could see for himself."

"Yeah," George said. "All you got to do is look at him."

"The law is not concerned with the obvious," Reilley said, glancing contentedly at his timer. The meeting was fourteen minutes, or $46.66, old, and still mired in the preliminaries, with George and Ethel more confused than when they came in. "You have to look at the conflicting interests that are involved here. There's your individual interest, your family interest, and your community interest. The conflict between those interests goes way back in history. A famous philosopher of the law—I forget which one—said that liberty can't be created or destroyed. It's called the Law of the Conservation of Liberty, which says there's only so much liberty in the universe and when someone gets more than his share it's because he took it away from someone else. The law is written on that principle. So anyway, over the centuries there's this shift of liberty from one side to the other."

"But what's that got to do with Wally?" Ethel said.

"Yeah," George added irritably.

Reilley smiled. "Let me explain."

Thirty-four minutes, or $113.34, later, Reilley closed his explanation of the Law of the Conservation of Liberty. "What we got to do here is convince the judge it's in Wally's best interest for you to take some of his liberty away from him and give it to you. You end up with more liberty than you had before and he ends up with less than he had before. Pretty neat, huh? How it works out so even? It's science, is what it is. The science of law."

"But does it mean we can have him operated on? If we want to?"

"Yep. If you say, 'cut him open,' that's what they'll do. 'Cause you'll have his liberty."

During the silence that followed, Ethel chewed her lip and thought. And during that silence George, who wasn't particularly good at thinking, watched Ethel think. And while George watched Ethel think, Reilley, who, being a successful lawyer, didn't need to think very much very often, contentedly doodled on a scratch pad as the second hand of his timer swept around, informing him with each circuit that he was $3.34 richer.

Ethel sighed. "What do we do next?"

"We get young Reilley in here and formulate a strategy." He leaned forward, pushed the talk button on the intercom and said, "Mary, ask Bobby to come in, will you?"

Bobby Reilley opened the door and came in with a steno pad and his timer. He put the timer on Reilley's desk and pushed the button.

"Bobby, I'd like you to meet Ethel Walder and her son George Walder. Ethel's husband Wally and I went to work at Allied on the same day. I was a shipping clerk going to night school and he was a draftsman or something. Anyway, Wally had this accident, which made him a little coo-coo, and Ethel needs to have him declared incompetent so she can take some of his liberty away from him. Now, I'm gonna represent Ethel in this matter and we need someone to represent Wally. That'll be you." He looked at Ethel with raised eyebrows. "That pretty much sums it up, doesn't it?"

Ethel looked dubiously at the skinny youngster standing by Reilley's desk. He looked like his voice might break if he spoke.

"I'll do a first-rate job for Wally, Mrs. Walder," he said, in a voice that cracked. "We'll beat this one."

"We're kind of all on the same team here," Reilley said.

"Oh. Well, that's what I meant. That we'll all beat this one."

"Right. And the first thing we got to do is get Wally to accept young Reilley here as his lawyer." Reilley looked at Ethel. "Think you can do that?"

On his knees on the kitchen floor, Wally excitedly opened the first box. In it were his charcoal, his pencils, his paints, several small canvases, and a stack of his sketchbooks. He rummaged in the box for a minute, then pushed it aside and opened the second, much larger box, which contained a dozen books about painting and drawing, several more canvases, and the parts of his easel. He looked up at George and Ethel like a kid who had gotten exactly what he wanted for Christmas.

"Oh, jeez, thanks," he exclaimed again. "Oh, this is so great! Oh, gosh, thanks Ethel, thanks, George."

"Don't thank me," George said irritably. "Wasn't my idea."

"You can have it as long as you behave," Ethel said in a kindly voice.

Wally rummaged among the sketch books, grabbing one and flipping through the pages, pausing now and then to look at a drawing. When he found the sketchbook he was looking for he sat back on his haunches and turned through the pages until he found the drawing he had been working on when Ethel had taken his art supplies away. He peered down in the box, found a pencil, and still on his haunches, immediately resumed work on the drawing, which was a still life of fruit in a bowl.

"Wally, did you hear me?" Ethel said patiently.

Wally nodded as he drew.

"I said you can have your drawing and painting things as long as you behave."

Scratch-scratch.

"Do you understand that, Wally?"

"He don't even hear you," George said disgustedly. "I told you you was makin' a mistake. He was makin' progress, then you go an' give him back his stupid damned art stuff."

"He wasn't making progress, he's been getting worse and worse," Ethel snapped. She turned her attention back to Wally. "Honey, I want you to put your things in your studio. Will you do that for me?"

Scratch-scratch-scratch.

"Honey, will you do it now? Please?"

Scratch-scratch-scratch.

"I told you," George muttered.

"George, if you can't say something helpful, just shut up."

Scratch-scratch-scratch.

"Wally!"

Wally started, looked up in surprise.

"Wally, honey, I want you to put your things in the studio. Right now, please."

Wally rose obediently and began dragging one of the boxes down the hall.

Ethel looked at George, as if to say, *see, smarty*. George shrugged, as if to say, *big deal*.

When Wally came back for the other box Ethel said, "Wally, George and I went to see Reilley and asked him to do something for you. We want you to hear about it. But it's okay for you to work on your drawings while we tell you. Would you like to set up your easel and draw something while we tell you about it?"

—

Wally opened his sketchbook and began to record the morning's discoveries, which came so rapidly that he didn't think he could keep up. The introductions around the long table, the long room filled with books, the interesting new faces, not to mention the familiar faces of Ethel and George and Wanda, which, because of their look of scrubbed uneasiness, seemed new. Judge Nutt's face was round and coarse, with thick black hair that grew right down to eyes that gleamed between dark wrinkles of skin; young Reilley's face was soft and pink and as intellectually empty as a doll's; the face of Reilley senior was jowly and dark and blankly contented; the court reporter's was disinterested and pretty; the staid, hardwood richness of the room in which they had gathered, a long, high space enclosed by shelves of so many books that it felt more like a library than a courthouse meeting room; and the sturdy hardwood table, which was long enough for eight chairs on a side. All of it, and more, waiting there for his discovering pencil.

Wally sat where Bobby Reilley told him to sit, and got busy sketching while the others arranged their file folders and pencils and notepads. He finished a quick study of young Reilley's face and glanced around for another subject. His gaze moved over book titles, taking in blocks of black lettering on sober brown spines, while Judge Nutt shuffled papers and the court reporter got her machine set up at a little side table and Reilley and Reilley arranged little piles of pages on opposite sides of the table. The geometry of the room—long, narrow, high—was, oddly, a recapitulation of the geometry of the books the room housed. That observation got Wally thinking about shapes, in particular about the pleasing dimensions of a book, which led him to a recollection of something he'd read, and liked, about the Greeks' speculations on the perfect shape, which they tried to express in their sculpture and architecture, and even in their philosophy. Inspired by the thought, he turned to a fresh page in his sketchbook and began drawing the shape of a book.

To Ethel and George and Wanda, drawing something was pretty much a normal thing for Wally to be doing, so they ignored his activity. Judge Nutt didn't see it that way. To Judge Nutt it was disrespect, pure and simple, and he wasn't having any of that bullshit from anyone, certainly not from some fucking whacko who was before him in a competency hearing. But before he could whip Wally into shape with a blast of his red-hot temper, the older Reilley leaned across the table and put his hand on the page Wally was working on and whispered, "Wally, we need for you to put that away now. We're about to start."

Judge Nutt glared at Wally for several seconds, then clasped his hands in front of him and began the proceeding.

The day went downhill from there. Not so much because of what happened as what didn't happen. What didn't happen was drawing. Wally wanted to draw so bad he could taste it. He ached to draw, was miserable with desire to discover all those interesting faces, those fascinating rows of books, the court reporter's machine, the window at the end of the room behind Judge Nutt, the coat rack, the flowers on the court reporter's little table. From time to time, when he could no longer stand not drawing he would surreptitiously open his sketchbook on his lap and begin scratching some image, and the judge, as if he was waiting for just such an opportunity, would bark, "Put that goddamned book away." And Wally would flinch and close the book on his lap. For a few minutes. This went on until ten-thirty, when the judge bellowed at Bobby Reilley to "get rid of that goddamned book or I'll throw your client's ass in jail, and yours with it."

Stripped of his pencils, his sketchbook, and even his ballpoint pen, Wally had to content himself with imaginary drawing, which he'd never tried before. Imaginary drawing turned out to be almost as gratifying as real drawing. But it was very, very challenging. For one thing, it took a hell of a lot of concentration. Much more than real drawing. To be successful he had to focus completely on the task, to the exclusion of everything going on around him. And he was successful; he was very pleased indeed with his first effort. He considered showing it to the others around the table, but didn't because he feared Judge Nutt would make him stop. He turned to a fresh sheet of imaginary drawing paper and began another drawing.

This activity occupied him entirely. He was aware only in barest outline of what was going on around him. Beside him was young Bobby Reilley; on his left, at the head of the table, was Judge Nutt; across the table was Reilley and George and Ethel and Wanda. When others came in to testify they always sat at the end of the table opposite Judge Nutt. Wally recognized some of them, and though he heard what they said he was too occupied by imaginarily drawing them to pay much attention to their words.

He noticed Doctor Ramsay come in and sit at the head of the table. He heard, but didn't listen closely, as young Ramsay enthusiastically explained his specialty to Judge Nutt. His interest in afflictions of the brain had led him into extensive research on the rare infirmity known as the Pablo Piccolo Syndrome. "The most noteworthy characteristic of that affliction is an obsession with drawing and painting," he said.

"This character has been obsessed with drawing all morning," Judge Nutt grumbled. "Couldn't keep his goddamned drawing book closed for three minutes. Crazy."

Doctor Ramsay nodded. "Exactly! They're like that all the time."

"Well, it must be a pain in the ass for people who've got to put up with it," Judge Nutt observed, glancing at Ethel, who nodded emphatically.

"It's a scientific fact that people who are obsessed with art don't fit in the world very well," Ramsay said. "For a long time we thought they were simply troublemakers and misfits. Of course they are troublemakers and misfits, but it turns out they're not doing it purpose. They just can't help it. Like Wally here. But now we know why. We've learned that their obsession with art has an organic cause that can be remedied by surgical intervention."

"No shit?" Judge Nutt said. "You can fix that kind of antisocial behavior?" He pointed at Wally, who was staring with great intensity into space as he completed an imaginary drawing of Judge Nutt's walnuty face "With surgery?"

"Yep. Well, not *every* time. No one bats a thousand. Let's just say we're right there with Ted Williams. A few die on us, some become permanently comatose, and some just sit and drool; but on the whole we've had pretty fair luck."

There was silence while Judge Nutt and the others absorbed this information.

"Can you fix criminal behavior with this technique?" Judge Nutt asked.

"Only one kind, so far. The criminality of artistic behavior. But we think we can do a lot more eventually."

"This has interesting potential." Judge Nutt asked. "What d'ya do?"

"Pardon?"

"It's a simple question. Open your goddamned ears and listen. What-do-you-do? Lop off the top of his head? Reach in and cut out parts of his brain? What?"

"Well—yes, more or less. Depends on what caused the condition. In Wally's case the condition was caused by injury, so we're guessing it might be something as simple as synapses short-circuited by bone splinters, and some unresorbed subdural hematoma—internal scabs, so to speak—and maybe some scar tissue. We need to go in and look around. When we see what's in there we can decide what we need to take out."

"So why in hell aren't you in there, doing that, instead of being here, wasting the court's time?"

"The patiient isn't keen on it."

"Which is what this proceeding is about, your honor," the elder Reilley interjected smoothly. "You may recall that we said in our petition that we wanted you to declare Walter Walder incompetent and to give Ethel Walder his liberty. It is her intent to use that liberty to have Walter Walder committed for brain surgery. By Doctor Ramsay, here."

"Ah-h-h, now I get it," Judge Nutt said, nodding. "This fiasco is finally starting to make some sense. We're finally talking about what this goddamned hearing is all about."

—

Roy twisted the cap off a bottle of beer, dropped the cap into the paper sack that Ethel had brought out to the patio to receive food scraps and paper plates. He belched. "Fantastic burgers, Ethel. As usual. You must get tired o' hearin' people tellin' you how you're the best cook they ever met. Well, I don't care, I'm gonna keep tellin' you that because it's the truth. If you wasn't already married, I'd come courtin'."

Ethel blushed, but looked pleased.

George, who sat on the other side of the picnic table, squinted into the sun, which lingered above the trees behind Roy. He tugged at the bill of his Mariners cap to shade his eyes. "So, anyway, the judge comes back in and sits down and says, as simple as you please, that he was taking Dad's liberty away and giving it to us. We can do whatever we want with him, is what he said. An' that was the whole shebang."

Ethel pulled the lemon pie toward her and began cutting it into wedges. "He didn't say we, he said me."

George shrugged.

"My oh my, look at that pie. One of *Ethel's* works of art. Real art."

Ethel slid the knife edge under a huge wedge, worked it onto a paper plate, put the plate in front of Roy. She smiled and allowed herself to feel good. As a matter of fact, she felt better today than she'd felt in many months. Getting past the decision, then obtaining the Judge Nut's permission to execute the decision, followed by Wally's surprising acquiescence—it all seemed to her like waking up optimistic and rested from a pleasant dream to find out the world really was as nice as the dream. She had finally crested her mountain of troubles, and now she was looking out over a vista of happiness and good times. That was what was ahead of them, now, she was sure of it.

"Look how she did that, how she slid that piece of pie right off the pan without even bending it¾that's a test of good pie crust. You have made a work of pie-crust art when it holds together like that. And when it's so good it melts in your mouth—like it does when it's Ethel's." Roy picked up a fork and dug a mouthful off his wedge of pie and deposited it on his waiting tongue. He rolled his eyes as he closed his mouth around the pie.

"Thank you, Roy. It's nice to have someone appreciate your cooking. Here, Wanda," Ethel said, offering a paper plate to Wanda.

"My, that does look good," Wanda said.

"When we gonna do it?" George asked.

"I haven't thought that part through," Ethel said. She slid another piece of pie onto a paper plate and looked around at Wally, who stood before his easel halfway down the sloping backyard, painting. "Wally," she called, "come on up here now and have some pie."

"He don't even hear you," George said.

"I prayed for Dad yesterday," Wanda offered, "while we was in the hall waiting for the afternoon session. The most amazing thing happened. While I was praying God come right into my head and pointed out to me that I was thinking of Dad like he was a little kid, and it was right. God told me we got to look out for him like he's a child. That it's right and proper to make decisions for him."

Ethel passed a piece of pie to George, then slid a piece off onto a paper plate for herself. "It's what I been sayin' for months. He's a big, overgrown twelve-year-old. And I don't need no little boy that I got to take care of all the time. I need a man."

There was an embarrassed silence, as if she had confessed something too weak and too personal to be talked about in public.

Beside her on the bench Roy sat a little taller.

"I think we ought to just go ahead and do it," George said. "Get it over with. We been waitin' for him to get better for months and all he does is sink deeper into that art sickness. If we keep waitin' we may never get him back."

"A little while longer won't hurt," Ethel said.

"It might hurt a lot."

She ate her pie, leaning ever so slightly toward Roy, just enough for her upper arm to touch his upper arm.

"Seems to me your Mom's right," Roy said. "Waitin' a little longer can't hurt."

After all those weeks and months of worrying about what to do, all those months of fear and despair, culminating finally in the judge's simple ruling, she wasn't in any hurry to use the power he'd given her, because she knew that when she made the decision it would unleash a cascade of events that would take Wally's well being out of her control. Of course she also knew that not making a decision was no longer possible. So it was simply a matter of timing. And the present felt, for the first time in a long time, full of possibility, and full of the excitement that comes with possibility, and she wanted to savor it for just a little while.

She did not deceive herself about that. She knew full well that some of the enjoyment of this moment came from Roy's unbroken support throughout the ordeal, for that support had given her something that had been missing from her life for a long time: a sense of the fullness of life that is possible between a man and a woman.

Twenty-two

"What d'you think?" Whipple asked. "Remind you of the first Whipple Gallery?"

He and Janice stood in the middle of a big high-ceilinged room with a black-and-white tiled floor. Plate-glass windows surrounded one corner of the room. One window faced Occidental Square, the other faced the park across the street. The windows were dirty and the floor was scuffed and dusty and the walls were nicked and gouged, though not badly. The location was perfect and it wouldn't take much to get it ready—some wall patching and paint, a new tile floor, new lighting, a sign, business cards, stationary, a desk, a few chairs. If you wanted to open a gallery this was as good a prospect as you could expect to find. Janice tried to revive some of the excitement she'd felt on the day she'd found the Kirkland location and began work on her own gallery, but the only feeling she could identify in the leaden lump below her heart was dread.

She walked over to the nearest wall, ran her hand over it's surface, and looked up into the shadows of the dark ceiling. She saw painted heating ducts and pipes. "How's the back room?" she asked, trying to be interested.

"A little small, but if we're careful about how we do the shelving, I think we can make it work." Whipple started toward a door in the back wall.

She followed him across the black-and-white floor and through the door. They emerged in a small room with unfinished walls and some crude shelves that would have to be demolished to make room for a work table and filing cabinets and proper storage racks for paintings. They came back into the main room and walked to the front door and turned and looked at the big walls and high ceiling once again.

"You don't like it."

"It'll be fine," she said.

"You're not very enthusiastic."

"Bad day."

"Bad month."

"I told you I wasn't ready."

"You will be. Let's go over to Hannibal's for a drink and figure out what we want to do with this place."

They went out on the square into light rain. Up the hill the top of Columbia Tower disappeared in a low gray sky. They walked across the glistening cobbles of the square, past benches that were now empty of the homesteading homeless, who were sheltering under the viaduct with their backpacks and grocery carts. They entered Hannibal's and walked past the bar to a table by the window. The barman came out of the back room wiping his hands on his apron and approached their table.

"Diet Pepsi for me," Whipple said.

"I'll have a white wine," Janice said. "House is fine."

"Chablis, sauvignon blanc, chardonnay," the barman said.

"I don't care."

"Did you get moved okay?" Whipple asked.

"I don't have much."

"Traveling light is the best way. That huge house Karen and I live in—it's just a container for all the crap we've accumulated. The more we own, the more it owns of us. Even the art, which is the only part I care anything about."

She smiled, looked out the window, and studied the gray sky. "I don't have that worry." She nodded at the rain. "It's early this year. Seeing it come feels good."

"Yeah—it's good for business."

She studied the cobbles of the square, observed how the gray sky was reflected in the rounded surfaces; noted that the gray was also reflected in the wet surfaces of the abstract metal sculpture in the middle of the square. When she was young and full of certainty and passion she saw the world the way she was seeing it now, as a mutable poetry of shape and form and color. Like Wally sees it. Wally sees everything that way. And in seeing the world that way, sees so much more than others see, discovers wonders that others can never see. And that thought led her to wonder how Wally was doing, and to wonder if his wife was happy now that the Janice Cushion Gallery was no longer there to poison him.

"You don't like this one, either," Whipple said again.

She turned back to him. "This is the best we've seen. It'll be fine."

The barman put a glass of Pepsi in front of Whipple and a stem of white wine in front of her and took the money that Whipple offered.

When the barman left she said, "I'm trying, Whipple, but I feel burnt out. I know all the things that I've got to do, and I know how to get them done. I'll be able to do what needs to be done when we get started. But right now it seems overwhelming."

"That's not burnout. That's depression."

"Whatever."

"How's your sex life?"

"It's fucked. So to speak."

He laughed.

She tried to smile. "Whipple, I don't hold you to your offer."

"Well, I'm holding you to your acceptance."

She looked out the window at the gray, two-dimensional world.

"How's Charles?" Whipple asked.

"He's fine. Off with high enthusiasm in a new direction. He's decided to take Patternism to the next level."

"Bet it's great stuff."

She shrugged. "He's never defeated. He fights."

"I'll say. I still can't figure out how the hell he got off the hook for thrashing Dillip. Or is he still on the hook?"

"He dodged that bullet. He's hoping the prosecutor will give up trying to talk that shrink into rewriting his report."

"Lives a charmed life, that fellow. He should have ended up in jail long ago. I saw Dillip the other day. His nose doesn't point the way he's facing." A pause. "Charles's got a very mean streak. He may be through with Dillip, but he's not through with you. He's still fucking you over."

"He's giving me shelter, a place to stay until I get on my feet."

"He's the one who knocked you off your feet. You sound like the woman who's grateful to her man because he got too tired to beat her up any more."

"It's not like that."

"He's using you."

"People use people. That's what relationships are about. The more you love, the more you use, and get used."

"That's one side of it. People who love also give."

"I think I get something from him. I always did. He never gives up—that's one thing."

"Yeah, you got something from him, all right. About this much dick. And a trashed gallery. Oh yes, and a hell of a lot of bad debt."

"What's it to you?"

"You getting belligerent on me?"

His needling had got her blood up, which, she realized, was what he had wanted. "No," she said tightly.

"Well I wish you would. You wear anger better than self pity. Now let's get down to business."

Twenty-three

"*Roy?*" George said incredulously. "You're crazy."
Wanda picked up the remote control device and clicked the TV off.
"Hey, I was watchin' that," George said.
"We need to talk."
"About whut?"
"About Mom and Roy. I told you I think they're havin' a—you know."
"Whut."
"You know—what men and women—"
"You're crazy. Roy couldn't get it up if he wanted to. And Mom—well, I happen to know that she'n Dad haven't screwed for fourteen years."
Wanda blushed. "How do you know that?"
"She told me."
Silence for several seconds. "Well, I don't care what she told you, the signs are obvious."
"Whut signs. Turn that TV back on, I wanna watch the game."
"The way he's over there all the time, for one."
"Gimme that goddamned remote."
"And the way he's always agreeing with her. Anything she says he jumps in and agrees with, and then looks at her like a puppy dog wantin' a pat on the head, and the way he's always giving her compliments about her cooking and how good she looks."
"Are you gonna gimme that fuckin' remote?"
"Don't you talk to me like that."
"Then gimme the fuckin' remote."
"And the touching. Don't you even notice how she sits beside him or kind of maneuvers around so she can stand by him and how she sort of leans at him, just a little bit, just enough to touch, and how he's always findin' excuses to put his arm round her shoulders, sometimes even her waist?"
"Okay then, I'll just turn the goddamned thing on by hand."
"I think they're—you know—doing it."
"Shit. Where's the thing? The thing to turn it on and off, the switch."
"I think that's the reason she won't decide."
"Is this it?"
"I been praying about it and God has told me Mom has decided she don't want to make Dad well again. That is why she won't talk about it."
"Goddamnit, now look what you made me do. How do I fix this fuckin' picture?"

God did not say anything to Wanda about an affair, because God doesn't care a fig about that kind of stuff. Wanda figured it out for herself, and just thought God was involved in it somewhere. But God did whisper in Wanda's ear that Ethel was stalling about making Wally well again. Wanda knew God wouldn't lie to her about that, or anything else, for that matter, but she did want to make sure she heard Him right, so during her lunch break on an bright fall day a few weeks after Judge Nutt's judgment, she got in her rusted-out 1975 Honda CVCC and drove it, rattling and smoking, up the hill on Juanita Drive to Mom and Dad's house to have a little chat with Mom. She didn't have a plan, had no idea how she'd broach the topic, just figured it would come out if she sat herself down at the kitchen table with Mom and started talking, woman to woman, about the important stuff in their lives.

She parked in the driveway behind Wally's Ford, which of course he was not allowed to drive anymore, and got out of her Honda and walked, as was her habit, around the house to the back door. As she came around the house she saw Wally standing at his easel down at the creek. His back was to her. She paused, poignantly struck by the scene. It was so sad! How badly she felt for Wally! His affliction was so unfair. But as soon as she had that thought, she was ashamed of it. God was not unfair. God had a purpose when He afflicted us with pain and suffering. Maybe to punish us. Or to make us stronger, so we can accept more pain and suffering later. For which we should just thank God. She walked down the slope.

"Hi, Dad, what are you painting? Can I see it?"

He didn't notice her presence. He continued painting odd little shapes in bright, garish colors.

"I said, *Hello, Dad.*"

He started and turned his head toward her. "Oh, Wanda."

She came up beside him. "My, my, that's pretty. What is it?"

He dabbed his brush into a bead of bright red paint on his palette, then stirred the bristles into a bead of yellow, creating a bright splash of orange. He darkened it with a daub of black, then stroked a little of it on the canvas.

"What is it?" she asked again.

Wally made another stroke. "A painting."

Wanda smiled. "I know it's a painting, Dad. I can see that. What are you painting? Flowers?"

"No. Just color."

"Oh."

He applied some more paint while she stood at his side, watching. "I want to see if I can compose a picture out of nothing but shapes of color that I see out there." He pointed with the brush. "Like how Piccolo and Brick did with Relativistic Polyhedralism, then Tubism, which of course all came out of Intractable Perspectivism. It's pretty hard to do."

"Sounds really hard. Which one is that."

He looked at her in surprise. "Well, it's Relativistic Polyhedralism, of course."

"Oh."

He mixed another color and began applying it.

She watched for a while, then said, "Where's Mom?"

He seemed to have left her, seemed to have gone back into his painting.

She turned and began walking back up the slope.

"Wanda, what's going to happen to me?"

She stopped and looked back at Wally, surprised. He had turned to face her, a palette and several brushes in his left hand, the big, wide-bristled brush in the other.

"You understand, don't you, Dad—about what's going on."

"Yes, some. They want to change me."

"They want to make you like you were before. They want to make you well. God wants you well."

Ethel hates my drawing and painting. So does George. They want to change me, to make me not want to do it any more. Judge Nutt told them they could. Everybody wants me to change. Is that what's going to happen?"

"God wants it that way."

"What would I do if I couldn't draw and paint?"

She didn't know what to say. He looked at her for a while longer then turned back to the canvas and daubed some paint on the brush and started working again. She watched him for a while, thinking about his words. She sighed. What to do, what to do. Though she'd already prayed an awful lot on this matter, she resolved now to pray even harder than before. She turned and walked up the slope to the back porch, climbed the stairs, and turned the door knob. It was locked. She knocked and waited. She was about to knock again when, through the lacy curtains of the backdoor window, she saw Ethel come smiling into the kitchen from the hall, tying her apron strings behind her. Then came Roy, buttoning his shirt. At that moment Ethel glanced at the backdoor, and stopped abruptly, the smile disappearing. Roy, who'd been laughing, stopped right behind her, and grinning, said something. Then he noticed the look on Ethel's face, and he looked at the backdoor. The grin faded. The three of them stood as still as figures in a photograph. Then Ethel broke out of the stillness; she smoothed her apron down, stepped to the door and opened it.

"Come in, Wanda. We were just about to have coffee."

Wanda stepped into the kitchen. She realized she had clenched her hands together over her Safeway apron so tightly that her finger nails were digging into her palms. She opened her hands, looked down at the red marks in her palms, and let her hands fall.

Roy hurriedly finished buttoning his shirt and began tucking it into his pants. "I think I better—I got to—"

"Yes, you do that," Ethel said. "Wanda and I have to talk about some things."

It took a cup of coffee and several minutes of edging around the subject before they got to it. But after they did Wanda found it surprisingly easy to just sit back and listen to, and even more surprisingly, to sympathize with Ethel. Not that she approved, mind. No way could she approve of what Ethel was doing. No way. Still. Once you heard the story from Ethel's point of view, once you got some idea of the terrible burden Ethel had been carrying for these many months—well, it was impossible to sit there at the kitchen table and listen to that woman's story and then just coldly condemn her for hungering for a man's support and for yielding to that man's touch when he miraculously came into her life and gave that vital support. Particularly since Ethel made it abundantly clear that she'd had her time with a man. But when the touching started to be on purpose, when it started to be needful, not just casually affectionate, when Roy started telling her what *he* needed—well, by then she had started something that had a life and a will of its own. She discovered that by listening to Roy tell her of his need she discovered her need to respond to his need. And most importantly, she discovered that she was not yet through with life.

After Ethel emptied herself of talk she got up and brought the coffee pot to the table. She refilled Wanda's cup, then her own, and resumed her seat. She stirred sugar and milk into her cup.

Wanda drew a deep breath. She had to ask the question. "But what about Wally, Mom?"

"I think about that all the time."

"What are you thinking?"

"That I got to choose."

Silence for several seconds, then: "What, Mom?"

For the first time since they sat down Ethel's voice grew plaintive. "You got to realize that Wally's become someone else now. He is another person."

"What do you have to choose, Mom?"

"Whether or not to get Wally's head fixed. And whether I want Roy or Wally. And I don't know which one I have to choose first."

Twenty-four

Wikka got her calculator out of her purse and thumped it down in the middle of the tiny table in the middle of what was now a bedroom, a room which, eight decades before, had been an office to which another fat woman in a long dress—the young mother of the white-haired old man in the shop downstairs—had come every day to add columns of numbers by hand. Wikka settled herself on that dead woman's now-rickety chair, which Charles and Boyce had salvaged from the mountains of trash that had occupied the room for many of those intervening decades. She opened her notebook.

"It's all right in here," Wikka said grimly. "See for yourself."

Carnita had no idea what all those numbers meant. "Do we have any money or don't we?"

"We do, at this moment, but if we spend it on a kitchen we won't."

"But I need a kitchen, and I want a kitchen," Carnita said, with out-thrust lower lip, off of which several metal ornaments dangled. "Look at that." She pointed to the food-encrusted hotplate, which rested on a knee-high wood box. "That's the kitchen."

"You could come back to the apartment," Wikka said. "We have a perfectly good kitchen there."

Boyce, who reclined, naked, thin, and exhausted beneath a sheet on the gray striped mattress ticking, turned his tattooed face and looked hopefully at Wikka, then at Carnita.

Carnita pulled her bathrobe closer around her. "There's no way I'm gonna leave Boyce. No way."

The hope went out of Boyce's expression. He looked at the ceiling, and deciding he'd better get some rest while he could, he closed his eyes.

Wikka tried another angle. "What about Greece? We need a lot of—"

"It's gonna take a little longer. 'Cause I want that kitchen. Oh, yeah, an' a bathroom."

"A bathroom?"

"And there's three of us going to Greece. When we go."

"Three of us. You're bringing Boyce."

"Of course. I love Boyce. You can be his business manager, too."

"What do I manage? He's never sold a painting."

"When he sells one he'll need a manager."

Wikka sighed. "What kind of kitchen?"

"I don't know. A kitchen. Sink, stove, cabinets. And don't forget the bathroom. With walls. And a shower. I'm getting tired of peeing and washing myself in front of everyone. Washing yourself from a bucket is a drag."

"We're talking thousands here," Wikka said.

"Oh, yeah, and don't forget a hot water heater."

"We're talking thousands," Wikka said again.

"No problem. I'll get busy soon and paint some more pictures."

"You keep saying that."

"I'll get started again soon."

Wikka positioned her hand over the calculator keys and tapped some numbers, paused, studied the display, wrote the numbers in the notebook, then tapped some more. While she was doing this Charles came to the office door, bringing with him a scent of turpentine. In his left hand he clutched a bunch of brushes, in his right, another brush, which glistened with fresh paint. His jeans and shirt were flecked with paint.

"We're out of white again," he announced. "Put it on the list."

Wikka looked incredulously at Charles, then looked indignantly at Carnita. Was she actually hearing what she thought she heard? She watched Carnita dutifully rise and pick up the black jeans she had dropped beside the mattress on which Boyce reclined. She reached into one of the pockets and got a piece of paper, which she brought back to the table. She found a drawing pencil in a pile of papers she'd raked off the table onto the floor and wrote "6 beg tubs whit" at the bottom of the list. She handed the list to Wikka.

"I almost forgot about the paint. Charles uses a lot of paint. He's working day and night."

Wikka opened her mouth to protest this outrage, but she was so shocked that nothing came out. Helplessly, she took the list into her hand and looked down at it.

"Charles needs it right away."

Wikka realized then that it was too late to intervene. Nothing Wikka could do now would change anything. Heartsick, she closed her book on the numbers. Carnita no longer listened to numbers. Nor to her own creative demon. All Carnita could hear now was her appetite for Boyce and his beastly penis. Wikka felt sick, unneeded, abandoned, betrayed, used. And vulnerable. Oh, yes! Very, very vulnerable: if Carnita no longer cared about the numbers, then of what use was Wikka and her calculator? She folded the paint list, stuck it in her purse, picked up her calculator and dropped it in her purse with the list, and pushed herself to her feet. Without another word she lumbered out of the little room and across the long open space past the cone of daylight in which Charles worked at an easel.

―

Shelley led the way from the foyer into the painting-filled room, followed by Carnita, then Charles, then Boyce, who carried one of Charles' recent paintings. Tiny Tim Leuter brought up the rear. From near the fireplace Shelley and Tim and Carnita and Charles watched Boyce remove the paper wrapping from a four-foot by four-foot Patternistic work done in a style that looked faintly Vovoic. He placed the painting on the easel and stepped aside.

Silence for fifteen seconds, then an appreciative "Hmm" from Tim, with a glance and a raised eyebrow at Shelley, who nodded approvingly.

"We've talked about getting another Vovo for some time," Shelley said to Carnita. "You may remember that we committed to buying the purple and yellow one you had at Janice's last show. Which, unfortunately, didn't survive."

"Well this one did," Charles said. "And for my money it's better than anything she's done before."

Carnita frowned fiercely, opened her mouth to say something, but snapped it shut with the tinkle of metal lip rings.

The silence grew while Tim and Shelley studied the painting on the easel. Shelley approached it, then Tim.

"It certainly is a mature, confident work," Shelley said. "Suggests the painter is a master of her medium. What do you think, Tim?"

"Oh, yes. By all means. Mature. Such an elegant mastery of the medium."

"Took the words right out of my mouth," Charles said.

Carnita reddened and stalked to the farthest wall and pretended to admire one of the paintings thereon, until she realized that it was the only Charles Gas in the room, whereupon she moved to another.

"How much are you asking for it?" Shelley asked.

"This is the best work Carnita's ever done," Charles said. "As a matter of fact—and you're probably not aware of this—*this* painting right here is the first work ever done in The New Patternism."

"The *New* Patternism? I've never heard of that movement."

"Of course you haven't. Because this is the first work ever done in that style."

"Really! How much for it?"

"The New Patternism is gonna be big. Monstrous. And you're the first to see it. And maybe the first to own one."

"How much?"

"For a Carnita Vovo? In The New Patternism? The entire bionic works, that's how much. Caps and bridges, platinum and gold. All of it."

"Oh, my!" said Tim Leuter.

"How much is one of Piccolo's early works worth right now?" Charles asked, then answered his own question. "Millions, that's what."

"Vovo is not Piccolo," Shelley said. "No disrespect, of course—I love Carnita's work, but no one is Piccolo. Besides, Piccolo's dead and Carnita's alive."

"Look. Investing in art is a long-term proposition. She ain't gonna live forever."

—

"What the hell are you bitching about?" Charles said. "This was your idea. Remember?"

"Yeah, but you didn't need to say—"

"If you'd stop thinking about Boyce's dick for five minutes maybe you could get a painting started. Maybe even finished. Then you could swap *it* for Boyce's dental work."

"Hey, man, I'm gittin' tired of all this talk about my dick. It's 'barrassing."

"*Em*-barrassing," Charles said.

"Whutever."

"Yeah, but what you said—you didn't have to say what you said the way you said it," Carnita said, with a pout.

"What'd I say?"

"You know. About that piece of shit being the best work I ever did."

"That piece of shit is better than anything you ever did. And it just bought Boyce a mouth full of new teeth."

"False teeth," Carnita corrected him. "No gold, no platinum, no bridges, no caps."

"*False* teeth is a hell of a lot better'n' a mouth full of hurt. Right, Boyce?"

"Yeah, man. False teeth can't hurt me like these fuckin' teeth are hurtin' me right now."

"After all that talk about platinum and gold he ends up with plastic teeth. Big fucking deal."

"You on the rag?"

"What if I am?"

"I got painting to do," Charles said. He rose and stalked out of the office-cum-bedroom.

"Are you?" Boyce said hopefully.

Carnita smiled lovingly at the man she loved, shook her head, rose, and began unfastening her black jeans.

Charles walked across the studio to the kitchen, a colonial-style assemblage of white cabinets and gray countertop that took up twelve feet of the brick wall beside the enclosed bathroom, which took up another ten feet. He opened the refrigerator, got bread and salami and lettuce and mayonnaise, which he took to the table. There he sat and constructed a sandwich and ate it with a beer. When he began to hear the usual grunting and wheezing and groaning and banging and thumping and whimpering he rose and turned on the radio, then walked the length of the studio to the front wall of the combination bedroom and sitting-room he and Boyce had constructed for Janice, and into which they had moved all of her possessions. Within a few days of her arrival Charles had moved his few rags of clothing into her chest of drawers and his body into her bed. He got his parka and came back to the center of the studio where his easel and a half-finished painting rested in the circle of anemic light spilling down from the skylight. He looked up at the gray of low scudding clouds and zipped his parka against the chill; and tried not to think about approaching winter. He went back to the kitchen, tuned the radio until he found some classical, turned the volume up, then returned to the easel and studied the painting.

Twenty-five

One storm after another swept in from the southwest, bringing torrential rains and gusting winds. El Niño. Meteorologists showed it on maps when they presented their forecasts and newspaper writers mentioned it in their articles about river-valley flooding and TV news presenters talked about El Niño in every broadcast, and pessimistic voices muttered gloomily that it was one more proof of global warming. Perhaps they were right. Who knows? Perhaps the unprecedented storminess of early fall was caused by global warming causing El Niño.

But Wally wasn't interested in speculations about the weather. He was interested in doing something about it. He wanted to paint it. Of course he knew from experience that painting rain is logistically complicated. At the very least you need a nice big umbrella. Which he didn't have; so he erected his easel in the kitchen by the window that overlooked the back yard. Roy, who seemed to be around the house most of the time these days, observed that being separated from the outside by a window isolated him from his subject and limited his point of view. He suggested a golfer's umbrella. As a matter of fact, he proposed rather grandly that the two of them get in his car right then and there and drive down to the pro shop at the Willow Run Golf Club and he'd buy Wally exactly what he needed to get him out of the house and closer to his subject.

When they returned, Wally popped the umbrella open and hauled his easel across the sloping back yard through the downpour. In a normal September the creek was little more than a trickle of clear spring water. Now it foamed brown and turbulent right up to the edge of the lawn. He erected the easel on the foot bridge, then came back through the rain to the house and got a canvas and ran back and put it up on the easel. Then he realized that if he left the easel unsheltered while he went back for his paints and brushes the canvas would be soaked before he got back. He took the canvas down and put it under his arm and was turning to go back to the house and figure out a way to bring all of his materials out at one time when he saw Roy come out the back door with the paint box and the brushes and a small table. Roy helped Wally arrange the table and even got some bricks and a piece of plywood to make a little shelter on the table for the paints and brushes, and then duct-taped the umbrella to the easel. Wally thanked his friend once again and set to work as the rain drummed on the big red and white umbrella.

Roy went back inside and took off his wet jacket and went to the bathroom and got a towel and came back and stood at the kitchen window drying his white hair and watching Wally.

"I keep wonderin' what's gonna happen next," he said.

Ethel finished wiping down the countertop, got the cooling rack out of the cabinet, opened a drawer, got a pair of hot pads, and went to the oven and pulled the door open. She removed the cookie sheet and brought it to the counter where she placed it on the cooling rack.

Roy turned and faced her. "What is gonna happen?"

"I don't know," she said.

Roy watched her carry the other cookie sheet to the oven and put it inside and close the door. Then she went to the sink and turned on the hot water. Roy dropped the hand towel over the back of a chair and came to her and put his arms around her as she leaned over the sink.

She looked over her shoulder at him, her hands busy in the sudsy water. "What d'you think you're doing?"

"I'm feelin' you up, that's what."

"Well, you can just stop it."

She brought her arms closer to her side, but not so firmly that the gesture told Roy to really stop it. She wiggled a little, as if in annoyance, but stayed where she was so Roy could move up against her. A shiver ran through her when he buried his hands in her breasts. Every time he did something like that she was shocked at his brazenness, but not as shocked as she was at her own acquiescence. Until Roy came along no one had touched her like that in so long she could scarcely remember what it had been like.

"Roy! For goodness sake, stop that."

Which, since she did not move, Roy understood to mean, "Do *not* stop that."

"Wally's gonna walk in on us one of these times."

Which Roy understood to mean, "Did you lock the back door?" He kissed the damp saltiness of the roll of fat that extended across her upper back, murmuring, "No he won't, I locked it."

She sucked her breath when he started raising her dress.

"Not here," she murmured.

Roy knew what that meant also. He stepped back and she turned from the sink and, drying her hands on her apron, led the way to the bedroom.

Roy pushed himself up on his elbow and looked down on Ethel's face. Her eyes were closed and her breathing was normal again. His gaze wandered down the length of her naked body, a glowing mound of white against the colored sheets. He was still amazed at his behavior, but not as amazed as he was at the appetite she had awakened in him. Think of it! At seventy-five, getting it up for a hot and heavy affair with a married woman. The thought was as exciting as the fact. An adulterer at seventy-five. And without Viagra! By god, *that* was living. There was still some kick left in the old mule. Adultery. He listened as the word echoed in his mind and wondered once again how much regret he should be feeling. A little, at least, but try as he might, he didn't regret anything. What was to regret, anyway? It wasn't like he was cuckolding a friend. Wally had been his friend, it was true, but Wally was gone, his body taken over by the another soul, a weird, a—well hell, an *artist*, a *demon*, that's what.

"You never answered me," he said.

She knew what he was talking about. "Yes, I did. I said I didn't know."

"That's not an answer."

She sighed, picked his hand up and placed it on her breast. She turned her head toward him and he leaned over and brushed her lips with his.

He wasn't going to give up. "What if Wally never has that surgery, what if he never changes." He moved his hand over her breasts.

"Do you actually think we can we keep on like this?" she asked.

"Yes."

"Well, I don't. I think about it all the time and I get so confused I don't know up from down. George and Wanda already know, and the whole neighborhood's gonna know sooner or later. It won't be long before the whole world knows. One of these days even Wally might know."

"What if Wally has the surgery and gets back to normal?" he said. "What then?"

"Then I'll have to make some decisions," she murmured.

"What decisions?"

She had been looking up at the ceiling. Now she turned her head and looked into his eyes. "You know what decisions. I'll have to choose which one of you gets me."

"I want you. He doesn't."

"Oh, yes he does."

"He only wants his paints and brushes. That's all he thinks about."

"That's because he's sick right now. When he gets well he'll want me."

"Not like I want you. He hasn't wanted you like that in years and years. You said so."

"He wants me, even now, but in his own way." She looked back at the ceiling, then closed her eyes and thought about the way Roy wanted her and the way his hands moved over her breasts.

"The way I want you— that's the best way," he murmured.

Silence.

"It is, isn't it? You said yourself that you'd forgot how good it was, how important it was."

She didn't say anything.

"You think you can give it up? Again?"

Silence.

"What if we just stay the way we are? We both get you that way. He gets you the one way he can and I get you another way."

"We've been over—"

"Why do we have to change him at all? The way he is now is the way he wants to be. Is that so bad?"

She looked at him again. "Keep him like this forever?"

"Why not? It's the way he wants to be. Then we can be the way we want to be."

She looked back up at the ceiling, closed her eyes. "The three of us? Like this? I don't want to talk about this anymore, it's gonna make me sick."

"You just got to get used to the idea of it. When you do, it'll make sense." Roy rolled his legs out of bed and pushed himself to his feet and stepped over to the window and lifted one of the metal slats of the blinds and looked out. He stood, naked, but warmed and lazed by the exertions of sex, drained of all appetite, content with the moment. Happy, even. The rain thudded out of clouds that swirled down into the treetops.

"What's he doing?" she asked.

"Painting. Standin' under that umbrella, painting. He looks happy."

Twenty-six

Reverend Stammer hoped Wanda's visit had nothing to do with the gossip that had been going around about Ethel Walder and her neighbor, Roy.

"I need to talk to you," Wanda said, "about what God has told me to do."

Uh-oh. This could be more dangerous than Reverence Stammer thought. When one of his flock talked about what God told them to do it was a sure sign they were cooking up something wacky. And probably violent. He stood in the entry hall, pipe in one hand, a piece of paper on which he was editing one of his poems in the other, while he cast about for a civil way to get rid of her.

Which was a mistake, for she perceived his hesitation as an invitation to continue; she edged around him and went into the tiny living room which also served as his office. She sat down in a straight-backed chair before his desk and clasped her hands in her lap, ready to talk business. God's business. The air was close and warm and stinking of rancid pipes and stale tobacco smoke.

He followed her apprehensively, slid behind his desk and sat, facing her. A goose-necked lamp focused its light on the clutter of papers on the desk. His poetry.

"What it is, is this. Mom—not my mom, she'd never—it's George's mom—she's—see, she and—see, Roy—"

Wanda stammered, stumbled, and finally stopped, her face aflame with embarrassment, unable to say the words to her minister. As a matter of fact, she couldn't bring herself to say the words to anyone, not even to George. Even when she tried telling her best friend Stella down at the Safeway she couldn't say it.

While she tried to communicate the shameful problem to Reverend Stammer, without actually talking about it, of course, he tried to think of a way of getting her out of his house before she managed to communicate anything to him, because her communication of the problem would thereby involve him in it.

Wanda saw that he wasn't reading her mind like she had hoped. She drew a deep breath and began again. "You know Roy Sharp? The big, tall old man with a purple nose? That sits in the back? And doesn't come very often?"

Reverend Stammer nodded cautiously. He had indeed seen him. He had even spoken to Roy Sharp a couple of times, though he never knew his name until this moment.

"Well, it's them."

Silence.

"So I didn't know what to do. About it. Until God told me. Which is what I need to talk to you about."

Reverend Stammer didn't want to know what God told her.

"Mainly because of Wally."

Reverend glanced around, but saw no escape.

She sighed. "Poor man. He doesn't know a thing about it. He's happy as a clam if he can just paint. That's all he wants. To paint."

Reverend Stammer poked around in the papers on his desk for his pipe before discovering he had it in his hand.

"God told me that Wally's got to act like a man if he is to be saved from this. And the only way that's gonna happen is for him to get that brain surgery the doctors want to give him. So guess what Ethel's not gonna do?"

He couldn't guess.

She went on as if he'd guessed and missed. "She's not gonna let him have that brain surgery, that's what she's not gonna do, because she doesn't want him to be able to see how she's¾well, you know."

Reverend Stammer fidgeted with his pipe.

"'Course she never actually told me, not in so many words, that she's not gonna make Wally get that surgery, but it's as obvious as the nose on your face. So after God told me he wants Wally to act like a man and take charge of his life—and take charge of his wife, like a man's supposed to—I knew God was telling me to do something, 'cause no one else was there when God said it, and I know George won't, so I got this idea, which I know God put in my head, 'cause I never could've thought about it myself."

Reverend Stammer had never in his whole life heard God say a single word. Not one. So he was more than a little skeptical when people talked about God talking to them. It was his experience that people who talked about God talking to them were about to cause a lot of trouble for someone and were setting God up to take the fall for it. He tamped tobacco into the bowl of his pipe, more nervous now at the thought that it might be him the trouble was heading for.

"What I'm thinkin' of doing is this. I'm thinkin' of calling this hot line they got downtown that's for abused spouses and tell 'em that Ethel is abusing Wally. For not giving him that surgery the doctors say will make him well."

Reverend Stammer lit his pipe, blew a cloud of blue smoke into the air above the desk. Well. Wasn't as bad as he'd thought it might be. At least God hadn't told her to murder someone.

"That way she'll be forced to let the doctors give him the surgery he needs. And I was wondering what you thought. Whether it seemed like the right thing to do. What do you think?"

Reverend Stammer was relieved. He tamped and lit his pipe again, thinking that this little episode of familial dysfunction was more or less harmless. He didn't detect any of the hatred and violence that he usually saw when adultery cropped up in his congregation.

"I don't see no other way," Wanda continued.

He rolled his eyes thoughtfully up, drew on his pipe, expelled another cloud of smoke.

"So. You do think I ought to just take the bull by the horns and do it. But I think I should warn Ethel first. You know, give her a chance to repent and stop what she's been doin'. God wasn't very specific about that part of it."

He ran a pipe cleaner through the bit of his pipe, stuck the pipe back in his mouth, shrugged thoughtfully.

"Yeah," she murmured. "I agree."

—

"No way, Jose," George said emphatically.

Wanda put her hands on her hips. "Well, it's your mom and dad involved in this, not mine."

"I said I ain't goin'. An' I'm not gonna talk about it, neither, or listen to you talk about it, so you might as well just shut up about it."

She sniffed. "You were the one tellin' your mom and ever body else, all year long, ever time you had the chance, that Dad had to have this surgery. Had to have it. Now you won't even talk about it."

"Get out o' the fuckin' way."

"You're just gonna sit there in front of that TV and let your dad¾well, just be made a fool of like that by your mom and that Roy?"

"Yes, I am. 'Cause it's none o' my fuckin' business. Now get out o' the way. I'm busy trying to watch—shit, now what the hell happened? Washington had the fuckin' ball just a minute ago and now look, the Ducks got it on the five. Shit."

The telephone rang. Wanda went to the telephone stand, which was the company headquarters of Septic Concepts. She made a motion, which he ignored, for him to turn the volume down, then picked up the telephone handset.

"Septic Concepts," she announced musically. Pause. "Yes, we do that. All the time." Pause. "No, there's no extra charge for Saturday." Pause as she scribbled something on a piece of paper. "We'll have one of our trucks there at three. Thank you."

She came back to her position between George and the TV, which caused him to have to lean off to the side to look around her again.

"You got a job up on the plateau."

He looked up at her. "The Huskies are playin'."

"The lady wants you there at three."

"Shit."

"I'm going over to talk to your mom. Then I'm goin' to work. I won't be home 'til seven."

"What about supper? Who's gonna fix supper?"

"I'll bring some fried chicken from the deli."

———

Wanda got out of the car and smoothed her Safeway apron down over her belly. She looked up at the house, was sure she saw Roy's big purple nose in the front window. As she walked up the driveway she heard the back door slam. It *was* Roy, she thought contemptuously, and now he's high-tailin' it for home. The image of him fleeing from the embarrassment of her witness to his adultery made her feel powerful. She liked the feeling, though she certainly didn't believe it was an appropriate feeling for a Christian woman to experience. Her being a woman and all, an' Roy bein' a man. She was more used to, and comfortable with, God's natural order.

She went around to the back door, tapped, and waited. Ethel's face appeared in the window, then the door opened and Ethel stepped back and permitted her daughter-in-law to enter.

"I was just about to make some coffee," Ethel said coolly. "Please have a seat."

Talking to me like I'm some stranger she just met, Wanda thought. It was what she expected. They'd talked only twice since she had confronted her mother-in-law about the adultery and both times the conversation had been short and cool. She went to the kitchen table and pulled out a chair and sat and clasped her hands in her lap around her purse and while she waited to see what would happen next, watched Ethel pour some water into the coffee maker, slide the filter tray out, add a filter and some coffee, then slide the tray back in.

"Nice of you to drop by," Ethel said. "How's my son?"

"Oh, he's fine. He's on a job right now, up on the plateau."

"Um."

The silence lengthened while they listened to the coffee maker burp and gurgle.

"How's Wally."

"Same as always."

"Um."

Silence.

"Is he painting today?"

"Yes. The TV."

"The TV? I thought Wally took all the TVs to the garage."

"He brought this one back in this morning, said he wanted to paint a pitcher of it."

The coffee maker gurgled and burped more urgently, and the smell of fresh coffee floated through the air. Ethel got up and went to the cabinet and got cups and a plate of cookies and brought them to the table with a carton of milk and a bowl of sugar. She poured the coffee and resumed her seat.

Wanda drew a deep breath. It was time for God's business. "How's Roy?" she asked, to introduce the subject.

Ethel stirred sugar and milk into her coffee. "I suppose he's all right," she said coolly.

Wanda picked up an oatmeal cookie and took a bite. It was a very good cookie. Ethel's cookies were the envy of every woman who'd ever tried one. She ate the rest of it and got another one.

Crumbs popped out of her mouth as she mumbled: "I come to find out what you're gonna do about Wally."

Ethel paled. She had been asking herself that painful question continuously for a year; and the question had become even more painful now that Roy was also asking it. But it had never been as painful as at that moment, when Wanda asked it. Wanda had stumbled into the moment when the pressures had reached the maximum possible levels, when she could not accept even the smallest increment of additional pressure. The innocuous question, meant to be an opening to a discussion of what God wanted, stabbed her like a spear.

Wanda dipped her second cookie in her coffee, and ate it while she watched Ethel struggle for composure.

"I don't know—I been thinking—" Ethel's eyes blinked rapidly at the tears welling in her eyes. Her voice broke, her words weakened and trailed off into silence. She watched Wanda eating cookies as cool as you please while the ground heaved, while the world came unstuck, came flying apart, and accusation became judgment and judgment became sentence and sentence became execution. She burst into tears.

Wanda stuck the rest of a cookie into her mouth, brushed the crumbs from her bodice and lap, and rose and went to her sobbing mother-in-law and leaned over and hugged her and said, through the little crumbs of cookie that jumped out of her mouth: "It's okay, Mom, it's gonna be fine, you'll see. God's looking out for all of us."

Wally heard the wailing and sobbing, and he was getting ready to go and see what was the matter, but first he had to finish this little corner. He'd finally got the texture right, after struggling with it all morning. He'd had to lay a thick layer on because thin paint, which was what he preferred to work with, ran down the plastic face of the TV screen. Even thick paint had not worked well until he'd finally figured out how to make the paint stick. He'd gotten some sand paper from the garage and roughed the screen.

He heard Wanda talking soothingly, then Ethel's hiccupping sobs came stronger. Then Wanda's voice broke and her sobs mixed with Ethel's in a despairing counterpoint. He knew he ought to go and see what in the world was the matter, but the painting was going so well after the frustrations of the morning that he had to keep going. For just another minute or two. Then he'd go and find out.

He pushed himself up from his knees and found a tube of white and squeezed a little out on his palette beside the shades of gray that he had already mixed. He'd painted the screen with layers of slightly different shades of gray and was topping it all with careful, minute flecks of white. But it needed more white. Getting the little flecks of white to lay right was the hard part. He was about to get on his knees again in front of the screen when the two women, looking like the Women of Troy, burst out of the kitchen and grabbed him in their arms and pressed their fat soft breasts against his back and chest and pushed their wet faces into his neck, front and back.

"Don't worry, Dad, it's gonna be okay," Wanda sobbed.

Wally raised himself a little so he could look down over Wanda's head at the TV screen. And thought, it's not working, it needs more white.

Twenty-seven

The light grew dusky as the afternoon waned and the rain drummed more loudly on the skylight. As the yellows went flat and the reds and greens darkened toward black Charles gave up on natural light and turned on the floods. He painted for a while longer, then took a break and put a pot of water on the range, and while he waited for the water to heat, stepped back into the big open space between the kitchen and his easel and looked back at the long brick wall. On it were his newest paintings, the first works of the New Neo-Post-Post-Modernistic Patternism school, which he had founded a couple of weeks after they let him out of the Bayview psycho ward.

Charles knew he might have a problem getting people to accept New Neo-Post-Post-Modernistic Patternism—the thirteen syllables didn't exactly glide off the tongue—but he wasn't gonna change the name, because that's what it was. He'd tried the name on Janice, but she was so busy selling out, as usual, that she just said, "You're crazy," as usual. Boyce, who in his before-Carnita incarnation would have said something envious and stupid and irrelevant, which would have had the merit, at least, of provoking an argument, now wallowed in oblivious, glassy-eyed pain. And all Carnita said was, "Your shit looks like the shit I was doin' a year ago," which of course was a fucking lie. She could never, never, **NEVER**, not in a lifetime of monastic dedication to the sole purpose of raising the level of her work, approach his level of artistic integrity, originality, and quality. **Nev-er-ev-er**.

Still. Scrutinizing the paintings like this. All of them at one time, under those brilliant 6000° K floods. He had to admit he glimpsed the barest hint of a glimmer of similarity; an elusive, almost-impossible-to-detect resemblance between what he was doing now and something he had seen in her work. Elusive. But there. There to puzzle out in coincidental form, in coincidental juxtaposition of color, in coincidental range of color, in coincidental shape, in coincidental repetition of pattern. He chewed his lip: quite a bit of coincidence, he thought uneasily.

It had been Carnita's outrageous lie (that his shit looked like her shit) that made Charles think of representing one of his New Neo-Post-Post-Modernistic Patternism paintings as her's and trading it to the Leuters in exchange for Boyce's dental work. It had been a shocking thought: a piece of *his* work carrying *her* name? He'd rejected the ridiculous idea, of course. But it wouldn't stay rejected. It kept popping up in his consciousness. It was on one of those days when the painting was going well and his confidence was on the flood that he found the generosity of spirit to let himself realize that it made sense, because something needed to be done about Boyce's health. He'd lost forty pounds since Carnita moved in and the pain from his teeth had grown so intense that it was impossible for him to eat anything but warm rice pap spiced up with the tartness of aspirin. He was sinking rapidly, and most of the time was so pale even his tattoos looked bleached.

Charles had broached the idea to Carnita, who had squinted suspiciously and said, "You're crazy." But she'd gotten interested when he pointed out that a healthy Boyce would be more energetic than an unhealthy Boyce.

Charles poured a cup of coffee, then dragged a kitchen chair to the middle of the big open area between kitchen and studio space under the skylight and sat and sipped the steaming coffee and viewed the wall covered with his paintings. When he finished the coffee he rose and cleaned his brushes and went to the bedroom he shared with Janice, when she let him, and got one of her umbrellas. He looked at his watch. It was time.

—

"Bullshit," said Charles.

"Does too," said Carnita.

"Bullshit," Charles reiterated. "Inspiration has nothing to do with art."

"Well how about—" She twisted her face into such strenuous thought that for a moment she resembled Popeye, except Popeye had no metal embedded in his face. "Okay then, how do you explain—um-m-m, let's see—how do you explain—Piccolo?"

"Hard work."

"What about—Arto. What about him?"

"More hard work. All hard work, as a matter of fact. If you'd read Leon Arto's autobiography you'd know that. In there he wrote, 'Inspiration is bullshit. Genius comes out of labor, not inspiration.'"

Charles settled back in his chair and resumed his browse of *Teenage Beauty Contests*, satisfied that once again he had demolished a Carnita Vovo stupidity, even if he had to use a made-up quote to do it. That didn't weaken his satisfaction, of course, for while the quote was technically a lie, it was essentially true; it would have been just like Arto to say that, if he'd thought of it.

Suspiciously: "Did he really say that?"

Charles glanced up disdainfully, but didn't disdain to answer.

"Well, I don't care what you or Arto say, I can't work unless I'm inspired."

Charles resumed his study of a picture of Miss Teenage Wichita, whose private parts were almost obscured by a diaphanous all-but-invisible bathing suit; a wet, shrink-wrap, see-through thing that you could scarcely see on the tight tanned skin. That was what had attracted his attention: the brevity of the bathing suit. That and the photographer's subtle eye for light and shadow, evidenced by his breathtaking skill in modeling her *mons veneris*, which rose in sensual triangularity off the page in a stunning perfection of form. A Greek perfection. If the architects of the Parthenon had seen it they would have blushed at their own crudeness. This photographer understood art. And he also knew what the mother of this young girl wanted the readers to know about her.

The stirring in Charles' groin made him think about Janice, who had been rejecting him in recent weeks. Of course that had the effect of rekindling his appetite for her, which he had to admit had been on the wane. He hoped wistfully that she was having a good day for a change. Most evenings she returned from work so down or so pissed she wouldn't even talk to him, much less let him get near her. In the first few weeks after his release from Bayview things had gone well. They'd slipped into the manic life they'd shared thirty years before, when they'd painted and argued and screwed all day every day. And then Whipple finally got to her with his sweet-talking business bullshit until he had lured her out to help him set up another gallery—and of course that did it. In spite of Charles' warnings she'd bounced back into a job and a skirt and uptightness like she was on a rubber band.

"Well, I can't work without inspiration," Carnita said again, in case Charles hadn't understood.

Another grunt came from down the hall, followed by Tim Leuter's voice: "The hammer."

Carnita closed her eyes and shivered: "Why does he have to do that?"

"Because they're just stumps. He has to break 'em up with a chisel, then dig the pieces out."

Another grunt, this one desperate, then a tink-tink-tink-tink-THUNK, followed by a strangled, gurgly scream, then silence. Then Tiny Tim's voice: "Did his heart stop again?"

Shelly: "No, he only fainted."

"Good, maybe he'll be still for a minute. Christ, I never saw anyone wiggle and jump about like this fellow. Cowardly, is what I call it. For a while I thought we were going to have to waste money on anesthesia."

Carnita had grown even paler than normal. "Charles? Is Boyce gonna be okay?"

"Don't worry, he's okay."

"God! How long are they gonna take?"

"As long as it takes."

"But Jeez, it's been hours already."

From the other room: "Hold his mouth open."

"I can't. The blood—his jaw's too slippery."

"Get the wedge then."

Silence.

"Hurry up, I wanna dig these last three out before he wakes up Oh, shit. Look, the sonofabitch bled on my shirt. Fucker bled all over me. Look, it's ruined."

"I told you to wear the plastic apron. Take it off. Here, let me have it."

The sound of running water.

Charles turned the page and found Miss Teenage Ponca City. Tawny-skinned. Dark-eyed. Black-haired. His groin stirred to life again. What a great magazine! Marking the place with his thumb, he flipped through the pages, looking for a subscription mailer he could rip out give to Carnita to give to Wikka. He didn't find a mailer, but he did find that several of the pages were stuck together, making him think that something really good must be on those pages. He turned back to Miss Teenage Ponca City, examined her closely, decided that her mother had definitely gotten this girl a wax job. So they could veil the girl's depilated treasure with even skimpier pieces of cloth and flimsier strings than they had used to shelter Miss Teenage Wichita's treasure. Looked like mosquito netting. Making a bathing suit out of mosquito netting: he was impressed.

"Hurry up. I can't do this alone. His damned head's flopping all over the place."

"All this blood, I hate it. I don't know why you insist on doing this on Sundays."

"It saves a couple of hundred bucks is why. Now hold his head. There's only three more."

Tink-tink-tink-THUNK.

"Oh shit, I'm gonna puke," Carnita gasped. She jumped up and pushed through the glass door and across the sidewalk to the curb, where she offered her breakfast to traffic hissing by in the rain.

Charles rolled up the magazine and rose and stuck it in his back pocket, then went to the magazine rack and looked for other numbers of *Teenage Beauty Contests*. He found one and was immersed in it when he heard the sound of shuffling feet. He looked up and saw head-lolling, cross-eyed Boyce, one arm around Shelly's shoulder, the other around skinny, bloody-chested Tim's shoulders, grinning lopsidedly to show the white of his new teeth, only you couldn't see the white for all the blood.

"This should not be news," Wikka said, tapping the open page of her notebook, which rested on the table in the center of the new kitchen. "I've been warning you for weeks."

Charles leaned forward and looked at the two columns of numbers. He noticed a pattern: the numbers became smaller from the top of the page to the bottom.

"Yeah, but you could've warned us more often," Carnita said. "Then we would've had time—"

"I warned you," Wikka said patiently, "every time you spent a nickel. I warned you about how much those fancy lights cost, about how much the kitchen was going to cost, about how much the bathroom would be. I warned you about buying all this food and all that paint and canvas. None of which *you've* used." She looked coldly at Charles as she added, "Which have been used by someone whose work *doesn't* sell, while the artist whose work *does* sell isn't painting anything."

"I can't work without inspiration," Carnita pouted.

"It's time to get inspired."

"She lives here, she pays her way," Charles interjected. "That's the deal."

"She is paying everyone's way."

"You can't just get inspiration," Carnita explained. "That's not how art works. Inspiration comes when you—when you—when you get inspired."

"Our deal was she buys the food and paint and pays the rent," Charles continued. "It was her idea to buy a kitchen and a bathroom and all these flood lights. I was perfectly happy pissing in the old toilet."

"I *need* a bathroom. And I'll need light when I start painting again. And I need a kitchen, too."

"You can't boil water," Wikka said.

"Anybody want cookies?" This from Boyce, aproned, his grinning white teeth surrounded by the paisley counterpoint of tattooed chin and cheeks and nose, a plate of chocolate chip cookies in one hand, the coffee pot in the other.

"Apparently nothing I say will influence any of you. Okay, so be it. I know my duty and I've done it. I have just told you the same thing I told you last week. And the week before. The money is running out. If we don't get some money pretty soon, I won't even be able to pay the rent on my apartment. Then I'll have to move into this pig sty."

Wikka, grim-faced, arms crossed over pillowy breasts, let everyone think about that for a minute. Charles, sitting on a stool, raised his eyebrows, pursed his lips, leaned back, and thought about it. Carnita pouted. Boyce plopped the plate down on the table, right in the middle of the silence, next to Wikka's calculator. He took a cookie, and still grinning whitely, bit off half, and chewed with enough ostentation to show off the taste of the cookie *and* the whiteness of his grin. Abruptly, Charles rose and went out of the office and walked across the large floor to the brick wall and switched the floods on. He stood looking at the paintings for a couple of minutes while the others in the office watched him.

When, years later, they wrote their memoirs, they would tell different versions about what happened next. Charles would say he came back into the office and instructed Carnita to tell Whipple that she had enough work for an exhibition. Carnita would protest that she had no work to show Whipple; and he, Charles—in the interest of their co-operative community—would say that he would permit her to show *his* paintings as her work. Carnita would demure, saying her work just didn't measure up to his, but Charles would insist: they lived in *his* cooperative and he, as their leader, had responsibilities. He would make whatever sacrifice was necessary to keep it together. Tearfully, Wikka would congratulate him on his nobility.

Wikka would describe the event a little differently. In her version Charles would beg her, Wikka, to let him show his trash as Carnita's work. He would plead that he'd been studying Carnita's style for months, to learn how to paint better; and he had become such an adept student of her technique that not even Whipple would question the authenticity of the work. Charles would plead that he wanted Carnita's name on his work, because it was such an honor. Wikka would relate that she was appalled at the very idea, and as long as she had breath in her body she would protect Carnita's good name. At which point Carnita would interrupt and say she'd do it. For the money. She wanted money to take Boyce to Greece, where she could get inspired and resume painting. And of course she would insist that Wikka come along to manage things.

Carnita would remember it differently. She would remember that she was astonished, then sickened, that the dirty old sonofabitch could even think such a thing was possible—put her name on his shit? Okay, it was true she'd already put her name on one of his pieces of shit, but that had been for a good cause: Boyce's health. But she'd never do it for money. There were things you just didn't do for money. Then, in Carnita's version, Wikka would begin to cry, saying she would never get to Greece, never, never, never; and then Boyce would close his tattooed lips down over his new white teeth and frown and ask how she expected him to learn how to cook Greek food if he never went to Greece. And of course the filthy old sonofabitch who caused all the problems in the first place would beg her to "please do it, please, please, please do it, it's my only chance to sell my work." Well, what was she supposed to do? Like, how could she say no to all of them.

Decades later Boyce wouldn't even remember the incident. He would remember that all he thought about in those first months of painless teeth was cooking and eating, and all he did, when he wasn't screwing Carnita and eating to keep his strength up, was read about food and cook food.

—

Whipple took two lattes from the young man and gave him some bills. He closed and locked the door and came back into the main room. "The thing is," he continued, "I'm having a little problem understanding this *retrospective* business."

Janice hit the button and the projector ejected one slide and dropped another into the slot. A new image appeared on the screen, of a painting all in blue. She looked at him and waited for him to finish. He gave her a latte and slouched comfortably down on the sofa. He'd stripped off his tie and kicked his shoes off.

"I just can't get excited about a retrospective—not for the grand opening."
"What are you talking about, then? You agreed to this weeks ago."

"Well." A shrug.

"You loved the idea."

"But Leon is so predictable. A Leon Arto retrospective is suitable for a museum exposition, not a gallery opening. A gallery should show what is good art, not what was good art. And besides, what are we going sell? Half the work you want to show is not available."

"If you didn't like the idea, why didn't you say so? Why are you bringing this up now, for God's sake? You were with me on this, you said it was a brilliant idea, great PR, and sure to draw a crowd. And now that I've gotten commitments to show all these paintings you start bringing up objections."

He shrugged, sipped, smiled placatingly, "Guilty as charged. You're right on all counts. I wasn't thinking clearly. The thing is, I hadn't seen the show assembled until this evening." He nodded at the screen. "I haven't really looked at Leon's work for a long time. It comes across as a bit passé, don't you think? A five-foot canvas painted solid blue? A canvas painted solid red? One that's all yellow?"

"Good art is never out of style. The purpose of a retrospective is to remind us of that. That was our message, remember? The timelessness, the universality of art, our dedication to finding tomorrow's good art."

"Yes, of course. Still."

She watched him get up, hike his trousers over his belly, pad across the new tile floor to the desk, get a half-sandwich, and return to the sofa. The white walls and the white-painted windows shimmered in the blue light reflected from the screen. He sat and looked up at the square block of blue.

"Okay, Whipple, what's really going on?"

He smiled lazily, almost apologetically. "In the final analysis, art is product. It's a product that people with a lot of money buy to decorate their houses with. It is decorative product. Artists know that, but they don't know how to productize it without admitting the romance, the mystique, is just marketing. That's why they deal with us. We're the packagers."

"What the hell's that got to do with Arto's work? Something's going on here. You were in love with the idea two weeks ago."

"That was then. Before I got a look at the assemblage of his work. And before this other thing came up. This other opportunity."

She was beginning to understand that his objections to an Arto exhibition had nothing to do with Arto's work. "Okay, what other opportunity?"

"Wikka came to me with one of Carnita Vovo's new paintings. I liked it. It's far more polished than anything she's done before. She's got fourteen new pieces—enough for a show."

"*Carnita?*"

"She wants a show, and soon. She said if Whipple won't do it, she'll take it elsewhere. Of course Whipple has to do it. Whipple's is the face of Seattle art and the place for Carnita Vovo's work. She's painting with amazing maturity now. I can't image how she developed so fast. I was amazed at her progress. Her brush work is masterful."

"*Carnita?*"

"Why didn't you tell me that she's finished all that work? You see her all the time, up in rabbit warren you live in with Charles."

—

Up in the rabbit warren Janice was screaming, "How could you *do* this to me? *Why* did you do this to me?"

Charles blinked. Those were the only words he understood in all the screaming. And she was screaming—with a blue-veined, red-faced, teeth-clenched fury. He was dumbfounded; he'd never heard such a sound from that mouth. An animal scream, a scream of primal anguish. Shouts he'd heard, yes, and bellows of rage. And snarls. But never anything as frightening as this. It was almost like she really did love him. Was it possible that he was indeed something more to her than a dick with a man attached (which, deep inside, was the way he always thought she thought of him)?

"Why, goddamn you?" Janice screamed.

Shakily: "What are you talking about?"

Still screaming: "You know what I'm talking about, you fuck head!"

Charles looked helplessly around him. Carnita was a woman, perhaps she knew. But Carnita was obviously as astonished as he. She just stood there in her black bathrobe, open-mouthed, a glass of milk in one hand, a sandwich in the other, her face metal gleaming yellow. And then Janice stopped screaming. The cords of her neck relaxed, the red splotches on her face faded. She started crying, the first evidence a pair of tears running down her cheeks. She sobbed, wilted into a heap, and disappeared into some convulsive unknown grief.

Twenty-eight

It wasn't Ethel's night noises that kept him awake. He was used to her snoring. Something else was stealing his sleep. When he began to experience occasional sleeplessness, in the weeks after the hearing, he thought perhaps it was because he feared the surgery they all wanted him to undergo. But after much thought over many nights he became convinced that the surgery, while dangerous, could not really change him. He did not believe anything could change his need to draw and paint. Nonetheless, nighttime unease and the sleeplessness continued and he just couldn't figure out why.

He had thoughts like these only in the deep quiet of the night, never in the daytime. In the daytime he was too busy with his painting and drawing—those important explorations that consumed every moment of his waking hours. Discovery is like that. It devours you. The process of uncovering, the stripping away of obscurity, the difficult and necessary work of clarifying relationships between objects, the reasoning out of causalities and the points and counterpoints of space, time, shape, texture, color, was so intensely mental that, once he got going on a painting or a drawing, distraction by other concerns was simply inconceivable. In the daytime he was so busy painting and drawing that he couldn't think about anything else.

A shock of recognition got his heart to racing: the answer was right there in front of him. It had been there all along, and he was amazed that he had not seen it. He smiled at the dark ceiling. To discover what was causing his sleeplessness all he had to do was pick up his pencil and draw. Understanding would flow out of the pencil. That was his path to discovery, and he would discover his fear by drawing it. The recognition that he could draw his way to understanding this puzzle as he drew his way to understanding the other subjects of his drawings and paintings got his heart pounding so loudly he thought the racket must awaken Ethel. His fatigue melted away and he felt energy fueling his limbs. He tossed the covers back, swung his legs out of bed, stumbled over the heap of clothing he'd left at bedside, stepped into the darkness and crashed right into the chest of drawers that he'd walked around every night for thirty-three years, fumbled for the doorknob on the wrong side of the door, finally got the door open and went down the hall to his studio and turned on the light and grabbed his sketch pad and some pencils and went to the kitchen. He opened the sketch pad on the table and looked down at the last drawing he had completed, a self portrait. As he studied the sketch his confidence rose: he knew how to discover with a pencil. He sat down, flinched when the cold plastic met his bare ass, and turned to a clean page.

It wasn't as easy as he thought. Uncovering and exorcising the cause of his anxiety by drawing it was turning out to be very hard indeed. Harder even than the mind drawing he had taught himself that day when Judge Nutt took his sketch book and pencils away from him. He looked at the clock. He'd been at it for an hour and a half and all he had to show were a few unimaginative sketches. Instead of discovering his problems in the lines of new and revealing drawings, he'd found himself sketching familiar images: Pete's face as he'd looked down on him and scolded him about moving while he was in the machine; the face of Doctor Ramsay as he'd stood with a pointer before a half-dozen radiographs and MRI scans of a skull; a portrait of Roy and Ethel, sitting side by side on the bench of a picnic table, looking like American Gothic with purple nose and pink pendulous cheeks; George in his slack-jawed TV-watching profile; Wanda in her Safeway apron, looking even more primly tight lipped than Ethel, and more like Ethel's twin than she did in the flesh; and another self-portrait, this one a sketch of himself sketching himself.

He realized the house was getting colder, and that all he wore was the T-shirt in which he had gone to bed. He went back into the bedroom where he stood for a moment listening to Ethel's noises. He thought about climbing back under the covers to her warmth, but he was too restless to sleep. A walk. A good long walk would leave him peaceful and relaxed. He would walk and think. He got his clothes and came back to the kitchen where he dressed.

He left the house and walked down the long driveway to the road. Above him a full moon floated in its bowl of sky, its pale light intermittently penetrating the tree tunnels through which the roadway curved. The night was silent except for the crunch of his shoes on the graveled shoulder and the hum and swish of infrequent cars and the clatter of his feet exploding through wind-blown mounds of maple leaves. He walked the two miles down the hill to the junction at Juanita Bay. There he went to the right, following the abandoned section of piling-supported roadway over the wetlands along the lake shore and then past the park where he'd painted many hours away and up the hill and into the small-town neighborhoods along Market and down into the Kirkland business district. It was only when he got to the bottom of Market, where it ends at the boat ramp in the heart of town, that he realized his feet were taking him to Janice's gallery. But the gallery wasn't a gallery anymore. It was a shop that sold cards and touristy gifts. He stopped across the street from its darkened street-level windows, looked up at the windows of what had been her apartment. He'd come to see her a couple of weeks after the gallery closed and had learned from the clerk at the art-supply shop down the street that she was living somewhere in Seattle. He wondered once again what she was doing and wished she was there behind those windows, because he needed to talk to her. A single car came around the corner two blocks away and headed in his direction, passed him, and continued south on Lake Washington Boulevard. He began walking.

Three hours later he was on the I-90 floating bridge. The moon was low in the western sky, the lake flat and black, the bridge wet from a passing shower. The cars and trucks of the early-morning commute roared by toward the city across the mile of lake spanned by the many lanes of the two floating bridges. Wally walked at a steady pace, following the red tail lights rocketing away from him. He was only peripherally aware that his legs were beginning to tire, that his feet were sore. His focus had gone outside of himself: he was once again immersed in the problem of how to paint the night, when your eyes see only shades of gray and black, except of course for the tiny little islands of brightness created by humans—orangy-yellow splashes of street lighting, red taillights, the bright specks of yellow that modeled the hills of the city rising out of the lake. And how to render water that was as black as ink; how to convey the Technicolor vividness of red taillights volleying away from you like tracers into the night. His mind swarmed with observation, questions, discovery. There was no room for the fear that had dogged his sleep.

He made his way up over the hill and down into the Rainier valley, then up Rainier to Jackson Street, and down the gentle grade toward the waterfront. Passing under the overpasses of I-5 and then along the eastern boundary of the International District, past the Vietnamese shops and stores, coming finally to the King Street Station in the old heart of the city with the sun behind him. Tired, footsore, no longer observing and discovering; moving in a daze now; weak and hungry and ready for the sleep that had earlier eluded him. He crossed the street, intent on resting in Occidental Park for a few minutes before calling Ethel and letting her know he was all right; that he had just gone out for a walk and had lost track of the time. She would be very angry.

He limped through Occidental Square, over still-wet cobbles between the fronts of galleries, restaurants, a bank, all with darkened windows, and across Occidental Street to the cobble-stoned park with trees and benches and sculptures. No one was sleeping on the bench nearest the street. He crossed the street to the bench, sat on the dew-dampened slats, stretched his legs out before him, crossed his arms over his chest, and was asleep before he even relaxed.

Voices woke him. Strange, coarse voices superimposed on sounds of traffic. Wally raised his head and opened his eyes. The day was bright and unseasonably warm. Sharing the bench with him were two pony-tailed men in soiled jeans and coats. At their feet were bedrolls and knapsacks. Their smell was strong and unpleasant. Wally stretched his legs and yawned. The benches in the square block of park were occupied by professional indolents—like his two companions—and by clerks and salespeople and shoppers out to take the noonday sun with their sack lunches. The scent of new bread from the open doors of the bakery on the western boundary of the park contributed to the sensual laziness of the day and reminded him that he had not eaten.

The indolents who shared his bench looked him over, perhaps wondering why this not-dirty, not-smelly, not-badly-dressed old man was sleeping on a park bench. "You got any cigarettes, man?" one of them asked.

Wally shook his head. "I don't smoke."

"Any spare change?"

"Ethel won't let me carry money." He smiled and stood. Feeling the soreness of his feet and calves, he limped over to the drinking fountain, where he drank long, to take the edge off his hunger. He thought about Ethel once again, and resolved to call her immediately. She would be angry, as usual, but not as angry as she'd be if he put it off and the police started to look for him again. He walked stiffly past the bench on which he'd slept, and the two young indolents, who eyed him. When he saw a break in traffic he crossed the street to Occidental Square. As he entered the Square he saw, on windows facing the street and the square, an arc of silver and black lettering that identified the establishment as a branch operation of Whipple Galleries of Fine Art, Inc.

He'd met Whipple when Janice took him to Whipple's Kirkland gallery over a year ago. Curious, he went to the window and looked into a large room with high white walls. Two young women in jeans and T-shirts were raising a painting against the wall. It was the only painting in the otherwise empty room, and though he did not have a clear view of it, the painter's style looked familiar. One of the women reached around to the back to loop the wire over the hanger, then they lowered the painting against the wall. They went into the back room and returned with another painting. Wally wanted to find out more about this. He went around the corner to the door. On the glass was a sign announcing the opening—that very evening—of an exposition of the newest work of Carnita Vovo. Carnita Vovo? Wally was puzzled. The two paintings were Patternistic, to be sure, and the flamboyant colors suggested the palette of Carnita Vovo, but these paintings were much more controlled and far more thoughtfully structured than any work he'd seen by Carnita Vovo. He tried the door and found it locked. He went back to the window and watched the young women hang a third painting. He studied the paintings again. There could be no doubt about it, these were not the work of Carnita Vovo. They were Charles' work. He tapped on the window to get their attention so he could explain to them that they'd made a mistake, but they only glanced once over their shoulders at his tapping. Thereafter, they ignored him.

"You could make a lot of money doin' that, man."

Wally handed the dirty-faced young man the piece of paper on which he had created a sketch. Wally had managed to portray his dirtiness as an integral part of his personality. This greatly impressed the young man.

"Seriously, man, this is good." The young man studied the bearded face that glowered at him from under a Mariners cap. "This is one mean dude." He giggled and handed the drawing to the other man on the bench, an equally-smelly, equally-dirty fellow with a long greasy ponytail and a matted blond beard embedded with bread crumbs.

Wally began a sketch of the fountain and a leafless maple tree under a lamppost in the middle of the park. The light behind him brightened as the streetlights came on. In the sky above, the orange was spreading from the west and the powdery blue behind the orange was degrading to purple. He looked over his shoulder toward the window of the Whipple gallery. All of the interior walls were hung now with paintings and the two young women wore skirts and high-heeled shoes. They were still moving around, doing things, but now they moved under Whipple's direction. Whipple, short and round and pink and completely bald, was immaculately dressed in a gray suit and vest and red. He was saying something to one of the young women and the other was dragging a table out of the back room. Wally returned his attention to his spiral notebook and the sketch of the fountain.

He'd spotted the spiral notebook in an alley trash can, and naturally he'd picked it up and opened it, and luckily found that most of the pages had writing on only one side. He'd gotten a pencil from the first person he asked. After that he passed a very pleasant afternoon in the park, drawing people and trees and benches and features of buildings. Most people had ignored him, even when he shared their bench and drew pictures of them. Except the professional indolents. They were curious and unselfconscious enough to crowd up and talk among themselves as they watched him draw. One had been so impressed he'd invited Wally to join him for dinner at The Good Shepherd Mission over on First. Wally was tempted, having had no food since the day before; but he declined when he found that you had to stand in line until six, then go in and listen to some preaching, which he didn't really mind, except he was told it would last at least a half-hour and that it would take another half-hour to get through the food line and a half-hour to eat. By the time he finished eating he'd have missed part of Charles' show.

"Hey, man, I got a idea. How we can make some money."

The dark-bearded young man leaned closer to Wally, to get his attention. His smell was strong enough to make your eyes water. Wally leaned away from the young man and continued drawing.

"See, what we do is this. We go over to the Elliott Bay Bookstore—lot a foot traffic there—or maybe over at that restaurant on King Street, and make a little place for you to like, sit or something, then you draw a picher of me or Jim here. You know, to get people interested. Oh, yeah, an' we can tape some of these pichers up on the window an' make a sign sayin' for sale or somethin', and maybe we say for three-fifty? Is that enough?"

Wally kept drawing.

"But the paper's got lines on it," Jim objected. "An' words on the other side. An' the edges is ragged where he tears it outa the book."

"Well, shit, so what? They don't have to look at that side. We can go three-fifty, easy. Even if the paper's got lines. Look at this, for Chris' sake." He held up one of the drawings to prove his point.

Jim nodded, convinced.

"Okay, three-fifty it is," the dark-bearded one said. "How we gonna split it?"

Jim pondered. Three-fifty divided three ways. Wally drew.

"Okay, how 'bout this. I get a buck, Jim gets a buck, an'—what's his name, anyway?"

"He told me Wally."

"Wally here gets the other buck. 'Cause he's doin' the drawin'."

Jim nodded his agreement to the equity of the proposed distribution and Wally drew.

Twenty-nine

"She just ignores me," Charles complained.

"A positive sign," Doctor James said. "Shows there's hope she might regain her mental health."

Charles had just visited Janice in the craft room, where he had tried to engage her in conversation while she glued little pieces of tile into a metal frame, to make a trivet. She had acted like he wasn't even there, so he'd gone to Doctor James' office to see if he'd tell him what to do about it.

"She makes me feel like I'm not even there. Every time I visit it's like that."

"She's shutting you out. Because she doesn't like you anymore. That is a positive indication, of course."

Charles looked miserably down at his hands.

"She talks to *me*," Doctor James continued, with a satisfied air. "Loquaciously. With bubbly enthusiasm at times. I've discovered in that apparently wacko lady an intelligent, witty, altogether charming conversationalist, even when she's stoned. You've noticed, of course, that we keep her stoned. It's to control her depression. She says she likes being stoned because she doesn't think of you when she's stoned." He knitted the fingers of his hands together over the mound of his vested belly. "You should hear some of the stuff she says about you when she gets to talking about her sex life. All about your impotence."

Charles bristled. "I'm not impotent."

"She told me all about it."

"It's not impotence. Sometimes a man just don't want to fuck."

"A real man always wants to fuck. Impotent men don't. But we're not gonna talk about your problems, because you haven't got any money. Back to Janice. I tell her she has no responsibility for your impotence, though impotence usually is the fault of women. Not in your case, though. In your case it's because you're a drug addict."

"I'm not a drug addict."

"I told her none of your preversions surprise me. The minute I laid eyes on you I knew I was looking at a prevert. What surprises me is she ever saw anything worthwhile in you, even when she was a vulnerable, innocent child and you were a preverted child molester."

Irritably: "The word's *per*-version. And I was never a perverted child molester."

Doctor James, with raised eyebrows: "You'd know all about *pre*version, wouldn't you. Well, if you weren't a *pre*verted child molester, what kind of child molester were you? She was pretty graphic in her descriptions of what I'd call preverted child molestation."

"She wasn't a child."

"Semantics. What's a child? But this is not about you, anyway. You're way beyond redemption, but she's worth saving."

Charles' insides were churning with what he thought might be guilt.

"How much longer before she's back to normal and she can leave?" he asked.

"She has to leave soon—she's broke."

"You were willing to keep me indefinitely."

"I was sheltering you from the prosecutor until we could get you certified as temporarily insane, in exchange for your cooperation in providing material for my book. Remember?"

"Oh, yeah."

"Having you here for observation was necessary for my book. Otherwise I'd have handed you over to the cops in a microsecond."

Charles left Bayview and walked the two miles back to the Co-op. There he tuned the radio to classical music, to drown out the sounds coming from the office-cum-bedroom, and smoked a jay while he arranged a new canvas on the easel under the skylight. He picked up a piece of charcoal, confronted the white, and raised the charcoal to begin a layout. His head, however, seemed confused about what the hand was about to do, so after a minute of standing there he dropped the charcoal on the work table and got a sketch book and went to the kitchen and put it on the table and prepared a cup of coffee. But he was too tense, too nervous to sit. He had always been like this before a show, but the anxiety this time was intensely complicated by his feeling of guilt over Janice's condition. He went to his easel, picked up the charcoal again, and made a sweeping diagonal line. But he could think of nothing to add to the line. He raised his hand, but that appendage wouldn't help at all. Sighing, he dropped the charcoal on the work table and looked up at the skylight. The orange was deepening to red, over patches of blue. It was almost time.

From the office-cum-bedroom the sounds of love-making intensified; finally, after forty-five minutes of bumps and thumps and panting and grunts, they were entering the familiar endgame: urgent feminine whimperings of ow, ow, OWW, oh, OWWW, accompanied by louder and louder and faster and faster thump-slap-thump-slap-thump-slap-thump-SLAP-THUMP-SLAP-SLAP-SLAP-SLAP-SLAP. She would come soon and you would know it when she screamed. As a matter of fact people down the stairs and across the street would know it. Jesus. Charles shook his head disgustedly. Enviously. And went to the bathroom and turned on the shower. When he finished he toweled himself dry and wiped the mirror off and looked at his face and decided he wouldn't bother shaving. Not for *this* opening. He grabbed his clothes into a bundle and came out and found Carnita waiting with a towel wrapped around her torso. Ignoring his nakedness, she slipped around him and turned on the shower.

    Ignoring him: yeah, lately, women were doing a lot of that. First Janice. Now Carnita. But he understood why Carnita ignored him—she was embarrassed, because she knew he wouldn't do what she was about to do. Not that he gave a fuck what went on in the dimwit's brain. If she had a brain. Of more interest, and some concern to Charles, was what was happening to Boyce. His new teeth had brought changes that no one could have foreseen. As far as Charles knew, Boyce had not even picked up a paint brush since he got his teeth. Hadn't offered even one of his stupid and unsolicited criticisms of his—Charles'—work. Indeed, the only thing he seemed to have any passion for was food. And of course Carnita's snatch, when Carnita could get him up; which was pretty much when she wanted him up, now that he was healthy; which seemed like all of the time; which of course could be the reason neither one of them got around to painting any more.

    He went to Janice's bedroom, which, in her absence, he had taken over, and kicked through the clothes on the floor until he found some jeans that were not too dirty, a shirt that didn't look like he had painted in it very often, and some socks that had a memory, at least, of being clean. In a minute he was dressed. He combed his hands through his hair and called it good, grabbed his ancient paint-speckled Army-surplus parka, and left.

Thirty

"I was shocked of course," Whipple said. "I blame myself—I should have seen the signs and sent her home to rest. Not that she has a home. She went back to Charles Gas, you know, to that desolate cave of misery that he calls an artists' cooperative. Which I'm sure didn't help her problem one bit."

At the mention of Charles Gas, Dillip darted a look for his bodyguards. One—a burly fellow in a baggy suit—stood at the door comparing the faces of people entering the gallery with a picture that he held in his hand: a picture of Charles Gas.

"After what he did to her. And to you, for that matter. Your nose looks good, by the way—isn't it marvelous what they can do with reconstructive surgery?"

"You didn't invite him, did you?"

"Certainly not. I eighty-sixed him decades ago."

"Where's Pietro?"

Whipple looked around, saw the baggy suit at the door. He pointed. "You mean that one?"

"No, no, that's Guido. Pietro's the tall one."

"Maybe he's in the back. I'm sure he's around here somewhere."

"I don't like this. Shit, where is he?"

Soothingly: "It's all right, no one's going to hurt you."

"Easy for you to say, you're not an art critic."

At that moment Pietro came out of the back room, zipping his fly.

"There he is," Whipple said, patting Dillip on the shoulder. "See, I told you. Everything's going to be okay."

"Thank God. For a minute I had this awful premonition that Gas was already here, taking out my bodyguards one at a time." He shivered. "God! Why do I do this? Hanging around galleries is so dangerous. When's she coming, for God's sake? I need to get out of here."

"You know Carnita. Whenever she gets here, she'll be here."

"I hate going to galleries."

Einstein said good theories are always straightforward and simple. $E = mc^2$ for example. But apply his energy-mass equation to the real world and see how simple it really is. It was turning out that the Nominal Theory of Good Art, which postulates that the goodness of art depends on whose name you put on it, became just as complex as soon as you started applying it to real life; which is what Charles was doing as he sucked on a joint and strode down the brightly lit canyon of Fifth Avenue skyscrapers toward Occidental Park.

Like any good theoretician Charles knew theories are mere speculation until you test them through real-world experience. As a validation of the Nominal Theory of Good Art he was considering the success of Pablo Piccolo. Was it mere coincidence that *all* of the work with Piccolo's name on it was good art? Could it not be—indeed, didn't the laws of probability argue that it was in fact quite likely—that much of the work of Pablo Piccolo was good *because* his name was on it?

In his excitement at reasoning out this new theory he had begun to walk very rapidly. Recognizing this, he made himself slow down; he didn't want to make the same mistake he'd made at the other show he and Carnita Vovo had shared: getting there early and watching all those red dots appear one by one on Carnita's title cards had driven him nuts. And then he remembered that red-dots-on-Carnita-Vovo-title-cards was, in fact, what he wanted to see on this night. Because her red dots would be his red dots. He smiled. So far so good: the Nominal Theory of Good Art was panning out.

It was seven o'clock when he entered Occidental Park. Light from the yellow globes of street lamps lit the park, though not brightly enough to disturb the slumber of a score or so of professional indolents who had finished a busy day of indolence and who had already bundled themselves in blankets and sleeping bags for a well-earned night of rest in their park-bench lodgings. The bakery was closed, as was the cigar store, the toy store, the kitchen shop, and every other retail shop in the neighborhood except the convenience store on the east side of the park, which supplied park residents with necessary victuals such as cigarettes and beer and cheap wine. Straight ahead of him, across the cobble-stoned park, was Occidental Square, on the nearest corner of which was the newest of the Whipple Galleries of Fine Art, Inc. It wasn't far from Whipple's first Occidental Square gallery, which was the first gallery that he, Charles, had wrecked. For his handiwork on that evening he'd been forever banished from all Whipple galleries. For years that punishment had seemed extreme. But now he didn't even want to show his work in a Whipple gallery. On this night he was showing the work of Carnita Vovo in a Whipple gallery, and who knew—if the fates smiled he would, perhaps, thereafter create the work of someone else and show that in a Whipple gallery. If he could find the right name to put on it. It was turning out that everything depended on name. Just like the theory said.

Even from a block away he could see the gallery was alive with people. The bright color and the movement of all those people cheered him and gave him confidence. He advanced through the park, spotted an unoccupied bench in front of the bank a hundred feet across the cobbled square from the gallery. Perfect: from there he could see everything. He went to the bench and sat, pulled the hood of his parka up over his head to fend off recognition, and jammed his hands into parka pockets.

He could see, above the heads of the crowd, the tops of six of his Carnita Vovo paintings. As the crowd shifted, openings appeared, fully exposing paintings and sections of white wall. Over a period of several minutes he discerned, in those flashes of white and turbulent color, one livid little spot of red on a title card, and then another; and each time he saw one of those splotches of color his heart lurched and fluttered.

He began to imagine himself in there, surrounded by the same worshippers who surrounded Carnita; began to feel the warmth of all that admiration. But he managed to console himself with what he could imagine they were saying about his work. Look at that one there: the fat lady in the big floppy wide-brimmed hat, talking to the tall skinny guy; pointing at one unsold painting, then another. And there comes Whipple, sales pad in hand.

The full weight of this wondrous scene suddenly hit Charles. My god! the fat lady and the skinny man are actually deciding which painting to buy! "Oh, sweet bleeding Jesus," he groaned aloud, faint suddenly from the shock of this epiphany: he was witnessing an art buyer actually buying his work; not trading food for it, or drugs, or an old Nissan beater. He could not remember the last time he actually saw an art buyer doing that. This sacred moment he would remember all of his life. Even in his last moment of life he would remember this as a new and sacred beginning to what is left of his life. This floppy-hatted fat lady and her skinny husband will hang one of his paintings and look at it each day through all of the decades of life that remain to them, and they will come to love it because they will discover therein more and more of the important something that induced them to buy it, and it will become a family treasure, and it will pass down into the family of their son, who will by then be a middle-aged insurance salesman, and he will tell stories of how long it's been in the family, and—But wait! Look! Oh Christ, she's decided: it's to be Number Four. Fat lady, you have a good eye: Four's the best of the lot. And now there are only two unsold—though he can't be certain of that because seven are not visible to him; but his statistical analysis of the situation suggests that since all but one of those he can see are sold, it is likely that of the ones he doesn't see, all but one are sold. Feverishly, he rethinks his statistical analysis. God! Almost sold out! Imagine a Charles Gas show selling out. It's gotta be a big mistake. Stoned on pot and emotion, he giggled foolishly. It is a big mistake: that is what his Nominal Theory of Good Art is all about.

His blood was hot and the bad side of him was starting to get the upper hand. He could hardly restrain himself from going in there and correcting the mistake; could barely keep himself from crashing the gate with paints and brush and angling "Charles Gas" precisely across the lower right corner of every one of those paintings.

But he didn't budge. Didn't move a muscle. With steely determination he made himself sit right there and believe that all those people knew they are admiring the work of Charles Gas. Because he knew that if he went in there he would discover they are in fact admiring the work of Carnita Vovo. And he feared what the bad side of him would do if confronted with that reality. Out here he can inhabit a fictional, parallel universe in which all those art buyers are buying his art; in there he will inhabit the miserable, real universe in which it is impossible to admire his art unless it is Carnita Vovo's art.

Speak of the devil: there she is. The knot of her worshippers has loosened. The admirers draw back momentarily, as if to show her; as if they have just finished preparing her; as if they are the artist and she is the art they have created: all in black—hair, blouse, jeans, lipstick, gloves, cape—except for golden flashes from her metal-spangled snow-white face. Funereal black framing pallid dead innocence. A concoction of the phony-baloney despair she, like so many of her nitwit generation, wear like a uniform but are too inexperienced and too dim to even conceptualize, and which, on her, is as contrived as her art. A cliché. Like her art.

—

Since he got his teeth and gave up art Boyce has been happy—and he knew why. It was because he no longer had pain or hunger. When he gave up art, he gave up pain and hunger. And Boyce was not stupid: he made the correct conclusion: that art is a gigantic fucking fraud, and he no longer gives a fuck for it. In fact, he stayed with it as long as he did only because, with his paisley-ed face and rotten teeth and malnutrition he was fit for nothing else.

He didn't like to think about his life in art, because it amounted to reliving a nightmare of pain, of humiliation, of hunger. The thing that surprised him about his life in art was that he ever thought it was important. Because art's not important. Art is decoration, that's all. What's important is being able to eat and to taste what you eat, and that what you eat tastes good.

But Boyce, being a man of integrity, gave credit where credit was due. He recognized that art gave him a thrill once in a while. Like when he discovered the Aushaus Grupe. Shit like that. But even Aushaus Grupe shit never gave him one thrill anywhere near as thrilling as the thrill he gets every time he bites into a Big Mac or sucks down a chocolate ice cream soda like they make in that little café down on the second level of the Pike Street Market. Not to mention something like the moussaka he made two nights ago. Or ground lamb sautéed in olive oil and garlic and sage and scattered over a plate smeared about a quarter-inch thick with lemony creamy hummous rich with tahini nuttiness and a bite of garlic, topped of course by chopped parsley and scooped up to a watering mouth on a toasted slice of french bread, which is better'n pita any day, because its crunch is the perfect counterpoint to the pillowy nutty smoothness of hummous. With maybe a little tabbouli on the side, to sparkle the mouth. Or a nice omelet with feta and a splash of green Tobasco. Compared to that, art is shit.

Take this show, for instance. Why do these people fight each other to give their money to Carnita for this shit she didn't even paint? He didn't know. Not that he worried his head very much over why a fool is a fool. He's been so busy with food that he's only dimly followed the events that led up to this evening's deception. And he didn't care. He was here because Carnita wanted him here, and it was workin' out fine, because they got food on the tables in back. And not bad food, neither. Some tiny little sandwiches with shit like cucumbers in them and little-bitty pastries with meat inside and some tasty Italian sausage—hard, thin little slices of it, which his new teeth just loved to mash up into a fatty pulp redolent with a spicy meaty tartness—and a half-dozen good cheeses that release a whole spectrum of rich mustiness, one even smells like cum, which surprised the hell out of him, though he had to admit it didn't taste like cum. It tasted pretty good, in fact, especially when stacked on one o' them crispy slices of new apple sprinkled with sugar and lemon. Galas, he thinks they are. And the wine's not bad, neither. For a opening. He was in the back a couple minutes ago talkin' to the skinny little queer who catered the food—Lawrence, he called himself—complimenting him on the cheeses and the wine and findin' out if there was any more food back there that he didn't know about. The queer had blushed and thanked him, then went on to say that most people just don't give a shit what they put in their mouths, but he cares what goes in his customers' mouth, not to mention his own mouth—at which point he smirked, then said he can tell that Boyce is a discriminating man, that he cares what he puts in his mouth. And by the way, he just loves what Boyce has done to his face—those paisley blues and reds surrounding that manly mouth and those lovely portable teeth. The pass passed right over Boyce's head, unnoticed, because by then he was eating more of the soft white cheese that smelled like cum, this time with some scrumptious imported strawberries, and thinking resentfully about how much time he slaved over a hot stove in the Co-op fixin' food for people who stuff it in their mouths with about as much respect as they have for the shit that come out the other end a few hours later.

All these fools—for that's what they are—elbowing one another, pushing at one another, being ugly to one another, just to get close to Carnita because her name is on the bottom of those canvasses Charles painted. He saw the Leuters at the fringe of a knot of fifteen or twenty people who had coalesced like bacon grease around Carnita. He noted how happy the Leuters looked. He waved, grinning big to show them their handiwork, but so intense was their zeal to get close to the Queen of the Evening that they didn't even see him.

He discovered Wikka had come to his side and was talking to him, which surprised him, he being the owner of the penis that was now such a big part of her daughter's life. He gave her some teeth, but she didn't notice the flash of white. She had other things on her mind, things so important that she didn't even realize she was talking, on purpose, to Boyce, who, being a man, has a predatory red aura to go along with his malign penis. He figured for a second that maybe she'd forgiven him for that penis, then realized she was preoccupied by thoughts of money, as usual. She had her calculator out, was holding the thing up for Boyce to look at. Her eyes were shining and her fat cheeks, beneath the metal dangling from her eyebrows, were rosy with pleasure.

—

Philip Dillip was so full of hope now that Carnita had arrived that for the moment he forgot he was in a gravely dangerous situation, surrounded as he was by a crowd that was likely to contain an artist. He'd even had a chance to greet her with a quavery, "Hello, I'd like to talk to you about your work. Privately." And then she was gone, whisked away by Whipple, who said over his shoulder, "Sorry, Philip, but I must steal her, a buyer just has to meet the creator of his wonderful new painting. I'll bring her back, I promise." Of course he hadn't brought her back, he'd taken her to still another buyer who wanted to talk to the painter of the work they'd just paid thousands of dollars for.

The term *hopeful* misstated Dillip's mental state. In fact, he was obsessed. As obsessed as he was the first moment he saw her. Even though she wass no longer the helpless innocent he favored. She stopped being so helpless and so innocent when success came. Success stripped her of innocence. Now she has the hard worldliness of a practiced victor. The metal components of her face still gleam, now like an accoutrement of war. As natural on her as tits. But, notwithstanding the scars and the metal and her transmogrification, he still wanted her. If anything, he wanted her more than ever. But there was that damned unruly mob surrounding her. Even with Pietro and Guido beside him, going into that mob could be suicidal. And where the hell are they, anyway? Are both of them back there with that queer?

—

"Draw yer picher fer a buck, man."

Charles looked at the man, who had moved into position between him and the gallery. "What?"

"Draw yer picher fer a buck. Like this."

Charles watched the dirty-faced bum unroll, with dirty fingers, a piece of notebook paper with ragged edges and hold it out to him, at arms length. The drawing was right in Charles' face, so he couldn't help looking at it.

"Just a buck, man."

Charles' stomach lurched, just like it did whenever he saw the work of a much better artist than himself, which of course didn't happen very often. The last time was just before he went berserk and tore up Janice's gallery. He blinked at the drawing. A magnificent head, made more magnificent by the artist's genius in composing his art on a ragged scrap of paper, which was the perfect medium for the unruly head. Instantly, he hated it and he loved it. Hated it because, by existing before his eyes, it set a standard he could not meet, loved it because it was just so fucking good. And he couldn't help thinking: it figures, the best art is out on the street, at a buck a shot. He raised his eyes from the drawing, expecting to communicate with an artist of sensitivity and intelligence. But all he saw was another dull-eyed indolent who looked like the other professional indolents who had taken over the park: a smelly squat creature with dirty skin, yellow beard, and tangled yellow hair that flared crazily from under a black watch cap.

"It's only a buck, man."

"Show me your artist."

"Hunh?"

"Show me your artist. Where is he?"

The bum wheeled and yelled across the square: "Hey Jim! Wally! This guy wants the artist! Does that mean you, Wally?"

They hadn't sold a single picture in front of the restaurant. Not that Wally noticed, or even cared. All he wanted was to draw, and he had a pencil and a notebook full of pages that had writing on only one side, so he had what he needed. He went along with his new friends because at the moment they had parallel interests: he wanted to draw and they wanted him to draw. Moreover, they were interesting people to be around. Wally'd never been with people like them before, so he drew picture after picture of them, to learn something about them, while they got crankier and crankier because everyone turned them down. When they hadn't gotten a customer even after they lowered Wally's price to a buck, it became clear that the people entering and leaving this particular restaurant were sports fans, and therefore too under-developed artistically to be a viable market for Wally's product. While Wally sketched Jerry and Jim, the two indolent art marketeers talked about going to another restaurant. Maybe a higher-class place. But their talk was just talk. The endeavor was starting to seem too much like work to hold their interest. It was at about that time that Wally decided he wanted to return to the gallery for one more visit before it closed. Since Jim and Jerry had no appointments for the rest of the evening they joined Wally in a stroll back to Occidental Square.

When Wally heard Jerry's yell he was standing with Jim at the side window of the gallery, looking in at one of the paintings. He was explaining Patternism to Jim. He broke off and came around the corner to see what Jerry wanted and immediately recognized Charles.

"Hello Charles, I was hoping I'd see you here," he said, as he approached the bench.

"I'll be damned. That *was* your drawing, just like I thought."

Wally offered his hand. "I loved your show. Though I confess I don't understand why you put Carnita's name on the paintings. When I asked a couple of people they laughed, like I was being funny. Why did you?"

Charles jumped to his feet, grabbed Wally's hand, pumped it. "How did you know? Who told you? How did you know that it's my work?"

"Well—by looking at it."

"No shit?"

"It's terrific work, Charles."

Still pumping Wally's hand, almost hysterically now, Charles exclaimed, "No shit? You liked it? And you knew it was mine? You could tell it was mine?"

"I want to know about Number Seven. How in the world did you get the yellows to come through the blues like that without it going to green? When it does that it just shimmers off the canvas. It's really amazing."

"Seven? You liked Number Seven?"

"It's the best one."

"No, no, not Seven. The best one's Number Four. But seven's good, yes, definitely, it's good."

"No, Charles. Number Four's lovely, but Number Seven's better. Let me show you why."

"Hey man, you said Wally here was gonna draw yer picher, so you owe me a buck."

Wally and Charles had started across the square toward the gallery, both talking at once. Jerry hurried along behind them. He grabbed Charles' sleeve.

"Hey, man, pay up. You owe me a buck."

—

Pietro and Guido had disappeared. And with their disappearance the awful peril of his situation dawned on Dillip. He'd been a fool not to see it sooner. Gas had used his, Dillip's, obsession with getting into Carnita Vovo to blind him to the trap. Gas had erased Pietro and Guido and he, Dillip, hadn't even noticed. Rubbed them out, one at a time. Dillip imagined their bodies, crumpled and bloodied, in the back room. Now nothing stood between him and Gas. All this horror because of his obsession with Carnita Vovo. He wished he'd never heard of Carnita Vovo. He felt panic rising in him again, binding his chest so tightly he could hardly breathe.

"Don't panic," he muttered tensely as he darted his gaze over the room. Oh God, where's it coming from? Would it be Gas himself? Was the pretend artist already here, pretending now to be a buyer of art? Such a perversity would be just like him. Ohmigod! There, coming out of the crowd. He sucked his breath. A tiny little man with a face like a puppet emerged from the crowd, looked coolly at him for several seconds, then moved toward him. A sinister, freckled, big-eyed face with a wide red slash of a mouth. Could this be a Gas executioner? He looked the part.

"Mister Dillip, good to see you again. I'm Doctor Tim Leuter, art collector and dentist. I've been wanting to thank you for a long time. We never miss your column. My wife and I have a valuable collection, thanks to your investment ideas."

Dillip had seen that sneer somewhere. He shivered, felt the panic rising in him, felt himself losing control. "Don't panic," he muttered through clenched teeth.

"Yeah, I know what you mean. Takes time, doesn't it? Look at Carnita. Who'd have thought she could improve so much in so short a time. It's like looking at her work ten or twenty years from now. She's improved immeasurably, don't you think? So immeasurably that Shelley and I bought another piece, even though it's not at wholesale and even though we couldn't get Whipple to budge an inch on price. This is our third Vovo. It's a big investment, but once she dies, we'll be sitting pretty. 'Course that may take a while, her being so young and all. But you never know with this generation of artists—drugs, AIDS, bad eating habits. Gotta be positive about these things. Death can come at any time, eh?"

Death! At any time! What a sadistic thing to say! "Don't panic," he breathed.

"You're right, of course. No need for panic. Patience always wins in the end, eh? Like death. Especially for artists. It's no wonder they all die young, they live like swine. Unhealthy miscreants is what they are. Pigs. You should see their teeth. Green stuff growing on them like on the bottom of a boat that's been at sea for five yours. Of course, you know all about artists. Fortunately for us art buyers death comes early to artists. But the secret is, you have to read the right art critics to find out which art to buy. Except for a couple of bad decisions, which we made on our own, like trading dental work with Charles Gas for one of his paintings, if you can call 'em that, we'd be batting a thousand."

Gas again. He's Gas' man, all right, you can tell by the way he's toying with me. Now that Pietro and Guido are out of the way, he knows he's got me. But maybe—just maybe—I can turn that against him. Just maybe, if I move now, if I go for it, I just might make the door. Courage, Philip! Courage! Just fifteen feet, and you'll be in the open, and once in the open you've got a chance.

At that moment the puppet-faced assassin's attention was diverted by the approach of a frizzy-headed woman a foot an a half taller than he was. Dillip saw the opening and made his move. He bolted for the door, making it in four steps, only to find himself face to face with Charles Gas! By then his heart was pumped so full of adrenaline he couldn't have fainted if he'd wanted to. Now he understood the diabolical completeness of the trap: the puppet-faced assassin inside; Gas outside, waiting. With a cry of horror he spun and hurled himself at the crowd, through which he clawed and slashed, flinging art patrons aside like rags. On the other side of the crowd Pietro, who'd just returned from the back room, looked up from zipping his fly just as Dillip exploded through the crowd. Reflex took control of Pietro, just like reflex ought to take control of a good bodyguard in a moment of unexpected danger. He threw a right that landed with all the power that his two-hundred-and-forty-pounds of work-out-hardened muscle was capable of unleashing—which in Pietro's case was enough to drive a 20-penny spike through an oak plank—smack on Dillip's nose, and as the nose snapped and popped, Pietro's left was already launched toward its rendezvous with Dillip's ear. The one with the lobe bitten off.

Thirty-one

Screams, obscenities, the thuds of meat slamming meat; stunned art patrons herding up like panicked cattle, swaying first against one wall, then another; paintings crashing to the floor; a few patrons scampering through the door before a surge of the crowd clogged it tight; a sturdy pair of matronly women seizing a tiny puppet of a man and pitching him through the plate-glass window; the crowd scrambling out over the sill and the crumpled, bloody body of the tiny man.

These fragments Whipple passed on to the policeman as attendants slammed the back door of the first ambulance and drove off with strobes flashing and sirens beeping and booping. Behind the second ambulance, into which attendants slid other wounded art patrons, a police car flashed blue lights. In the shadows of the car's back seat one could see Boyce's profile.

"It wasn't Boyce," Carnita raged, "it was that fucking Charles Gas!"

The cop studied his notes. "Yep, this has LaFree written all over it. Fits like a glove."

"It wasn't Boyce, it was Gas!"

Whipple put his arm around her shoulders to quiet her. "Take it easy," he murmured. "Everything's going to be all right. Only three paintings were destroyed. We can afford that."

"THREE? I thought it was only one! That's—that's—" Wikka, who'd been standing behind Carnita, fumbled in her handbag, found her calculator, punched some numbers into the keypad. Her eyebrow bangles and her cheek rings quivered and jangled. "Omigod, that's $30,000!"

Carnita put her face right in the cop's face and yelled: "See, you dumb shit? I told you, he's out to get me!"

The cop addressed Whipple: "It adds up to LaFree, all right. His rap sheet's got wrecked art shows all over it. We think he's the character that wrecked the Cushion show in Kirkland. Appears he may be a serial art-show wrecker."

"He only wrecked one other show and that was my show and it wasn't Boyce that did it, it was Charles Gas! It's Gas that's the serial wrecker!"

The officer scribbled something in his notebook, turned a page, wetted the end of his pencil with his tongue. He looked at Carnita with raised eyebrows. "Now, what about you? What's your name?"

"My name? I'm the fucking artist whose show Charles Gas wrecked, that's what my name is!"

"And what might that be?"

"Jesus Christ! No. No, don't write that. It's Carnita. C-A-R-N-I-T-A. Vovo. No, not Vulva, you idiot, Vovo! V-O-V-O."

"Got it. Now, what'd you see?"

"I didn't see nothing, but it had to be Gas. He's out to get me."

The officer shook his head. "I can't write that down. It's not evidence. I only write down evidence. Like LaFree being the serial wrecker."

"Evidence? You want evidence? Wrecked paintings isn't evidence?"

"Did you actually see Charles Gas beat the shit out of Mister Dillip and those other folks? Or wreck some paintings?"

"Well, no, but it had to be Charles Gas!"

"Lady, what did you actually see? With your own eyes."

"I didn't see nothing! I was with a buyer when all this screaming started and then people were running around and jumping out the window. But it had to be Boyce. I mean Charles!"

—

The door slammed back against the brick wall. Carnita Vovo entered and strode murderously across the studio toward Charles, who stood at the easel with Wally, a brush in one hand and a cut-off beer can in the other. The gold in her face glittered with her rage.

"It was *you*, you bastard," she snarled.

"What."

"You had to wreck it, didn't you."

"Wreck what."

"My *show*!"

"You're fucking crazy. I didn't even go inside. Did I, Wally. And it wasn't your show, anyway, it was my show. Why would I wreck my own show?"

"Can I try it, Charles?" Wally asked.

"It was not your show, it was *my* show," she yelled.

"That was my art you were showing, you dimwit," Charles reminded her.

Wally took the brush from Charles' right hand, dipped it into the cut-off beer can in Charles' left hand and turned to the easel, where he began stroking paint on the canvas.

"My name is on that shit so it is MY SHIT!"

Charles' face was now as red as her face and his blood surged as hot as hers. He'd just about had it with this bitch and he was ready—man, was he ever ready—to finally, completely, and irrevocably kick her ass. But he did nothing. Because she had him. She had silenced him, without even understanding how, by simply rubbing his nose in his own theory. Victorious, she turned and marched off to the office-cum-bedroom.

Wally got a brush from the coffee can and picked up the palette. He daubed at a glistening ribbon of yellow and began laying paint thinly on the canvas.

Charles watched Carnita stride across the studio. Only then did it occur to him that Boyce was missing.

"It's hard to lay it on thin enough, but I think I got it this time," Wally said.

"Hey, where's Boyce?" Charles called.

She spun around: "Jail! For you, you scumbag!"

"Or do you think it's still a little too thick?"

"For wrecking my show?"

"For wrecking *my* show! And for beating the shit out of Philip Dillip."

"He did? He beat the shit out of Dillip?"

"No! He didn't do nothing. *You* did. *You* beat the shit out of Dillip."

She went through the door to the office-cum-bedroom and rolled the TV stand out of the way and started dragging clothes out of the chest and flinging them to the bed. Charles handed the can to Wally and walked over to the doorway. He watched her, thinking guiltily that he ought to say something in acknowledgment of Boyce's sacrifice, which was what Boyce's misfortune seemed at that moment to be. But he instantly realized that he, Charles, hadn't done anything to apologize for. Boyce wasn't taking the rap for him. Boyce's calamity was as blameless as nature—in confronting this latest misfortune Boyce was confronting nothing less than his own karma. His present circumstance had become his destiny many years before when he'd been caught with a pocket full of Aspergum in grade school, which had a zero-tolerance drug policy. The resultant rap sheet, the tattoos, failure at art, falling into Carnita's web—these were his destiny. And Charles had to admit there was a grinding logic in that destiny. Everyone knows that if you've been arrested it's likely you'll be arrested again. Look at the record—it's what happens. So hey, you couldn't blame the cops for figuring they had their man when they found Boyce. A man with a rap sheet that goes back so many years, right there at the scene of the crime? Plus, he's a certifiable weirdo. An even more damning piece of irrefutable evidence. It was practically an open and shut case. Boyce would just have to do his time.

"What are you doing?" he asked Carnita.

"What's it look like?"

He watched her for a while, then: "Where you going?"

She jammed one handful of clothing after another into a bag until it was full, zipped it shut, then jerked another bag up on the bed and opened it.

"Greece?"

She dumped a box of clothing into the bag and pressed it down. "As soon as I get Boyce out of jail and I get my money out of Whipple."

"Our money."

Still leaning over the bag, she paused and looked up at him. The light coming in the doorway from the studio floodlights was hard and low and the way it glinted against the gold in her face made him think of a lizard. He almost expected her tongue to come flipping out. But her tongue did not come flipping out. Nor did she respond with words: her smile said it all.

He spoke uneasily: "You're remembering our deal. Aren't you."

She closed the bag, dragged it off the bed, then squatted beside a box of Boyce's things and began pawing through it.

"You're not gonna skip. Are you."

She took socks out of the box and pitched them to the bed and returned to digging in the box.

"If you skip I'll blow the whistle."

Dragging a shirt out of the box and tossing it to the bed, she said, "So blow. Who'd believe a fucked up dried up old drug addict pretending to be an artist? Who never sold a fucking painting at retail. And if by a miracle you did convince one of my buyers that you painted my shit I imagine he'd be real happy you told him how you cheated him out of his money."

He watched her drag an old pair of jeans out of the box, then another shirt. "I raised the bar," he said weakly, knowing as soon as he said it how foolish it sounded. But he continued, because it was all that he had left to say. "You'll never be able to get over the bar. No way. They want my work with your name on it. You'll be going backwards if you deliver your shit with your name on it."

That lizard smile: "You really don't understand, do you."

But he did understand. His Nominal Theory of Good Art was already reminding him of what he already knew: her name is what they want. He watched her close the suit case and stalk past him and across the big open space of the studio and through the door. Only then did he become aware that Wally was standing behind him, talking.

"—show me how you decide which part of the patterns you paint first? I want to learn how to do it vertically, up through all those layers, the way you do it. Instead of horizontally. Please, Charles, I need learn how you do that."

———

And Wally did learn. He learned so quickly that he didn't appear to be learning at all, he appeared to be remembering. Their practice canvas became a painting, and as they possessed the white canvas with their paint, it possessed them, reinforcing the change that was occurring in their relationship. They were becoming peers. With neither of them realizing it, the teaching session became a work session.

To Charles, observing Wally's intensity of focus and the quickness of his development was like looking at his own development in fast-forward, like seeing the decades of his own life compressed to hours. But, while Wally's unconscious virtuosity disconcerted him, it was not as disconcerting as the fact of their collaboration: that they were working together on the same canvas at the same time amazed him; that their hands painted what their collective mind realized amazed him. Even anonymity, that primary demand made on the artist by Charles' Nominal Theory of Good Art, was not as hard to accept as collaboration, with the self denial that any collaboration demands.

Because self is the starting point of art. It is the starting point and the middle point and the ending point. It is the all of art. Self, my, me. Art is me, I—it cannot be us. So how the fuck was it possible that such a fine, strong piece of art came out of their collaboration? How was it that the canvas resting on the easel the next morning appeared to be the work of one hand, one mind? Where had the coherence of their hands come from?

Charles let his head fall against the sofa back and gazed up at the pink and blue of a bright new sky framed by the enclosing grid of the skylight. He stretched his legs to let some of the fatigue settle out. He heard Wally drop his palette and brush into the litter of cut-off beer cans and squeezed-out paint tubes that covered the table.

"Charles."

"What."

"Help me with this, Charles."

"It's finished. Leave it alone."

"But—"

"It's finished. All you're doing is moving paint around. You're gonna fuck it up."

Silence. Charles raised his head, looked at Wally, who stood before the easel, arms crossed; looking pale, stooped, hollowed out. Gazing worriedly at the painting. Charles' eyes moved to the canvas once again and he felt—in spite of his exhaustion and his headache and the soreness in his shoulders and neck—the aesthetic lift that always came when he gazed upon a piece of good art. But that one problem remained: how could it be good? A single ego creates art, not two egos.

Which brought another question to the foreground: whose name should this art carry? He had already decided it was too good for Carnita Vovo's name, even if he was still doing Carnita's art—which he wasn't. And naturally he viewed his own name as the kiss of death. So what name would this art carry? Perhaps a concatenation of names. A collaboration, so to speak. Perhaps Wally Gas? Or Charles Walder? Or Wally Charles? A faint smile: "Gimme that two-oh, Wally," he said, and rose. He approached the canvas, took the brush Wally offered, but gave it back. "No, the sable." Wally handed him another brush. Charles daubed it in a patch of black on the palette and leaned over the lower right corner of the painting and lettered the name "Wally Charles."

He straightened and said, "This means it's finished. Now leave it alone."

"Okay."

"You look like shit, man. C'mon, let's get some food, then some sleep."

Wally followed Charles across the studio to the kitchen, like he always followed Ethel from his own tiny little studio when she came to tell him he needed food or sleep. He sat in the chair that Charles pointed at, like he did when Ethel pointed at a chair, and watched Charles open the refrigerator and get a gallon of milk and put it on the table with a couple of glasses, which he poured full. It was then that he realized he had not eaten for nearly two days. He picked up a glass of milk and drank it down.

Charles opened the refrigerator again. The drawers were full of fresh vegetables and there was a package of chicken, some beef, the remains of a leg of lamb that Boyce had baked a couple of days before, and eggs and ham and bacon. He settled for eggs and bacon. In a few minutes he'd fried a pound of bacon and scrambled a dozen eggs and buttered a pile of toast. He put a couple of plates and forks on the table with the skillet of eggs.

After eating the eggs and bacon they slept—Wally on the broken-backed sofa under the skylight and Charles in Janice's bed. Charles woke in the afternoon, thinking about Carnita. He looked up at the dark underside of the roof, listened to traffic on the street below, and wondered if Carnita would go through with it; and knew, of course, that she would. No way she wouldn't. Not even if he apologized for wrecking her show. Because she had finally gotten it, finally understood that this was the perfect pay back for all the shit he'd handed her. Even a twit like Carnita could see that it was the perfect pay back. And Wikka was there to help her remember it. What about Boyce? He smiled sleepily at the ceiling. Right. Ask Boyce—who's in jail brooding about being in jail because he's blamed, once again, for wrecking a gallery, which he thinks Charles wrecked. Janice? Sometimes the gold-spangled twit listens to Janice. Naw, not if revenge on Charles Gas was what she'd have to give up. He yawned, turned on his side, wished he didn't have to piss, because he knew if he got up he might as well stay up; wished that Janice was there beside him. He wondered if she was still mad at him, wondered if she still loved him, wondered if she was ready to talk to him.

Thirty-two

"She still won't talk to me," Charles said. "She won't even look at me."

Doctor James nodded. "She hates you. It's a healthy sign, of course, because it proves she's sane. If she ever stops hating you—well, that would be crazy."

"But how long is she gonna be like this?"

"How long is she gonna hate you? As long as she keeps being sane, I guess. I'm optimistic on that score because she seems to enjoy hating you. We psychiatrists see that as a healthy sign when we see a patient begin to enjoy something. And there's another positive thing about hating you: hate motivates. You should see how her production in crafts goes up after one of your visits."

"She's only pissed. She doesn't really hate me."

Doctor James smiled. "All of this is academic. It doesn't matter, you see, because mute or not, you get her back. She has no money, and the state's informed us they don't care about her, so this afternoon she's outa here."

Charles chewed his lower lip. Finally: "But will she go home with me?"

"I certainly wouldn't if I was her. But she's broke—so any port in a storm, as they say. Apparently it's your place or the street."

—

The streets were jammed with cars in the full aggressive rush of the evening commute. Janice walked beside him down the long hill into the sun, her hands in her coat pockets, imagining that he wasn't even there, behaving like his imagined absence was exactly the circumstance she desired, while he talked compulsively to prove he was there—and got no response. Nothing. She refused to acknowledge him in any way. Not when he told her the show sold out, not when he told her that Boyce was in jail for wrecking the gallery and beating the shit out of Philip Dillip, not when he told her that Carnita had moved out. Only when he mentioned that he and Wally had painted all night did she respond, and then only minimally—a mere flicker of surprise. He'd gotten to her with that one—mentioning Wally out of the blue like that—and though she recovered without so much as a glance at him, he knew he'd found the leak in her dike. He began digging at it.

"He saw my stuff when they were hanging the show and recognized it instantly. Isn't that a kick?"

No response. They continued walking.

"We were going in the gallery to look at my paintings when the shit hit the fan. I knew they'd blame me, so I turned around and high-tailed it for home."

Silence.

"He followed me like a puppy."

Not the blink of an eye. No sign she even knew he was there beside her. She squinted into the dying sun as if her only occupation at the moment was to witness the day's last glorious minutes.

"He wanted me to show him how I layer patterns and we ended up painting all night. He's a space case, all right, but he's also an amazing painter. I never saw anybody focus like he focuses or learn like he learns. And then turn it around and show it to you better than you showed it to him."

Though she gave no sign, he knew that he'd made the connection. She was plugged in, all right; listening intently, wanting him to continue. You could see it, just barely, in a movement of her eyes or the flare of her nostrils. He made her wait—to intensify the need. They stopped at a corner and he looked off at the purple mountains squatting under the reddening sky, and when the light turned, stepped briskly out into the street, forcing her to hurry to catch up. They walked another block before he spoke again.

"We finished a painting."

More silence. This time he waited for two blocks while he felt her wait become impatience.

"A four-by-four canvas. We never even had to talk about it. It seemed like we knew what the other one was going to do next."

He let her take that in, let his silence play against her silence. They walked wordlessly while traffic hissed and rumbled around them. After a several minutes he continued.

"Twelve hours. I don't remember even taking a break. My legs were aching when we finished and I could hardly lift my arms. Wally wanted to keep painting, but I made him stop for breakfast."

The hill sloped more sharply now. Ahead of them the street bridged over the freeway, which passed along the base of the hill, and beyond the freeway, the square mile of downtown, with its mushrooming stacks of steel and glass. In the distance the ball of the sun had dimmed enough for eyes to gaze upon it, and it was sinking slowly toward the Olympics through a sky clotting up with red. A breeze had sprung up, and though the air was cooling noticeably, they were warmed by their walk.

"I never worked with anyone on a painting, not even with you. Because one person makes art, not two. But Wally and I made art. Our little committee of two produced a fine piece of art." Pause. "And I still can't explain how." He sensed she was ready. "What d'you think?"

She tensed and drew a breath as if to respond, but he didn't notice, for that question about Wally, toward which he'd been leading her, had also led him unconsciously toward a triggering of something in his own head: an unforeseen liberation of every insight and information that he'd stored therein about Wally, and now every fragment of it cascaded down into his consciousness in the form a shocking realization. Their collaboration wasn't really a collaboration at all; it was Wally painting that canvas, with Charles following along.

"I figured him out, Janice."

Janice listened to his explanation of Wally, laughed at him, and then said, in the first words she'd spoken to him in many days, that as usual he didn't know what he was talking about. Wally was crazy. He was a wonderful, lovable, harmless old crazy who'd been made crazy by a bathroom door smashing him on the head. He was a good painter because it was his craziness to be obsessed about painting. Her sneering words did not persuade Charles—hell, he was also obsessed by painting, and that didn't make him crazy, did it? She laughed again. But he wasn't paying attention; he was already asking the next question: "How the hell can a head injury produce an authentic genius?" But Janice's words and her caustic laugh had exhausted her inclination to notice Charles: she clammed up and stayed clammed up until they got to the Co-op, where she greeted Wally with a hug, then viewed the painting he and Charles had executed. And was stunned by what she saw—so stunned she completely forgot how pissed she was at Charles.

—

Charles flushed the toilet, washed his hands and face, went to the kitchen and turned on the light suspended over the counter. He put some water in the tea kettle and while he waited for it to heat, loaded last night's supper dishes into the dish washer, then cleared the remaining bowls and cups and empty wine bottles off the table. Then he went to Carnita's TV, which rested on its stand under the skylight beside the easel on which the Wally Charles painting still rested. He studied the unlit screen for a minute. It was a huge screen—exactly what you'd expect Carnita to buy. The skylight allowed enough light to see some detail, but not enough to clarify or sharpen his perception, or even to show the layered color. He pushed the POWER button. Instantly a fuzzy brightness under lighted the layers of paint that Wally had applied.

Wally's soft voice came from the predawn murk behind him: "You want to work together on it?"

Charles looked over his shoulder, saw that Wally had raised himself on one elbow and was running a hand through his hair. He swung his legs off the sofa and stood and stretched. Charles looked back at the TV screen. Work together on it? Hell yes wanted to work on it with Wally. His hands itched to work with Wally, but not on this. Laying paint on canvas he knew all about. Watercolor on paper he knew all about. But painting TV screens? That was new territory. Moreover, this painting was too good, too important, to be his learning canvas. The tea kettle began to whistle.

"You want coffee?" he asked.

Wally moved to the paint table and picked up his palette and took a spatula from one of the coffee cans and began scraping the hardened paint off the palette.

"I said, you want coffee."

Wally looked up. "Yes. Yes, that would be fine. Lovely." Then he went back to scraping his palette.

Charles went to the kitchen and prepared a pot of coffee, poured two cups, added milk. He brought them back to his work area which, he realized with a jolt, he now regarded as Wally's work area, under the skylight. Charles handed Wally one of the cups, which Wally immediately put down on the paint table and forgot. He squeezed a ribbon of blue out on his palette, daubed a little black into it, mixed it, then leaned over the illuminated TV screen and resumed his work.

Charles watched for a half hour, then went back to the kitchen and made more coffee. He took two cups to Janice's bedroom and woke her.

"He's working on the TV again," Charles said.

She yawned. "So?"

"We need to talk about Wally. What are we gonna do with him?"

"What's to do? Let him paint." She turned on to her side and, facing away from him, closed her eyes.

He put his coffee on the side table, dropped his jeans and stripped off his shirt and climb into bed.

"I thought you were getting up to work," she murmured.

"I was," he said. "But he's taken over my place. And I didn't feel like painting next to him." A sigh. "He intimidates me."

When Charles woke and climbed out of bed it was afternoon and Wally was still painting. Charles went to the kitchen and helped Janice prepare their supper. When it was ready Charles went to Wally and told him to stop painting and come and eat. Obediently, Wally put his brush and palette on the work table beside the TV and followed Charles to the kitchen where they sat.

"Ethel won't let me paint like this at home. Not all I want, like here. She says the paint stinks and it costs too much. But I don't think that's really the reason. I think it's because she thinks painting's what's making me sick. She says I have Pablo Piccolo Syndrome. That's what Doctor Ramsay told her. But I think they're both wrong. I think I'm just crazy. Sometimes I wish I wasn't. But I'm glad I am."

The last sentence he spoke as he looked over his shoulder at the TV under the skylight. He started to rise, but Janice put her hand on his arm.

"After you eat your supper, Wally. You need to eat and then you need to rest."

"But can't I just turn it on and look at it?"

"Just rest a little, Wally. You've been painting all day."

Charles poured the pot of boiling water and spaghetti into the colander. He let it drain, then put the spaghetti back into the empty pot, added the sauce, stirred it around, and brought the pot to the table. Janice rose and got plates and silverware while Charles got wine glasses. He poured two glasses of wine, then poured a glass of milk for Wally.

"Doctor Ramsay says I'm not gonna be crazy for much longer," Wally said.

Charles coiled spaghetti on his fork and stuffed it in his mouth. "Yeah?" he mumbled.

"He says he can fix it. Ethel wants to make me do it. She didn't before, but she does now."

"Eat, Wally," Janice said.

Obediently, Wally picked up a fork and a spoon and began coiling spaghetti on the fork.

"How's he gonna fix it?" Charles asked through a mouth full of spaghetti.

"Cut my head open. Right here." Wally put his silverware down and traced the path of an imaginary incision with his left forefinger from his left temple across the top of his head to his right temple.

Charles stopped chewing. "No shit? They wanna cut your head open to make you forget about painting?"

Wally looked thoughtfully at Charles. "I don't think they can make me forget about painting. They believe it's a sickness and the doctor thinks he can make me well."

Silence for several seconds. Not a hand moved, not a jaw chewed.

Then from Charles: "Wally, what the fucking hell are you talking about?"

Wally told them about the operation, while Charles and Janice stared in horror. Then Wally bolted down his spaghetti and rose and went back to his TV painting.

"What are we gonna do, Charles?"

"Nothing, that's what."

A long silence as they watched Wally.

"Charles—are we committing a crime by letting him stay here?"

He shrugged. "Who's to tell anyone he's here? He can stay if he wants."

"If she's his guardian, like he says—maybe it's like he's a kid. Or something. Maybe it's kidnapping if we let him stay here."

"They'll cut his fucking brain out if we hand him over. The fucking savages."

"But we don't really know that."

"The fucking savages," Charles snarled. "We're not telling 'em."

"But how can we keep him indefinitely? How do you do something like that? Charles, this could be serious. This could be kidnapping. Or something."

"You already said that."

Thirty-three

Reverend Stammer reluctantly mounted the stairs, hesitantly pushed the doorbell and waited, hoping no one was home. Almost immediately Wanda Walder, in her Safeway uniform, opened the door.

"Reverend Stammer, I'm so glad you called. Isn't it terrible what's happened? Everybody's so shocked."

"Any news?"

She shook her head. "Isn't it the awfulest thing? Mom's gone through so much in the last year and now this."

She led the way from the tiny foyer into the living room. The TV had been rolled from its position on the hearth in front of the fireplace out into the middle of the living room. Wanda stepped around it and went into the kitchen. Reverend Stammer followed, but as he came abreast of the TV its big forty-inch screen came into view, and he stopped and gaped, unable to believe his eyes. The screen was painted over by a test pattern, in pointillistic gray and white. It seemed to quiver and glow at the sixty-cycle rate of a real 1950s test pattern. Reverend Stammer was dumbfounded. Not so much because the screen was painted or that the subject was a test pattern, which of course he was too young to have experienced, but because it was breathtakingly, achingly, beautiful. He dropped to his knees before the TV screen. "Unbelievable," he murmured. He raised a hand tentatively to the screen.

"Everyone says that," Wanda said. "Dad did it. When he told Mom he was gonna paint the TV she thought he meant a picher of it. By the time she found out what he was doin' it was too late to stop him so she just let him finish ruinin' it."

"Unbelievable," he murmured again.

"I know. It's such a shame. It wasn't even three years old and it's ruined. The TV man said it won't come off."

"It's—It's—" The beauty of it rendered him speechless.

"I know what you mean. Do you think it was Satan made Dad do it? I do. I told Mom she ought to burn it up."

"Burn it up?" he murmured incredulously. *Burn this? If this, why not Pablo Piccolo's Immaculate Deception? Or—*

The sound of Ethel's voice reminded him of his mission of consolation. She had come into the living room and was saying something. He rose, turned reluctantly from the TV, went to her; and took her hand.

"I was shocked to read about Wally's disappearance. Any clue at all about what happened?"

"Nothing."

"The authorities are still searching?"

George's muffled voice came from the kitchen. "They're draggin' the lake this afternoon. The part where Forbes Creek comes in, 'cause he used to go there an' paint the lily pads."

Reverend Stammer's gaze drifted back to the TV; he couldn't keep his eyes off it. "Amazing," he murmured.

Ethel nodded. "The last thing he painted before he disappeared. It's just awful. I can't stand to look at it. Roy's taking it away."

George's voice, still muffled: "They think he might of drownded."

Ethel's face darkened. "He didn't drown," she flung over her shoulder. "He's just gone off somewheres to draw something and¾" Her voice tightened up and she turned away from Reverend Stammer and went sniffling back into the kitchen.

Wanda and then Reverend Stammer—after a yearning backward glance at the TV—followed her into the kitchen. Roy sat on one side of the table and George, his mouth working, sat on the other behind a cup of coffee and a plate of cookies. Cookie crumbs littered the table before him. "They say this happens all the time. Old people who don't know up from down wanderin' off an'—"

"Wally's not old," Ethel snapped.

"—an' then they find their bones a few years later in some ditch or other."

"Wally's not in some ditch. He's off drawing something."

"Well, old or not, he don't know up from down. That's for sure."

"I guess I could load the TV, now there's some able bodies here to help," Roy offered.

Alarmed, Reverend Stammer stammered, "You're not going to—you're not—you're—what're you—"

"The TV man said it's not worth fixing," Ethel sniffed from the sink where she had gone back to washing the cookie sheet and the mixing bowls. "I just want it out of here—it's such a ugly reminder of how we have all failed. Roy said he'd take it to the dump."

"I don't see how you can say we failed," George said. "We did ever thing we could think of to break him o' that art crap an'—"

"I'll take it," Reverend Stammer blurted, his voice unnaturally high and all but cracking with the unbearable tension he felt around his heart, which was thumping like a drum. Destroy this painting? One could live one's life—nay; one could live two, four, even five lifetimes—and never see such an opportunity: to save a magnificent work of art from destruction—and no less importantly, to save it for oneself. He had to have it!

"Works for me," Roy said. "C'mon, I'll give you a hand."

Ethel and Wanda watched them carry the TV down the driveway, Reverend Stammer stammering, "careful—look out—that crack, don't trip," urging Roy to "watch that low place," and clucking, "careful, careful, there's a rock off to your left." They gingerly deposited the TV in the trunk of Reverend Stammer's Toyota, whereupon Reverend Stammer hastily shook Roy's hand, waved to Ethel and Wanda, jumped in the Toyota, and sped off before anyone changed a mind.

"Well, my goodness," Ethel remarked in surprise. "He took that TV and left, just like that. And I made cookies for him."

"It sure was a short visit," Wanda agreed. "I was hopin' he'd lead a prayer."

They went back inside and reconvened the family meeting, which Reverend Stammer's visit had interrupted. They had just decided, as he arrived, that the police would take Wally right to the hospital when they recaptured him—"recaptured" was George's word, to which Ethel had strenuously objected, and which George had just as energetically defended—where they could hold him in the loony ward until the doctors were ready to perform the surgery that would make him well.

"An' another thing," George now declared in an I-told-you-so tone of voice, "you need to clean that art crap out o' here like I been tellin' you for I don't know how many months——just get it the hell out, 'cause it'll jes' contaminate him when he gets back from the hospital. If they ever find him to put him *in* the hospital."

"If you had eyes to see and ears to hear you'd know I been doin' that, Mister Know-It-All. This very morning Roy helped me clean Wally's supplies out of the den and we got all the TV reruns back in the shelves like he used to have it before his sickness. And Roy boxed the easel an' all the canvases an' sketch books." She reached across the table and squeezed Roy's hand. "Roy's been a rock. Don't know what I'd 've done without him."

Roy's nose purpled up with a blush. Feeling a bit like an interloper, he had been quiet throughout the meeting. He had wanted to leave when George and Wanda arrived, demanding a family meeting, but Ethel had insisted he stay. Just days before she had surprised him with a call, asking him if he'd come over and help her with some things, and when he did, one thing led to another and before he knew it she was back to being his lover; which was a bit of a shock, inasmuch as she had only recently ended their adultery, as she had then called their relationship. It seemed to be on again, though she did not refer to it now as adultery—now it was "us." As in, "What are we going to do about us?" Which made him a tiny bit nervous. And another thing made him a little nervous: she wasn't even acting guilty about their adultery. As a matter of fact she was being disturbingly defiant. He'd felt more comfortable with their adultery when she had all that hand-wringing anxiety about the dirtiness of it, and there wasn't any *us* talk.

"We need to pray on it," Wanda said. "Nuthin' good's gonna happen 'til we do that." She looked meaningfully at Roy, then at Ethel. "And I wouldn't be surprised if there ain't some other things some of us need to pray about."

Ethel tightened her lips and raised her head defiantly.

George said, "Whut."

Roy's cheeks purpled up to match his nose.

The ringing of the telephone broke the tension. Ethel got up to answer it. The eyes of the other three expectantly followed her to the counter where she lifted the handset from its cradle. They watched as her eyes rounded and her face paled and she brought her hand to her mouth.

"I don't understand," she whispered.

Silence for several seconds.

"Whut," George said.

She waved her hand for silence as she listened. Then, weakly, "Yes, yes, of course. You do what you got to do, but please be careful—and call as soon as you know."

"Whut," George said again.

Looking dazed, Ethel placed the handset in its cradle and came back to the table. "They think Wally was kidnapped. Some woman called the police, wonderin' if there was a reward. She said she saw his picture in the paper—said he was a prisoner in some artist co-op, is what the policeman called it. Where that Cushion woman lives."

"I told you we should be prayin'.'"

Thirty-four

"Do you know why you're here?"

Charles brought his head up and blinked groggily: "What?"

"Do you know why you're here?"

Charles' head drooped and his eyes thudded shut and he began snoring. But something deep inside willed him to rally. His head bounced up and he glared, wild-eyed, at the Doctor Jameses, both of whom had almost escaped back into that dark corner of his unconsciousness where they now hovered most of the time. But Charles wasn't letting them escape this time; this time he was holding on to them and getting to the bottom of whatever the fuck was going on here.

"Here?" he wavered determinedly.

The Doctor Jameses nodded in unison.

So far so good: an answer. Progress that, for a moment, calmed Charles. But it also confused him, for five seconds later he could remember neither the question nor the answer. With enormous effort he focused on Doctor James' two faces floating as benignly as Buddha's visage above two bow ties and two checkered vests.

"Are you through being violent?" the two Doctor Jameses asked in one voice.

Violence: the discordant music of shattering glass, the woody explosion of the door, Janice screaming and the struggle, the slashing lights and bellowed curses.

"Are you?"

Charles tried to raise his right hand to scratch an itchy place in his matted white hair, but couldn't.

"You're still confused," both Doctor Jameses noted at the same time.

Charles nodded gratefully. Finally, someone was making sense.

"Perhaps you're still too confused to understand what is happening to you."

Now they were making headway: Charles nodded vigorously.

"Do you like the confusion?"

That was an easy one: Charles shook his head vehemently.

"I can clear it up for you."

Charles perceived this to be an invitation to dialog, so he croaked, "Okay."

The Buddha faces of Doctor James smiled in unison. "Okay what, Charles?"

Shit. There it was again, this problem with dialog, in which the other guy makes references to words just spoken—and of course you have to remember what it was if your response is going to make any sense at all. Concentration distorted Charles' features, but it didn't do a bit of good. He had no idea what was okay. He waited helplessly.

"Are you being obstreperous again, Charles? Because if you are, I'll ask the attendant to take you back to your room and leave you in your straightjacket for the rest of the day. And maybe even give you another shot."

Attendant? Charles didn't know what he was talking about—and yet, the words did trigger something. A dim something that was almost, but not quite, recollection; a vague dark thing that made him shiver with horror. Dread flooded his gut like they'd taken a can opener to his belly and opened him up and hosed him full of it.

"Charles, do you understand that as long as you are violent we will keep you in the jacket and give you shots? Do you understand that, Charles?"

He seems to be making sense, Charles thought fragmentally.

"Because you are the patient, Charles. And we don't let the patients be violent. The only ones who can be violent are the attendants."

Violent, erratic lights, stunning in their brilliance against the violent darkness. His face slammed down against coarse oily-smelling planks. His arms jerked behind him, the muscles and ligaments of his shoulders popping and screaming with pain as his hands were hauled up to his scapulas, almost to his neck.

"Are you ready to behave?"

Charles thought for a moment, guessed that a nod might be what both of the Doctor Jameses wanted—and was happily right.

"Good," said the Doctor Jameses. "In that case we'll see if you can behave without the jacket. If you still behave properly even when we tell you once again what happened to Janice, we'll let you stay in your cell without the jacket. And this is a test, Charles. Hope you pass."

Janice? What happened to Janice?

—

"What difference does it make whether you can lift your right arm?" Doctor James asked.

Charles had complained about the pain in his shoulders. He dropped his arms.

"You'll never paint again, anyway. They don't let lifers paint."

"I'm not a lifer. I didn't do anything."

"Denial again. That's another thing wrong with you. It's one of your biggest problems. Not that it matters—where you're going everyone's in denial. Your criminal self-deception will fit right in. Might even be an asset as you fight to survive in that savage jungle. It's all brutality and death in there, you know. But back to your question. Janice is better, I think, though it scarcely matters—she's facing the same fate you're facing. If I was her I'd be wishing they had let me die. She was a mess. You should have seen her—you couldn't tell the color of her hair for all the blood." He stopped and smiled. "But of course you did see her—you were right there."

Charles tried to scratch his head, but couldn't raise either hand. He winced at a stab of pain in his shoulders.

Doctor James watched him and mused aloud: "You are a perfect validation of the principle, 'control of symptoms equals cure.' That's a quote from my most recent book, you know, the one you helped me with. Which I call 'The Principle of Cure of Violent Tendencies by Violence.' You are a veritable poster boy for my book."

"What about Janice?"

"She doesn't have a problem with violence. Her problem is the company she keeps."

"I mean, is she going to jail, too?"

"Oh, sure, if she survives her wounds. She's in this up to her eyeballs."

"I want to see her."

Doctor James laughed heartily. "You are one nervy sonofabitch, I'll give you that."

"You are one lucky sonofabitch," Doctor James said with a rueful chuckle. "Cats should have as many lives as you have. The prosecutor was so pissed at the injustice of releasing you that he had a stroke. In fact, he's downstairs in intensive care, not expected to live."

"Good," said Charles, threading the belt through the waist loops of his paint-stiff jeans.

The attendant had just brought Charles' personal effects—jeans, shirt, sandals, a pocket knife, an empty billfold, some cigarette papers—to Doctor James' office. Doctor James sat in his big leather chair behind his big mahogany desk, watching Charles change from his prisoner attire into his free-man attire. He had just informed Charles that since the office of the prosecutor was no longer paying for his confinement the hospital was kicking him out.

"How about Janice?" Charles asked, as he tucked his shirt.

"Another injustice. It seems her former employer, that same Whipple fellow that went your alibi, told the cops she was here in my ward when the alleged kidnapping occurred. Naturally, the cops were very annoyed to have their case wrecked. They're still trying to salvage it by reconciling the inconsistency. They want to change the dates on the hospital records. But the hospital's talked some judge into stopping them, because the changes will screw up their billing system and the hospital would have to send out a bunch of refunds." He smiled. "They're still trying to find something to pin on her, of course, but in the absence of a criminal record there's not much they can do. It looks like another case of a potential criminal getting away with something because the cops' hands are tied."

Charles had sat and pulled his shoes on. Now he stood and donned his coat. "Was that an answer to my question?"

"Frankly, I have no idea," Doctor James said frankly. "What was your question?"

"Can Janice go home?"

"I have no idea. You'll have to check with the folks down in ICU."

—

"Talking is hard," she murmured sleepily. "The morphine—I can't keep things straight—I keep dozing."

"You don't have to talk," Charles said.

"I want to take this thing off, but the light hurts my eyes. Are the lights on?"

Charles got up and went to the door and turned the lights off.

"The curtains, too."

He closed the curtains and came back to the chair and sat and watched Janice lift the black sleeping mask from her eyes. The top her hairless head was swathed in bandages. She squinted at the brightness she perceived in the gloomy room.

"See what they did to me? I saw myself for the first time this morning. Pretty, aren't I?"

"You look fine. A little bruised, but that'll go away and you'll be as beautiful as you were the first time you seduced me. The rest of you looks great, too, I might add. Tits, ass, everything. Matter of fact I think you might've lost a couple of uninteresting pounds in here."

Sleepily: "How would you know? I'm all covered up."

"I been feeling around under the covers while you were asleep."

"I can believe that." Her smile faded slowly. "The worst thing is my left cheek—they said they might be able to get it back by putting some hip bone in there, but I don't know. Operations. It hurts so much now. And even if they can fix it there's that awful crease in my forehead, which they can't do anything about. What should I do, Charles?"

"What do I know?"

"I got another headache this morning. When one of the nurses turned on the TV. I puked and thought my head was exploding—" Her words trailed off and her eyes closed and she dozed for a few seconds. Then her eyes opened. "I like the morphine. I'm still high from this afternoon. Can you tell?"

"What I'm hearing you say is you don't feel like screwing."

"Nope."

"I might as well go."

"Yeah, I guess so."

He grinned. "On the other hand, since I got nothin' better to do I guess I might as well stay. In case you change your mind."

Her lopsided smile faded and her eyes closed for several seconds, then opened again. "Charles—what about Wally? What happened to Wally."

"I already told you I don't know—they just released me."

"Find out, will you?" Her voice grew softer as she drifted toward sleep. "I'm worried—"

Thirty-five

Ethel's voice, from the living room: "He's still sick. He can't have no visitors."

Wally looked anxiously across the kitchen table at Roy. "Who's that at the door?"

"Nobody important," Roy said soothingly.

The man's voice came louder: "That you, Wally? This is Charles—I come to see how you're doing." Then, ingratiatingly: "I just want to say hello. That's all. Then I'll leave."

"Wally can't have no visitors," Ethel said, "so you can leave right now."

Looking pale and thin in over-sized pajamas and robe and a big white turban of bandages, Wally pushed himself away from the table, rose unsteadily, and shuffled toward the doorway that separated the kitchen from the living room.

Roy jumped up and came around the table. "Wait a minute, Wally, you ain't supposed to be movin' around without your walker."

Wally stopped in the doorway and peered across the living room. Beyond Ethel was a white-headed man who seemed to be looking right at him. "Who's that?" Wally whispered to Roy, apprehensively.

"It's Charles, man—I came to see you. You okay?"

Wally stared at the white-headed man for several seconds, then murmured apologetically, "I don't—my memory—"

Ethel spoke up: "You're doing just fine, honey. There's some things ain't worth remembering."

"I remember you—I just can't put a name to your face. You work down at the Safeway—with Wanda."

"Sweetheart, this man's leaving, so why don't you go on back in the kitchen and finish your supper."

"We made art together, man. Good art. Remember the Wally Charles?"

"He don't know nothin' about art," said Roy, who now stood with his arm round Wally's waist, steadying him. "An' we're gonna keep it that way. So you just do what Ethel says and leave. And don't come back here no more. We don't need your kind here." He slid a glance at Ethel, to see if he'd overstepped himself again. Her expression told him he hadn't.

"Janice says hello," the white-haired man said.

Wally wrinkled his face in confusion. "Janice?"

"Don't want her kind here, neither," Roy declared, emboldened now to take the lead in ejecting Charles.

"Janice from the gallery, Wally. She taught you to paint."

"Paint?"

"He don't know what he's talkin' about, Wally, so don't let it worry you," Roy said. "Now come on back to the table."

Wanda wedged past Roy into the living room. "Want me to call the cops, Mom?" A carbon copy of Ethel, she stood with arms crossed over pillowy breasts, jaw tight, lips thin.

Reverend Stammer and George followed Wanda through the kitchen door. Reverend Stammer had just arrived minutes before, having been coerced away from his desk and his poetry by a plea—nay, a command—by Wanda that he lead a prayer of thanksgiving for Wally's recovery. Now he spoke, shocking everyone in the room with the unprecedented vehemence of his rebuke. "Sir, your presence is disturbing a sick man."

Charles took advantage of Ethel's distraction, as she looked in surprise at Reverend Stammer. He slipped past her, confronting Wally before Roy or George could even think of blocking him. Charles grabbed Wally's limp right hand and started pumping—as if to prime Wally's memory.

"C'mon, you remember me, Wally. Charles Gas. Remember the Wally Charles? Remember how we worked all night on it? We made good art, man. And how I fixed bacon and eggs when we got up? Remember? And the TV—oh, man, Carnita's TV!"

Wally, wincing and tugging feebly to free his hand, rolled his eyes fearfully at Ethel. He had grown pale. Now the uneasiness that had come to him with the appearance of this intense, demanding man gave way to nausea and before he could even warn them he was going to puke, he spewed his supper all over himself and Charles.

Roy's arm tightened around Wally's waist. "See what you done?" he bellowed. "Now you get the hell outa here."

"Sir, you have abused your welcome. Please leave."

"Aw Jesus, Wally—oh Christ, what the fucking hell have they done to you?"

"I'm calling the cops right now."

"You fucking murderers! You goddamned motherfucking cocksucking murdering fucking Nazis, look—look what you've done—LOOK—"

A few minutes later a cop car lurched beep-booping into the driveway, but Charles had already scrambled out the back door and was running across the footbridge. And they never caught him, for it required all of them—even the cops—to get Wally settled enough to swallow one of his blue pills. Within minutes he was dozing in his recliner in front of the new TV, soothed by the familiar laugh track of a *Mayberry RFD* tape.

Later, as Reverend Stammer walked down the driveway, the questions that had plagued his peace since he'd rescued the TV were troubling him again. The questions demanded answers, but he'd found no answer. He kept asking himself how it was possible that James Stammer, a seminary-trained expert on the human condition, *and* a published poet, had overlooked Wally? It was inconceivable that a man with sensibilities as refined as his could have known a Wally Walder for the last two years and not perceived the titanic talent swelling therein, waiting to explode so brilliantly into the world—brilliantly and, alas, briefly. How could an artist of profound expressiveness and sensitivity (himself) completely overlook all the signs and signals of an emerging artist of even profounder powers than his own? The evidence of Wally's genius was inescapable; it presided now over Reverend Stammer's tiny living room on its alter, facing his desk, which he'd turned so that when he looked up from his poetry he would see it; and seeing it, feel an aesthetic lift take him high, higher than any drug could take him, there to flow out of him through his fingers into *his* art, giving his poetry a life-energy it had never known. He wished once again, oh so fervently, that he had let himself know this man; wished that in the all-too-short interval of Wally's ascendant genius he, James Stammer, could have—was it so farfetched?—could he perhaps have been Wally's artistic collaborator? Charles Gas had been his collaborator, or so he said, and if that awful man why not a man of genuine refinement, such as himself? Oh, what they could have shared! Had he recognized Wally's genius early on, wouldn't everything have turned out very differently? The inevitable question, and the most difficult one, reminding him of the unspeakable (and unbearable) accusations of that ghastly Gas: would knowledge of Wally's genius have changed the course of events? Would Wally Walder still be painting? Or was it simpler than that? Was Wally Walder on some deterministic path ordained by his karma? Perhaps he was a shooting star and not a sun. Reverend Stammer got in his Toyota and drove off, grateful that he had before him the solace of his poetry.

Thirty-six

Wally took his cup to the break room where he filled it with coffee.
"Welcome back, Wally."
Wally turned and saw another face that he should have a name for, but didn't. Nodding cautiously, he moved aside to let the matronly woman get at the coffee pot. Her familiar manner made him believe that he'd known her for a long time. But he didn't have a clue what her name was, or what she did. He supposed she was one of his colleagues.
"Gosh, Wally, how long has it been?" When Wally looked like he was waiting for the rest of the question, she added, "Since you were injured?"
"Oh." He started to respond but realized he couldn't remember that, either, though he'd been thinking about it that very morning as got off the bus. "Too long," he murmured vaguely.
"I'll bet. Feel good to be back?"
"Yeah."
Wally walked back to his cubicle, trying to remember the woman's name and how long he'd been gone. He sat in front of his terminal and with his mouse moved the cursor to the calendar icon and clicked. His empty calendar appeared. He counted back through the empty months to the first appearance of an appointment. He closed his eyes and whispered the month and year over and over again, then wrote it on a Post-It and stuck the scrap of yellow paper on the side of his computer terminal. Then he clicked the intranet icon and when the home page came up, opened the Employee Directory. He scrolled down through pictures until he came to the woman's. Of course! How the hell could he forget Marcia Sloane? Marcia had been his admin for five years. He closed his eyes and whispered her name over and over again.
He returned to his project, which Kimberly had given him right after—shit, now he'd forgotten her name: the HR woman, the one who got him back on the payroll and then showed him to his new cubicle; what the hell was her name? He opened the Employee Directory again and scrolled down until he came to Joan Campbell's picture. He sighed: she'd been with the company for twelve years.
Reaching for his coffee he caught the brown of Kimberly's suit in the corner of his eye. Thinking she was coming to see him about another project, he turned. But the long hall was empty. She'd disappeared into one of the offices. He had not recognized her that morning when she entered his cube a few minutes after—what was her name? Joan something-or-other?—had left him off at eight-thirty. Kimberly had showed up in a stiff brown suit and

patent-leather heels, her hair efficiently short and her once-pointy breasts modestly subdued beneath the sober weight of a double-breasted jacket. She hadn't even put her brief case down. Hadn't smiled, nor even said hello. Just got briskly to the point. "Henceforward, you are responsible for maintaining the Employee Directory and the Company Style Guide," was what she said. Which of course had shocked him, these being menial chores that were lowest-priority activities in any tech pubs group (stuff like that he'd always given to an intern or to one of the more talented admins). During the few seconds she'd been in his cube, he hadn't said a word. For that matter, she hadn't said many, either. Not even "Welcome back, Wally," or "Let's talk later, Wally." Just said a few words and then she was gone. In a hurry. Okay, he understood; he'd had his share of busy days around here. No doubt she'd be back later when she'd put out all the fires she was obviously fighting, to chat about a more challenging project for him, something so thorny that it would require the skills of a toughened, wily, battle-tested tech writer like himself. But after their brief encounter she didn't notice him again, though she was coming and going around his cube for the rest of the day.

And now that he'd had a whole day back on the job he was beginning to think maybe he didn't really want a thorny project. Not for a while yet. He'd passed a surprisingly pleasant and dreamy afternoon trying to find a solution to the problem of hyphenating compound adjectives. And of course the related quandary of how to apply hyphenation to reduce noun stacks, the dreaded bane of technical writers—and novelists, too, he'd been led to believe. There was a lot more to understand about hyphenation than most people thought.

His guts were rumbling again. The French fries and the cold pizza left over from the software group's lunch meeting, and the carrot cake someone had brought in for a birthday celebration on top of the lunch Ethel had packed for him. And the coffee. A lot more coffee than Ethel let him have. He'd have to watch that, he thought as he went down the hall and pushed into the crapper. He entered a stall and dropped his trousers and shorts and hadn't even got his cheeks situated before a gassy, ripping explosion echoed hollowly. He raised an eyebrow. That was a close call.

He came back to the confines of his cube with a fresh cup of coffee. Feeling better. Even liking the coziness of his new cubicle. Gray walls a body-length wide, a body-length long, a body-length high. A gray, plastic-topped corner desk with a beige computer terminal and a beige keyboard and a beige computer tower below the desk. A swivel chair, in gray fabric. A single bank of gray drawers. A hanger for his coat, which hung against one cubicle wall. Not the office he'd once occupied, but of course they'd had to move his stuff out so Kimberly could move in.

Sometime later he realized that he had so lost himself in the problem of compound adjectives and noun stacks that he'd lost track of the time; if he didn't hurry he'd miss the 540. He shut down his computer, grabbed his hat and raincoat and umbrella and hurried to the row of elevators in the hall. An elevator was filling with his colleagues, most of whom he couldn't remember, though they apparently remembered him, for they waved and smiled and yelled, "Hold it for Wally," and "Run for it Wally," and other friendly encouragement. As he pushed in, he returned their greetings with nods and "How are ya?" and turned to face the door so that he would not have to make conversation with people he knew he knew, but didn't know. When the elevator opened on the lobby he was the first out. He strode quickly across the marble floor past the Starbucks counter and pushed through the big revolving door in time to watch the five-forty roar off into rainy traffic. The next bus would be the six-ten. He popped his umbrella open and walked to the corner where he waited for the light. Pedestrian traffic spilled out of office towers along Fifth Avenue, and the motion of raincoated and umbrellaed men and women against the lights of cars gave energy to the night. The street was a slick black mirror reflecting the myriad hues of that teeming vitality in glittering and shimmering polygons. But Wally wasn't noticing motion or light or pattern or shape. He had nothing on his mind as he headed across the street except the shelter at the bus stop in the next block, and supper, and what was on TV tonight.

At the newsstand near the shelter he bought a paper. Inside the crowded shelter he turned to the TV section. But the light too dim for his aging eyes to read the newspaper's ten-point Times-Roman. He left the Plexiglas and aluminum enclosure and crossed the sidewalk to a recessed doorway where he stood in the abundant and cheerful light provided by the window displays of *Whipple's Art Outlet*, which, according to a huge banner sign hanging over the entrance, was a new discount art gallery "dedicated to providing low-cost art solutions, in the form of off-goods art and art seconds." An arc of dignified silver lettering on the door identified the establishment as a division of Whipple's Art Galleries, Inc. Wally noticed none of this. He was occupied with the complex problem of selecting TV programs (from the thirty or forty that were available for every time slot in the TV schedule) for he and Ethel to watch that night. For years this had been his reading material on the long bus ride from downtown Seattle to the wilds of Finn Hill. And it was no mean task. It required all of one's attention to make the right choices. He was disappointed to see that by missing his bus he was also missing a re-run of Murder, She Wrote. He was still marking the most important programs for the seven-to-eight time slot when he was distracted by movement in the window. He glanced to his right, observed a young woman doing something to a painting on the easel in the window. When she stepped off the window stage Wally saw that she'd taped a big red tag to the painting, which announced an inventory-reduction price of "ONLY $99.99!!!" Wally looked at his watch. Another ten minutes. He wondered what Ethel had fixed for supper, and whether he ought to call her and tell her he'd missed the five-forty. Deciding she'd probably worry, he left the shelter of the recessed doorway and walked to the pay phone a half-block down the street. He picked up the handset, dropped a quarter and a dime in the coin slots, poised his finger over the keypad—and discovered that he had no idea what his telephone number was. He sighed, replaced the handset, removed his hat to scratch his head and remembered elatedly (yes! remembered!) that Ethel had taped it on the inside of his hat.

—

"Well, are we gonna just go on and on like this?" Roy asked insistently.

"I already told you what we're gonna do," Ethel said primly. "And now it's time you went home. Wally'll be here in twenty minutes and I got to fix supper. You can come over later, for supper and TV, if you want. It ain't right for you to be here when he comes home."

The telephone rang. She answered it, listened for a few seconds, then said, "Take your time, Sweetheart, supper'll wait." A pause. "Okay, I'll tape it." Another pause. "She was? Well, I can't wait to hear about it. Okay. Bye, Sweetheart."

Roy stood beside her, his arms crossed, leaning resentfully against the counter.

"Are we gonna just go on like this?" he asked again. "Waitin' for telephone calls?"

"Waitin' for telephone calls, indeed! Don't be silly."

Roy's cheeks purpled up almost as much as his nose; from anger, as well as embarrassment. "Well, damnit, sharin' a woman's just not my style."

Ethel had moved to the sink and started peeling potatoes. She looked over at him and said sharply: "You are not sharin' me, as you so-delicately put it."

"You know what I mean."

"And you know what I mean."

"Well, he does sleep with you."

"He's my husband."

Roy left angry, but also chastened. Every time he brought The Subject up he left feeling as foolish as a teenaged boy caught—well, caught doing shameful things, like masturbating. No, not exactly like that. More like someone whose childish jealousy has just been exposed to the world. Which wasn't the case. It wasn't childish jealousy. His feeling was perfectly reasonable. He climbed the stairs with heavy tread and opened his back door and went inside, turned on the light and filled the teapot before going into the living room and turning on the TV. He plopped down in his recliner and pushed back, took up the remote and surfed through twenty or thirty channels. He stopped at *The Bathing Suit Channel* and watched nubile women—girls, really—jump around on the sand of a lovely beach, probably in South America or someplace where they allow you to dress, or undress, like that.

Usually he didn't watch this program for very long because it was always the same stuff, but this one had a sort of artistic touch to it, in the way the camera guy used slow motion to reveal so much more of the girls' personalities as they threw themselves at a volleyball. When the teakettle started whistling at him he pushed up out of the recliner and went into the kitchen and fixed a cup of tea. Tea. He'd never had a cup of tea in his life until he started having his adultery with Ethel. Maybe she's right about this adultery business, too, he thought, as he carried the cup into the living room. Even he had to admit their adultery was not the invigorating thing it had been. Maybe it was time to stop. He had to admit that it would feel a lot more comfortable playing cribbage with Wally if he wasn't still having his adultery with Ethel. Still. He wistfully sipped his tea. A seventy-five year old man doesn't get that many chances at adultery. Not with an attractive woman like Ethel. The tide of his self pity began to recede as he became more interested in the pubescent girls arcing back and forth across the screen, and he began to feel the familiar stirring of energy in his gut and in his pants. His blood rose a bit and he smiled. By God he wasn't through yet. Not by a long shot. She was too fine a woman to give up on.

Thirty-seven

"March is the cruelest month, not April," Charles said, shivering. Naked and chilled to the bone, he stood at the big window on the west wall of the office-cum-bedroom. The window looked out on steel and glass towers, between which he could see the Sound resting like a huge puddle of quicksilver—metallic gray against a darker landscape that was growing even darker now that the sun had dropped below the Olympics, draining the world of color and warmth.

"You keep changing positions," Janice complained from the bed where she sat naked, cross-legged, pencil in hand, looking down at the sketchbook.

"Because it teases us with a few warm days after months of living in this icebox, and then it betrays its promise with another month of cold." He looked over his shoulder at her. "Hurry up."

"Hold your head right there. And hold that angry expression. It's you."

"It's also difficult. You got two more minutes."

Looking back over his shoulder he watched her hand darting over the page, saw the features of his head and shoulders fill out beneath her hand. He studied her face, which he did often when she was not aware of his scrutiny. He was still trying to fathom the disfigurement, which seemed greater now than when he had seen her in the hospital—because the swelling was gone, he supposed, revealing more dramatically the absence of the cheekbone prominence that was evident on the right side of her face. The lopsidedness of her face accentuated the vertical depression above her left eye. To keep that lazy left eye open she had to arch her eyebrows, which gave her a perpetually quizzical look. Which added to the impression that her air of distraction already gave one—that maybe she was a little bit wacky. Which of course was true. It had not taken him long to come to that conclusion. He'd assumed that her facial disfigurement had done it—had tipped her over the edge. But now he wasn't so sure. For one thing, she didn't seem to care about it.

"Hurry up, I'm cold. You got one more minute."

But he gave her more than one more minute. He gave her as much time as she needed to finish the drawing—probably ten minutes. When she dropped the pencil on the sheet and arched her back and stretched, flexing her fingers, he moved, shivering, away from the window and picked up his jeans and sweatshirt.

She rolled off the bed and found her palette on the chair by the door, where she'd put it after he'd offered to pose for a half-hour in exchange for one fuck—in the midst of which activity he had breathlessly observed that her enthusiasm suggested she was making out better than him on this deal—getting her ashes hauled and getting a half-hour of posing, whereas all he was getting was his ashes hauled; in answer to which she'd breathed, "Don't you dare come yet." But he did come, muttering, "I couldn't help it," and she'd hugged him and said, "It's okay, that was all I wanted." But of course it wasn't—he could tell from the energy in her hands and arms as she rubbed his back—so, after he'd rested for a minute he'd worked his way down, with lips and tongue, over her breasts and belly and into that pungently moist pubic darkness between her legs, where he rooted around until she'd gotten hers. And then she'd pushed him aside and bounded off the bed and grabbed her pencils and the big sketch book and instructed him to stand looking out the window, and he had protested that it was cold by the windows, and she had demanded that he keep his word, and he'd complied, grumbling about what he had to go through nowadays to get laid.

She went out the door and across the studio to the big easel under the skylight. She stood looking at the painting for a few seconds, then set to work. Charles came out of the office-cum-bedroom with socks and a pair of sandals and sweatshirt and sweatpants. He approached Janice and dropped them at her feet.

"Get your clothes on. It's cold."

She gave him a distracted, uncomprehending glance, and went back to work.

"Hey! Put your clothes on."

"In a minute."

"Now."

She sighed impatiently, put her palette down, sat on the broken-backed sofa, pulled the socks on, then rose and stepped into the slippers and immediately picked up her palette and brush and faced the canvas.

"The sweatshirt."

She ignored him.

"The sweatshirt, goddamnit."

She put the palette and brush down and pulled the shirt over her head, and before she could pick up the palette and brush again Charles thrust the sweatpants into her hands. She pulled them on and turned back to the painting.

Charles went to the kitchen and put the teakettle on the range. He opened a cabinet and got a package of pasta, which he put on the counter, then went to the refrigerator and studied its contents for a minute before removing broccoli, some parmesan, a package of ham. After he filled a pot of water and put it on the range he moved out of the kitchen and faced the long flood-lit wall and studied the paintings thereon.

—

Janice stepped up to the canvas and raised her brush.

"Did you hear me?" Charles asked.

She nodded.

"So answer: why's he coming around like this? Being so friendly."

"I think—I don't know, maybe he wants to look at your paintings," Janice murmured absently, as she daubed her brush into a puddle of yellow on her palette. "How do I know? He might want to show your work."

"He hates my guts. Besides, I know why he's coming around, and so do you. He's sucking up to you; he wants to fuck you again. You can see it a mile away."

She brushed paint on the canvas. "He never fucked me. Never even tried."

Charles stared at her for several incredulous seconds, then: "You're lying." Silence. "You said he did. You used to tell me that all the time."

"Because it pissed you off." She stepped back from the painting to the work table where she thrust the brush in a can of thinner and swished it around.

"I don't believe you."

"I liked the effect it had on you," she observed, dropping the brush she had just cleaned into the coffee can and lifting another out. She flexed its bristles as she studied the canvas. "You were a lot friskier after he'd been around me for a while."

"That's disgusting."

"I can tell what you want. When you talk about Whipple wanting to fuck me you're the one wanting to fuck me."

"That's bullshit. I just want to figure out why he's coming around acting to nice to me, that's all."

"I think he wants to fuck me."

"Ha! That's what I thought."

"You want a roll in the hay, right?"

"I might. Interested?"

"What's in it for me?"

"The usual? Half hour of posing?""A wannabe artist," Whipple said wistfully. "That's the way I remember her twenty-five years ago. A sexy long-legged little-girl artist wannabe without a shred of talent, who finally discovered that she had no talent and gave it up and became a pretty-good business woman. I thought her work was second rate, so you can see why it's taken me a while to start taking her seriously. And now look at her. I still can't believe how rapidly her work is evolving. Her paintings are solid, sellable stuff—as sellable as Vovo's. And she's a perfect story—young artist gives up the struggle, sells out, gets a job, then in mid-life throws away success and takes the big risk all over again—the risk everyone wants to take and few have the guts for—and thereby finds real success. Appealing, no?"

Charles shrugged irritably.

"Of course there's no way I'd show the first ten pieces. She's still finding her voice in those. Maybe the next four. But the last four? Oh, yes, those for sure. That's where she's finding herself. Don't you agree?"

Of course Charles agreed. An idiot could see that the last four represented her breakthrough. All you had to do was look at the long wall and that fact jumped out at you. He knew better than Whipple how rapidly her work had evolved. He looked at that wall every day, and the longer the row of paintings grew, the more demoralizing it was. As demoralizing as Whipple coming in here this evening with his fucking bottle of champagne and telling Charles he wanted to show Janice in his Occidental Square gallery in the summer. Whipple didn't add, "not you," but he didn't need to. It was implicit—and evisceratingly, crushingly, numbingly, devastatingly disappointing. He had begun to let himself think that maybe, just maybe, Whipple was coming around not only because he wanted to fuck Janice but because he might be a little interested in his, Charles', work. It had not crossed Charles' mind that Whipple was thinking of showing Janice's work. Well, maybe it had, but he had managed to suppress that thought.

Whipple raised the champagne stem to his lips and drained it. He poured it full again, nodded in the direction of the skylight, under which Janice stood at her easel, painting. "She makes you feel good. Just watching her paint. You must be very proud of her."

Charles couldn't take it any longer. He got up from the table and stalked over to his work table, which he'd moved away from the skylight (he'd traded the skylight position to Janice for sex). On the table was Wally's TV and another TV that he'd found in a dumpster and had started painting.

Whipple looked at him studying the larger Wally TV, then looking at his own and scratching his chin. "I still want to buy it, you know."

"It's not for sale," Charles said, without looking up

"Everything is for sale, Charles. The discussion should be about price."

"It's not for sale."

—

"Sorry about this," Whipple whispered to Charles. "It's the only way he'd agree to come."

Charles glowered down the stairwell at the three baggy-suited, burly, surly-faced young men clumping up the stairs toward him.

"He refuses to go to openings, now," Whipple murmured behind his hand. "This is our only shot, so please don't say anything threatening—or make any sudden moves. Try to be nice."

Charles grunted and glared as threateningly as he could at each of the young men as they entered the door at the top of the stairs. They in turn scrutinized him, looking for bulges in his clothing. Satisfied they were looking at no one more threatening than an unarmed old man, they moved into the room. One followed the perimeter toward the right, the other to the left. The third, apparently the one in charge, walked out into the middle of the room and stopped a few feet from the easel where Janice worked. Charles tensed as the young man approached Janice and looked her over. She glanced at him and continued painting. Deciding she was harmless, he turned away from her and took position in the middle of the long room, his hands in his coat pockets, his eyes darting alertly. When the two burly young men finished their perimeter investigation they came back to the top of the stairs where Charles and Whipple waited. The young man in the middle of the room joined them, said something in a low voice, then went down the stairs.

Charles, being an artist, had already sensed the nearness of an art critic. Whipple knew this, of course, so he kept a close eye on him.

"Make it fast," Charles grumbled to Whipple, then stalked past Janice's easel to his own work table.

At that moment the burly young man who had gone down the stairs led Dillip and a fourth burly, baggy-suited young man through the doorway at the top of the stair into the studio. The two biggest, burliest young men positioned themselves between Charles and Dillip. Dillip eyed Charles between their bulky shoulders.

Charles had not seen Dillip for months, and he was shocked—as well as pleased—at the change. Dillip's hair had turned white, the skin of his face had deteriorated from an unhealthy sallow chubbiness to an unhealthy sallow looseness, and the remains of his nose pointed off to the right, as if it was trying to lead him into a right turn. His left ear was as knotted as a punch-drunk fighter's and the scar tissue over both eyes formed thick Neanderthalian ridges.

"Why does he have to be here, you didn't tell me he'd be here," Dillip whispered to Whipple. His eyes never left Charles, who—though his face still bore a scowl—had taken up his brush and palette.

"This is his studio, Philip."

The men advanced into the center of the room. The two biggest came first (their eyes never leaving Charles), then Dillip and Whipple, and finally the other two burly young men.

"What's that?" Dillip asked, pointing at Charles' worktable.

"That's Charles' current work."

"It's two TVs," Dillip said. "What's he doing, repairing TVs now?"

"You're looking at the backs, you have to look at the fronts to see the work. But we didn't come to see that." Whipple spoke to Charles. "Charles, will you please turn the floodlights on, so we can see the wall?"

Charles glared at Whipple, then Dillip, like he might be getting ready to say or do something very inhospitable; but he didn't: with clenched teeth, he walked stiff-legged past the bodyguards and the art critic and the gallery owner toward the light switch on the brick wall. The burly young men gracefully changed position to keep themselves between Charles and Dillip.

"What is he doing to the TV?" Dillip asked.

"Painting the screen. Let's go and look at Janice's work."

"Painting the screen?"

"Yes."

Dillip began to feel safe enough behind the meaty torsos and muscular arms of his body guards to behave like an art critic. He gave a little snigger of contempt and said, very loudly: "Painting TV screens? Who ever heard of painting TV screens?"

Whipple, growing alarmed, tried to deflect Dillip's attention back to Janice. "The reason I wanted you to come up here is to see the transition of Janice's work and the incredibly rapid evolution of talent that the transition reveals. When you see her current work in the context of that evolution, her enormous potential becomes evident—which is the theme I intend to exploit at her first show. Take the first painting, for example, the one on the end, which she executed just a week after she got out of the hospital—"

"I gotta see those TVs." Grinning, Dillip moved away from Whipple toward Charles' worktable. The burly young men moved with him, carefully keeping position between Dillip and Charles, who had turned on the floods and remained standing, arms belligerently crossed, by the brick wall.

Charles didn't move a muscle; just stood by the light switch, muttering his mantra to himself: *don't move don't move don't touch the motherfucker, don't move don't move don't touch the motherfucker*: a prayer for Janice. He reminded himself that he did indeed love Janice, and for her he could do it, for Janice he could forego killing Dillip.

Dillip came grinning around the worktable. Thinking of all the ways that painted TV screens were absurd, he was ready to critically destroy the art, and by association, the artist who'd painted it. His mistake was looking at Wally's screen. It stopped him in his tracks. He stared incredulously at the test pattern, went limp with astonishment, forgot entirely the purpose of his scrutiny of this painted TV screen, which was to ridicule it and its creator. He was overwhelmed by the first genuine aesthetic experience he'd had in months. The feeling was so clean and shockingly uplifting that he forgot to breathe. He became light-headed and reflexively put his hand out to the TV to steady himself; but his hand missed, and he stumbled off to the side, toward Janice, who stood obliviously at her easel, painting. One of the burly young men lunged clumsily forward to catch his off-balance boss and, tripping, pushed him instead, sending Dillip sprawling face down into Janice's easel, which collapsed. The painting tumbled off the easel, its corner neatly spearing Dillip's right hand. He screamed. Janice, startled out of her painting trance, stumbled back against the old sofa and fell. Blood gushed from Dillip's wounded hand. The burly young men crowded around their screaming boss.

Charles, thinking they'd hurt Janice, dashed across the studio toward the huddle of black suits surrounding screaming Dillip. A pair of the burly young men hauled Dillip to his feet just in time for him to see Charles hurtling toward him. He screamed again, turned, lunged into one of the burly young men, and the pair of them fell, in a tangle of arms and legs, into the collapsed easel. Everyone in the room heard the pop of Dillip's left tibia as it exploded under the weight of a pair of the burly young men who, intent on rescuing their boss, tripped and fell on him.

—

"I don't know how I've survived unscathed as long as I have," Whipple reflected. "Art's a dangerous business."

"Don't I know it," Charles said.

They stood at a window looking down into the street where the red lights flashed, watching the attendant close the back door of the ambulance. He hurried to the driver's door and climbed in and drove off, siren beeping and booping, lights flashing red. The burly young men stood in the street looking at one another.

Whipple sighed. "This is gonna cost us."

"This is art. It comes with the territory."

Whipple turned away and ambled, hands in pockets, back toward the easel, which Janice had reassembled, and on which she had replaced her canvas, which miraculously survived the altercation with almost no damage. There she stood, painting, as if nothing had happened. Charles followed him. Whipple fell to the sofa. Charles went to his work table and looked into the pot pot. He rummaged therein until he found a nice roach, which he affixed to a roach clip. He lit up and came to the sofa, where he offered it to Whipple.

Whipple gave a wan smile. "Haven't toked in twenty years. Might as well."

"I need to know something," Charles said through a stream of blue smoke.

"What?"

"Did you—you know, fuck her?" he asked, nodding at Janice, who worked, her back to them, five feet away.

Whipple smiled. "Why d'you care? That was half a lifetime ago."

"I don't care. I just have to know is all."

"I thought about it, but I couldn't. She was so young and innocent, it seemed like—well, you know. Like child molestation."

"Um."

Charles sat down beside Whipple and the two of them watched Janice paint.

"It's a shame," Whipple sighed.

"What?" Charles asked.

"Dillip hurting himself like that. He'll wreck her career, now."

"She doesn't give a fuck about career. She just wants to paint."

"Her work won't get out. Dillip won't let people buy it."

Charles drew on the roach, held his breath for a few seconds before expelling a cloud of smoke. "I have an idea about that."

"What."

He handed the roach clip to Whipple and began telling him about the Nominal Theory of Good Art, and about a new artist he was about to invent, by the name of Candice Pillow.

Thirty-eight

Kimberly was the best manager at Atlas Software, and it wasn't because she worked twice as hard as other managers—she didn't. Nor was it because she forced her team to work twice as hard as other teams—they didn't. She was a good manager because she intuitively understood the manager's job, which is brain-dead simple: you create and maintain a suitable work environment and then you put competent people in the environment and tell them the result you want and get out of the way and let them work. And if they don't produce what you want them to produce—well, you get rid of them and find other people. She'd known, for instance, exactly what Wally was suited for when the HR people made her take him back, and that was what she had him do.

He started out doing it pretty well. After only two months back on the job he'd succeeded in untangling the adjectival-hyphenation knot, the results of which he published in *The Atlas Software Style Guide for Internal Technical Publications, Rev. 7.5.01*. And while it was true that he'd not made much progress on solving the intractable noun-stack problem, he cut himself a little slack on that one—because of the difficulties he'd run into in updating the content of the Atlas Employee Directory. In fact, he was sure he'd have completed his work on the noun-stack problem had he not gotten side tracked by the aesthetic flaws he'd begun to see in the Employee Directory.

Curiously, his first inspection of the Directory, soon after he returned to work, gave him no hint of the crippling problems that would later become evident. And, frankly, there should have been no aesthetic problems—for the Directory had the simplest possible design: it comprised a home page with an alphabetized list of names, each of which was a link to an employee picture and a one- or two-line bio. Nothing can be simpler than that. Yet over the weeks, as he performed his duty of occasional updates of the site with bits of information and pictures of new employees, design irregularities began to emerge. He began to see that some of the pictures were slightly out of focus or poorly composed, that there were annoying little incongruities of color, that some alignments were askew, that certain design elements had disturbing proportions. On the whole the flaws were minute, even insignificant—or so he thought when he first encountered them. However, as the weeks passed he became increasingly sensitive to even slight irregularities; so much so that finally he could no longer ignore them. One day it came to him that he had to redesign the Employee Directory. He went to the supplies room and rummaged around until he found a spiral notebook and a box of colored pencils. Excited by his discovery, he hurried back to his little gray cubicle and shoved aside stacks of noun-stack research papers and immediately began sketching changes to the Directory GUI. The next day he gave the sketches to the Atlas Web Master to implement. The Web Master, a pimply-faced lad of seventeen, of course told him to fuck off. But that little setback did not discourage Wally. He simply continued his work of improving the design, but on paper, through his sketches.

His on-going effort to improve the aesthetics of the Employee Directory web design was the reason he was waiting in a chair outside of Kimberly's office on that spring day, his sketch book open in his lap. He'd been waiting for an hour, but he was happy, for time didn't matter when he was sketching his ideas about improving the web site.

"Wally, Kimberly will see you now," Dan said as he put the telephone handset back in its cradle. He selected a file folder from the pile on his desk and rose and led Wally into Kimberly's office and placed the folder on Kimberly's desk and turned and left the room, closing the door behind him.

Wally looked around. The office was much bigger than her old office, which had once been his office and which she'd occupied until her recent promotion to Worldwide Vice President of Operations. This office was much bigger and grander. There was a leather sofa and chair and a glass-topped cocktail table and a maple desk with matching book shelves. Kimberly, not one to waste time, was already pouring over the contents of the file folder. Without looking up, she gestured toward a chair positioned before her desk. Wally sat and as he waited for her to finish reading the contents of the folder he occupied himself with the design problem he'd been working on while he waited outside the office. When Kimberly looked up and addressed him he was once again deeply immersed in the drawing.

"Wally, I like to get right to the point in these matters."

Wally looked up and waited.

"It's not working. The fit just isn't there."

Wally was amazed. As busy as Kimberly was—managing the vast operational structure of a worldwide company—how in the world could she find the time to understand a relatively minor issue like the aesthetics of the Employee Directory web page? He was impressed, and happy that she agreed with him. He smiled broadly.

She offered a poignant smile in response. "Sometimes it's just the square-peg-and-round-hole problem. Neither the peg nor the hole is to blame. The problem comes from putting the hole and the peg together."

Wally thought about this and nodded vigorous agreement. She was right, by golly: it wasn't that the pimply-faced youngster was a poor web master or that the elements the youngster put together in his design were unbalanced and the color scheme garish—he just lacked the experience to understand that he was trying to shove a square peg into a round hole. Wally made a note of the phrase, to refer to when he needed to keep himself focused on a problem.

"Though I have to admit you did a great job on the adjectival-hyphenation problem."

Wally blushed at the praise.

"But in this fast track world we work in today, we have to have those kinds of successes all the time or we won't survive as a company. And that's what concerns me about the noun-stack problem." She raised a hand to restrain a protest he had no thought of making. "I know you had other work as well—I believe you also had the Employee Directory—"

The conversation continued in that vein—actually it not so much a conversation as it was a philosophical ramble on the unfair burdens on management, punctuated by pauses at which she seemed to want him to nod his head—but he wasn't really listening. His mind, having slipped once again into autopilot mode, had taken him where he wanted to be, which was back into his Employee Directory web redesign. He didn't even take in the fact that she stopped talking, closed the file folder, and pressed a button on the corner of her desk. Nor did he notice that the door immediately opened and Dan entered and approached the desk and accepted the file folder from her. Only when Dan touched his shoulder and said, "Follow me, please," did he realize that the meeting was over. Wally closed his notebook and stood and was about to say "Thank you," but Kimberly was already studying the contents of another open file folder. He followed Dan out the door and down the hall toward the office of the HR lady. She was waiting for him, smiling sympathetically. Wally wondered what she had to do with the design of the Employee Directory web page.

"Come in, Wally," she said gently, and closed the door behind him.

—

Still wondering what had happened, Wally stepped out of the elevator and walked into the big high-ceilinged lobby. He went past the line of people standing before the Starbucks counter and out the revolving door into gray morning rain. The box, which he carried under one arm, contained his cup, his colored pencils, his spiral notebook of GUI designs, his lunch of salami sandwich, apple, and three chocolate-chip cookies. He stood in the rain for a while before he realized his head was getting wet. This prompted him to open the umbrella and move to the corner and cross the street. It wasn't until he got to the shelter at the bus stop that he remembered that buses went to Finn Hill only during the morning and evening commutes. Placing the box on the bench, he searched his pockets for a quarter and a dime. All he found was his bus pass (Ethel still let him carry only lunch money, unless of course she made his lunch for him, in which case he carried no money at all). But it didn't bother him that he had no money to call Ethel. If anything he was relieved, because he knew how she'd take the news. She'd be upset. She'd ask questions. He sat on the bench and tried to answer what he knew would be the first question. What *had* happened? They'd fired him—that was what had happened. But why? That would be the second question, the one he didn't understand. Maybe he had done something bad. But if he had, he didn't know what it was. He was never late, so it couldn't be that. And as for his work ethic—well, he was in his cubicle at eight-thirty, sketched GUIs all day long, and left at five-thirty.

He sat for some time on the cold bench watching cars and trucks and buses hiss by in the rain, trying to puzzle out the reason why Kimberly fired him. After a while he lost interest in the question and got up and went to the window display behind the shelter, which he'd begun noticing in recent weeks as he waited for his bus. The storefront was two floor-to-ceiling windows separated by a recessed doorway. He stood before one of the windows looking at the artwork displayed on several easels. The words *Whipple's Art Outlet* arced across the window above his head in silver lettering. After he'd studied the paintings in each of the windows for some time he went inside, where a nice young man with purple hair and tongue rings wanted to know what he wanted. Wally told the nice young man that he liked the paintings very much, but he didn't have any money to buy anything. But he'd still like to look around, if it was okay. The purple-haired, tongue-ringed young man shrugged and went to the back and kicked his feet up on his desk and opened the comic book he'd been reading before Wally interrupted him.

Wally spent the rest of the afternoon browsing over hundreds of pieces of art seconds. It was the most enjoyable day he'd had in—well, he didn't know how long. He left the shop only when the purple-haired, tongue-ringed young man approached him and lisped, "You gotta go, 'causth I wanna clothe now." When Wally went outside he realized he'd missed the first two of the three afternoon Finn Hill buses. In the shelter he found the box that contained his cup, colored pencils, notebook, and lunch. He sat and opened the notebook on his lap and on a fresh page started a sketch. And it wasn't a sketch of the Employee Directory web site. It was a sketch of the purple-haired, tongue-ringed young man.

—

"You're healthy as a horse, Wally." Pete stepped back from the examination table and removed his stethoscope and slipped it into a pocket in his white jacket. "Except for the ten pounds you've gained since you went back to work. Are you still walking every day?"

"I got out of the habit for a while, but I started again."

Pete was leaning against the cabinet, his arms crossed. "You know why Ethel wanted this examination, Wally?"

Wally nodded.

"Can you tell me?"

"She's worried because I'm drawing again."

"That's right. It appears you've had a relapse."

Pete waited for Wally to respond, but Wally just sat on the examination table in his T-shirt and shorts, legs dangling, staring at the picture on the wall.

"Do you know why?" Pete asked.

Wally's eyes came back to Pete's. "Fine composition," he said.

Pete looked puzzled for a moment, then glanced over his shoulder at the picture. He turned back to Wally.

"I was asking if you know why Ethel's concerned about your drawings."

"She thinks I'm getting sick again."

"Are you?"

"I suppose. If she says so."

"What are you drawing?"

"The Employee Directory web design sometimes, but mainly things I see."

"The web design? But you were laid off."

Wally nodded.

"Why are you doing that? Are they paying you?"

He shook his head.

"Why did they fire you, Wally?"

"Ethel says they fired me because I was wasting my time on drawing, instead of solving the noun-stack problem." He hesitated. "Would you like to see some drawings?"

"Ethel already showed me your notebook. Very impressive work."

"You liked them? Really?"

Pete nodded. "Wally, do you remember what you were doing before Doctor Ramsay operated on you?"

"A little."

"Tell me about it."

"Ethel says I was drawing and painting and it made me sick."

"What do you remember?"

Wally told him he couldn't remember specific things. However, he had this feeling every time he tried to do something with his colored pencils that he'd done it before, because it seemed so easy, like it just flowed out of his pencil. And he told him how much pleasure it gave him to see the thing take shape on the paper.

"Okay, Wally. Go ahead get dressed, and when you're finished come to my office."

Pete stepped out of the room and walked down the hall to his office and opened the door. Ethel, seated on the sofa, looked up at him. He went around his desk and dropped into his chair.

"You believe me now, don't you."

"I'm afraid so." He looked down at the opened file folder, studied one page, then another. He looked up "I can order some tests, but I don't think it's necessary. There's no question. It's the Pablo Piccolo Syndrome."

"Don't need no tests."

"When did you first see the symptoms?"

"I had my suspicions before he was fired, when he started turning off the TVs and doodling with a pencil and paper, and when I asked him about it he'd say he was thinking about that web design. And then when I looked in that notebook with all those drawings I knew it." Her voice tightened and her eyes watered.

Pete watched her for several seconds. "What about you?"

"Me?" she asked, surprised that anyone would ask that.

"Yes. How are you doing?" Pete waited.

"I'm okay. I just don't know what to do, is all. We already tried operating on him and it didn't do no good. Should we try it again? I don't know. And even if I thought it was the best thing for him, will I have to go through the legal stuff again to make him do it? And if it didn't work the first time, why would it work the second time? And what happens if this condition he's in right now gets worse and worse."

"No one can tell you that, Ethel."

"Because if it gets worse, how am can I leave him alone to go to work? Which is what I got to do to support us. Because there's no way he can hold a job."

"I'm no expert on the Pablo Piccolo Syndrome. We need to talk to Doctor Ramsay."

At that moment Wally opened the door and came into the office.

"Good news, Ethel," he said. "I'm in the pink of health."

—

"Well, if Ramsay says we need to operate, then we probably need to operate," George said. "He's the expert, ain't he?"

Ethel glanced at Roy, as if to say *See, I told you what he'd say.* She looked back at George. "As usual, you weren't listening to what I said. His exact words were, 'Well, we can always try it again.'"

"For Christ's sake, Mom, what in hell else can we do? How—at your age—are you gonna take care of a hundred-and-sixty-pound seven-year-old? An' where's the money comin' from?"

"George, don't you talk to Mom like that," Wanda said sternly. "She's got enough on her mind without you going on like that." Wanda turned back to Ethel. "Mom, why don't we pray on it right now, and see what God thinks. Reverend Stammer, would you please lead us in prayer?"

Reverend Stammer, who'd stood silently in the farthest corner of the room during the family meeting (to which he'd only reluctantly come) hoping they'd forget he was there, had prayed that Wanda wouldn't want to pray, because there was no telling where that would lead. He looked at Ethel for a way out.

"I don't need no prayers right now," Ethel snapped. "What I need is for someone to say something like an idea of how we can deal with this without cutting his head open again. It just might kill him."

Though he'd been invited to the family meeting because he was almost a member of the family, Roy knew his place. He wasn't blood, or married to blood, so his role was that of observer, who could offer advice or comment only if invited. It felt like Ethel was inviting his support now. He cleared his throat. "Well, it seems to me," he began cautiously, "that Ethel's got a point about—"

"Well I say we give Ramsay one more shot at it," George said as he pushed himself away from the table. He stomped down the hall toward the bathroom, swearing just loud enough for everyone in the kitchen to hear his opinion about the stupidity of women.

"Mom, I think God's already showed us the way we gotta go," Wanda said gently, extending her hand to touch Ethel's. "He's given all kinds of signs—isn't that right, Reverend Stammer?"

George rescued Reverend Stammer from having to respond.

"Goddamnit, Dad! What in hell are you doin' to that TV? It's brand new, for God's sake! Mom, he's at it again!"

Thirty-nine

Reverend Stammer relit his pipe. Before him on his desk was a scatter of papers covered by penciled lines and red corrections—poems he'd been revising for submission to *Popular Poetry*. He dispersed the cloud of blue smoke with a wave of his hand and looked at the altar across the room. On it was the TV he'd rescued from Wally Walder's treacherous family. He still shuddered when he remembered how close the priceless treasure had come to destruction at their infidel hands. Vandals, sacking Rome, were no more destructive than these vulgarians. They still had no conception of the enormous talent they'd so blindly brutalized. Even now, as their poor victim was miraculously showing fluttery signs of artistic revival, they were preparing to stamp it out again by putting him through another, and more radical, ordeal of mental extinction. But Reverend Stammer did not want to think about the Walder family any more. He'd thought a great deal about the situation already and had concluded that Wally Walder's future was none of his business. It was a painful but inescapable conclusion. He recognized, of course, that inasmuch as Wally was one of the flock, he deserved the shepherd's attention. The problem was, Wally's family were also members of the flock, and they outnumbered Wally three to one. Four to one, if you counted Roy, who, because of his continuing infidelity with Ethel Walder, was practically family. So there you had it. Wally was out voted: democratically speaking, their interests clearly outweighed his. No matter how you analyzed the situation, it always came out the same way. It was the old problem of the interests of the many colliding with the interests of the one.

Reverend Stammer was grateful that this day was the first Thursday of the month, and therefore the day of the Art Walk. Putting the unpleasant matter of Wally Walder's ongoing ordeal out of his mind, he rose and got his jacket from the closet and opened the front door and walked down the steps to his car. He drove down the long hill to Juanita Junction and turned south on Market, then up over the hill through the oldest section of Kirkland to the lakefront business district.

He parked a block from Central Way and Lake Street, which was the heart of gallery row. The air was soft and sweetly warm and beginning to take on the color of sunset, and the sidewalks along Central Way were alive with strolling art lovers from all over the Seattle area. Reverend Stammer had attended the First Thursday Art Walk every month since he'd graduated from divinity school and landed the shepherd's job in his current flock. He always started at the Wagner Gallery, which was the one closest to Market Street, then worked his way down Central Way, then down Lake Street, through some twenty galleries. It was the most gratifying and stimulating part of his life—after his poetry.

As he wended his way through the couples strolling along Central Way toward Market he came to a knot of people that jammed the sidewalk in front of the Whipple Gallery. Curious, he paused and asked an elderly gentleman what was drawing their attention.

"The TV, of course. It's incredible."

Reverend Stammer's heart fluttered.

The elderly gentleman went on enthusiastically. "A magnificent thing—a work of genius. By a fellow named Wally. Just Wally, that's all. Every heard of him?"

"I—I—a *TV?*" Reverend Stammer stammered.

"It's marked NFS, but I tried to buy it anyway."

Reverend Stammer clawed and elbowed his way through the knot of art lovers.

"It's no use, they won't sell it," the elderly gentleman called after him.

Reverend Stammer couldn't believe what he saw when he managed to shove two old ladies aside and take their places at the window. A TV with a huge screen rested on a shoulder-high platform, positioned in such a way that it was visible to viewers in the room as well as to the people standing at the front window. The screen's test pattern in pointillistic gray-and-black-on-white was a stunning revelation, transcending beauty, transcending aesthetics. As a matter of fact, it was off the scale of any conceivable standard. It was as perfect as—no, it was more perfect and more powerful than the TV Reverend Stammer had on his own altar at home. A sign on an easel beside the TV announced, simply, *TV by Wally, NFS*. My God, it was true, Reverend Stammer thought as he pushed his way toward the door: Wally had painted two TVs before they lobotomized him.

"Okay, buddy, hold it right there," a tall, burly, crew-cut young man in a tight T-shirt shouted at him over the heads of three art lovers who stood between him and the door. The young man stood in the doorway blocking them all.

"But I have to get in there," Reverend Stammer cried.

"So does everyone else, buddy, so just cool yer jets an' take a number," the burly young man said.

"A number?"

"Like the sign says."

Reverend Stammer made his way back through the crowd and saw the sign "Take a number." Below the sign was a number dispenser. He pulled a tab out the bottom. Number three-hundred and seventy-one.

Behind him he heard the burly young man calling, "Three-ten! Three one zero!"

At eleven o'clock, two hours after the other galleries closed, the street was empty of pedestrian traffic, except in front of the two taverns, the restaurants, and the sidewalk in front of Whipple's Gallery. There Reverend Stammer still stood in a knot of stubborn art lovers, waiting for his number to come up.

"Three-hundred and seventy-one!"

"That's me," Reverend Stammer called, pushing his way toward the door.

The crowd parted, grumbling, and he found himself in front of the burly young man.

"You again. Lemme see yer number."

Reverend Stammer gave him the ticket, which the young man studied for a moment before grudgingly nodding. Reverend Stammer slipped past him into the gallery. He went to the TV altar, where he stood in the back rank of a silent crowd of worshipful art lovers, too overcome by the emotion of the moment to shove his way through to the first rank.

After some time of worshipful study, he became aware that someone was at his side, talking to him and tugging at his jacket. "What," he said impatiently.

"We're closing."

Reverend Stammer looked at the bald, gray-suited man. "But I just got in," he protested.

"Sorry, we close at eleven-thirty."

Reverend Stammer looked back at the TV and murmured wonderingly, "I thought I had the only one in the world."

"Pardon?"

Reverend Stammer couldn't take his eyes off the TV. "I also have a Wally TV, and I hate to admit it, but I think yours is a little better. Perhaps because mine was his first."

Incredulously: "You have a *Wally* TV?"

Reverend Stammer, still staring at the TV, nodded. "His first."

"My God! There's another one!"

Whipple topped off Reverend Stammer's half-empty champagne stem and refilled his own. He returned the bottle to the ice bucket, which rested on a silver tray in the middle of the cocktail table, and leaned back on the leather cushions of the sofa.

"Amazing story," Whipple said wonderingly. "And you say they've decided to put him through another surgery?"

Reverend Stammer nodded. "Wally's daughter-in-law told me today that Doctor Ramsay thinks he's figured out why it didn't work last time. He says he was too conservative, that this time he'll perform a second-stage lobotomy. At first the family didn't want to do it, but when Doctor Ramsay said he'd do the whole thing for half-price, they agreed. It appears they need Wally back in gainful employment. Besides, they can't afford the TVs."

Whipple shook his head. "Such a loss for the world. And yet, in a zero-sum world a loss for one is another's gain. It is not a loss for you, because, artistically speaking, Wally's a dead man. I heartily congratulate you on your admirable foresight in rescuing that first TV. Mark my words: Wally's first work of Test Patternism will one day be more valuable than Pablo Piccolo's first work of Tubism. I'd love to own the second one as well, but Gas won't sell it. Like you, Charles is indeed lucky."

There was a knock at the office door.

"Yes?" Whipple called.

The door opened and the burley young man appeared. "Mister Gas is here. He wants to see you before you leave."

"Send him in, Mike. And Mike, after you bring the beds out of the back room, please make sure the cross bar is properly installed on the back door. This morning when Charles woke he noticed it wasn't and he was very upset."

"I know, sir—he told me all about it. One other thing, sir. Mister Gas wants his bed in the main room, next to the TV. That okay with you, sir?"

"Of course. Just pull the draperies on the front windows before you set it up." Whipple watched Mike close the door, then said to Reverend Stammer, "Mike is a top-notch art guard. A dedicated young man. Eats and sleeps with the Wally TV. It's never out of his sight, which of course is a Gas requirement." He leaned forward in his chair, to emphasize the seriousness of his next words. "You must also take care, my friend. Your own TV is beyond priceless. Were I you, I'd move it to a more secure environment than your house. Or better yet, I'd begin negotiating the terms of a tour of North American and European art museums. Like Gas has done. Then they will take care of it for you and you'll get income from it."

"So this fellow Gas owns the Wally you're showing?"

"Yes, indeed." Whipple told him that Wally had painted the TV in the Art Cooperative in the hours just before he was recaptured and taken in shackles to the hospital.

The door opened and Charles came into Whipple's office. "Whipple, I'm bringing another man in until the show's over," he said with brassy self assurance. "I expect you to cover the cost. With all those people coming and going we've got to have better security."

"No problem. I was thinking the same thing. You were certainly right about the Wally TV—draws patrons like flies."

"What about the Pillows? Are they still selling?"

"You saw the red dots when you came in. Tell Janice that we sold another three. Now come in, my friend, I want you to meet Reverend Stammer. I have discovered that both of you belong to a very exclusive club. It seems Reverend Stammer also owns a Wally TV. In fact, he owns the first TV that Wally painted."

Charles' jaw dropped. "No *shit*? He painted *two*? Fuck! What does that do to the value of mine?"

"I wouldn't worry about it. Two isn't very many more than one, really."

"It's twice as many."

"True, but, technically, still only one more than one. Sit down Charles. Let me pour you a glass of this Dom Perignon."

"He's painting another one now," Reverend Stammer offered.

"Shit. That'll make three. That's got to depress the price—but, hey, wait a minute—his wife lobotomized him."

Whipple spoke as he poured champagne. "It appears the doctor screwed it up. The lobotomy did not take."

"Christ."

Whipple related the story of how Reverend Stammer came to possess Wally's first TV, and also about Wally's relapse back into art.

"I knew it was too good to be true," Charles groaned. "My fucking luck."

Whipple looked at Reverend Stammer. "Tell him what you told me."

Reverend Stammer told Charles about Wally's family's reaction to the loss of his job, ending with the family decision to let Doctor Ramsay operate again, if he'd do it at half price and with a money-back guarantee. "It seems that Ramsay convinced them that Wally can be cured by a second-stage lobotomy."

"There's no way he can do art after a second-stage lobotomy," Whipple added. "After that all he'll be capable of is going to work and watching TV. So you see, there's nothing to worry about, Charles. It's true that there'll be a third Wally TV out there—the one he's working on now—but that's still only one more than the two that now exist." He looked at Reverend Stammer. "Reverend Stammer, how near completion is his newest work of Test Patternism?"

"It's not clear to me that he'll ever finish it," Reverend Stammer said gloomily. "They're just letting him do it to occupy him until Ramsay can operate."

"Perhaps I should visit the Walter Walder family," Whipple said. What he didn't say was "I believe I can persuade them to let him finish it. And then perhaps I can persuade them to let me buy it from them. Then there will be three of us in your little club."

—

Reverend Stammer wished he hadn't let Whipple talk him into setting up the meeting. It had gotten off to a bad start and it got worse from there. Now Ethel was listening with tight lips, pink cheeks, and a baleful gaze that never left Whipple's face, a gaze that said *I don't like you*. And George, utterly bored with the situation now that they'd all decided to save his father by having him lobotomized, was wishing they'd finish so he could go home and watch the Mariners kick Oakland's ass. Wanda had simply sat with arms crossed over her ample breasts, a carbon copy of her mother-in-law, her expression making sure that everyone in the kitchen knew that only the need for family solidarity restrained her from getting up from the table and walking out on this slickly satanic creature. Roy, of course stood by the sink, which was his usual position at these family meetings, watching Ethel's reaction so he could react likewise.

Whipple was a smooth talker, no question about that, but Reverend Stammer knew his smoothness would be wasted on the Walders. He'd done his best to convey to Whipple how completely the Walders detested art, but apparently he'd not gotten through to him, for Whipple had managed to do every possible wrong thing from the moment he entered the house. First, he'd kissed Ethel's hand out there on the front porch, which had so shocked the poor woman that she could only watch open mouthed as the gray-suited, red-tied, bald-headed art mogul slithered snakelike around her into the living room and greeted Wally, who was so preoccupied with his work on the fifty-four-inch TV that he scarcely acknowledged Whipple's greeting. Then the art dealer had volubly, perhaps even excessively, admired the newest Wally TV, which of course darkened the brows of the whole family. Then he chatted with Wally about art (as if Wally was even listening), which got Ethel to exchanging urgent whispers with Wanda and Roy. Then Whipple had compounded his thoughtlessness by going on and on to everyone in the room about what a great talent Wally possessed, which of course reddened every Walder face with anger. Now all Reverend Stammer wanted was for Whipple to just please shut up so they could slink out of the Walder house before someone wanted to pray or something.

"I suppose much of what I've said about the art world has seemed irrelevant to your lives, Mrs. Walder, but I assure you that it isn't," Whipple was saying, probably for the third time.

"I still don't know why Reverend Stammer brought you here," Ethel said coldly.

Reverend Stammer, in the farthest corner of the room, reddened. He didn't either.

Whipple showed his gleaming teeth in a smile. "I do go on, don't I. All right, then, I will get mercifully to the point. I am here to ask you for the next Wally TV. That's it. That is all I want. Will you sell it to me?"

Whipple's audacity—or the outlandishness of his request—stunned everyone in the room, except George, whose fidgeting had gotten more and more aggressive (the game was probably in the third inning by now and who the fuck knew what he'd missed). He spoke up for the first time: "Are you sayin' you want to buy that TV he's ruined?"

"George, I'll handle this," Ethel said.

"Indeed I do," Whipple owned.

Roy, who had more experience in the entrepreneurial world than the others—having been the successful proprietor of *Roy Sharp's Sure-Sharp Saw-Sharpening Shop* for thirty-five years—was emboldened by the turn of the conversation to matters of finance. He interjected: "Just how much are you willin' to pay?"

Naturally, Whipple—being an art dealer—did not want to pay what the art was worth. "I was thinking—ten thousand?" Then, when he saw Ethel and Roy exchange glances, he hastily added: "But I'd listen to a counter proposal—if you care to make one."

—

The afternoon was waning when the deal was struck. As Whipple wrote the check for fifteen thousand bucks, Reverend Stammer murmured wistfully from his corner—as if to himself, "It would be nice if Wally had a chance to paint a few more TVs before Ramsay operates again."

Everyone looked at Reverend Stammer.

Reverend Stammer reddened and murmured at his shoes. "Sorry. Stupid of me."

George, who had watched with big eyes as Whipple drew the third zero on the check, immediately saw potential in the comment. Without a flicker of hesitation, he exclaimed, "Fuck yes! Let's go down to Costco right now and buy some TVs!"

Of course Whipple's first thought was that the TV he'd just paid fifteen thousand dollars for would be devalued, perhaps dramatically, by the production of a continuous stream of Wally TVs. But he knew he had paid so pitifully little for the third Wally that he'd still be way ahead of the game if there were dozens of Wallys in circulation. Moreover, he realized that if he played it right, he might obtain exclusive right to market Wally's work, and thereby get fifty, or maybe even sixty, percent of the take.

"It is a thought," Whipple said smoothly. "Like I said before, Wally's pretty good at TV painting. And folks will pay for that." To emphasize his point, Whipple scribbled his name across the bottom of the check and pushed it across the table toward Ethel.

Everyone watched Ethel pick up the check and count the zeros.

"We could go down to Costco right now, if you want," Whipple suggested. "I'll buy the first three TVs."

Roy and Ethel exchanged glances.

"Well shit! Let's do it," George exclaimed.

"Just you hold your horses," Ethel said irritably. "This is goin' too fast."

"Too fast?" George said. "The man said he'd buy the fuckin' TVs. How can that be a bad deal?"

"Ethel, I'm out of white again," Wally said from the doorway to the living room. In his left hand he held his palette and several brushes. In his right he held up a wrinkled, flattened tube.

"We are not gonna do any such a thing," Ethel said to George.

"Jeezus H. Keerist!" George exploded. "The man is offerin' you thousands and thousands of dollars. Fer nothin'! Alls you gotta do is put some fuckin' TVs in front of Dad and let him paint 'em and when he's done haul 'em away. It's a fuckin' money machine!"

Ethel's face reddened. "George, I'm gonna wash your mouth out with soap if you keep talking to me like that. If this—this—deal is a bargain, it's a bargain with the devil. You are askin' me to sell Wally's soul."

"Amen!" Wanda interjected. "We should not even be talkin' to this man. He smells of brimstone."

George rolled his eyes heavenward.

Reverend Stammer saw the endgame now, understood its inevitability, and was deeply saddened. But he was also relieved that it was almost over and he could return to his desk and his poetry.

Whipple, sharp observer of human nature that he was, realized with dismay that he had completely misjudged Ethel: she was not for sale.

Roy, leaning back against the counter with a somber expression, had been quiet for a long time. Now he stepped away from the counter. "Wally," he said, rather forcefully, "let's go get that tube of white."

Ethel looked at Roy with surprise.

They all watched Wally walk through the kitchen to the back door and turn and face them. Ethel approached him and took the palette and brushes from his left hand.

"Mister Whipple," Roy said, "Ethel is where the buck stops, an' she is sayin' there's nothin' more to talk about right now. When Wally finishes your TV, we'll call you. C'mon Wally, let's go get that paint."

—

Roy stood in the doorway that led to the living room, watching Wally paint the TV. Behind him Ethel still sniffed and snuffled and blew her nose. After their brief, sharp quarrel, which Roy had precipitated by his words after he and Wally came back from Kirkland Art Supply and after he'd berated George and Wanda and sent them home. She'd collapsed into a chair and sobbed for ten minutes, a blubbery wail that sounded like complete capitulation to despair—perhaps because of Roy's betrayal, or maybe because the load just got too heavy. Or maybe both. Now Roy stood back from her collapse and let her cry.

"I'm not that bad," she murmured, finally. "Not like you said."

"Well—maybe not yet," Roy allowed. He took his seat at the table and picked up his cup of tea, which had gotten cold. "Depends on what happens next."

"All I want is for Wally to be like he was. That's not bad."

"Yes it is, because you're never gonna get your Wally back."

"It might work," she pleaded.

"It didn't before. No reason to believe it'll work now. You've lost him. He is gone."

"No. I *haven't* lost him. Wally's there in the living room, inside the person who's paintin' that TV. We just got to figure out a way to get him out."

Roy picked up a pencil and began doodling on a piece of paper, Ethel watching. The pause between their exchange of words lengthened into a silence.

"*You're* not gettin' that syndrome, are you?" she said, trying for a conciliatory smile.

He looked up at her. "Ethel, Wally's never gonna be like he was. He ain't a sick man that needs to made well by some doctor cuttin' out part of his brain. He's a worm turned into a butterfly, and butterfly's don't go back to bein' a worm no matter what you do to their brains. It come to me while I was watchin' him paint. A sort of peace was settlin' in me and it got me to wonderin' why. I figured it out while I looked at what went on here this afternoon. Wally is what he is, an' he can't help it—the joy he gets from his paintin' is just like that butterfly movin' about without any purpose but flapping its wings—it is what that creature *does*. An' painting is what Wally does." He raised his hand to forestall her protest. "Reason we don't like it is he doesn't notice us enough for us to be important. The thing he notices is his discoveries, an' paintin' is how he makes them discoveries and how he shows us what he's discovered. For him, that is everything. He doesn't hear much of what we say—the voice he hears is the one inside of him, talking to him about his discoveries. We don't like it that that voice is more important than us, an' we don't like them pichers because they're what comes out o' that conversation 'tween him and that voice."

"What are you *talking* about?"

"We been tryin' to get the old Wally back but we can't, because he's as dead as my poor Grace is dead."

She rose and went to the sink. "I don't want to hear this."

Roy went back to his doodling. "All of us has been tryin' to fix this problem, like it's something happened to us. But it ain't. It is something happened to Wally. He is a worm changed into a butterfly. When we remember that, we will look at this situation and know what we got to do."

Roy dropped the pencil on the table and rose and went into the living room and lowered himself into Wally's Lazy Boy. He pushed back. The leg support rose and he settled himself to watch Wally, who kneeled before the fifty-four-inch TV with his palette in one hand and a brush in the other, carefully placing immaculately perfect tiny white dots of paint on the screen.

Soon Roy heard the rattle of pans in the kitchen, and then Ethel appeared in the doorway. "I'm frying some chicken, Roy. You'll stay for supper, won't you?"

"Ethel, you know I'd never pass up an opportunity to eat your fried chicken. Sure I'll stay. Thank you."

Ethel came into the living room and stood behind Wally and watched him for a minute, then said proudly, "It's very pretty, Wally."

But Wally didn't hear. He was discovering something very important in the conversation he was having with himself about the shapes and colors he was laying so meticulously on the face of the fifty-four-inch TV.

Made in the USA
Charleston, SC
16 April 2010